# THE POWER

Also by Howard E. Goldfluss
*The Judgment*

# THE
# POWER

## Howard E. Goldfluss

DONALD I. FINE, INC.
NEW YORK

LIBRARY OF CONGRESS CATALOGING-IN-PUBLICATION DATA

GOLDFLUSS, HOWARD E.
  THE POWER.

  I. TITLE.
PS3557.O363P68   1988      813'.54      87-46269
ISBN 1-55611-087-1

MANUFACTURED IN THE UNITED STATES OF AMERICA
10 · 9  8  7  6  5  4  3  2  1

*To Rebecca Ann, who didn't make the first one—to David Michael—and to the memory of Rose and Albert.*

## ACKNOWLEDGMENTS

To the list of union leaders that provided me with valuable background material for *The Judgment* and *The Power*, add the names of *Vincent Sombrotto*, President, National Association of Letter Carriers; *Henry Chartiers*, President Emeritus, Local 32-E, Building Service Employees; *Philip Caruso*, President, Patrolman's Benevolent Association.

Three class acts.

# Part One

# Chapter One

MICKEY GOLDMAN loved it—this thunderous response from the thousand or more members of the Civil Service Coalition who packed the Sheraton Centre Ballroom. His voice controlled them, pitched as it was high and angry as he attacked the incumbent governor of the state of New York.

"And we've had enough of Arnold Beale, of the antilabor presence in Albany. Imagine the callousness of this man to veto a cost of living adjustment bill that would have given our retirees a minimal substance income. But at least he's consistent. He opposed minimum safety standards—he opposed minimum wages—he knocked out grievance procedures for state employees. He would, if he could, transport the worker back to the nineteenth century. *He's got to go!*"

After evoking their emotions, he placed his palms downward to hush them.

"This afternoon we have with us the remarkable team that will *do* it for us—and for all of the people of the state. I don't have to tell you about them. They've made their positions clear. They are our friends. Beale is our enemy. The C.S.C.

works like hell for its friends, and we'll elect them in November."

The roar from the floor rose louder than before as the Democratic candidates for governor and lieutenant governor stood with clasped hands over their heads.


Mickey Goldman knew when to get off, to quit when he was ahead: "So welcome them, the next governor and lieutenant governor of the state of New York, Jon Klyk and Loren Sturdivant!"

Mickey told them as he clasped both their hands aloft, "Hold that position—your arms may get tired, but as long as it takes—it takes."

They cheered for a full five minutes, but Loren Sturdivant's arm was not tired. She felt transported by the adulation—and the aura of power that came with it. Klyk was smiling, undoubtedly pleased with the reception, but his emotions did not reach the intense pitch of Loren's. And while Klyk was an attractive figure—tall and brawny with white hair reflecting the light—all eyes were on her. Loren Sturdivant was almost as tall as Klyk—and she stood erect in a beige suit that clung to her, emphasizing her womanliness. Her deep blue eyes flashed, and her raven hair, shoulder length and radiant, flowed with the turn of her head. With legs to rival a Rockette's, the impact was more than beauty—it was a genuinely sexual magnetism that had them all but transfixed—and she knew it and she used it.

This, though, was a moment to savor especially. Leaving the podium with her running mate, the gubernatorial candidate, she felt so good she wondered if it really could ever be better, and then quickly reminded herself that this was only the beginning, the start of an ascendance to the kind of power, with all its potential for accomplishment on a major scale, that she had once considered possible only for a man like her late husband, but now—

The sharp report and sting in her arm, courtesy of a man she had never met, cut short her triumphant fantasy . . .

By most standards Clarence Brown, Jr., should have been a contented if not altogether happy man. He was an intelligent, successful accountant, married to a good woman; he had two good-looking kids; he lived in a fine home. But for all of his life that he could remember, Clarence Medford, Jr., was neither content nor happy. Moreover, he suffered from acute depression.

It would not have been difficult to trace Clarence's problem to a life forged and plotted by his father, though his acquiescence made him an accomplice. Once—just once—he expressed his own desires to his father, when he told him before leaving for college that he had no interest in joining his father's successful accounting firm. Clarence Brown, Sr., dismissed that notion with a wave of his hand and frost in his voice—more than enough to quash Clarence's rare show of will. Thereafter his life followed his father's charted course.

When his father died Clarence inherited the firm and a considerable amount of money. But liberation came too late. By now his malady of self-hate had gone too deep to accept or to exorcize. On a business trip for a corporate client in Charleston, South Carolina, he happened to pass a gunsmith's store; and Clarence, who had not so much as held a gun in his life, purchased a .38 Smith & Wesson revolver. Simple identification was required in Charleston, but a permit was needed in New York, and he was fully aware that he could submit no valid reason to persuade the police department to issue such a permit to him. Nevertheless he successfully secreted the weapon in his baggage and got through the *not*-all-seeing X-ray detector at the airport, thereby violating New York penal law by possessing and carrying an unlicensed gun.

5

After that he really did not understand why he kept it on his person all the time . . . he just felt the need to have it always within reach. He liked to finger it in his pocket, getting a little relief from the head-splitting tension that was building, making of Clarence Brown, Jr., a walking bomb ready to explode.

That Saturday afternoon of Jon Klyk and Loren Sturdivant's celebration found Clarence on Seventh Avenue in the city of New York, in front of the Sheraton Centre. Work now being his only outlet, the only temporary relief from the pressure in his head, he put in six-day weeks and tried to squeeze in a Sunday here and there. This day, though, he had reached a state where even his work could not relieve him. He felt compelled to leave his office, to walk somewhere, anywhere . . . and while he walked the anger and the hatred inside became too powerful to submerge. They demanded a target. He patted his pocket to feel the gun holstered at his hip under his suit jacket.

Short and stocky, in his better days a country fair athlete, he moved gracefully, and as he moved his destructive urge increased with the tempo of his steps. When he found himself in front of the Sheraton he entered the lobby. As usual it was packed, but he had been there before and he walked through the lobby and the shops toward the escalator in the rear, which led to the ballroom. He knew from working in the area that the chances were good that at least one of the rooms would be hosting a function on any given Saturday.

He used the escalator and found that he was right when he saw hordes of people on the floor with ID cards affixed to their lapels or dresses; he heard a booming voice through the loudspeaker and the applause of those in the room.

He saw the sign: C.S.C. Annual Shop Stewards Meeting. Please Pick Up Credentials at the Desk. For security reasons it was intended that those who entered the ballroom should first check in at a long desk—two tables actually—in front of the ballroom entrance. The tables were supposed to be

6

manned by at least ten people who checked credentials and gave out ID cards to those who were authorized to enter.

But Clarence saw only a man and woman who were joking with each other, and the security precautions that were taken hours before when the mass meeting started were now forgotten. He passed through the entrance unquestioned.

The room was jammed—more than a hundred tables were filled—and he joined the people who were standing at the sides. He watched and listened as Jon Klyk, the Democratic candidate for governor, finished his address to enthusiastic applause and walked off the dais, following Loren Sturdivant. He was first struck by the resemblance between this man and his father, which merely ignited the bomb that long had been ticking. He saw Jon Klyk as a personification of all the forces against him that caused his awful pain and suffering. He watched Klyk closely . . . and saw in this tall, smiling, handsome man—so confident and self-possessed—everything he felt he was not and everything he wished he were. But it was more than envy that he felt—people like Klyk who had it made, who enjoyed the fruits of life, conspired to deprive him of *his* rights to the same. And so it followed, through his twisted thought processes, that Klyk was the proper focus of his imperfectly buried rage, and that the elimination of Jon Klyk would at last relieve him of his undeserved pain and frustration.

Now he moved determinedly to the circle of well-wishers surrounding Loren Sturdivant and Klyk as they moved slowly toward the exit, and he managed to squeeze himself into a position in front where Klyk would have to pass by him. He tugged at the holster and felt the cold metal in his hand. He waited.

But not for long. Klyk finished his conversation with a persistent hanger-on, and glancing at his watch, surged forward behind his running mate, Loren Sturdivant. Clarence Brown, Jr., drew the gun from under his coat. A tall man standing behind him saw Clarence's movement and yelled a warning, striking Clarence's arm as he pulled the trigger.

Loren, who at that moment was a few feet ahead of Klyk, felt the sting of the bullet in her left arm and looked in shocked disbelief as her blood ran in an irregular pattern down her arm. The crimson stained the light beige of her jacket. Several men jumped on a totally unresisting Clarence and twisted the gun out of his hand. Klyk, in a rage, struck Clarence repeatedly in the face while the others held him down. Finally they pulled Klyk off, but only after Clarence's jaw was fractured and his teeth were broken and loosened.

The terror and uproar of those around her, as well as what had just happened to her, seemed to have no effect on Loren. Although she was losing blood and felt weakness taking over her body, she maintained a fixed smile on her ashen face while saying to herself, over and over, "I will *not* faint . . ."

They sat her down, someone supplied a scarf to be used as a tourniquet and Klyk held her, though from her appearance of calm it seemed he was more in need of comforting than she.

The ambulance attendants came and persuaded her to lie on the stretcher, and she was taken in the elevator down to the street level and then into the waiting ambulance.

A police escort led the way, and Klyk followed the ambulance as it screeched through the streets to Roosevelt Hospital. The Emergency Medical Service paramedic loosened the tourniquet and applied a pressure bandage to the wound. She was chalk white now and found it difficult to talk.

"Who's in this ambulance?" she weakly asked the paramedic.

"Just the two of us, Mrs. Sturdivant," he said, indicating the other E.M.S. man watching her, "and the driver and another man up front."

"No one else?"

"No."

"That's good," she said. "I can pass out now." Which she promptly did.

"This is one tough lady," the E.M.S. man said, looking at his partner and shaking his head in admiration.

She awoke to see the face of a pretty, smiling redhead who looked like a typecast mid-'50s college co-ed. Loren's eyes glanced at her nameplate attached to her medical smock.

"Dr. Eileen Shanahan?" Loren asked.

"That's me, Mrs. Sturdivant."

"Are you my doctor?"

"I'm one of them."

Loren was now fully aware of the throbbing pain in her upper arm.

"You're smiling at me, Dr. Shanahan," Loren said. "I hope that means good news."

"Excellent news, Mrs. Sturdivant. You are a very lucky woman."

Loren, who had not formed the habit of prayer in her lifetime, now realizing the truth of the adage about atheists in foxholes as applied to the recent demonstration of her own mortality, closed her eyes in acknowledgement of the Almighty's protection, along with a spoken "Thank God."

"I'm sorry . . ." she said quietly to Dr. Shanahan.

"Don't be sorry, Mrs. Sturdivant. I thank him all the time. This white coat takes you just so far."

Loren nodded. "How lucky was I?"

"Lucky enough to suffer the minimal consequences of being shot. The bullet entered the outer aspect of your left arm at its fleshiest part. X-rays show that it missed the humerus and passed through the flesh and exited without touching a nerve or tendon or bone. *And* it passed through cleanly—there were no fragments of the bullet that we could find. You should have no limitation of motion. We'll have to immobilize it temporarily with a sling. And there will be some pain for a while. The only permanent effect will be scars where the bullet entered and exited—here, and here, but the scars won't be large enough to be unsightly, and cosmetics will camouflage them and, if you like, plastic surgery will eliminate them."

"Why would I want to do that?" Loren asked.

"If I were as beautiful as you, Mrs. Sturdivant, I guess I would try to eliminate *any* flaw."

"Not if you were running for office, you wouldn't," Loren said.

Dr. Shanahan looked puzzled, not operating on Loren's wavelength. Loren was, of course, not about to hide the scars. Hide them? To the contrary, she would display them as a badge of honor and courage. To Loren's way of thinking, these were million-dollar wounds.

"Try to rest now, Mrs. Sturdivant," Dr. Shanahan was saying. "We've given you tetanus shots and these pills on the table are Demerol. The pain is going to get worse before it goes away, though I assure you it will. Take one now, relax and let it work. You'll be out of here tomorrow."

As the doctor handed her the pill and a cup of water, Loren rose up and kissed her on the cheek.

"You're great," the candidate said.

Dr. Eileen Shanahan beamed as she walked out of the room.

# Chapter Two

THE Demerol was working but Loren fought sleep. Strange, she thought, she had offered thanks to a supreme being that she was not sure she believed in, but if it wasn't his action, then it was a remarkable coincidence of events that had protected her to the time and place where she now found herself.

Nearly incredible, one might well say. What other way to characterize the way her life had evolved in the last few months? From being the spouse of a great man—or at least one who everybody said was destined for greatness—and consigned to operate in his shadow and vicariously share his celebrity, to her present situation, widowed and a candidate for the second highest elective office in the state . . . well, as fiction it would have been altogether implausible. Her husband, the highly respected, even revered, Judge Alan Sturdivant, had to have had as his mistress Andrea Blanchard, a lovely jet-set favorite who provoked him into an act of sudden violence—her murder. He had to have been chosen to preside at the trial of the innocent young man accused of the crime. And then to have succumbed to his conscience and collaborated in his own self-destruction. But all that was only prologue to the even more unpredictable . . . her husband's elimination as a previously favored candidate for the governorship, leading to *her* emergence as a candidate for lieutenant governor on the same ticket with Jon Klyk, her husband's former rival. Pieces in a bizarre pattern of events that led to a bullet intended for another that would have killed her instantly had it entered her body a few inches to the left . . .

She found it difficult to accept that God moved the hand of that would-be assassin or diverted his bullet. Easier to see her life being spared as part of a scenario not predestined by fate or divinity but by the special gift she had been given and had always known she had. The pattern of her life must be leading, she felt, to the power that Alan Sturdivant had been given and had failed to use.

Lying in her hospital bed, she promised herself she would not make his mistake.

Jon Klyk, the Democratic candidate for governor of the state of New York, and Charlie Sweeney, the New York State Democratic chairman, also known as—what else?—the "Boss," waited for the nurse to allow them to enter Loren's hospital room. The two men were the classic odd couple. Klyk, nattily dressed, had kept himself in good shape, and with his ruggedly handsome face that had wooed and won women voters for the twenty years that he had been mayor of Buffalo, he appeared nearly typecast for his role. Charlie Sweeney was older and shorter, with a hairline that had receded to virgin scalp and a bulging stomach that defied the efforts of his vest to contain it. After some fifty years of smoking three packs of cigarettes a day, his voice sounded like unstrained gravel.

The reason for the delay was cosmetic, not medical. Loren was not about to allow herself to be seen by either of them except at her best, and Loren Sturdivant's best was, indeed, considerable. The nurse applied her makeup and combed her hair according to Loren's directions, and even in a hospital gown with her left arm in a sling, she was still a knockout when the men were finally permitted to enter her room.

They both kissed her; in fact, she had real affection for both of them, if for different reasons. With Klyk she had had a brief sexual dalliance after her husband's death, both of them enjoying it and both of them knowing when it was over, but the aftermath led to a formidable bond of friendship. After the Democratic Convention nominated them by acclamation, the Boss was elated with a ticket that was exciting and appealing, and while he was always aware of the vagaries of political campaigns, he was as optimistic as he could allow himself to be—until one of those vagaries came to pass the previous day when his candidate for lieutenant governor was shot. Hopeful as he had been, he also knew that the race would be close and the loss of the dynamic Loren Sturdivant, even for a while, could be disastrous . . .

Loren seemed to read his thoughts. "Cheer up, Charlie, I'm leaving this place in an hour."

"Yes, good, but you're going straight home to rest for the next three days. We'll cancel Schenectady, Utica and Troy and reschedule them for the end of the month—"

"Not on your life," Loren said.

Klyk joined in: "Good God, Loren, you just didn't catch a head cold. Getting shot has got to slow even you down a bit. Give me a little credit, I can carry the ball for a week."

Loren laughed. "And you'll do a fantastic job. But you're both putting me out of action without reason. I know how I feel. I'll be at that rally in Schenectady tomorrow night."

"With the arm in a sling?" Klyk asked.

"Especially with the arm in the sling. Do you know how many votes that sling will earn us? I don't intend to lose one of them."

Sweeney shook his head, but Klyk stopped him with a wave of his hand.

"Forget it, Charlie, there's no talking to her. She's the boss."

Sweeney let that pass. But to himself he was thinking the same thing.

Loren finally contacted her mother in Palm Beach. Cynthia Phillips did not fall apart on the phone as her daughter assured her that she was fine, but then again, Cynthia Phillips never fell apart. She was much like her late husband Arthur Phillips, both of them towers of strength, and they had taught Loren well. To an outsider the Phillipses were cold people, but in their fashion Arthur and Cynthia Phillips loved each other. For them the WASP no-show-but-felt emotion worked, but for Loren's marriage it failed. Alan Sturdivant craved affection—or at least displays of affection—and when Loren could not satisfy his craving he sought it elsewhere.

Loren did not hold herself entirely blameless for his relationship with Andrea Blanchard, which ultimately led to Andrea's destruction. Nor did she consider herself blameless for her own strained relationship with her older daughter, Melody, who was now sixteen and had turned sullen and unforgiving after her father, who she revered, died violently in prison. Never mind that he had brought much of it on himself, a loving daughter needed a living target for her hurt. Loren understood all that, but it hardly made things easier when her daughter looked at her like she wished she were dead. Ten-year-old Donna felt no such resentment and openly adored her mother, but it couldn't make up for Melody's estrangement. Loren knew she needed to do something now to avoid a permanent break, but the demands of the campaign left her so little time . . . Both girls, of course, had been exposed to the screaming headlines recounting the details of how their father, a Supreme Court judge, killed his mistress and died in jail, how he betrayed his family and his name. There was no way she could protect either of them from the lurid story, but with it all she knew that Donna would survive it. She was not so confident about Melody.

It wasn't just the understandable antagonism toward her that Loren was concerned with. Time, she felt, was a curative. But Melody had always been an introspective and moody child, and after Alan's death her gloom seemed to deepen and she hardly spoke. She was a beautiful child, the image of Loren, and she should have enjoyed the pleasures of growing up as much as any sixteen-year-old, but instead she seemed to sink into its pitfalls . . .

Cynthia now put Donna on the phone, and Loren's spirits were lifted by Donna's voice that spoke words of love and concern. They looked forward to seeing each other in two weeks, when Cynthia and Donna planned to join her in New York during a break in the campaign schedule.

Cynthia took the phone again, and the anticipated bad news about Melody came pouring out.

Even while her father was alive Melody found it difficult to relate, not only to her mother and her grandmother but to her peers as well. The family was advised by a child psychologist that she needed to change her surroundings to a "semistructured" and "disciplined" environment, and he suggested Mount Olympus, a highly regarded prep school in the Connecticut valley of the Berkshires. They followed her advice, Melody resisting, but her outlook did not improve, she was still sullen and uncommunicative. And now there was this new source of worry that had crept in.

"I'm afraid we've got a serious problem with Melody," Cynthia was saying.

"We've always had a problem with Melody, mother."

"Yes, but this is something we never had to face before."

Loren waited for the shoe to drop and said the words her mother had trouble with.

"It's drugs, isn't it?"

"How did you know?"

"Not difficult to guess, mother. How bad is it?"

"I don't know. I spoke to the headmaster yesterday. Nobody would be specific. They only admit that they suspect it. I'm flying up there tomorrow and I'll have more information for you after I speak to them . . . Hasn't she called you?"

"No, mother, Melody hasn't called—and we both know the chances are she won't."

Cynthia allowed herself a rare display of emotion. "It breaks my heart that she—"

"That she doesn't love me?" Loren said. "Wouldn't call her mother after she'd been shot? Well, it doesn't do too much for my heart either, but these aren't ordinary circumstances. When all this is over I should have some time. Things will get better between us, I'm sure they will . . ." This was said more to cheer up her mother than out of conviction.

Loren shook her head as she handed the phone to the nurse, who returned it to its cradle. She had, face it, chosen her course, knowing what its consequences were going to be. But the question nagged at her . . . Was she not only risking her relationship with Melody, but sacrificing Melody herself?

The nurse, whose nameplate read Bella Kaplan, R.N., was a thirty-five-year veteran and a grandmother seven times; she took Loren's hand and held it tight.

"Excuse me for intruding, Mrs. Sturdivant. I know this is none of my business, but I couldn't help but overhear. May I say something?"

"I would appreciate it if you did," Loren said and meant it.

"Years ago, before women emerged as human beings, we didn't have this problem. Life was accepted drudgery, home and children. We had no choices to make. But we're having to make choices now, and accept that sometimes sacrifices have to be made—"

"Like the love of our children?"

"Well, it depends on . . . I mean, some can have it all, some can't."

As Mrs. Kaplan adjusted the arm sling, Loren looked out the window without seeing, then turned to her.

"It's a damn heavy price to pay, Mrs. Kaplan. Maybe too heavy."

The nurse shook her head. "Only you can decide that, Mrs. Sturdivant. But keep in mind that until very recently women have paid a heavy price for burying their own identities for their husbands and children, and *that* may have been an even heavier price."

Loren smiled. "You're quite a philosopher, Mrs. Kaplan. And I'd like to accept what you say, but sometimes I question my own motives . . . Am I being too selfish—?"

"Maybe. If you throw it all away now, give up your goals and devote the rest of your life totally and completely to your children, well, it might make you feel good and noble, but for how long? Frankly, ma'am, I for one . . . and I'm one of very many, I assure you . . . would hate to see it happen. You are *unique*. You have a special opportunity here . . . Women have always failed politically in this state. You won't, you can't. Forgive me for going on like this, but I think I know what you're going through. I went through it in my own way. A lot of us have, and maybe we have some regrets. But I think the greater regret is crying later about what could have been."

And then an interesting, altogether unexpected, tableau took place, as the tough WASP candidate for lieutenant governor of the state of New York, originally from Virginia and Palm Beach, and the Jewish grandmother, originally from Orchard Street on the Lower East Side of New York City, embraced like long-lost sisters. And Loren Sturdivant, the "Iron Lady" who had lived through a loveless marriage, who had been abruptly widowed in an international scandal and had just narrowly escaped her own demise, finally gave in and allowed herself the indulgence of breaking down, tears flowing, while held in the arms of the nurse—until there were no more tears left to cry.

# Chapter Three

AS the 747 raised itself from the tarmac of El Dorado
Airport, reached its designated elevation and turned
north, Terry Wilbur watched from his portside window seat as the city of Bogotá faded from view.

"Goodbye, Bogotá," he said to himself. "I'll be back. You
better believe I'll be back."

He relaxed in his seat and smiled. How sweet it was
. . . only seventeen and on his way to becoming a million-
aire—check that—a multimillionaire. It wasn't that difficult
to find the key. All it took was that good old American
ingenuity and imagination. You had to make things happen,
and you had to take chances. Otherwise, you wound up like
the rest of the geeks.

Okay, so you had to hock your Rolex. Now you can buy
a dozen Rolexes. You've got one kilo of pure coke in the false
bottom of that bag. You have a buyer in New York, a guy
with twenty-five grand waiting to pay you for this trip. And
it's just the beginning. The connection in Bogotá was solid.
And they were always ready in New York to pay for pure
Colombian coke. He watched the sun's rays silhouetted
against the moving clouds. He thought of the money, the

beautiful money that would give him the broads and the good times and the power. What a future!

He thought about Mount Olympus. Should he stay at the school? Why not? Leaving school now, besides being unexplainable to his parents, would make no sense. As a matter of fact it was a perfect front. It wouldn't be too tough to maintain passing grades, even though he planned to take frequent trips. Besides, he had plans for future business transactions on the campus. Some two-bit civilian now had the concession and was peddling "blows" on the campus—well, he had found his connection in Colombia, he had found a buyer in New York and he could find out where the factories were and how to retail the stuff. He would learn how to cut out the drain of the middle man.

His happy thoughts were interrupted by the trilling light voice of the hostess.

"Anything to drink, sir?"

He turned to eye her. God, she was lovely. His eyes slowly left her hips and paused at the blouse, which was bursting. That body, that face, would belong to the type of woman that his money and the power that went with it soon would buy. It was going to be a great life in the great big world.

"I'd like a Scotch on the rocks."

"So would I," said the young man seated next to Terry. He appeared to be a little older than Terry, with his long hair tied in a ponytail, a small gold earring through his pierced right ear and three large gold chains circling his neck. His jeans were torn, as was his shirt, which hung loose. From his worn sneakers to his scraggly black beard, he looked to be a classic member of the Beat Generation of the sixties. Except for those heavy gold chains.

The hostess, mindful of the regulations about the sale of alcohol to minors, only had Coke or 7-Up in mind when she approached them. Now she looked at both of them more closely. Well, the beatnick type was at least eighteen . . . the other could pass. The hell with it. She poured the two Scotches from the small bottles into plastic glasses and added the ice.

"That will be three dollars each, gentlemen." Terry Wilbur moved first.

"It's on me, friend," he said as he handed the stewardess six one-dollar bills.

"Why, thank you," the other said, flashing white teeth beaming through the blackness of his beard. "I'll get the next one."

Terry smiled and extended his hand. "By the way, my name's Terry Wilbur."

"And I'm Vinnie Prago."

They shook hands and sipped their drinks. Terry moved cautiously. "How'd you like Bogotá?"

"I didn't have much time to enjoy it. My business took up all of my time."

Terry was almost certain now that they were in the same business and changed the subject. "Those are great chains, man."

"Yeah," Vinnie said, "feel good when I wear them. Know what I mean?"

"I'd like to pick up something like that."

"No problem," Prago said, "I'll give you the number of the guy in New York. Just call him. He'll come to you."

Prago motioned the stewardess for refills, which she poured and Prago paid for. He waited until she walked away. "I don't even have to give him bread, if you know what I mean."

Terry nodded. The second Scotch on an empty stomach caused his head to float with the airplane. He smiled and looked cautiously to the side and behind him before he whispered. "The stuff's good as money, isn't it?"

"Better," Vinnie said, "much better. You get more for it than the dollar. The trick is to always have some handy. Hold some back. Never sell it all."

"Yeah, but where can I store it?"

Prago smiled. "You know," he said, "I hope you don't mind, but I've got to tell you that I'm a little bothered by all these questions."

Terry felt it was time to make his move. "I need your help," he said, "and maybe I can be of some help to you. I think we were in Colombia for the same reason. Maybe I'm going about this the wrong way, maybe I'm screwing myself, maybe if I work with you we both could be better off . . ."

Prago's smile vanished, then reappeared, punctuated by hostile eyes. "How do I know you're not a narc?"

Terry laughed. "Me?—a narc? Look Vinnie, I'm what is called a preppie. I go to Mount Olympus in Massachusetts. My father, for God's sake, is *Assemblyman* Daniel Wilbur, majority whip of the Assembly—"

"Hey, I heard of him. He's an asshole buddy of Mayor Klyk—"

"You keep up, I see. Yes, they're both county leaders—"

"So if Klyk gets elected governor, your old man will be an even bigger cheese than he is now."

"Probably."

"Then what the hell do you need all this for?"

"Because, number one, I'm bored out of my skull, and number two, the bread my dad gives me doesn't come close to buying the lifestyle I want."

Prago had his reservations; he looked at Terry but said nothing.

"Look, if I were a narc, would I be telling you things that you can check out as soon as we land?"

Prago touched his lips with his fingertips, looked straight ahead and finally turned to Terry. "What have you got in mind, kid?"

Terry's *sotto voce* could not camouflage his excitement. "I can bring in an unlimited amount anytime I want, as long as I pay up front. But I don't think I'm getting enough at this end."

Vinnie bent close. "Are you holding this trip?"

"Yes."

"How much?"

"A kilo."

"First time you've done business with your source?"

"Yes."

"A kilo on the very first trip . . . quality?"

"Ninety percent."

"So what's the problem?"

"Mostly it's that I don't know what I'm doing yet. Like I said, I think I'm selling too low."

"How much?"

"Twenty-five grand."

"You're right. We're talking more than fifteen thousand grains. Worth more than a million on the street."

"That's what I wanted to know . . . How come the big difference?"

"Because after you sell it the wholesaler processes it. He takes it to his factory, adds the adulterants and cuts the purity as the quantity gets lower. This way he gets to use more of it and nets more bread."

"Give me a specific," Terry said.

"Jesus. Okay, he buys your kilo at ninety percent pure. Then he sells it in ounces, about 438 grains, cut to forty percent pure. But he also sells it in grams, 28 grains at fifteen percent pure. And he can reduce it even more to twelve percent pure—that's in the form of blows, four grains for twenty dollars, mostly used by the street sniffers and the kids on the campuses. The demand all over the country is so big that we can't keep up with it. So like I say, as the purity goes down, the profit goes up. Shit, you don't have to be Einstein to dig it."

Terry shook his head. "I'm taking the big risk and they're making the big money."

"You've got it, bunnie. For the risk you're taking you're getting a double dose of shit."

Terry swore softly. "Maybe it's not too late. Vinnie, let's hook up together. Get me a buyer—better yet, get me in a position where I can make the real bread. I promise you won't be sorry, I can always bring it in. Bogotá is *sure.*"

Prago touched his fingers to his lips again before he spoke. "I can't promise you anything. Have to talk to the people in New York—they've got to check you out first. They don't fool around. Once you're in you don't get out. Understand?"

A flash of fear sped through Terry, but it was quickly displaced by greed. "No problem . . ."

"Tell you the truth," Prago said, "I don't know how they're going to take to your father being that big shot politician, being close to maybe the next governor. Could scare them off—and then again, they may like the idea. Could work two ways . . . When do you meet with the buyer?"

"Tomorrow night."

"Did he give you an advance?"

"No."

"You mean you did all this without front money?"

"Yes—kind of stupid, right?"

Prago smiled. "Not stupid—inexperience. But as it is you lucked out because you don't owe the buyer nothin'. Call him and tell him you didn't score. I'll have a buyer for you tomorrow. There'll be more money, and just maybe my friends will work you in, get you better involved."

Terry shook Prago's hand and for the rest of the trip talked about his great future. Prago listened, or pretended to.

As usual, air traffic over Kennedy caused a delay and they landed an hour late. Vinnie Prago told Terry that he had someone meeting him and offered Terry a ride into the city, which Terry accepted. He also had to sweat out customs.

"Smile," Prago counseled, "and don't sweat. They see

sweat—they see fear. Look the inspector in the eye. Do you have anything you can declare?"

"Two bottles of tequilla."

"Good. Take the bottles out and show them to him, even if he doesn't ask you." Prago appraised this tall, thin kid with the sandy hair and the blue eyes and the trace of a wispy moustache, who was dressed in blue slacks, a blue windbreaker and expensive-looking Oxfords.

"You look straight, God knows. Regular all-American boy. I'm not holding, so it doesn't matter with me. So here's how we do it. I won't look them in the eye, I'm going to be real nervous. They do spot-checks. The inspector is going to take one look at me and he'll be convinced that I should be searched. He'll go through my bag. You'll be behind me. He'll look at you. You'll be cool, you'll smile. He'll pass you on. But make *sure* you're right behind me in the line. Got it?"

"Got it."

They waited the normal time for the bags and then proceeded to the customs area. The customs agent, after quickly eyeing Prago, made him empty all the contents of his bag on the counter—even examining his rolled-up socks. He then examined the bag itself. Terry, right behind him, put on a happy face, as ordered. He only hoped that his pounding heart wasn't as loud as it seemed to him. If his bag were examined that carefully he was dead . . .

Prago, though, had hit it on the button. The inspector eyed him casually, and after he did the routine with the tequilla bottles the agent passed him through with only a cursory glance at his opened bag.

When they hit the street Vinnie Prago pointed to a battered brown 1979 Ford. Standing at the door was a man dressed like Prago—but older and bigger. He waved to them.

"Terry," Prago said, "this is Willie. He's one of our people. Willie, meet Terry . . . I think he's going to join our operation."

Willie shook Terry's outstretched hand, took Prago's bag and put it in the rear trunk. Terry held onto his bag, took it with him to the back seat, where Vinnie joined him.

Terry decided to stay over at a hotel in New York and rent a car in the morning since it was a long drive to Mount Olympus and he was too bushed after the long air trip to try it now.

"Fellas," he said, "just drop me at the closest good hotel in the city. I need a good night's sleep."

Neither responded. Instead Willie abruptly drove the car off onto a service road and stopped. Vinnie Prago grabbed Terry's bag and felt for the bottom.

"What the hell are you *doing?*"

Terry tried to wrest the bag away from him—stopped abruptly when he saw that Willie had turned around in the driver's seat and was pointing a 357 Magnum at his face. Prago found the coke, put it on the floor and spoke for the first time since they had entered the car.

"Terry Wilbur, my name is Al Ziwicki. This is my I.D. card. It has my picture on it. The gentleman pointing that gun at you is Gus Catonas. He has the same kind of card with his picture on it. We are federal agents and we work for the D.E.A., the Drug Enforcement Administration. You are under arrest. You are charged with being in violation of Section 841 of Title 21 of the U.S. Code, in this case possession of a controlled substance with the intent to dispense it. You have the right to remain silent. You have the right to an attorney and if you can't afford an attorney one will be provided free of charge. Anything you now say may be used as evidence in court. When we arrive at our office you will be permitted to make a phone call. Place your hands behind your back, please."

Terry reacted in stages—first sheer terror—then anger—then lachrymose self-pity.

"*Now* you give me my rights? After you set me up . . . you guys are a bunch of—"

Ziwicki, alias Prago, produced handcuffs from a side pocket in the car door and cuffed Terry's hands behind him. "I suggest that you don't say anything more, Mr. Wilbur." Ziwicki's eyes were distinctly unfriendly. "It's really a terrible state of affairs. You just can't trust anybody these days."

"Look—I'll give up the buyer."

Ziwicki smiled. "How do you think we got you?"

"But I can't go to jail—goddamn—I can't . . . please . . ."

Gus Catonas, who had said nothing so far, finally weighed in with: "If you can't do the time don't do the crime."

After that profundity nobody spoke, and the only sound in the car was Terry's quiet sobs until they reached the D.E.A. headquarters on West Fifty-seventh Street, where Ziwicki and Catonas checked in with the district director.

"How did it come off?" the director asked.

"Perfect," Ziwicki said. "There were a few hairy moments at customs. In spite of what I told him the kid was nervous as hell, but they didn't pick it up and passed him through."

The director nodded. "If customs had gotten him we would have lost him. A big shot politician's son is too big to lose."

"I guess you're right," Ziwicki said, "but I wonder why we don't all work together more . . . F.B.I., customs, Alcohol and Tobacco, us and others. We're all in competition, like we're working for different countries."

"No," the director said, smiling, "just different fundings."

The process of printing the pedigree inched along, and it wasn't until 1:00 A.M. that they delivered Terry to the custody of the Metropolitan Correction Center, where he slept not a wink and was awakened by a U.S. marshal at 6:00 A.M. and driven to the Federal Courthouse at Cadman Plaza in Brooklyn. He was then arraigned before a U.S. magistrate, formally charged and bail was fixed at $100,000.

# THE POWER

Afterwards they returned him to the Metropolitan Correction Center. He had called his father an hour after he was arrested and now called him again, this time to inform Assemblyman Daniel Wilbur of the high price of his precious son's immediate release.

# Chapter Four

D ANIEL WILBUR'S County. That's what his fellow members of the New York State legislature called Choctaw. He wasn't merely its representative in the assembly. He was the current heir of the Wilbur's— the famed Wilburs of Choctaw—who owned the only productive industry in that quiet wooded county nestled in the foothills of the Adirondacks. Wilbur Glass, 150 years old, manufactured the finest product of its kind in the U.S. and was still going strong. If you were not a farmer, you worked for Wilbur or the retail outlets that serviced farmers and Wilbur employees because those were the only sources of income in Choctaw.

The Wilburs ran the county as benevolent despots, contributing magnanimously to the public good, which was, as they saw it, their good as well. What was good for Wilbur was good for Choctaw.

The Wilbur influence over the lives of every man, woman and child within the county lines was formidable—awesome, some might say. Consider Daniel Wilbur's entry into politics. When he reached the ripe age of twenty-five he expressed his desire to his father, Daniel, Sr., that he represent the county as its assemblyman. Senior was a rock-ribbed Republican, as were all generations of Wilburs—as had been all the legislators from Choctaw throughout county history. Senior transmitted notice of his son's ambition to Bryan Crawford. Crawford, age fifty, had been Choctaw's assemblyman for sixteen years and had put his years of seniority to good public use.

Nonetheless, when Daniel, Sr., proposed, Daniel, Sr., disposed. Crawford was to step down on request—after all, Senior had picked him in the first place. Crawford had benefited from Wilbur's benevolence for sixteen years. It had been a good run, now he would turn over the reins to Daniel, Jr., fresh out of college and figuring a career in politics would be *neat*. At first Crawford failed to read Wilbur's diplomatic nudge and even offered to help Daniel, Jr., begin his political career until the realization hit him that for Junior to begin meant for Crawford to end. Daniel, Sr., even assured Crawford he would never in the future be wanting, that a vice-presidency of Wilbur Glass awaited him at generous compensation, but Crawford remained obtuse—by Senior's lights, at any rate. His self-esteem would be badly damaged, Crawford declared. Further, it would be bad for the party if the minority leader, with all the power, prestige and patronage attached thereto were to just step aside for a young man who would start at the very bottom in legislative influence.

Daniel, Sr., unmoved by such logic, took a harder line: "Look here, Bryan, *you* don't own that seat. *We* do. We rented it to you for sixteen years. Now we're terminating the lease."

But Crawford would not see the light. He even tried to persuade the old man that because of the prestige of his position in the assembly he was not a nonentity and he was not about to terminate his dreams at the age of fifty. At which point matters began to unravel. Daniel, Sr., told

Crawford that if he did not step aside for Junior he would be destroyed.

Crawford responded by telling Senior to drop dead, or words to that effect.

And the battle lines were drawn in what appeared to be a one-sided war. The Wilbur clan, however, suffered an initial setback when the Republican party of Choctaw County refused to order Crawford to dry up and blow away for the wet-behind-the-ears Daniel Wilbur, Jr. After all, the assemblyman from Choctaw was also the party leader, and even the awesome power of the Wilburs could not overcome that.

Daniel Wilbur, Sr., correctly assessed the situation. Running Junior against Crawford in the Republican primary would be too risky. Daniel, Sr., was fully aware of the truism that politicians vote in primaries, the rest of the people vote in general elections. The cold reaction by his fellow Republicans to Junior's bid convinced him that the way to go was definitely not through the Republican party. Then where?

Obviously Junior would be a *Democratic* candidate, the thought of which was almost a blasphemy. Never mind— Daniel, Sr., would deal with it and explain it later to his loyal but puzzled adherents. Having so decided, he sought contact with the Democratic chairman. The problem, or opportunity, he faced was that the members of the Democratic party of Choctaw County could meet in a phone booth. After some investigation he discovered that the party chairman was a barber in Stylesville, the county seat, who drank every liquid in sight and on occasion, when caught short, satisfied his need with a multipurpose bay rum that he used only incidentally on his customers' heads.

When this happy individual was finally discovered, he was made even happier by Senior's most generous offer to buy his barber shop. The chairman, having never seen so much money before, did the following in rapid succession: (1) he sold; (2) he called a County Committee meeting (the sole members of which were his wife, his sister-in-law, his dead brother and his maiden aunt); (3) he resigned as chairman; (4) he placed in nomination Daniel Wilbur, Jr., as his successor, who was elected by acclamation and (5) he floated away from Stylesville on a sea of booze never to be heard from again.

Daniel, Sr., now owning a party, proceeded to use it. He cajoled with his money, persuaded with it, threatened with it, and before long the rallies for Junior's candidacy began to be respectably attended. Naturally, all the plant workers, their families, and the stores and businesses servicing them, had an interest in pleasing Wilbur, Sr., and the guilt over giving old Bryan Crawford the shaft after serving Choctaw so well for so many years was short-lived.

To his credit, Daniel, Jr., was quite a presentable candidate. He spoke well, smiled a lot and said things he was told to say in a manner that convinced the voters that he knew what he was talking about. He also proved he could take it, a useful capability for the most ego-bruising business extant. An outraged Crawford called him the "peach-fuzz candidate"—one of the milder epithets directed at him—but Daniel showed a remarkable stability of temperament that was to work to his advantage all his political life. He did not strike back, he just concentrated on the "issues" (there were none), and let Crawford rant on. Meanwhile Daniel, Sr., worked his money magic, spending almost a quarter of a million dollars to satisfy his son's ambitions. After the votes were counted the good folks of Choctaw had elected a Democratic assemblyman for the first time in county history—by a margin of 310 votes out of 50,000 cast.

Crawford immediately demanded a recount, claiming fraud, and questioned the amazing coincidence that the head of the County Board of Elections, who tallied the official count, happened to be a foreman at Wilbur Glass; although always a Republican, he had been promoted by Wilbur during the campaign to an executive position in the front office. There was also some talk of ballots having been seen floating on the surface of Choctaw Lake and then disappearing into its depths. Nobody, however, could prove anything, and the results stood and Daniel Wilbur, Jr.'s, career was launched.

To most everybody's surprise he proved to be a damn good assemblyman. He did not overwhelm with his brilliance or his oratory, but he was pragmatic and therefore quietly effective. He learned early in the game that a politician cannot afford to be a dreamer. He kept a low profile with his colleagues at first, and he utilized the formidable advantage of his father's unlimited funds in wise and more or less ethical ways. No one was more aware than Daniel, Jr., that his colleagues had to run every two years, and that the cost of being sent back by the voters again and again was an expensive proposition that could very easily drain the average man.

Daniel quietly surveyed those colleagues around him. A specified number of these received phone calls from Daniel, Sr., informing them that Wilbur Glass, always interested in good government, found them to be exceptionally qualified, and would he or she accept a modest contribution? No strings, of course.

The kind offer was never declined, and the message was delivered clearly—*be good to Junior*. It was not mere coincidence that the recipients of the Wilbur largesse were powerful or potentially powerful members who could advance Junior's career. Committee assignments—leading to committee chairmanships—were of course the sole province of the speaker, but the speaker listened to the members of the Democratic delegation, especially those he relied on, who talked to him about debts and obligations and how they could be paid. Daniel, Jr., had plenty of years ahead of him and he was a patient young man, content to wait a long time, if necessary, for repayment. He waited with quiet confidence, though, knowing that the unwritten law of the game compelled repayment.

At the beginning some of the Republican veteran legislators were, naturally, resentful of the peach-fuzz candidate who had dislodged Bryan Crawford, an old friend and colleague who as minority leader bestowed many favors on them. But time and Wilbur money eroded such sensibilities. Contributions from Wilbur Glass were made without regard to political affiliation, and with each check hostility withered and finally disappeared.

Junior helped, listening to the solons and doing what his father and the speaker "advised." He also kept on smiling at everybody, kept quiet unless it was absolutely necessary for him to speak and tried not to let his mind be cluttered by independent thoughts. The reward of such wisdom projected him slowly up the legislative ladder until the assemblyman from Choctaw was eventually named chairman of the Ways and Means Committee—extremely powerful because no piece of legislation could hit the floor before Ways and Means released it. Neither the state Democratic chairman nor the speaker of the assembly lost a night's sleep over whether Daniel Wilbur, Jr., would do anything other than what he was told. A bully fellow.

Except Junior, despite appearances, was not a fool. On the contrary, he played the game according to its rules, and each move he made was well calculated and shrewdly executed. He did his homework—though he didn't make a point of it—and was fully informed on the intricacies of legislative issues. *And* he never forgot his constituency. He maintained an office in Stylesville and saw the people in that office two nights a week and on Saturdays for fifty weeks a year, rain or shine, even if he had to commute between Albany and home. And unlike some of his colleagues he actually liked his constituents, and they liked him. After his fourth term he ran unopposed.

As the years passed he lost some of his hair and added girth and wore horn-rimmed glasses and passed gracefully into the era of middle age. His marriage to Dora Abernathy was a happy one . . . Dora had the same likable disposition, was just as nondescript physically, and when their union produced a handsome male whom they named Terrance after Dora's father, their world was complete. But the complications in her pregnancy made it unsafe for Dora to go through another, and so their progeny stopped with Terry. He was their world, and since he had an exclusive hold on their love and affection, they granted him every wish and denied him nothing, which doubtless explained in part his growing up to be a wimp with the backbone of a fig leaf.

Terry's parents accommodated each shortcoming by improvising. When Terry could not hack it at Stylesville High they searched for a school more attuned to his specific needs. They settled on sending him to Mount Olympus in Massachusetts after hearing from the headmaster that the children of prominent families often found their way to Mount Olympus because ordinary schools simply could not deal with the stress their parents' social status placed on them. Claptrap, the headmaster might say in private, but when he told Daniel and Dora Wilbur that Mount Olympus was especially set up for students in Terry's position, he told them precisely what they wanted to hear. Terry was immediately enrolled, and through a subtle hint by the headmaster a donation to the Building Fund was included, as well as sizable endowment sums courtesy of Wilbur Glass.

In fact there was no compelling academic reason for Terry to leave Stylesville High. He had the intelligence to prevail academically, except he chose not to. The approach of Mount Olympus suited him fine. A "progressive" school, its philosophy was that a student should be permitted to absorb knowledge at his own stress level, which often translated to: "Never flunk a kid whose tuition is paid up."

Terry's desires exceeded his father's generosity. He dreamed of the good life—the women, the Italian sports cars and the first-class travel, and he wanted it yesterday. The fact that he was merely seventeen did not dissuade him from reaching out to try to find the means to change those dreams to reality. The cocaine business beckoned. Its vista was opened to him by José Rivas, a classmate at Mount Olympus who was fully qualified to indoctrinate Terry on the subject. His presence at Mount Olympus was made possible through the wealth accumulated by his father and his uncle, who were most respected citizens of Colombia—and partners in the manufacture and export of pure Colombian coke. Blood might be thicker than water, but not thicker than greed, and in an incident involving staggering amounts of money, his uncle placed a well-aimed bullet between the eyes of his father, killing him instantly. According to custom his uncle assumed responsibility for José's welfare, and after José returned to Colombia his uncle married his mother, thereby keeping it all in the family and providing renewed stability to young José's life.

Before José left for home he made a commitment to Terry Wilbur that he would supply him with all the cocaine he needed—at the lowest wholesale price—if he ever was inclined to travel to Colombia for that purpose. They shook hands on it in an almost tearful farewell, and in Terry's mind a new world opened for him with the handshake. He was obsessed with the thought of it, could hardly sleep through the excitement, and within a month he made the trip, raising the necessary funds for the purchase price and transportation expenses by hocking his solid gold Rolex watch, which his doting parents had bought him in Switzerland.

Abruptly the door to his new world closed when Terry was busted.

The shock to Daniel Wilbur, Jr., and his wife Dora was cruel if not unexpected. Terry clearly was not able to cope; each had had an unspoken premonition that the other shoe would drop sooner than later.

But as might be expected, the arrest of the son of the chairman of the Ways and Means Committee on a drug importing charge was front-page news across the state and out of state as well. Daniel Wilbur's colleagues were, of course, supportive if careful. After all, the alleged crime was not a popular one. The media was not as kind. The mail ran ten to one demanding that Terry be punished and that no special consideration be given him. Dan Wilbur treated it all with equanimity. Although the process of posting bail and meeting his son as he was discharged from the Metropolitan Correction Center amid the scores of TV commentators, cameramen, reporters and news photographers would have been enough to devastate most men, Wilbur seemed to take it in stride.

During the long drive from New York to Stylesville there was only one point in the conversation when Daniel's fuse almost blew . . . when Terry was explaining his motivation.

"You see, Dad, I couldn't help it. I didn't want to bother you. And it wasn't just the money. I was bored at Mount Olympus. I wanted to do something . . . exciting."

For a moment Daniel had the salutary impulse to stop the car and use Terry's head as a punching bag. He quickly suppressed the urge, however, recalling the advice of the psychiatrist to play it cool, let the young man know he was loved no matter what, et cetera.

The rage that boiled in his gut showed in the contracted muscles of his face and the abrupt flush that went with it.

Terry, giving passing notice, quickly returned to the subject that most concerned him—himself.

"If they send me back to that jail I'll kill myself. I want you to know that, and I want mother to know that too."

And thereby Terry, by his mysterious logic, transferred his guilt to his parents and made himself the victim—which he had managed to do pretty much all his life. And it worked especially well with his father, who, after all, had known similar paternal indulgence. More than he might like to admit, Terry's father saw something of an early version of himself in his son.

"Terry, no son of mine is going to jail." Saying it, he

believed it to be God's honest truth. All problems were decided on a quid pro quo basis. It was just a question of how many markers had to be called in to accomplish his purpose, and in this case he was prepared to call in all of them. By canceling the indebtedness of his rich and powerfully connected friends and acquaintances, he would, he felt, get their cooperation in saving his son. After all, they were all honorable men . . .

Terry was less confident. When they arrived at Stylesville he kept to his room, ate little and treated his parents to the sounds of his anguish, threatening again and again that he would do himself in if he were jailed. To escape this barrage of nonstop self-pity and save his wife from the nervous breakdown she was quietly edging toward, Daniel Wilbur drove Terry to Mount Olympus, and after depositing him in his room made straight for the headmaster's office, knowing that his meeting with Dr. Cyrus Pringlehof, B.S., M.S., Ph.D., LL.B., J.S.D., would not be pleasant.

Dr. Pringlehof was a tall, gawky man with a long neck and an oversized Adam's apple that bobbed when he talked. He wore pince-nez, which were particularly unsuited for his face. His brown hair was combed straight back. He favored a tweed jacket, blue or gray, and a pair of slacks, blue or gray, the two never matching up. He wore only bow ties, of which he owned two—white polka dots on a blue field, and white polka dots on a gray field. Wilbur early on had heard from veteran legislators that a bow tie somehow signaled that the wearer was not entirely trustworthy, a bit too slick and quietly arrogant. He had never put much stock in this sartorial omen, but in the case of Pringlehof, he allowed the possibility.

Framed on the wall above the headmaster's desk, in large classical letters for all to see and admire, was: "Truth is the secret of eloquence and of virtue, the basis of moral authority, the highest summit of art and life." The author was not named. Dr. Pringlehof took no precautions against the reader of this prominently displayed eloquence from concluding that those words were written by himself—actually they were the creation of the French essayist, Ami Frederick-Amiel.

Daniel was suspicious of a man who wore his morality on his sleeve or his wall.

"Dr. Pringlehof," he began, "I'm sure you've heard about the unfortunate events involving my son Terry."

"Yes, it was very disturbing to us too . . ."

Wilbur eyed the headmaster closely, but said nothing, waiting for the man to make his move, which he did after a measured beat.

"It creates a bit of a problem for us, Mr. Wilbur."

"Oh? What problem is that, Doctor?"

"Well, you are of course aware that the standards of Mount Olympus are high. I'm sure you understand that the publicity of Terry's arrest has caused consternation to the many families that trust their children to our educational and moral supervision."

Although he had expected something like this, Daniel Wilbur was surprised at Dr. Pringlehof's apparent lapse of memory. According to Daniel's code, men of honor did not require a reminder of past favors still to be repaid. He proceeded to the task of reminding the headmaster.

"Dr. Pringlehof, are you suggesting that Terry leave Mount Olympus?"

"Unfortunately, Mr. Wilbur, that may be a better path for all of us to follow."

"Well, before we follow any paths, I think we should consider that in view of our close relationship—the Wilbur family's long-standing financial support—and especially in view of how Drayton Hall happens to be standing on this campus, you forego any thoughts of Terry leaving at this time, voluntarily or involuntarily."

His mention of Drayton Hall was intended to and did jog the memory of the eminent moralist. When first appointed headmaster, he had the dream of building the finest and largest and best-equipped gymnasium in the East. It was to be named Drayton Hall, after the school's founder, Joseph Drayton. While the doctor never had difficulty in raising funds from the alumni association, he did have a major problem persuading the state of Massachusetts to cede twenty acres of public land that abutted the boundaries of Mount Olympus. The state was adamant in its resistance, and since the sprawling campus was overbuilt to accommodate the ever-increasing enrollment, and since the acquisition of this particular land would have been the only space available for the projected construction, Pringlehof's dream appeared doomed. But then, in going over the lists of influential parents, his eye fell on the name of the Honorable Daniel Wilbur, Jr., Ways and Means Chairman of the New York State Assembly. The thought crossed his mind that such a man, although he was a legislator from another state (all his Massachusetts contacts had turned him down), could have access to those people of Massachusetts who had been so arbitrary in saying nay to his request that public lands be converted to private use. After he had driven to Albany and presented his problem, he was overjoyed by Daniel Wilbur's quiet assurance that he could take care of the matter. And so he did.

Daniel did it not because he was fond of the headmaster, but because it *was* his son's school, and knowing his son's proclivities he thought it foresighted that the headmaster be in his debt.

By a happy coincidence Daniel was president of the National Organization of State Legislators, and his vice-president was a powerful legislative figure in Massachusetts, Daniel having also been influential in getting that gentlemen the vice-presidency. And so the gentleman owed him. It still wasn't easy, but finally the state of Massachusetts took a second look at Pringlehof's request, and he got more than he had hoped for—not the sale of the property but a ninety-nine-year lease at a most moderate rental. Drayton Hall was built, a testimony to the institution of political muscle.

Pringlehof had been hoping that Wilbur would not bring up this past favor, no matter how important, because, after all, one had nothing to do with the other . . . "Yes, sir, Mount Olympus will always be grateful. But I'm sure you agree that the very association of drugs with our campus would violate every standard we seek to maintain. Our highest priority is building character . . ."

Daniel Wilbur hardly ever swore or lost his temper. But the pressure that had been building inside him since Terry's arrest and his concern for his wife's health finally caused an eruption.

"You, sir, are a hypocritical son of a bitch. Drugs on the campus? You know damn well that drugs are rampant on your campus. How did Terry make his connection in the first place? Don't trifle with me, Doctor. Things that have been done for Mount Olympus, and for you, can be undone."

"Is that a threat, Mr. Wilbur?"

Wilbur did not respond immediately. Instead, he locked his eyes on Pringlehof's, and the stare-down contest began. But it was no contest. Pringlehof blinked quickly and averted his eyes, and they both knew that Daniel Wilbur had won.

Wilbur resumed his soft approach, which was more characteristic of his style.

"I would request that you do not consider expelling Terry. Not just now at any rate. I want him to stay here until his problem is resolved. After that, he will leave of his own accord."

He did not wait for Pringlehof's reply, but turned and walked out.

Dr. Cyrus Pringlehof was left standing among his plaques, his trophies, his laurels, his certificates. Covering the walls were all those good words and phrases he tried to live by. He took stock of his position. Wilbur had just told him to compromise his standards. He had expected him to wilt under the threat of the considerable power he could exert—blackmailing him, in effect, with threats of retribution. Well, Dr. Cyrus Pringlehof was made of sterner stuff, was he not? He would expel Terry Wilbur immediately, it was the only proper thing to do. And if doing the proper thing would place him in personal jeopardy, well, so be it.

And then, having gone through the cleansing motions of conscience, he reached into his desk and found hidden under some old files a piece of paper on which were written five words: "The ultimate truth is survival." Those words he did not appropriate from another author. Those words he wrote himself. Words truly to live by. He dropped the subject, eliminated it from his mind. No action would be taken on Terry Wilbur.


Had Daniel Wilbur not come on so strong, and had Dr. Pringlehof not proved to be so "practical," young Terry Wilbur might have been better off and, down the road, the shocking proceedings against the top executive of the state of New York might have been headed off, or never have happened at all . . .

# Chapter Five

TRUE to her promise, Loren Sturdivant kept her campaign dates in Schenectady, Utica and Troy. Her arm remained in the sling. She didn't solicit pity, but she wouldn't disdain whatever extra mileage might accrue for the reminder of her close call.

It was by now obvious to Boss Sweeney and every other informed party sachem that she was the star. Her rallies consistently outdrew Klyk's. While Sweeney never believed in looking a gift horse in the mouth, he would have preferred the top of the ticket be the drawing card. After all, although they ran as a team, he was not convinced that Loren's appeal was enough. But she was going to lead the statewide ticket— no question about it, and it worried him. He called the labor leader Mickey Goldman, his closest advisor and confidante, and they set up a dinner meeting at Neary's.

Neary's Pub and its diminutive Irish owner always made Sweeney feel at home away from home. The roast beef was the best in town, and Sweeney most appreciated the privacy. When he and Mickey Goldman arrived, they were instantly recognizable, since both had done guest stints on Sunday network TV interview shows. As soon as they were seated in the back, a lady with a snootful at the bar left her equally smashed husband and headed in the general direction of Sweeney and Goldman. Neary was prepared, however, for such invasions, and he motioned to Sean, his oldest son, who, unlike his father, was distinctly not diminutive but built like an oak tree. He stood in front of the lady, and as she tried to peer above him or move around him she realized that she might as well have been dealing with the Great Wall of China. He told her that Sweeney and Goldman were off limits in a voice loud enough to deter her or others similarly inclined. She promptly retreated back to the bar and the warning claxon had been sounded.

Mickey Goldman was also a large man with a shock of gray, unruly hair and a weather-worn face. He towered over Sweeney—they were indeed the odd couple. But each trusted the other, and it was only to Mickey Goldman that Sweeney would express his fears.

"Mickey," he said, "she's a winner. No doubt about it. She's going to take Jim Collins easy. Collins was a nothing when he got into office and he's still a nothing. Beale realizes it. He's distancing himself from Collins and I don't blame him."

Sweeney was referring to James Collins, the incumbent lieutenant governor of the state of New York and former chairman of the Republican party in Kings County—better known as Brooklyn. The Boss's assessment of Collins was generally accepted. Collins had represented the one Republican district in Kings in the state senate, and in the interest of a balanced ticket Beale, who was the power in Rochester, chose the lackluster downstater to run with him. Beale won big—and Collins slipped through narrowly in a primary, clutching Beale's coattails. Even then, his opponent had to be as much a nonentity as he.

"So what's the problem?" Mickey asked.

"The problem is I can't say the same about Jonny Klyk,

44

and unless we transfer some of her pulling power to Jonny we could lose the top spot. Look—you don't like Beale, I don't like him either, but he's an incumbent governor who took sixty-five percent of the vote last time and he knows how to fight dirty. He's never going to let the voters forget that the late Alan Sturdivant was our first choice. We've got to face up to the fact that Jonny cannot match Sturdivant's stature."

Goldman smiled.

"You're talking of course about Sturdivant before his fall from grace."

"Yes, of course—he would have been valueless—worse— after the scandal of his conviction. But my point is that without that he would have destroyed Beale. Look—Jon Klyk's been my friend all my political life. He was great as the mayor of Buffalo—he could win forever there. The people sort of adopted Klyk because he was one of them. The good looks, the wisecracks, the drinking with the boys— even the womanizing and the divorce didn't hurt him. Nothing really could hurt Jon Klyk in Buffalo. But this is a different ballgame. Statewide we're obviously dealing with a more complex and diverse electorate—and the thought nags me that the voters will be concerned about how strong a governor he would be and how much time he'd spend attending to business."

"That thought has occurred to me also, Charlie," Goldman said.

"Well," Sweeney continued, "if that's the problem we have to solve it. Maybe he'll grow into the job—that's happened before. But we've got to get him elected first. Frankly, I don't see the response at his campaign rallies that I see at hers. It worries me. A lot."

Mickey Goldman sipped his beer. They ate silently. This was not the first time Sweeney had called Mickey in as a trouble-shooter—and no one was more perceptive than this old labor leader who had fought the political wars on the labor battlefields, the toughest training any politician could hope for.

An idea had already started forming in Mickey's head, and when it jelled he broke the silence. "Have they scheduled any joint appearances?"

"No, except for the night before the election at a rally in New York. They're appearing separately all over the state, the two of them together couldn't cover it all before the election."

"Then you'll have to eliminate some of their stops. They've got to be on the same platform—together—all the time from now on in. When they appeared at my rally she was devastating, and Klyk got the overspill. It's no longer necessary for Loren Sturdivant to tell the voters 'Elect me.' What she's got to tell them now is to 'elect *us*.' "

"She's been saying that."

"But it's more effective when they're standing together with their hands clasped. That's got sex appeal. The 'team' concept has to be implanted in the voters' heads. People love a romance, or even a hint of one. Anyway, I understand that the both of them had a thing going for a while there."

"I don't even want to think about that."

"I don't say advertize it on the Goodyear blimp. Just let the thought float out. Look, Charlie, I keep going back to the late forties in Argentina. I was there on a labor junket. I saw what Evita did for Peron, you should forgive the expression. Without her, he was nothing. Talk about charisma. She wooed them, she tantalized them, she seduced them, and because of her they waited in line to vote for her husband—a no-good fascist bum. I thought I'd never see the likes of her again. Well, I have. Loren Sturdivant has the same animal magnetism, but more important, she radiates sincerity. She tells them, 'Believe me, accept what I'm offering,' and she delivers them. So what if the tail wags the dog? In this case that's how the cookie crumbles."

Mickey softened his tone. "Look, Charlie, to tell you the truth I don't really know how to figure her. Maybe under that cool and tough exterior beats the heart of a crusader. Maybe she's more like her late husband than we've suspected. Up front he appeared to be callous and unfeeling, but in fact, if you remember, down deep he was a caring and charitable man . . . No question, she's not easy to read. I think I believe that a part of her feels for the underprivileged and the poor. It wouldn't much surprise me if in a private place where she couldn't be seen or heard she sheds tears for people who need help. But I also think that another part of her is all driving, even ruthless, ambition which won't let conscience or morality get in the way of what she's got her heart set on. She'll never be *my* friend—tell you the truth, she scares me a little. But she's not one of those what-you-see-is-what-you-get. Unless she's conning an old con man. Always possible, of course . . . Anyway, she's a helluva an asset for the ticket and *that's* what counts now. We'll worry about the other stuff tomorrow."

Sweeney was impressed. Charlie Goldman was one smart fella. But his solution would create new problems. Klyk would go for it—he wasn't that uptight about the billing. But Loren was her own woman—she was spending her own money, which made her hard to control. Word had gotten back to Sweeney that in the last weeks of her campaign she planned to target certain heavyweights in industry who had always been friendly—more than friendly—to the Democratic organization.

"I've got some problems with Loren Sturdivant . . ." Sweeney began.

Mickey Goldman understood what he meant, but for him Loren Sturdivant's Populist notions, even if newly acquired, set off the drumbeat in an old union war horse's innards. When he heard that her upcoming targets were the toxic disposal industry for its disregard of public safety and the electric utility industry for asking unconscionably high increases in rates and the Public Service Commission for granting them—well, he "kvelled," which he explained to Sweeney was Yiddish for the way a grandmother might feel at her grandson's bar mitzvah.

Sweeney had to take a more pragmatic view . . . The people who were involved with the industries that Loren was planning to do a number on were old dependable contributors. One didn't survive in politics in New York State or anywhere else without support in every class of society; Sweeney bore no prejudice against the rich and powerful. Klyk was similarly inclined, and it violated the basic sense of loyalty ingrained in both these men who had graduated from an old school that taught that one never bites the hand that feeds or perpetuates one in office.

"I understand your problem, Charlie," Mickey said. "I know what you're talking about. But as Coach Vince Lombardi is supposed to have said, 'Winning isn't everything—it's the only thing.' You've got to give her her head. She's not going to listen to you anyway so don't waste your breath. Klyk's going to be the tail on her kite. He's got to bite his tongue and make it look like she speaks for both of them. I hate to put it this way, but with this girl you gotta take it or leave it."

"You don't look too broken up about it."

"No, actually I'm enjoying it. I like it that she's sticking it to you establishment types. How she got to be a Populist, I don't know. But I don't *think* it's a ploy. I've seen political phonies in action, and I may be many things but I'm not naive. No, I believe she means it. Her sincerity is contagious and you *want* to believe her. Anyway, no question you're sitting on a coming political superstar. She'll give your party a governor."

Charlie Sweeney puffed at his cigarette, shook his head. "I don't know. You're asking that I risk future support from old friends and bet it all on a woman—God bless them, but as candidates they haven't exactly been smash hits in New York. I don't know why, but—"

"I know why," Goldman said. "Women scare people—other women included—and institutions too. All kinds—political, media, corporate and, sorry to say, labor. We're all scared to death that women are going to move into seats of power without even considering that they couldn't do any worse than we have."

"Then why is this one so different?"

"Why? I'm not sure, but Loren Sturdivant manages to get across terrific confidence and competence without regard to her gender, at the same time never losing her attractiveness as a woman. It's rare, but we've got a few examples . . . the late Clare Boothe Luce and Margaret Thatcher, except Sturdivant is no stone-face like Thatcher. She gives off heat . . ."

Sweeney accepted the strategy, mostly because he had no choice. He called an emergency meeting of the campaign committee and Loren's individual appearances were merged with Jon Klyk's. Klyk was no fool. He knew exactly why this was done, but nobody understood more than Jon Klyk that politics was the business of winning. He did not resent Loren. On the contrary he welcomed her help and her money because when the war was over and the dust was settled she would make him the governor of the state of New York. So he would be elected holding onto her skirts. Big deal! He'd been in politics too long to mope over a bruised ego. And as for ruffling feathers of old friends—well, he planned to take care of that by getting word to them, in-directly of course, that campaign rhetoric was one thing and after the ball was another. After all, *he* was going to be the governor, not her, and there was one old saying that the lieutenant governor was as important as a tit on a bull. She would have little or nothing to say in his administration. As tradition had it, she'd be lucky to get through the door of his office.

* * *

They took to the road—Loren the star attraction—and after they finished the so-called Southern Tier (Elmira, Binghamton and Jamestown), the new polls reflected for the first time that Klyk had a slight lead.

It could not have happened without the energy and pull of Loren Sturdivant. If she wasn't inspiring the crowds she was attending skull sessions. She was *totally* involved, and it soon became obvious to everyone—Klyk, Sweeney, the county leaders—that Loren Sturdivant had taken charge. She was now giving the orders, and since success speaks for itself they grudgingly went along.

They were now linked, which, of course, ran to Klyk's benefit. But in Schenectady she put him on the spot, and according to the game plan he had to grin and bear it. The auditorium held over two thousand people, and it was standing room only. The local Democratic leader had done his job; he realized that Loren now was a celebrity and he worked it. Loren had hired professional public relations people who had organized a claque of about fifty women and placed them at a strategic place in the auditorium where they could be most effective. A like number of men were in another part of the house. Klyk was at one wing of the stage, Loren the other. The lights dimmed. The party chairman introduced them both, and they entered from each side.

A spotlight shone on each of them, and as they walked to center stage, the spots merged and they stood in the classic pose—arms extended, hands clasped. Then the women's claque started: "*Lo-ren, Lo-ren, Lo-ren,*" and from the other side, louder and deeper: "*Lo-ren, Lo-ren, Lo-ren,*" and the fever caught and now it was a legitimate solid sound of "*Lo-ren.*" She let it play—and when she was satisfied that it had hit its peak, she threw kisses and, still clasping Klyk's hand, sat down with him.

Charlie Goldman was there at Sweeney's request. He gave

his standard rouser—an anti-Beale, prolabor speech, but he held back on the fire and brimstone. This was Loren's show. John Klyk was on next; he delivered his message well—he always had been an outstanding speaker—and received respectable applause when he talked about the issues.

But that was not why they were there—not in Schenectady, not in any of the other campaign stops. The party chairman introduced her. She rose, and as she walked toward the lectern it started in the back . . . a wave of sound that moved slowly forward and crashed onto the stage.

Loren was careful never to let her clothes detract from her beauty or the lines of her body. She was slim, and the royal blue, knit dress trimmed on the sleeve with yellow braid clung nicely to her. The top button was open—just one button, but enough. Just right. The lectern was especially built to be low enough so as not to hide too much of her from public view. She dispensed with the opening remarks—Klyk had taken care of the amenities. She didn't need media advisers to act and *feel* like more than a politician—she held out new and special hope, plus inspiration. She seemed to sense the special needs of the particular audience—aided, of course, by some briefing. But she went beyond the conventional wisdom of local sachems. That was for losers.

Minutes earlier the applause, the shouts and whistles were deafening. Now, because she signaled it, the silence was overwhelming. She let that silence play the way she had the noise . . . savored it, drew on it, let the moment take over . . . and then with masterful timing began:

"We have reached a point in this campaign where we must speak out. No more generalities—no more campaign oratory. We need to let our hair down."

And she reached behind her head and pulled the pin that held her hair in a bun, and her hair fell free and she stood there looking at them—smiling at them, blue eyes out of alabaster skin framed by the free-flowing hair. She had indeed created a moment, and however contrived, it came off altogether natural. She had the skill of any great actress.

"There are so many things that are happening that go contrary to the interests of the people of this state. The present governor carries blame, but *we* are not blameless, because we have all allowed the powerful and the rich and the greedy . . . oh, yes, the greedy . . . to fill their pockets with little or no resistance from anyone, *including* you and me."

She pointed at Jon Klyk. "Our next governor, Jon Klyk, will bring an end to all that." Translation: Jon Klyk and *I* . . . translation: *I*.

The gesture with her hand, pointing to Klyk, signaled applause that was begun by the claques and picked up by the rest.

"During these next weeks, starting here, tonight, we are going to be painfully specific. Tonight, for example, I want to talk about the public utilities industries and more particularly the utility that services this area, Mid-State Electric. We now know that Mid-State installed nuclear power reactors *without* satisfactory safeguards, and that the Public Service Commission of this state has looked the other way. The truth of it is that the people in this area could well be in mortal danger, and *no one* is doing anything about it. Enough. I care. *You* care. I'm now going to name the two villains of the piece—Jesse Case, the man who speaks for the utilities, and, sad to say, the incumbent governor, Arnold Beale, who speaks more for such private interests than the public good.

She went on to develop the "unholy conspiracy" between the two, and then proceeded to name other villains on her list. Klyk's concentration wandered after she named Case. Klyk knew that she knew that Case had always been his strong supporter, financial backer and political pal. He had mentioned Case to her more than once. She knew that Case had the same relationship with Charlie Sweeney. He sat on that platform, watching and listening to her with the famous Klyk smile painted on his face, but inside he was boiling.

Case had always taken pains to maintain his anonymity, which Klyk and Sweeney respected because they understood that his strength needed a low profile. Of course Case had been mentioned and vaguely attacked by environmental groups and occasional pieces in the press, but it was always passing, it didn't last.

But this would last. This public attack was intended to make him a campaign issue. It brought him out of the shadows.

Klyk liked Loren, at one time had more than liked her, but this compromised him and she knew it. Case was the chief national lobbyist for the public utility industry. They paid him a million a year and he was worth every dime. *Time* magazine, in a not entirely derogatory piece, referred to him as "the Congressman no one elected" and described him only half in jest as "having more influence than any member of the House." Case didn't appreciate the publicity, but when asked to comment he smartly denied nothing, merely smiled agreeably and said he hoped he was of service "to all concerned."

Even after the Three Mile Island accident occurred Case had passed his quiet word to certain members of Congress that their reactions to what could have been a major catastrophe should be tempered. It was no coincidence that meaningful legislation responding to the public clamor over the near catastrophe never reached the floors of the House or the Senate. It was also no coincidence that two of the members of the Nuclear Regulatory Commission were Case's former business associates . . .

Instead of fearing him or walking around him, Loren Sturdivant decided early on that her tactic would be to get on Case's hit list and exploit *that* for all it was worth. After the Three Mile Island accident, and the one at Con Edison in New York and the reports of others throughout the nation, Case backed a media blitz that sought to assure the public that these incidents posed no lasting danger, but were isolated aberrations. Loren financed a poll that indicated his message was not being bought by the public. So, it seemed, Case ruled by fear. Good. It would show courage to take him on. She was also aware that money fought money; she would match Case dollar for dollar. She would enlighten the public about the Jesse Cases in government whom the people did not elect to any office but who hovered over the legislative bodies of the nation exerting influence contrary to the public interest. She would let the voters know what the battle was about and who wore the white hats and who the black hats.

In Schenectady she opened the floodgates. She charged Mid-State Electric with cheating the area and putting its residents in mortal danger. She recited in rousing style chapter and verse of every piece of legislation that Case had scuttled that would have been consumer-oriented. Her staff had researched it most thoroughly, and the shouts of indignation and anger that she brought forth from the audience proved she was on target.

When she had built them up to a peak, she moved from behind the lectern, removed the mike from its stand and walked, or stalked, across the stage. The spot followed her, and when she stopped she looked out into the hushed audience.

Goldman sat there as transfixed as any of them, and understood, perhaps more than any, how well this lady had mastered her art.

She reduced her voice level when she continued, starting at a slow tempo, accelerating as she built her point . . . "The thing about Jesse Case is that he does his dirty work in the dark, and what makes it worse is that he has the present governor and too many legislators eating out of his hand. Let me give you a horrible example. Have you ever heard about the Nuclear Liability Limitation Bill? Of course not. Nobody publicizes it because *Jesse Case wrote it*. He has gone to legislatures all over the country, to legislators that he has in his pocket. He has them introduce and pass it, and governors like Arnold Beale sign it into law. The bill provides that if the utility companies get sloppy and allow a little mishap such as the nuclear leak at Three Mile Island, which could only poison you, injure you, make you and your children permanently ill or perhaps kill you, your compensation from the company for their unfortunate mistake would be limited. Does that upset you? Well, Case is trying hard to slip it through the legislature of *this* state, and if he does, Arnold Beale will most assuredly sign it."

There, eyes flashing, arm extended, fist in the air, she brought them again to a near-fever pitch.

"Do we have to let this happen?"

The crowd responded: "No!" She let the collective feeling hang there and then subside before she continued.

"We have no choice. On election day we must rid our-selves of Arnold Beale and Jesse Case and all the minions serving him, people who care little about the welfare of the people of this state. But Jon Klyk cares—and Loren Sturdiv-ant cares—*we give a damn. Indeed, we do.*"

She raised her hands again and motioned for Klyk to join her and they resumed with "Lo-ren—Lo-ren" on and on while the house lights went up and the candidates stood and milked it dry.

Mickey Goldman was once again hit with the notion that her attraction was largely based in her sincerity . . . She projected it, and when she manifested righteous indignation it came from her heart. She convinced them that she was not being just political, but was herself caring and concerned. Did she mean it? If not, it was one hell of an act . . .

Again his mind returned to the forties and Evita Peron's beloved *camasillos*, who adored her and gave her a blank check. And while he liked what Loren Sturdivant was now saying, and as he watched in wonder the effect she had on the men and women who were now standing, some on their seats, and shouting her name, he also worried about a woman-on-horseback who could, somewhere further along the road, lose her love for the people and use her power for something else . . .

Bennet Sloane watched from the left wing of the stage with the rest of Loren's coterie, waiting for her to finish. As a member of her campaign staff, his was the exalted position of arranging for transportation, not only for her, but for all those who traveled with her.

He watched as Klyk and Loren waited for the inevitable picture event and press interview. By his reckoning, this would take at least fifteen minutes, more than enough time . . . He moved to the side and out a door and made for a store he had observed advertized a pay phone. He deposited the coin, dialed the number and heard the voice.

"Jesse Case."

Try as he would, Sloane could never suppress the pride he felt in working for Jesse Case. In no way did he equate his spying on the Sturdivant campaign as unethical. Nor did he consider it a betrayal of the trust Loren had placed in him. Bennet had a different, if convenient, perspective on his conduct. It was, he reasoned, the Jesse Cases that made the nation really work; ergo, any measures taken to advance Case's interests were admirable. Indeed he was so taken with the aura of Jesse Case that whenever he spoke to him he found himself stuttering before he could express his thoughts.

"She just fin—finished, Mr. Case."

"Was it bad?"

"It was ver—very bad, Mr. Case."

"For Christ's sake, Sloane, take a deep breath and then talk. What did herself have to say?"

"Well—named you, Mr. Case."

"Named me as doing *what?*"

"Well . . . she mentioned your—interest in the Nuclear

Liability Limitation Bill." A mouthful, and said without a stutter. He was getting better, he thought with some pride. Case was good medicine.

"Okay, what else?"

"She said that you worked against the interest of the people, that you had Governor Beale in your pocket and that you had some legislators there too. She made you a target."

At first he heard nothing but Case's breathing, finally his voice: "Was Klyk there with her?"

"Yes."

"What was he doing during all this?"

"As I remember it, sir, he was smiling."

"Another pause—and then in a controlled voice: "All right, Bennet, very good. I want you to continue. Be careful, don't get caught. Call when you think it's necessary. I'll handle this."

"Yes, sir."

Bennet Sloane walked slowly back to the auditorium, feeling contented. As the special assistant to Jesse Case, now on undercover assignment, he felt needed, important. Ultimately he hoped to make C.E.O. of a major corporation; that had been his goal from the time he graduated the Wharton School of Business, a goal shared by many other graduates. One of his professors, who had retired from the business world, predicted that Mr. Sloane was the most likely to succeed. "Why?" asked a colleague. "Because," said the professor, "he's especially qualified in the best way that business understands and accepts. He can kiss ass better than anyone else in his class. He'll be a C.E.O., you bet on it."

And so it came to pass that Bennet Sloane climbed the ladder in double time, using the expertise described by his professor. When he joined Case Enterprises fresh out of Wharton he resolved that he would dedicate every waking hour to making Case need him and rely on him—for anything, everything.

Case had a good deal of contempt for Bennet Sloane. Indeed, there were times that Case had to admit to intimates that the reason he dismissed Sloane so curtly after giving him his marching orders was that too much of Sloane at one time could very well make him puke. Sloane was accomplishing his purpose; he had worked himself into the very position he wanted. Whether it was his current assignment or any other he got it done. Sloane had no social life, nor did he desire one. His was a twenty-four-hour dedication to Case Enterprises. Case understood what he had in the young man—fawning or not—and he hid his contempt as well as he could, not always succeeding. After all, Sloane was a type who asked to be exploited; Case accommodated him.

When Case first heard about Loren's plans to attack him and others, he assigned Sloane to infiltrate the Klyk-Sturdivant headquarters. All political campaigns welcomed volunteers such as Sloane appeared to be, and Sloane, using his customary zeal and persistence, worked his way up into a more important inside job in the campaign. In fact, he worked so hard and such long hours that Loren offered him a paying position, which he declined—opting only for expenses, all of which he duly reported to Jesse Case.

Had anyone at headquarters thought seriously about it, he or she might have been at least curious about where his treasure came from and what his game was in working sixteen-hour days with no remuneration. He deflected such curiosity by planting innuendoes that he was independently wealthy, and nobody checked him out. There just was no time in a compressed and time-pressured political campaign to do security checks on such diligent workers, and so Sloane was accepted if not liked, since anybody with normal instincts and even a moderately sensitive stomach could not really *like* Bennet Sloane. Now, of course, he was especially motivated to keep on top of matters because a threat to Case was a threat to his future . . .

\* \* \*

Jesse Case looked out at the panorama of New York Harbor from his corner office on the seventy-fifth floor of the World Trade Center. Few views rivaled it, and he pondered many hairy problems and solved them while watching the harbor's activity. Loren Sturdivant's words didn't especially bother him . . . he would take care of her in his good time. But what appeared to be Jon Klyk's passive support of her attacks did. Always a cautious man, he felt nagging doubts about a man whom he had always considered close to him and who in many instances had been the recipient of his benevolence. He sniffed a double-cross, yet he hesitated to conclude that it was—he knew that Jon Klyk was not stupid, and pulling such a double-cross in the midst of a highly contested campaign could be suicidal. He decided to speak to Klyk, give him an opportunity to explain before he drew up the blueprints to lower the boom on the mayor of Buffalo. If Klyk did indeed turn out to be a foolish ingrate, then he deserved what was now planned for him.

On the other hand, Case understood Loren Sturdivant's move. She was going to be the good guy, he the bad guy. She could afford to go that route because her dominance over Collins, her Republican rival, was clear and everyone knew it. But Klyk beating the incumbent Beale was even money at best, and it was obvious that the last thing that Klyk needed was the full force of Jesse Case's enmity.

He called Klyk, who was not in, and left a message with his secretary that he expected to hear from Mayor Klyk immediately.


Another young man at the Schenectady rally walked forward and followed Loren Sturdivant as she moved toward the wings of the stage, surrounded by well-wishers. He managed to climb onto the stage, and although a small crowd was around her his six-foot-four height made it easy for her to spot him. He smiled at her, and she smiled back.

Scott Morgan knew how to win smiles from the ladies. He had been endowed with that gift at birth; and the blond, blue-eyed, all-American boy used his gift. He was more than pretty, he was bright, moved well, was articulate and immediately likable. Originally he had planned to practice law in Schenectady after graduating from Albany Law School and passing the bar. He did join a law firm, but after a short time he came to grips with the realization that settling down in Schenectady was not for him. He didn't know where he was going, just that he had to go somewhere else, and although only curiosity prompted him to attend the rally, the first glimpse of Loren Sturdivant filled his head with insistent ideas and plans.

When she noticed him, she had been talking to a corpulent lady who was showering her with praise as well as unwelcome touches and pats. She had just exclaimed to Loren that she was going to vote for her *forever*. Normally Loren focused her eyes directly into those of each admirer, making the recipient feel she was her only concern at that precise moment. But she could not help but avert her eyes to look at this beautiful young man smiling at her and apparently trying to edge closer to her through the crowd. Again she faced the lady, peripherally watching him nearing her. She should have moved on to the others, but she dallied long enough for him to catch up. Now she faced him. She clasped his hand. He said something but she wasn't hearing it . . . Something awakened in her during that brief moment—something that had been lying dormant for a long time. Her eyes never left his face as he continued to talk to her in low tones, and she wondered at the fact that this boy, who was young enough to be her son, was having this startling effect—this surging of the juices she had believed were diverted elsewhere. She continued to clasp his hand in hers . . .

She brought herself back to reality, began hearing his words . . . "So, Mrs. Sturdivant, that's why I believe I can be of some value to your campaign."

Of great value, she thought.

"What did you say your name was?"

"I'm afraid I didn't. It's Scott Morgan."

Loren motioned to one of her aides. "Jerry, take Mr. Morgan's phone number."

Scott handed his card to Jerry but his eyes never left hers. Then, her hand free, she proceeded on to the others who were waiting for her, but as he turned his back to talk to Jerry she glanced at him until he moved out of sight. She was tingling; she *desired* this young man. Given the opportunity, which was hardly likely, but given it . . . she permitted the fantasy to dance in her brain for a brief moment, until it became ridiculously concrete—herself and this Scott Morgan making love—and she shook her head, took a deep breath and moved to the next prospective voter.

# Chapter Six

THE two figures shivered in the cold New England night air. The tall boy pushed the barn door, but it didn't give. He tried again, and finally the third time after he used the full force of his body the door opened wide enough for the short and slightly built girl to follow him into the barn.

Terry Wilbur held the paper bag in his left hand and guided the girl to the rickety stairs leading to the hayloft. He had forgotten to bring a flashlight, but the full moon acted like a beacon through the crisp autumn air and illuminated the interior of the barn. She sat shivering in the hay, patiently waiting for Terry.

As she watched him take the paraphernalia out of the bag, Melody Sturdivant, daughter of Loren, thought only of how low she had come and how she hated herself for her weakness. She had always been conscious of the bloodlines she carried. The Phillips were traditionally strong, self-reliant and proud. With the exception of her late father, the fallen judge, the Sturdivants's history was much the same. But like her father she was mortgaging her self-esteem. In finding Terry Wilbur at Mount Olympus she found another who resorted to inhaling the white powder as the way to deal with life. She detested him, but she stayed with him, had sex with him, snorted with him and escaped with him. For her, their relationship was a form of punishment—Terry Wilbur was what she deserved, the symbol and substance of her own loss of self-respect. And was it part of her revenge against a father who had disgraced her and her mother? Maybe the school shrink was right, but who cared?

At first what Terry promised seemed no lie. But after two months of use she woke up in the morning and the need for the drug grabbed her by the nape of the neck—it owned her. Larger doses were needed, and then they did not satisfy her as her tolerance increased with her addiction. Her only goal in life was her next fix. She appeared anorexic, had stopped eating, weighed scarcely ninety pounds, and now she had sunk to the level of mostly downers and few highs—and always excruciating pain, physical and mental.

She and Terry Wilbur were out of it most of the time. Then Terry heard about free-basing from one of Dr. Pringlehof's "motivated" students at Mount Olympus. This, he was told, was an "incredible new high," something that they had never experienced before and that would fill the need they could no longer supply. When he first told her about it she thought of nothing else, and the three days it took him to find the opportunity to steal the liquid ether from the infirmary were an eternity to both of them.

The barn was in a mini-forest in an obscure part of the campus—long abandoned for any purpose except use by students for midsummer-night trysts. But with the change of seasons adolescent ardor was displaced by goose bumps, and the barn was vacant until the warmth of spring.

Now the cold was teeth-chattering, penetrating their sheepskin-lined coats. Melody watched with deep-set eyes as Terry opened the bag and removed the bottle of ether, the raw cocaine and the glass pipe. He concentrated on the instructions he had been given:

"Put the coke in the bowl of the pipe. Pour the ether into the bowl. Very little because ether is highly flammable. Use the cigarette lighter, cook it until a paste forms in the spoon. Light it and inhale it slowly. The high you get sticks with you . . ."

He poured the ether into the bowl. The kid had told him a little. What was a little? Two drops? Three? Ten? He'd forgotten to ask. He poured what he thought was a little and lit the cigarette lighter.

They heard a sharp crackling noise—a small explosion— before the flame shot to the ceiling of the barn which was just a few feet over the hayloft. Terry panicked and dropped the lighter and the spoon as fire engulfed the hay. Flame burned Melody on the left leg. She screamed, and Terry's manly response was to scream even louder. He then scurried down the ladder and ran out of the barn, leaving Melody behind. She rolled over the edge of the loft and fell eight feet below onto a pile of hay that had been left there years before. Her pants were still on fire as she ran out of the barn, but she still had the presence of mind to get out of her coat, wrap it around the bottom half of her body and roll on the ground—something she had learned as a child. It saved her leg and maybe her life. The fire was out, and now she was on the ground screaming in her pain and her fright and her misery—it had all come together for Melody Sturdivant. Gradually her cry became a whimper as she shivered and finally passed out.

The fire quickly consumed the barn, and the trees dried out by the rainless summer went soon after. The heat was intense as the flames climbed the wooded rise and cast a red-and-orange light that lit up the campus. The volunteer fire department and the police responded quickly and did their jobs well, but the police found Melody with not much time to spare . . . Although she was fortunate that the wind was blowing the flames away from her, there was still the danger of her being overwhelmed by the intense heat. The firemen worked through the night, and when the dawn showed, the wooded area was flat and the trees were charred remnants.

Through it all, cool man Terry, who had run off to his room, had never considered returning to find out what had happened to Melody.

Loren, located by Dr. Pringlehof in an Albany hotel, immediately canceled the next day's scheduled rally and chartered a helicopter to the Mount Olympus campus. She rushed to the infirmary and found the doctor waiting for her.

"It could have been worse, Mrs. Sturdivant," he told her. "She reacted very well, smothering the flames with her coat. She has serious burns on her leg, but I doubt there will be permanent damage."

"Thank God."

The doctor seemed reluctant to go on.

"What else, Doctor?"

"Well," he said slowly, "I can't be sure, but I suspect Melody has another problem."

"Please, Doctor . . ."

"In examining Melody I observed inflammation of the tissue in her nostrils . . ."

Loren had suspected it, but she had to hear the doctor confirm it.

"I'll be positive when I do a urine analysis in the morning, but I suspect cocaine usage."

Loren's voice was flat. "Thank you, Doctor, I will take care of it. May I see her now?"

"Yes, but briefly. She's still experiencing some mild pain. Because of what I suspect I did not give her a painkiller at this time. I don't know when she last used the drug or the quantity she may have used. I did give her a mild sedative, though. She needs her rest."

"Thank you, Doctor, I understand. I won't be long."

She entered the infirmary room and saw her daughter, eyes shrunk in their sockets, face thin and chalk white.

"Oh, Mother . . ." A pitiful sound that tore at Loren's heart. She went to the bed and gently held her daughter in her arms, both saying nothing but at that moment knowing the breach between them was hugely narrowed. Loren felt a different pain, and no drug could relieve it. Pain at what had happened to their child, thanks to the sins of her parents. And, finally, her own tears came, silently, falling on the bare shoulders of her daughter.

They stayed that way, hugging each other, until Loren released her and pulled back, trying to smile through her tears . . . "It's all right, baby, not your fault . . . we'll talk tomorrow—"

"*No*, I want to talk about it now." And she did: all Loren knew but didn't want to know or face up to . . . the pretense of her parents, the disgrace of the father she had worshiped, his murder in jail—and then the drugs. And she named Terry Wilbur as her supplier—she'd be damned if she'd protect the little rat, and when she finished she collapsed into the deep sleep she so badly needed.

Loren called for the nurse, left the room and went to the physician.

"May I use your phone, Doctor?"

He motioned to a small cubicle. She closed the door and picked up the phone. A tired voice answered; it was late for the operator on duty.

"Please ring Dr. Pringlehof, Operator."

"It's two o'clock in the morning. Dr. Pringlehof is asleep, he left instructions—"

"This is Loren Sturdivant speaking. Wake him up."

Dr. Pringlehof was ready to kill. Of late he had been having difficulty falling asleep in any case, and the fire on the campus was one in a series of setbacks fraying his nerves. After the rough day and rough night he had just been subjected to—Good Lord, couldn't they leave a man in *peace*?

All those questions from the police and the fire-fighters—
questions he couldn't, of course, answer. When he saw the
illuminated clock showing 2:05 A.M. his irritation was undis-
guised.

"*Yes,* what is it?"

"Dr. Pringlehof, this is Loren Sturdivant."

"Oh, yes, Mrs. Sturdivant . . . You've no idea how sorry
I am—"

"I appreciate your concern, but that's not why I woke you.
I want you to understand that I expect Terrance Wilbur off
your campus within a week."

Pringlehof swallowed hard. "Mrs. Sturdivant, all the facts
aren't known yet. We—"

"All the facts necessary *are* known. Terrance Wilbur was
supplying my daughter—and who knows how many others—with cocaine and Melody is now an addict. She is too
sick to stay here. We will take care of young Mr. Wilbur in
our own time, but for now, I insist that he at least be dismissed. Other young people must not be exposed to him. I'm
sure you agree that this matter should be disposed of quickly
and quietly, without the unfavorable publicity that could
damage Mount Olympus."

And without giving him an opportunity to tell her
whether he did or didn't agree, she hung up, crashing the
phone on its cradle.

Dr. Pringlehof was furious . . . This was the *second* time
within the past month that he had been threatened by a big
shot. He was getting tired of it. To think that a person of his
stature had to be subjected to such abuse was intolerable.
Terry Wilbur's father had warned him of the consequences
if he expelled him. Loren Sturdivant was warning him of the
consequences if he didn't. It was too much. He would show
them; he would resign and let them find another with the
qualifications and ability of Cyrus Pringlehof. Discarding
that notion almost immediately, he turned out the lights but

passed a sleepless night trying to find an acceptable formula for balancing the outrageous demands made upon him.

As it turned out, Terrance Wilbur saved him. Terry was already gone, leaving the scene of the conflagration and running to his room only long enough to pack his things, get to his car and speed home to Stylesville in Choctaw County. Good old Dad would, as usual, save the day. Well, he always had, right?

# Chapter Seven

B OSS SWEENEY was not looking forward to this meeting. Jesse Case called him first, then Klyk, and they arranged to meet at party headquarters in Manhattan because the Klyk-Sturdivant team was scheduled for an evening rally at the Hilton.

Sweeney, of course, was fully aware of the problem and its implications. He and Jesse Case were old allies, going back some thirty years. Although Case stood to the right of Sweeney—especially to the right of his party—Sweeney had counted on Case for support at crucial times, and Case had delivered. The fact that he also delivered for the Republicans when they needed him was beside the point. The backing of thirty million dollars, and more important the knowledge of how to use it to its best advantage, gave Jesse Case a special status—if not respected, he was at least feared. Case had also been helpful to Jon Klyk as the mayor of Buffalo.

When Case walked into Sweeney's office he wasted no time getting to it.

"Let's get something straight, gentlemen. It's Loren Sturdivant or me."

Klyk tried to lighten the air. "That's pretty good for openers, Jesse."

Klyk's humor was a lead balloon. Case was there to settle the issue, not to be jollied.

Sweeney moved in.

"Jesse, the fact of the matter is that she's her own man. I'd be lying to you if I told you that Jon or I could control her—"

"Charlie, what exactly are you saying? Are you kissing off all the support you got from me in the past? Or are you saying that you really don't care if I stay neutral, maybe even tilt toward the other party?"

"I don't mean that at all, Jesse," Sweeney said quickly. "I'm no ingrate. What she's saying now is campaign rhetoric. Let's analyze what she's really said. She's never implied that you've committed a criminal or dishonest act. What she's said in effect is that you're a power broker—a powerful influence on state affairs and probably the most effective lobbyist in this state if not in the country—"

"I couldn't care less what she's saying about me. But she's definitely out to hurt people I represent. And what's worse, she doesn't know what the hell she's talking about." He turned to Klyk. "Jonny, you've got to understand she's spreading bull. What would she like to do, eliminate the public utilities? Do you know what would happen to the area if Mid-State Electric went down the tubes?"

"Sure, I know . . . But can't utilities exert the maximum safety standards to avoid catastrophic accident or an accumulation of pollution?"

Case's jaw tightened. Klyk was sounding more and more like Loren Sturdivant. "There's never been a catastrophic accident, as you put it. It still hasn't been proved that anyone died or even became ill from the Three Mile Island leak."

"We're not so sure about that, Jesse. Some reports I've read said there was an increase in strange illnesses in the area. Look, I've never gone back on a friend and I don't intend to start with you. But you've got to help me out a little. We've got to act like responsible leaders—"

"We *are* responsible, damn it. She's asking for stuff that would eliminate nuclear powered utilities altogether. And *that* would increase the cost of electricity to the average consumer. It's basic—the companies can't be in the black if expenses equal income. No profits mean no dividends—and eventually no company. If we go nuclear, we create jobs, and we make profits *and* produce cheaper power for people."

"Sounds good, Jesse, but look at Long Island—"

"They screwed it up on Long Island, I admit. They were in over their heads. They're thirteen years behind schedule and a hundred million over budget. That was amateur night. That utility is *not* one of my clients. Mid-State will do it right."

"What about disposal of nuclear waste?"

Case only looked at Klyk and said nothing, now convinced that Loren Sturdivant had gotten to Klyk.

He shifted his attention to Sweeney. "Charlie, I think we're all wasting our time."

But Klyk still tried to control the damage. "Jesse, listen, the truth is that I was caught by surprise in Schenectady. Loren never told me that she was going to attack you—"

"Never told you? Don't you people talk to each other? Don't you plan your strategy together?"

Klyk evaded it. "You have a right to be upset, and I intend to do something about it. I'll issue a statement that I hold you in high esteem and that a healthy public utility industry is essential for the economy of the state. All of which I believe. But I *won't* say that the present safeguards or the use of atomic fuel and waste disposal are up to speed to protect the public because I don't know that they are, and frankly I suspect that they aren't—"

"That won't do it, Jon. What I hear is a plan to saddle the industry with crazy safety standards that eventually would make it a state-run utility. Is that what you want?"

THE POWER

"You know it isn't, Jesse. I'm as opposed to government-owned facilities as you are. You know that. But I still believe we can watch out for people's safety and still earn a profit. You talk as if the two were oil and water."

Sweeney was getting very uneasy. Klyk's voice showed his irritation, and he knew Jon Klyk—you could push him just so far.

Case levered himself out of his chair. "I've got to think about this. I don't like what I'm hearing. Not one damn bit. Jon, I'm beginning to think that you're listening to that slut too much . . ."

Sweeney winced. He knew Klyk's regard for Loren Sturdivant. He'd also heard the rumors about their brief romantic interlude, now over, but, he suspected, leaving some warm memories. His concern was on the mark. The blood rushed to Klyk's face, and Sweeney, five-foot-seven and wide as a rowboat, moved as quickly as he could to stand as a buffer between the six-foot-three, 250-pound Jon Klyk and Jesse Case. When Klyk's Polish blood reached boiling he could be awesome. Like now . . .

Klyk swept Sweeney aside with the back of his hand and grabbed Case by the tie and lifted him off the floor. "Listen, you son of a bitch . . . you're talking about a lady who's got more class in one little finger than you'll ever have in your whole miserable life."

Case was gasping like a landed fish, and Sweeney was tugging hard as he could on Klyk's arm. "Jon, he's turning green. You'll kill him . . ."

Klyk finally got himself under control and released Case, who fell to the floor like a bag of laundry.

The mayor of Buffalo then walked out of the room without another word. Case, holding his throat and trying to catch his breath, managed to stand and he too then walked out, pausing only long enough to tell the New York State Democratic Chairman: "You're dead, Charlie. I'll bury you, your party *and* your candidate. Bet your life on it . . ."

74

Meanwhile Klyk walked into a private office to cool off. A minute before he'd been ready to compromise with Case, issue a public statement that could have been seen by the press as a division between Loren and himself—a possibly damaging move, but he'd felt bound to do it out of past-due bills. But Case had called Loren a slut. That turned him around. Maybe he still felt more for her than he'd admit— although it had been a short-term thing. Or maybe the "Loren" magic was getting to him too. Or maybe he approved of her position that real leaders had to put the people's interests above political cronies and allies, never mind the fallout . . .

Scott Morgan joined the campaign in Schenectady, and his abilities as a speech writer were quickly discovered and put to work. He worked closely with the candidates, researching the issues in all the counties they would cover in the last weeks of the campaign. It was an eighteen-hour-day routine. In Cayuga County they spoke at a street rally in Auburn, addressed a woman's group at Elmira and made a Chemung County stop. In one day they covered Cattaraugus County at Oleon, Chantaugua County in Jamestown, Chenango County at Norwich.

Scott thought he had a day off in Amsterdam before the last weeks' concentrated push, but it wasn't to be. His phone rang, interrupting his exhausted sleep, but when he heard his candidate's voice his mind focused like a conditioned reflex.

"Scott," Klyk said, "sorry to do this to you but I need you right away . . ."

Morgan was in Klyk's hotel room fifteen minutes later.

"I'm going after Mid-State Electric tomorrow," Klyk told him. "I'm going to take on Jesse Case."

Morgan raised his clenched fist. "All *right*." Case was not one of his favorite people, but up to now he hadn't advertised his feelings—at least to Klyk—because he respected the relationship that he thought existed between the mayor and Case.

Scott knew what Klyk wanted in a speech, and with Loren's people doing the research, he wrote a beauty in a hurry. When Klyk read the finished draft he was very pleased.

An overflow crowd greeted them at the rally, and this time Loren was the opening act and Jon Klyk the star. He built up to the climax slowly—just as Scott Morgan had written it—and then went to work:

"The time has come for the Public Service Commission of this state to account for caving in to every demand made by Mid-State Electric. In the early part of the year, the P.S.C. approved a 79.4 million dollar rate increase requested by Mid-State. It took unmitigated gall for Mid-State to make the request. But it took more unmitigated gall to grant it. The P.S.C. in this state is a farce—in the pockets of Governor Arnold Beale and Jesse Case. We're being looted—we're being robbed—we're being raped—and it's time to end it."

Then he stopped—and the crowd began to cheer as they watched Loren walking toward him, embracing him. Her magic had now literally rubbed off on him. Boss Sweeney, sitting in the first row and still concerned over Case's ability to take revenge for this attack and become an enemy forever, nonetheless was caught up in the moment, and he found himself standing and applauding like the rest of them.

Bennet Sloane sat patiently outside Jesse Case's office. It bothered him not a bit that he had been cooling his heels for forty-five minutes. Self-effacement was his forte—and because he was inconspicuous by appearance—short and balding with a face that was instantly forgettable—he fit his role perfectly. He was prepared to put up with disrespect and even contempt to achieve his eventual goal.

Finally the secretary's intercom buzzed and he heard her say, "Yes sir, Mr. Case. I'll send him right in." She looked at him, or more accurately through him, and pointed to the door of Case's office. Sloane had long ago given up trying to understand why people took an instant dislike to him, but it didn't bother him anymore. He smiled at the secretary, visualizing the day that would come when he was in a seat of power and the pleasure he would take in remembering her and others who put him down on his way up. He had a list, as did the Mikado's Lord High Executioner.

He walked gingerly into Case's massive office and closed the door silently behind him. The Persian rug covered the entire expanse of the floor. The desk was massive, made of carved mahogany by a European master. The picture windows, facing south and west, extended from floor to ceiling unencumbered by drapes or curtains, so that the vast expanse of sunlight and blue sky and water appeared to make the room twice its size.

Case sat in his chair, framed by this massive background. Bennet Sloane felt he was in the den of a potentate, His Holiness himself.

Case didn't ask him to be seated, although there were two comfortable-looking chairs on each side of the desk. In fact, he continued to peruse a report—allowing Sloane to remain standing in silence. When he finished, he placed it on the desk together with his glasses.

"I want you to quit the Klyk campaign," he said abruptly. "In the short time that's left until election day I want you to carry out another assignment."

"Yes, Mr. Case."

"Up to now we've been officially neutral. That's over. We're going all out for Governor Beale. Which means that we have to do everything to knock Jon Klyk out of the box."

"Yes, sir."

Case rose and looked Sloane squarely in the eye. "I want you to have something—something big—that I can give to the press the day before the election. I want it to be bad, so bad that his denial won't be enough. Do you get my meaning?"

Bennet Sloane got his meaning. A bombshell was wanted—to be exploded on election eve so that it could not be answered in time. It would have to be so devastating in impact that it could decide a close election. And Case specifically neglected to insist that the damaging item be true. It only had to have the appearance of being true . . . "I understand fully, Mr. Case."

"Good boy. Get on it. You only have two weeks."

His first efforts were fruitless. Klyk's occasional sexual dalliances of the past were known. A revelation of more of the same could produce at worst a public snicker followed by a larger yawn. But as with everything else that Sloane applied himself to, he pushed mercilessly, his bulldog style at full tilt. What, he thought, would be most damaging to a candidate in a close race? To offend a large chunk of the electorate. Get them mad enough to come out and vote again with adrenelin free-flowing. The target, of course, had to be a significant group—preferably one that historically had the highest proportion of "come-outs" on election day. The Jews. And what could bring the Jews out even more? Hints of anti-Semitism. Sloane also knew if he were to tar a candidate with that brush the evidence would have to be totally plausible—though not necessarily true. The seed had to be planted, and the lie would nurture itself and knock the targeted candidate out on his ass. When briefed, Case nodded in satisfaction. The Mole, as he privately thought of him, had never failed him. Some day this obnoxious young man would have to be repaid for his loyalty. But never—never—would he invite him home for dinner.

Case decided to give the story to his trusted friend Mortimer Fiske, publisher of the Syracuse *Ledger*. Fiske and he were old cronies who thought alike. Fiske also owned TV and radio outlets. By saturation coverage, the news services and other media would report the story immediately. After working out the time schedule with Fiske he called the governor.

"Arnold," he said, "I've decided to back you all the way. Watch the papers on election day. Klyk will be gone."

Arnold Beale was, of course, gratified—ecstatic—that he now was Case's candidate. The question did cross his mind as to why Case had waited so long to give him his endorsement, but he decided not to look a gift horse in the mouth. He did wonder what disaster Case had planned for his opponent. Naturally he asked no questions.


It took somebody as mentally and physically attractive as Scott Morgan to overcome the natural cynicism of Paula Lawson. As political reporter for the Syracuse *Ledger* she had a healthy skepticism about those connected with a pretty face crowned by brownish red hair. It was her paper's policy to back the governor and attack the Democrats, but she performed that task with intelligence and occasional acerbity. Although still in her twenties, her abilities were recognized, and she was called upon to be guest commentator on several television shows. To look at her, one might conclude that the vitriolic pieces she turned out were somehow out of character. In truth, they spoke her thoughts and feelings.

Because her paper knew her value, they allowed her to take potshots at both sides, but she was firmly notified that certain people were off limits. Governor Beale and Jesse Case were two of them. She could live with the hands-off on Beale, whom she considered relatively harmless, but Case she considered venal.

Still, she understood the practical aspects of the newspaper business and lived with it. If she quit and joined another paper, she was certain that if not Jesse Case there would be some other sacred cow protected by "editorial policy."

Comforting her in her conflict was the reasonable hope that she would soon be leaving the *Ledger* for greener pastures in New York—and possibly a future in television news. She was also aware of how quickly word spread in her industry if one was classified as "difficult."

But no such careful considerations applied where Scott Morgan was involved. His success with the opposite sex was not thanks to his matinee-idol features alone. He never came on to women—he respected them and truly liked them. Qualified to be called a "hunk," he was much more, and Paula Lawson appreciated his intelligence, his tenderness and his apparent sincerity. It was only a matter of time before they got together.

It happened in Syracuse a week before election day. She invited him to dinner at her apartment; nothing had to be said, everything was understood.

Dinner was short-lived, and the night was a fulfillment of the expectations of both.

In the early morning hours they were listening to Vivaldi, and she was stroking his face.

"Why," she said quietly, like an invitation.

"Why what?"

"Why are you so involved in this campaign?"

He raised himself from the pillow. "At first I thought it was a way of getting out of Schenectady. Now . . . to tell the truth, I've been educated about the government of this state, what's wrong with it and what can be done about it . . ."

"You're putting me on."

"It may sound naive, but the more I see how this administration works, the more I believe that Klyk-Sturdivant can at least begin to turn things around.

Paula left the bed and slipped on her negligee. "Scott,

what makes you think a new administration will really change anything? We're talking about political animals. Don't you know the nature of the beast?"

"Yes, I think I do. But Loren Sturdivant, and to my surprise Jon Klyk, are genuinely interested in doing something."

"Or appear to be, during the campaign," she said. "I could buy that about Loren Sturdivant. She's the new kid on the block, and she can afford to be pure as the driven snow . . . but Jon Klyk?"

"Maybe you're right, but consider that the people of Buffalo elected him mayor four times, and only the first one was close. I've checked on his record in Buffalo and I've talked to voters there. They say he cared about the needs of people. He had a bond with the electorate."

"Yes," she said, "but he also surrounded himself with cronies, including crooks. I agree he kept himself clean—he let his friends rip off the city. No mayor can be totally unaware of what's going on in his administration."

"A failing," Scott agreed, "but doesn't his joining up with Loren Sturdivant in taking on Jesse Case show some political courage—especially now? You know he's made an enemy of Case forever."

"True, but if elected he'll probably revert to type . . ."

She went to the window, listening to the rain, and finally came back and sat next to him on the bed. "Look, I've got a problem," she said slowly. "And you're a big part of it. There's something I should tell you, but if I do I'll have to give up information I discovered within the four walls of the Syracuse *Ledger*—a journalistic no-no. But if I don't, another political 'dirty trick' will be carried out, and this one, unlike Watergate, could work and turn an election around."

She searched his face for a reaction.

"Whatever choice you make is okay," he said.

"You bastard, you're no help. Oh, what the hell, I'm enti-

tled to one good turn a year. We'll talk while I make breakfast."

He followed her into the small kitchen.

"Have you ever met an individual by the name of Bennet
Sloane?"

"Yes, I've had that misfortune."

"How do you know him?"

"Until recently he was a part of the Klyk-Sturdivant campaign team, in charge of transportation, I think."

"He's no longer with you?"

"No—he disappeared, just didn't show up about ten days
ago, and we haven't seen him since."

"Didn't you ever wonder why?"

"Damn right we wondered why, and then we wondered
where he went, but more important, where he came from.
And then we got caught up in the campaign and he got lost."

"Bennet Sloane is a spy, Scott. He works for Jesse Case.
He's now in the process of completing a dirty trick that will
make Watergate look like kiddie time . . ."

It had happened a week before, she told him, when she
saw Sloane talking to her editor Morty Fiske. She had been
working late on a lead story about her impressions of the
Klyk-Sturdivant campaign. Sloane and Fiske? How come?
Why was Sloane here? She saw Sloane shake Fiske's hand
and watched Fiske take him to the paper's morgue and leave
him there . . . Watching from a distance, she saw Sloane take
out two files, scrutinize the clippings and make notes. He
was so absorbed that he didn't hear her as she walked up
quietly behind him, looked over his shoulder and saw the
large red stenciled numbers on the face of the files. At that
point he looked up but saw only her back. She went back to
her desk and waited. He was there for more than an hour
before returning the files and leaving.

She went quickly to the morgue. "K-192, K-1131 . . ." She
repeated the file numbers to an empty room, found them and
sat down to study them.

K-192 was the bulging file on Jon Klyk. Nothing there that she didn't know: a chronological history of Jon Klyk's entrance into Buffalo politics as an alderman, his ascendancy to Democratic leader of Erie County and mayor of Buffalo. At the time it made no sense. Why would a worker in Klyk's campaign have to go to a newspaper morgue to get information about his own candidate? Then she looked at the other file, K-1131, and found the name Stefan Klykowski. She recognized the name . . . She hadn't been born when the Nuremberg trials recorded his brutality for posterity, but she had done a piece on Auschwitz and had written in her article that if Auschwitz was the factory of death, Stefan Klykowski was its foreman; that he personally had terminated ten thousand Jews, including women and children; that he was convicted and hung . . .

And then the light flashed. She went back to the Klyk file and dug until she found it—dated January 23, 1949:

"Alderman Jon Klyk responded to the question from his Polish-American constituents last night at a Town Hall meeting. When asked why he shortened his name from Klykowski, he said: 'I didn't—my father did. It was Klykowski in the old country, but he changed it when he came here—or the customs people changed it for him. I use the name I was born with.'"

She read further. His father, Jerczy Klykowski, emigrated to the United States in 1913 from a town called Modzik. Back to Stefan Klykowski's file. Bingo. Stefan Klykowski was born in Modzik, a town so small that she couldn't find it on a map. Now she was on to what was building in Sloane's conniving little mind. It stood to reason that two Klykowskis living in the same village were related. Stefan Klykowski stayed in Poland and became a war criminal. Jerczy Klykowski arrived in America and became known as Jerry Klyk, American as apple pie, fathering four sons. The oldest, Jon, served in World War II and the Korean conflict and was honorably discharged with a chestful of citations.

If the Klykowskis were cousins, or even brothers, they had only their blood in common. Yet it was clear what Sloane was planning and the smear that Case would lay on through the paper. The name connection would be headlined—but it would only be at the middle or toward the end of the story that it would appear that there was no proof of any substantive connection. Never mind, the idea would be planted—and the Jewish electorate in particular could draw the intended inference. The damage would, of course, be devastating, especially in a close election. Paula had little doubt that her paper, favoring incumbent Beale, would run the story the day before the election—probably in the first edition that hit the stands in the afternoon. But whenever the story was run, she was sure that it would be timed so as to give Klyk insufficient opportunity to respond.

When she finished her story Scott shook his head. "I can't believe they could sink so low . . ."

"Believe it," she said.

He kissed her. "I know how tough this was for you, and what it took for you to do it."

She laughed. "Aw, sex with you wasn't all that tough."

Scott was already on her phone, calling the hotel to wake up Klyk. The candidate had checked into his Syracuse hotel late and had wanted to catch up on his sleep before the scheduled noon rally.

"How did you get the information?" Klyk said after he heard Scott's story.

"From a reliable informant."

"Can you give me the name?"

"I'm afraid not. It would be a breach of trust—"

"Okay, I'll take it from here. And Scott . . ."

"Yes, sir."

"I owe you."

\* \* \*

Abe Feldman had one foot out the door when the phone rang and his wife called to him from the door.

"Abe," she said excitedly, "it's Mayor Klyk."

He rushed to the phone. "Mr. Mayor—what a pleasure—"

"Abe, I've got a crisis here that you can help me with."

"Shoot."

Abe Feldman was incensed at what he heard. As chairman of the Buffalo branch of the Anti-Defamation League he knew who the anti-Semites in Buffalo were. And he knew that John Klyk was in the vanguard exposing them, rooting them out, refusing their support. This move by Case was a cheap shot and a fraud—to manipulate the Jewish vote . . .

He went to work immediately, calling an emergency meeting of his executive board, of which one of the directors was David Michael, who happened to be managing editor of the Buffalo *Pilot*, a pro-Klyk paper. Abe concentrated on Michael.

"We're being used by Case and nobody can tell me that Governor Beale doesn't know about this. We have enough trouble fighting Jew-haters without allowing our friends to be harpooned. Dave, let's stop this shit right now."

Dave Michael puffed on his pipe, but his exterior denied the fire he felt inside.

"We'll run it tomorrow, Abe."

The story hit Case hard—and by clear implication, Governor Beale. It traced Klyk's record on Jewish affairs and his relationship with the Jewish community, detailing how Klyk had repeatedly condemned anti-Semitic bigotry. The editorial, written by Michael, did the number on Case and Beale that Abe had asked for.

"In a story elsewhere in this paper we have exposed a cynical, dirty trick that was attempted by Jesse Case and others still to be identified. We had thought that Watergate had ended such tactics, but apparently there are those who will continue to drag American politics into the mud. We believe it is our obligation to search out and expose the vermin who would pollute our system. The scorn and revulsion of the electorate should be directed at any candidate who would allow such tactics. Any claim that Governor Beale was unaware of Case's actions insults the intelligence."

The Buffalo *Pilot*'s story hit the wire services and was carried statewide and beyond. The headline: "Another Watergate" got attention with one week to go. It was a shot in the arm to the Klyk campaign and a severe setback to Beale. The Syracuse *Ledger* promptly scrapped the "Klykowski Connection" story.

*Dear Mr. Case:*

*I wish to take this opportunity to thank you for the enlightening and beneficial experience of being in your employment. Even though the duration of my service has been brief I have benefited greatly from it.*

*I have, however, accepted a position in California that offers an opportunity I cannot turn down. Therefore I hereby tender my resignation, effective immediately, with sincere regrets.*

*Sincerely yours,*
*Bennet Sloane*

He signed the letter, stamped it and mailed it at Kennedy Airport. He caught the last flight to L.A. as a strategy for moving up in his new job, which he had had the foresight to arrange as a back-up in case of just such an emergency. He was not, he assured himself, defeated—just diverted.

# Chapter Eight

ALTHOUGH the Klykowski boomerang hurt Beale, it did not knock him out. On October 30, three days before the election, the New York *Daily News* still had Beale ahead by two points. Beale continued to drive home his message of stability and experience, which helped him hold his own.

The three Beale-Klyk debates were standoffs—Klyk a more attractive debater, Beale's position carefully programmed toward being tough on crime, holding the line on taxes, keeping his antiabortion position. Some polls showed only a one-point difference. A dead heat. The bookies made it a 6 to 5 pick 'em, and every political observer agreed that it was the closest race since they started polling in the forties.

Financial resources weren't a factor. Loren Sturdivant was personally the most affluent, and spent on the Klyk-Sturdivant campaign a record $15 million of her own money, but the power of the incumbency was considerable, and Arnold Beale raised enough to match her dollar for dollar.

In these last few days both sides reverted to the personal approach—Beale stressed his upstate origins in rallies at

Syracuse, Binghamton, Elmira, Ithaca, Utica, Jamestown and Plattsburgh; Klyk returned to his strongholds in New York City, Buffalo, Albany and Yonkers. In these last appearances he responded to the advice of young Scott Morgan, whose analytical mind he and Loren Sturdivant came to respect. Morgan said that the negativeness of Klyk's campaign through the attacks on Beale—although seemingly well-received at the rallies—was not having the desired effect on the total electorate. Morgan believed that a good proportion of the voters did not really give a damn about Beale being in the pocket of big business. In fact, it was his opinion that such an alignment was attractive, not only to those who had it made but also to the yuppies scratching under the Tiffany lamps to get there.

As for air pollution, he told Klyk and Loren at a strategy meeting that possible nuclear accidents, scary as they were, were not bread-and-butter issues. "We're in pretty good times now, but the recession of the seventies is fresh in everyone's mind. Voters give number one priority to feeding their bellies, to paying the mortgage and sweating to have enough left over to educate the kids. The stock market craziness doesn't help too much, but it's still fairly remote for the average person."

So at Scott's urging, Klyk and Loren reached out to Mickey Goldman and made him an important consultant. Mickey's area, of course, was labor, but his influence extended to private business because of his personal relationships with business and labor leaders. Scott was amazed at Mickey Goldman's built-in understanding of what made people tick, what the elusive man-in-the-street was looking for from those who governed. Mickey and Morgan now drew up proposals that had not been spoken of before—proposals that Klyk would implement in his administration. They talked about a homeowners mortgage insurance plan, which for a small premium could prevent foreclosures. And increased state aid to the disabled—a guarantee of medical care. And guarantees of state-financed treatment for the elderly suffering catastrophic illnesses. All adding to the "compassionate" role that the government would take under a Klyk-Sturdivant administration.

The response was more than favorable. Jon Klyk and Loren Sturdivant manned the phone banks with the other volunteers, asking instead of telling about individuals' problems and suggesting how government could help.

Beale wasn't asleep. He traded on his two terms of experience and the stability of the state, which wasn't in bad shape. It was true that he was generally seen as antilabor, but so were a lot of people who were fed up with labor's "gimme-gimme" stands in good times and bad. Mickey Goldman admitted it. Beale had another advantage. He had been generous in his appointments of members of the opposition party to key positions, and for the most part they were quality appointments, especially his appointment of a Democrat as chief judge of the court of appeals. So Beale had friends in Democratic circles, and collectible due bills—not in the form of open support for the candidate of the opposition, but in abstaining from any political activity for their presumed candidate, which was just as good.

In these last days Klyk found himself pushing causes fairly new to him—commitments to the homeless, to teenage mothers, to health-care improvement, but he felt comfortable with them, so comfortable that Loren labeled them both "closet liberals." And behind that was the basic truth that they shared an attitude of caring, although they differed on how to accomplish their ends.

Loren Sturdivant had made a 180-degree turn from her roots. Her father, Arthur Phillips, the classic capitalist, was a tycoon in the mold of the Rockefellers, Whitneys, Sturdivants, and Joseph Kennedy. In amassing his fortune her father's last consideration was the welfare of the populace. Nevertheless, as with the Kennedy offspring, she developed a social consciousness so out of step with the Phillips family history that had her father in his Maryland grave been made aware of his offspring's new philosophy he would have been referred to as "revolving Arthur."

Like, F.D.R., not only was her approach foreign to her history, but it seemed out of character with her own personality—or at least her persona, beyond which few if any had penetrated, including Jon Klyk, who had once shared her bed. Just how far did that fire in her eyes go when she spoke out about reform and the people? As close as they'd been in these past months, Klyk still could not read her. But he could distinguish the difference in their approaches. She was all out, get the rascals, and so forth. He was more restrained, not about to be labeled a flaming liberal. Scott Morgan agreed with Klyk, and convinced Loren to go along with Jon Klyk's moderate reformism that still left the voters with a choice. She wasn't satisfied with the degree of difference between the Beale and Klyk campaign positions, but she also appreciated that even a hint of a rift between the two at this stage would be fatal to the victory she was sure of.

Jon Klyk and Scott Morgan were less sure. There seemed to be no movement in the polls. The Jewish backfire seemed only to stop Beale from forging ahead, because he always had come up even with the Jewish vote, and although some of it was lost, all of it wasn't. The poll results showed that the poor and so-called underprivileged were strong for his opponent, but that had already been discounted. As for the rest, whether classified by sex or ethnic origin or age, or whatever, the results were surprising . . . one would think that Klyk-Sturdivant would have done better with them. But like the yuppies, they seemed less concerned with social justice than getting a piece of the pie and holding on to what they had. If the election had been held in the seventies, Scott said, it would have been no contest; a candidate with Beale's philosophy would not have had the staying power of a match in a hurricane. But then was then—now was now.

Nerves in both camps were frayed by uncertainty, and

while Klyk admired Loren he wondered what she used for a nervous system. She appeared serene and confident, without a trace of sweaty palms, headaches or butterfly-stomach.

Scott Morgan's doubts were nurtured by the best barometer—the flow, or the lack thereof, of political contributions immediately preceding the election. True, Klyk-Sturdivant wasn't hurting for funds, but contributions were solicited for "mood detection." People who dealt with government—industrialists, law firms, public relations types, contractors, builders and anyone who would profit from state funds—had a pressing fear of missing the boat. They tended to sense imminent victory better than most, and like an insider in the stock market they made their move on what they believed to be solid information. Since it was an undeniable fact that sizable contributions to political campaigns were not motivated by the totally pure in heart, the most uplifting sign was a sudden increase just before election, before the bandwagon left forever.

But the funds weren't coming in. Not enough, at least, to indicate the confidence out there in a Democratic victory. Still, the Republicans weren't getting it either.

Paula Lawson said it succinctly in her column: "This election promises to be the closest ever recorded in New York State's gubernatorial history. The polls show one percent either way, which in effect is a dead heat. The Almighty may very well decide this one." Meaning the Supreme Being could decide it by how he designed the weather conditions on election day. By tradition, the rural areas went Republican and the urban areas Democratic. If the weather was good in one area and not the other, the sun could very well shine on the winner.

Now, two days before election, it was obvious to Loren Sturdivant that all possible benefit from her public appearances was gained and that it would serve no purpose to hit the stump again. But she knew how important the starry-eyed volunteers were, and how important it was that their passion for her cause be maintained. So she went with Scott Morgan to all the headquarters throughout the state in a grueling nonstop forty-eight hours. She met and spoke to them at the coffee klatches, at the union halls, in the ballrooms and in their homes—thanking them and spurring them on. She had little or no sleep, because when she wasn't meeting with them she was traveling. And though she was bone tired, on the point of exhaustion, when she burst into a room where supporters had congregated she was indeed an "Evita," complete with smile and gesture and body language that inspired a feverish reception.

On election eve she managed to wipe out her opposite number, Lieutenant Governor Jim Collins, in a television debate—he had to be dragged to it kicking and screaming—after which she and Scott Morgan took the limo to the Carlyle Hotel. Once in her suite she allowed the weariness to take hold, and, fully dressed, she collapsed on her bed.

Her soft laugh stopped Scott when he walked toward the door. "If you're going to take advantage of me," she said, "now's the time to . . ."

"It wouldn't be any fun, you're too tired. It wouldn't be a fair contest."

She smiled. "You're probably right—but why don't you stay here tonight? Just in case there's a revival?"

He moved toward her bed, kissed her lightly, flipped the light switch and left her room. He understood she wanted him there for more than sex—she didn't want to be alone on the eve of the most important night of her life.

She had planned to have Cynthia bring Donna up on election day, after the voting, so that they could be with her when the votes were tallied. Melody was in a drug rehabilitation program in the city, and although she phoned her daily, it was too early in her treatment to consider release even for a day.

Scott was exhausted too, and used one of the adjoining bedrooms of the suite to collapse in, stripping to his shorts before hitting the bed and falling asleep almost immediately.

He slept through the night and missed his early morning appointments on election day. When he woke up he had to rub his eyes and try to focus on what he was seeing and feeling. Next to him, holding him in her arms, was the candidate for lieutenant governor of the state of New York—without a stitch.

"I thought you were so tired," he said.

"Not that tired. Now be a gentleman . . ."

As she moved him into position, he accepted the inevitability of it. He knew it was coming almost from the first time they met. But she, characteristically, chose the moment. Her lovemaking was performed in the same fashion as everything else she was interested in—intensely and with total commitment. He had enjoyed the pleasures of a good many beds, including the recent experience with Paula Lawson, but never was it like this—anyone better than this could very possibly kill him. They were not interrupted by phone calls . . . Loren had signaled the desk by pushing a button that no calls would be taken until further notice . . . and after they had satisfied each other they fell back into a deep sleep.

It was noon before he was awake. She was still out. He covered her with a second blanket that he had retrieved from the other bedroom and dressed silently. He walked into the sitting room and turned on the television. No news yet, of course; the upstate polling places were just opening. His interest at that moment was focused solely on the weather report, and what he heard was to his liking: New York City was forty-five degrees and partly sunny, cool but not uncomfortably so. No rain in sight. Upstate—snow in the northern regions and a heavy front from Canada bringing heavy rains in a southeasterly direction to reach New York City *tomorrow*. Beale country gets it today, and we get it tomorrow. If Scott had ordered it, it couldn't have been better.

He looked at the door of the bedroom where Loren was

sleeping, then left the suite and went directly to campaign headquarters.

She woke up at 2:00 P.M., turned on the phone and ordered breakfast. She had just replaced the receiver when the phone rang. It was the top of the ticket calling from Buffalo.

"Good afternoon, lady. It's just like you to laze away the day while I work my ass off just to get us elected. Do you realize that I started touring the polls at five this morning?"

She laughed.

"Loren . . ."

"Yes?"

"Whatever happens—win or lose—you were, and always will be, a real class act."

In spite of herself, mist filled her eyes. "You weren't so bad yourself. I never would have figured out why Case turned on you so suddenly and so late in the campaign until Charlie Sweeney told me you put the whole election on the line defending me. Talk about class acts . . ."

"I wish he hadn't told you."

"Well, you know Charlie, I think he cares about both of us and wanted me to know the kind of character you are. I won't forget it . . ."

The next call was from Scott at headquarters. A media event was set for 3:00 P.M. at the public school where she was scheduled to vote.

She showed up in a simple purple knit dress that accentuated her slimness and figure. She was still tired but had camouflaged the circles under her eyes with deft application of eye shadow and answered all the reporters' questions. She then returned to the Carlyle with Scott.

They heard the first real news at 4:00 P.M. It wasn't good. Beale was ahead in a test of 200 exit votes in the New York City suburbs by a disturbing five points. Naturally this was inconclusive, but Klyk sounded concerned when she called him, although she tried to play down its significance.

At 4:45 headquarters called with better news. They were

coming out of the woodwork in New York City. Voters were lined up at the polls, and watchers reported a 25 percent increase in voter turnout compared to the same time the previous year—which had been a presidential election!

At 5:15 P.M. the news turned bad again. Rochester, Syracuse and other upstate cities that were Beale strongholds, despite the sleet and the cold, were reporting record numbers there as well.

The confidence that Jon Klyk had in Scott Morgan's efficiency was demonstrated by Scott's being put in charge of the vote pulling operation that started at 3:00 P.M. in New York City. A military operation could not have been more efficiently planned or executed. Hired cars and vans covered the city, transporting voters to the polls from housing clusters, nursing homes and even hospitals where patients were ambulatory. Coffee and donuts were served. Senior citizens were aided in every possible way, and if nursing personnel had to be on hand, they were. Everyone who was escorted was treated with tender loving care before and after the curtains closed on the voting booth.

Results began to show by 8:00 P.M. All World Media, as a result of exit-poll numbers, predicted an amazing 75 percent Klyk vote in New York City and a smashing 80 percent in Buffalo. Yet Beale was piling up equally startling numbers in his areas of strength.

By 11:00 P.M. there was still no clear winner, and the paper ballots sent in by the servicemen and -women and absentees were the only votes left to be counted.

It was not until after midnight that the State Board of Elections figures were released. They heard it first in a newscast by Tom McPartland, the All World Media political correspondent: "We now can state with certainty that Mayor Jon Klyk of Buffalo has defeated incumbent Governor Arnold Beale in the closest gubernatorial election in New York State history. Governor Beale will no doubt call for a recount, but the figures that we have are truly amazing.

"Mayor Klyk received 2,527,385 on the Democratic line and 110,320 on the Liberal line, for a total of 2,637,705. Governor Beale received 2,252,623 on the Republican line, 218,020 on the Conservative line and 117,120 on the Right to Life line, making a total of 2,587,763. The total votes cast were 5,225,468. The margin of victory was 49,942, less than 1 percent—incredibly close.

"Political analysts will have a field day over what could have been done to change the result. Did Case's power-broker attempt to manipulate the Jewish vote rub off on Beale? Was it the weather? Was it Loren Sturdivant's celebrity? Was it a combination of all these and more? We'll never really know. But we do know that somewhere along the way one side worked a little harder or a little longer than the other. If this reporter had to guess, I would say that the popular "Evita," as some call her, Sturdivant put Jon Klyk over the top by her tireless and remarkable campaigning."

At 2:00 A.M. they were sure. The paper-ballot count was favoring Klyk. They had won. Beale did not concede, but everyone agreed that a recount would not do it for him. As Sweeney said, in the absence of massive fraud—and claims of irregularities by either side in the election were minimum—a recount would only reaffirm the winner and probably add to the winning margin.

The concession call from Beale came at 3:00 A.M., and with it Jon Klyk was the new governor of the state of New York and Loren Sturdivant the new lieutenant governor—the first female to win the office in New York.

They made their victory speeches at the Sheraton Centre, the statewide headquarters, and the ballroom was packed. The scene got to the new governor, whose eyes became wet, but not so the newly elected lieutenant governor, who stood dry-eyed—like a monarch responding to the adoring throng.

They stayed in the ballroom until 5:00 A.M., when the newly elected governor and lieutenant governor left the still-celebrating crowd and were given the privacy of the penthouse suite. Scott Morgan remained outside the door.

They said nothing at first. Jon Klyk had not yet digested the implications of his victory. Loren Sturdivant took it in her stride. But she, too, stood at the window facing east, savoring this moment as the first streaks of dawn illuminated the city.

Finally Klyk spoke: "For some reason, don't know why, I'm thinking now of a movie I saw a long time ago. The candidate in this movie won after a campaign as hard as we've just gone through. I remember that he looked like all the starch was taken out of him and he was as limp as I feel now. And then he turned to one of his advisors and asked, 'What do we do now?' The picture ended with that question, and at the time I thought it was a sappy ending. But now, I understand what he meant . . ."

"Maybe you're still in shock," she said.

"That's possible, but . . . being governor of the state of New York is one big job . . ."

"Jon, why do you think the people of Buffalo made you their mayor *four* different times?"

"My Barrymore profile?"

"I'm serious, *Governor.*"

The exhaustion was beginning to take hold. He yawned, finding it hard to concentrate. "I think," he said, "that maybe up to now the reason is I've tried hard to like people and wanted people to like me. It's not enough anymore."

They watched the dawn break and the day take over the

city. Suddenly Klyk shook his head as if to clear it. "Okay, Loren, school's out. Let's get at it."

"I'm right behind you, Governor."

And to herself, Just don't make the mistake of looking over your shoulder . . .

# Part Two

# Chapter Nine

WHEN the English settlers first saw the inlet on the south shore of what was later named Long Island, they were charmed. The bay was landlocked on three sides—Fire Island to the south, the banks of Fireplace Creek pouring in from Brookhaven on the east, and on the west Patchogue Indian Village jutting into the bay.

In the early eighteenth century, they met friendly Indians, the Unkechaugs, who aptly called this inlet Occumbomock—"opposite the fishing place." Fish were plentiful because the waters that had forged through the Great South Barrier Beach fed the inlet from the Atlantic. Whales were seen in great quantities, and the English developed the area into a place of fishermen and boat people thriving on the life and climate. For southern European immigrants who came later, the climate of Long Island was not that attractive, but to the English it was a distinct improvement. Eventually, in 1835, a Captain Bell who was in the business of dismantling wrecked ships came to the inlet on business, liked what he saw, bought up the most valuable property and made it his home. Which was as good a reason as any to name the village after him. Bellport, Long Island, became a monument to the good captain who had the foresight to invest in it.

Scott Morgan, on a less happy mission than the founding captain, was nonetheless charmed by the place as he drove east on South County Road on this June day, past large oaks, which had not been destroyed by the hurricane, and the old homes, white and stately, that reminded Scott of the antebellum South.

Like many before him, he felt compelled to park his car in Bellport and have a look around. He walked south on Bellport Lane toward the marina and dock. The homes were remarkably preserved, most of them the original residences of the whalers who had settled the village. He walked along the beach, looked across the bay. Just a few nautical miles away, gleaming in the sun, was the refuge of those who escaped the tension of the city—Fire Island. Scott's appointment by the governor as director of the newly created office of ombudsman brought him instant public recognition *and* responsibilities. It also played hell with his love life.

He walked on through the village, past neat, clean stores, went back to his car and proceeded east again on South County Road. Suddenly, the beauty of the green trees and shrubbery and lawns and oak trees dissolved into the bareness of brown earth, and he knew he was at Snyder's Flats before he saw the sign: Danger—Drink No Water In This Area."

For Sale signs stood forlornly in front of almost all the houses—put up long ago when there was some hope that others would buy them at bargain prices. It was an eerie feeling, like walking through a ghost town, except that this was an island of desolation, surrounded by the otherwise coastal beauty of the South Shore.

And why did they leave? There was no mystery here, or to island residents who could read a newspaper or watch TV news. The mystery was why the authorities, duty-bound to investigate a tragedy, had done next to nothing about it.

He parked the car, got out and waited. As prearranged, a large, red-faced man approached him.

"Mr. Morgan?"

"Yes—and you're Mathew Bradley."

"Yes, sir."

Bradley was tall, perhaps even taller than Scott, perhaps in his early forties, though it was difficult to tell; Bradley's face showed the lines of a man who either was older, or who had lived through too much sorrow.

"Thanks for coming, Mr. Morgan," he said. "I've written a lot of letters to a lot of people. Either they sent me back form letters or they ignored me. I don't know what you can do about it now, but at least you're here."

Scott looked at the desolation around him. "Is this where it happened?"

Bradley nodded and motioned Scott to follow him. They walked in silence about two hundred yards and stopped. "Take a look around you, Mr. Morgan. This was the storage dump, and this is where it all started."

Scott saw a ten-acre stretch of violated earth. Metal drums that had been buried were partially exposed, and a close inspection of them showed that some had burst at the seams, and surrounding those were sickly green-and-yellow scummy liquids.

Scott pulled a tape recorder from his pocket. "What you say to me now is important, Mr. Bradley. The machine is going to record it, unless you object."

"I don't."

"Tell it from the beginning."

"When it happened I was working as an engineer for the water authority. To really understand this you'd have to know the particular water problem we have on Long Island. We're one of the few areas of the state that relies on aquifers for its drinking water. Aquifers are water-storage layers deep in the earth that supply our well-water. Aquifers are supposed to purge contaminants naturally, in a process that takes hundreds of thousands of years. The water we drink here is hundreds, maybe thousands, of years old. But the quality of the water we drink reflects the condition of the land, because naturally purified water, when it becomes groundwater, must of course come into contact with the earth. Where we're standing now you can see the perfect example of how groundwater was poisoned by man. It was caused by the storing and the dumping of deadly toxic materials."

"Such as."

"Among others—dioxin. Barrels of the stuff were shipped from chemical factories in the New York City area. That's how they got rid of their waste. You can see these barrels, partially exposed, that were supposed to have been buried deep in the ground. You can see how the seams split, allowing the poison to cover the ground. It just seeped into the groundwater—and a deadly poison, Mr. Morgan, became part of the water that flowed from our taps."

"When did it first show itself?"

"It started with the birds, we saw a lot of dead birds on the ground. Then we got a lot of stillborn puppies and kittens. And then it hit humans—serious illnesses—in the area, in every home. I mean *every* home."

Bradley pointed to a large house. "This place doesn't look like much now, but it was a fine house. The lawns were green and the shrubs were manicured. The man who owned it was right proud of it. Two years ago he had a lung removed. Last year he died." He pointed to the house across the road. "The woman who lived there died in childbirth— and the baby was stillborn. The one next to it, he had kidney cancer. Everybody's moved away. The house next to it, their little girl had bladder problems. She's five. Should I go on?"

"Good God . . ."

"I could go down each house. No one was spared."

Morgan shook his head. "I can't believe this—"

"Oh, believe it, Mr. Morgan. That dump contained ten acres of death. If you had walked further in, you would have seen that some of the drums weren't even buried—just left on the surface where the elements were bound to cause the metal to deteriorate and the poison to seep out. When we examined the spillage we knew we were in trouble—arsenic, D.D.T. and chlordane. Poison. What makes it worse is that the sons of bitches took no precautions at all. About fifty barrels were dumped at the edge near the Westlands. A water main that starts here and runs right through to Bellport was found to contain dioxin. Between here and Bellport there's a small lake. You must have seen it on the way. Well, at one time you could drink the water in that lake. It's never clear anymore. One family had a house on that lake, and two of their girls developed pituitary problems. The boy grew a tumor on his pancreas and died last year. He was eighteen."

Bradley now had a glint of anger in his eyes. "Mr. Morgan, we have about seventy-five active members of a Rotary Club in this area. Four have developed uterine cancer, almost always fatal. It wasn't publicized out of respect for the privacy of the victims. I can see one case, or two, but four? In the same group? All getting it at the same time? You tell me that it's a coincidence."

"When did you all get out?"

"I was the first. They didn't believe me at first, didn't want to. I had to point out the deaths, and the illnesses, before they believed me and left."

They returned to the dump, and this time Scott followed Bradley well into it, seeing the sickish gray color of the earth with spots of orange and green reflecting the toxicity of the poisons that had been buried there.

Scott was convinced.

"All right, Mr. Bradley. Who owns the dump?"

"Good question, Mr. Morgan. The deed file at the courthouse lists the owner as Dispo, Inc., in care of an attorney at the attorney's address."

"Any other names on the deed?"

"No, the certificate of incorporation lists only the attorney and two other people, probably his secretary and an associate, as subscribers—the usual procedure used to hide the true owner. Are you a lawyer, Mr. Morgan?"

"Yes."

"Then you know the routine."

"Do you have his name and address?"

"Yes, but he won't talk to anyone. When I called him and asked for the owner's name he said it's a privileged communication between him and his client and to reveal it would be a breach of professional ethics—"

"Not always," Scott said.

Bradley handed him a piece of paper. "Here it is, Gerald Canfield, Esq., 18 Oak Road, Smithtown . . . Mr. Morgan, I'll be frank with you. I'm grateful you had the decency to answer my letter and come here personally to see this. But I don't know what good it's going to do. Canfield won't reveal his client's name to you, and even if he does, so what? The county has begun an investigation, made their headlines—and the name still hasn't been revealed. This acreage won't be used again, they tell me it was legal to dump here when they did, no crime has been committed, they say, and the story is over. They *murdered* people here, they ruined lives—and the story is over."

Scott grabbed his arm. "Mr. Bradley, the governor sent me here because he has a genuine interest in this matter. We will find out who's responsible for this, and where the blame lies. We'll get the son of a bitch and expose him, and if he committed a crime we'll see that he is prosecuted."

"We'll see, Mr. Morgan. I heard all this talk when the story first broke in the Long Island papers. Promises. He's protected by the law, and we're out of luck."

Scott knew there was nothing more he could say to reassure Bradley. The man had every reason to believe that the system was corrupt, that there had been a cover-up of the abomination at Snyder's Flats and that he was making token inquiries only to bury the matter once more on a pile of dust-gathering papers that would be moved from one pile to another until it was interred permanently in a dead file to be forgotten forever.

Too much talk. Time for action.


Ross Montgomery was not happy. As district attorney of the county he had no choice but to see this Scott Morgan character who was obviously representing the governor's office. He reread again the letter requesting the appointment. "Office of Ombudsman"—what the *hell* was that? Supposed to look after the people's interests, supposed to right wrongs? Another gimmick by the new governor or the lieutenant governor, or both, to harass officeholders and thereby give Klyk and Sturdivant a bright, shiny high profile.

Snyder's Flats again. God, when will this ever go away? His office had investigated it, found no laws were broken. All safeguards required by the Environmental Protection Authority were complied with. The waste was buried in stainless steel barrels that met the standards of the E.P.A. The government inspectors found no laws were broken. The poisoning of the water was tragic, but it was an inherent effect of the toxic waste problem. He had nothing to go to a grand jury with. At best, the people at Snyder's Flats had a civil suit, and not a great one at that, in view of the E.P.A. findings. He buzzed his secretary.

"Tell Mr. Morgan to come in." Scott had no sooner closed the door than Montgomery spoke up.

"Mr. Morgan, I'm kind of busy today, but of course I want to be courteous to you and the governor . . ."

Scott sat down without being asked to.

"We really appreciate that, Mr. Montgomery."

Montgomery caught the sarcasm. "My office investigated this incident when we first heard about it. We've exhausted every avenue of investigation, we've found no violation of the law—"

"Mr. Montgomery, do you know what they were burying?"

"Of course . . . toxic chemical waste. That's why they had to bury it—"

"But were you aware that Dispo, Inc., was burying the waste of one particular toxic chemical—tetrachloroethylene, which your county legislature outlawed in 1981 because it caused cancer in rats."

Montgomery, beginning to boil, was frustrated by his own ignorance. What the hell was this son of a bitch talking about?

"What do you mean, outlawed?"

"I *mean* that it was used as an active ingredient in cleansers used to degrease cesspools. In eighty-one, when the E.P.A. issued a warning about the potential danger, the Suffolk County legislature enacted Law 251, banning the use, possession or disposing of tetrachloroethylene. I'm surprised you aren't aware of that ordinance."

Montgomery now vaguely remembered that the legislature had passed some damn ordinance against the use of some damn chemical. He took little notice of it because it was one of those last minute bills that the county legislature enacted so that they could refer to it in their newsletters to constituents—a law forgotten as soon as it was passed . . .

"I'm very much aware of it," Mr. Morgan," Montgomery said, his voice rising, "but if you knew anything about criminal prosecution you would understand that I would have had to prove that the violation of the law began *after* the passage of the ordinance. Those metal containers have been in the ground since the seventies, and at the time tetrachlorine—"

"That's tetrachloroethylene."

"Good for you, Mr. Morgan. You can pronounce it and I

can't. But whatever, at the time it was dumped it was legal to use it, possess it and dump it. And this office doesn't prosecute people ex post facto."

"Very commendable, but shouldn't we look into the possibility that some of the tetrachloroethylene, and dioxin, and arsenic, and D.D.T., and chlordine were all dumped there as late as 1984? Only dioxin and tetrachloroethylene were outlawed. The others aren't—at least not yet—but people are dying of cancer out there. I'm not here to discuss legal technicalities. I'm asking you to help us stop the poisoning of more water on the island, the killing of more people and the deforming of more babies at birth—"

"You don't know what you're talking about. E.P.A. checked it out, and you people in Albany checked it out—"

"Not we people, Mr. Montgomery. We won't rest on what the previous administration did or didn't do. Look, wells were poisoned, people died, are dying. That's the bottom line. It's not a question of prosecuting criminals. All we want to do is discover who's responsible for all this and stop him from repeating it—in any damn way we can, even if he happens to be a big shot who has political connections with every public officeholder in the county."

Montgomery was on his feet. "I don't like your implication, Mr. Morgan. I've said all I'm going to say to you. Go to the feds, go to the F.B.I., for all I care. We've investigated this thing to death. It's over, the dumping is over, the people in Snyder's Flats have been evacuated. We're all heartsick over it but it's a closed chapter. And frankly we don't need a carpetbagger like you or Loren Sturdivant to make headlines for herself and dress up her 'Evita' image. Good day, Mr. Morgan."

"Will you at least tell me who owns Dispo, Inc.?"

"Good day, Mr. Morgan."

Scott left, convinced now more than ever that Montgomery knew more than he was telling. Including the owner of Dispo, Inc.

# THE POWER

\* \* \*

The signpost on the lawn, Gerald Canfield, Attorney at Law, was large enough to draw attention a block away. Scott parked in front of the ranch-style house and walked toward the entrance. Typical of many Long Island law offices, the building had once been a residence.

The door opened into a large foyer, where he faced a young girl sitting behind a desk.

"Is Mr. Canfield in?"

"Yes, sir, do you have an appointment?"

"No, but he was recommended to me very highly and I have a local matter that I'd like to discuss with him."

"Your name, sir?"

"Fred Peterson."

She flicked the switch on the intercom.

"Mr. Canfield, there's a Mr. Peterson to see you. It's a new matter."

Scott heard his reply on the intercom. "I'll see him in a few minutes."

Scott had been the beneficiary of a code between the secretary and the exclusive Mr. Canfield. "He has no appointment" meant that in her judgment the visitor was a waste of time. "It's a new matter" could mean "ready money," a "live one." Canfield relied on her hunches. For the most part she was right. Finally he buzzed.

"You can go in now."

Gerald Canfield's office was a lasting tribute to Gerald Canfield. Scott was especially interested in the photographs. One with the Suffolk County Republican leader, another with the local assemblyman, another with the United States senator, and one that interested Scott more than all the others—with Ross Montgomery, the District Attorney of Suffolk County.

Canfield fairly sprang off his chair to greet Scott. "Mr. Peterson, it's a pleasure to meet you. Please sit down, how can I help you?" A heavy man, his jowls and pot belly were too pronounced to be affected by his once-a-week eighteen holes of golf. He was, however, impeccably dressed— matched accessories, mirror-shined shoes, capped teeth, and a full mane of white hair, razor cut.

"Mr. Canfield, I'll come right to the point. First, I'm here under false pretenses."

Canfield's smile began to fade.

"Well, Mr. Peterson, it can't be all that bad . . ."

"That's for you to decide. I used Peterson because I doubted you'd see me if you heard my correct name—Scott Morgan."

The smile disappeared. Scott figured District Attorney Montgomery had called him.

"Mr. Canfield," Scott said, "I'm the director of the New York State Office of Ombudsman. I'm investigating the deaths and illnesses at Snyder's Flats. I want to know how and why it happened, but mostly I want to try and stop it from happening again. I'm asking for your cooperation. I'm asking you to give me the name of the principal stockholder of Dispo, Inc."

Canfield, an experienced trial lawyer, recovered quickly. His smile returned, ear to ear. He reached for a cigarette in a silver box on the desk and pushed the box toward Scott.

"You indulge, Mr. Morgan?"

"No."

"I wish I could say the same. I gave it up three years ago, then I went back to it. Crazy . . . Are you an attorney, Mr. Morgan?"

"Yes, I am."

"Then you know full well why I can't reveal a privileged communication brought about by the attorney-client relationship."

"Unless a criminal act was in the process of being committed. Then you know, Mr. Canfield, that privileged communication would no longer apply."

Canfield's smile widened. This chump was bluffing. The Snyder's Flats mess had passed every criminal investigation . . .

"There's been no crime committed at Snyder's Flats. What's more, I think you know it. Now you'll have to excuse me, I have some pressing business."

Scott didn't move. "Mr. Canfield, you're probably right about Snyder's Flats. At least no criminal act can be proved. But I was referring to something else. It concerns Dispo, Inc., and since the corporation names you as the addressee, it should concern you personally."

Canfield's smile was gone again. "Don't try to intimidate me, Mr. Morgan. It won't work. I've been around too long to fall for your shyster tricks. I want you to go. Now."

"No need to raise your voice, Mr. Canfield. I'll go. But let me leave this with you. According to the records of the State Board of Elections, Dispo, Inc., has been very generous in contributing to the election campaigns of certain state legislators, and equally generous to the campaign of former Governor Beale. Now I found that interesting, because I'm sure you're up on the election law and its provision for criminal penalties in case of specific violations."

Canfield waited.

"State law forbids any corporation from contributing more than five thousand dollars in a gubernatorial race. I looked at the records of corporate contributions, and what do you know . . . I found that Dispo, Inc., at this address, care of *you*, sir, contributed forty-two thousand in two successive years to Beale's campaign."

Canfield stayed cool, said nothing.

"There's more, Mr. Canfield. I've reason to believe that Dispo, Inc., is a one-person corporation, and that the true owner owns all the stock. You sign the checks as treasurer, but I don't believe you own any stock, and if any, a negligible amount. If that's the case, this person is the true owner of this business. According to the election law, the owner's name must be identified when making contributions to gubernatorial campaigns. Let me be specific—Section 14–120 of the election law states that 'no person shall in any name but his own, directly or indirectly, make payment to a candidate.' Now yours is the only name on record connected with Dipso, Inc., which has plainly violated the law by donating more than the five thousand allowable. We can do this two ways. You can give me the name of the principal and it won't be necessary to refer your name to the attorney general. Or they can call you before the grand jury and you can claim privileged communication there. You'd have difficulty with that, Mr. Canfield. I repeat, the privileged communication doctrine doesn't apply where a crime was committed and you were a participant in covering it up. The checks were sent from this office. You signed the checks. You couldn't possibly say you knew nothing about it."

Canfield sat down, almost an involuntary motion. "You don't want his name for violation of the election law. You want it for Snyder's Flats—"

"That's immaterial."

"And you're threatening me with this . . . gimmick."

"Going after a lawbreaker is not a gimmick."

Canfield kept silent.

"Look around you, Mr. Canfield. Your walls are covered with testimonials of the respect that your community has for you. That respect took years in the making. After the first newspaper story, all of this will be down the tubes. Don't risk that. Whoever he is . . . he's not worth your good name."

Canfield took a deep breath, wrote a name on a piece of paper, folded it, put it in an envelope and sealed it. He handed it to Scott.

So much for privileged communications.

Scott waited until he was back in his car before ripping open the envelope. The name written by Canfield was Paul Medford—Governor Jon Klyk's best friend in Suffolk County, the Democratic minority leader in the state senate . . .

# Chapter Ten

WILLIAM LLOYD KENDALL, United States district judge, eyed the press people warily. Not that he hadn't expected them to turn out. This was sentence day for Terrance Wilbur, who had pleaded guilty the first time he appeared before him, and as his attorney dramatically intoned, threw himself upon the mercy of the court. The press was there because the nineteen-year-old defendant was the son of the chairman of the Ways and Means Committee of the New York state assembly. They milled around the entrance to the courthouse, holding their cameras at the ready, waiting for Terry and his family to enter.

Judge Kendall was not an imposing figure—scarcely 140 pounds soaking wet. At times, he thought, it was an advantage to be so common in appearance. It let him pass now undetected through the throng of reporters and cameramen who would have pounced had they known he was the sentencing judge. A shy and private man, cases that drew the media made him uncomfortable.

His face was hardly ever creased by a smile, he was so absorbed in performing his duties. He parted his hair in the middle, the same way he parted his judicial philosophy. Not colorful, avoiding headlines whenever possible, he had a reputation for being eminently fair. His dedication to justice made him especially apprehensive when sentencing days came along, when he was faced with the age-old problem of balancing society's rights against the accused's.

The sentencing of Terrance Wilbur was no exception. Did the serious transgression of this nineteen-year-old require his imprisonment? Was he a threat to society, or was this an aberration not likely to be repeated?

Kendall was aware that the press was in his courtroom looking for the blood of young Wilbur. He was also aware of the clout of Dan Wilbur, and determined not to let either influence him. And all this was complicated by his own ambition. Like every federal judge sitting in the district court, he looked to the circuit court of appeals. He also was aware of how the system worked . . . be acceptable to the U.S. senator from his state. While technically the president made all federal judicial appointments, no appointment could pass through the Senate Judiciary Committee if the candidate's home senator vetoed him. And it was common knowledge that Senator Kenneth Hodkins and Daniel Wilbur, Terry's father, originally from the same area, were close as sin.

Of course Senator Hodkins did not contact Judge Kendall about the Terry Wilbur sentence . . . it would have been improper for the senator to make the call and equally improper for the judge to receive it. More important, the call was unnecessary. A young judge looking to ascend the judicial ladder would be committing professional suicide if he imprisoned the son of a close friend and political ally of the senator, especially where probation was a viable alternative.

The thought passed through the mind of Judge William Lloyd Kendall, and was instantly banished. The merits of the matter were all that counted, he instructed himself. Or at least all that he could allow to matter. Sometimes judges

were appointed without political consideration, and he was
one of them. His quiet, gentlemanly manner gave some the
impression that he was without emotion, incapable of anger
or sorrow or humor. Untrue. But for his own purposes he
developed the uncanny ability to conceal his reactions from
public view. Such self-discipline served him well.

In the hectic years of the Carter administration his quiet
dependability was brought to the attention of the president
by the attorney general, and he was named deputy attorney
general and finally appointed a district court judge through
an exercise of muscle from the White House. Charlie
Sweeney wasn't happy with the choice, not because he had
anything for or against Kendall but because he didn't know
him. He objected that Kendall was charged to New York
State when he lived in Washington, D.C., during the Carter
years. But Sweeney never fought his president too long or
too hard, and he "suggested" to the then U.S. senators from
New York that no objection be made, and Kendall was confirmed by the U.S. Senate.

But the next year the former governor of California beat
the man from Georgia and Senator Hodkins had no loyalty
to a Republican president. Now, if Kendall wanted a promo-
tion he would have to ingratiate himself with the powers in
the Democratic party of New York State. Kendall wasn't
good at that. But now, out of the blue, he had this opportunity to ingratiate himself with Senator Hodkins. Treating
young Wilbur with mercy would be a statement that he
"respected" Senator Hodkins's interest in the case. It would
not turn Hodkins into a full-blown supporter of William
Lloyd Kendall—far from it—but it would be a good and
promising beginning on the road to the appellate court.

Kendall especially felt the irony of his situation after reading the presentence reports and feeling inclined on its merits
to place Wilbur on probation. He had weighed all the factors
and did not believe a jail sentence was necessary. But he had
to query himself . . . was the senator's interest a factor at all

in his decision? He wrestled with that for a while, but on the morning of the sentencing he woke up at peace with himself, confident that such wasn't the case . . .

Actually, there were two sentences that he had scheduled for this day. He had put them down for 10:00 A.M., hoping he could deal with them quickly so he could resume with the complicated antitrust case he was trying that had been going on for two months and had at least another two to go.

The "Hear ye, hear ye" of the bailiff rang out clearly as he moved into the courtroom and walked the one step to his elevated perch of authority.

Mark Hammond took the Jesus Ferrano case because he considered it a payback to the Fates for his good fortune. The publicity from his successful defense of a man named Jorgenson had made his name known to millions. He had done a masterful job, and the press credited him with that, but the overwhelming drama of the presiding judge at the trial confessing to the very crime of which he was sitting in judgment was what evoked worldwide interest. And the fact that the widow of that judge who had been killed in jail was now the lieutenant governor of the state of New York kept the story alive.

Mark Hammond had the ability to capitalize on the consequences of that trial. His recognition was national, his fees large, and his marriage to top model Randy Spencer was a well-covered social event. There came a point, though, when he sat back and counted his blessings. Mark Hammond— born Moshe Himmelfarb—had become rich, had married a stunningly beautiful lady, had earned nationwide respect. He felt an obligation to repay the gods.

Fortunately for the Vietnam Veterans of America, they called him at just the right time. He was between trials and he arranged to have their delegation see him immediately. They came the following day, asking that he go to bat for a special guy who needed and deserved a lot of help . . . Jesus Ferrano was a drug addict—a condition directly caused by his Marine Corps service in Vietnam. He pleaded guilty to a drug sale charge, but it wasn't for profit, it was to feed his dependency. The clincher for Hammond was Ferrano's background. A poor kid from the New York Barrio, he was getting straight As at City College and had dreams about going on to medical school. But Jesus Ferrano, at eighteen, was subject to the draft and decided that since he was slated to go anyway he'd go with the best. He joined the marines. After a short training period he was sent to Nam, and like thousands of others, he only survived physically.

All of which was no defense for the sale of cocaine to an undercover federal narcotics cop, and Hammond arranged to have him plead guilty before Judge Kendall. Going to trial would have been suicide. His client had been arrested twice before for possession with the intent to sell. In the state courts each of those cases was reduced to a misdemeanor. The first time he was referred to a drug program, but it didn't take. He went A.W.O.L., and when he was busted the second time he was sentenced to one year at Riker's Island. After he served the required eight months, his Viet Vet buddies hoped that the sustained period of cold turkey would help him stop. But Jesus's problems were not just physical, and he soon returned to cocaine abuse. When he was arrested by the feds he surrendered passively, as though it was his ordained fate.

Hammond had refused any fee from the Viet Vets, and he spent long hours pouring over Jesus's medical reports and his army records preparing for this sentencing day . . .

As the clerk called out "United States of America against Jesus Ferrano" they brought him out of the detention pen. He was pale. Once stocky and muscular, he was now thin and pale. His eyes showed little understanding. Hammond smiled at him, but his client showed no reaction.

The young assistant U.S. attorney spoke first, reciting in

detail Ferrano's record as a chronic criminal—a drug seller—a scourge and a threat to society . . . "This is a recidivist that stands before you, Your Honor, who deserves no consideration. The government recommends the maximum sentence."

The clerk then asked Ferrano if he wished to speak. His face remained expressionless. "No, sir."

"I'll hear you, Mr. Hammond," Judge Kendall now said.

Hammond began in a soft, modulated tone. "On September 16, 1965, at the age of sixteen, Jesus Ferrano enlisted in the United States Marine Corps. He didn't shirk the draft, he didn't run away to Canada, he voluntarily joined the marines to serve his country. After basic training he was assigned to a combat unit and again volunteered, this time for hazardous mission assignments in Vietnam. He was wounded three times in his fourteen months in Vietnam. At the border of Quan Tri, in Operation Hastings, his left arm was splintered with shrapnel. In a rescue mission at Da Nang, a Viet Cong bullet pierced his leg. It was a flesh wound, and seven days later he was hit by shrapnel again, only this time he caught it in his leg and he couldn't walk. In July of 1967 they sent him home and hospitalized him.

"Now, I think this is especially important, Your Honor. Jesus Ferrano could have been discharged. But Jesus Ferrano is a special person. To his way of thinking, he was needed back in the hell of Southeast Asia. Sergeant Ferrano, at the ripe old age of nineteen, returned to Vietnam and was wounded a fourth time. He considered himself lucky . . . he only lost his toes. He'll always limp, but unlike so many of his buddies he still walks. He was awarded four Purple Hearts, three Silver Stars, three Bronze Stars, the Navy Cross and numerous citations. He was, Your Honor, a certified hero. He was in combat, not in the fleshpots of Saigon, *but in active combat for a total of thirty-seven months.*

"I respectfully ask Your Honor to bear in mind that prior to his marine service he was a particularly gifted student, as attested by the letters from his high school teachers who recommended him for a scholarship at several Ivy League colleges. I spoke to those teachers. They all said it was a tragic waste of human potential. But Mr. Ferrano *opted* to serve his country. Most everyone considered that madness. He believed in country, he believed in duty, he believed in honor. And this belief extracted a terrible price, a price he is paying now and will pay for the rest of his life.

"The legacy is described by psychiatrists as posttraumatic stress disorder. There's nothing unique about that. Most of those who saw action in Vietnam are affected by it. And it manifests itself in many ways. Jesus Ferrano, who never indulged in any drugs before he entered the service of his country, was given massive doses of morphine for his pain-wracked body, and shortly thereafter found he could not cope with life without the drugs.

"It's important, sir, to understand why. In addition to his other problems, he suffers from 'survivor's guilt,' a common phenomenon among those who came back from Nam alive. In Quan Tri, a man young as he, principled as he, brave as he, died in his arms. I tell you now, sir, that there hasn't been a day that this remembrance has not plagued him. He expresses guilt that he lived.

"In 1980 he was admitted into the V.A. hospital in the Bronx after a documented suicide attempt in the form of a valium overdose. After a period of treatment the doctors thought his depression was manageable and planned to discharge him. They were wrong. He jumped from an open window on the fourth floor and fractured his spine. Finally they let him go, but they barely saved his life when he was admitted to Montrose V.A. Hospital after he slashed his wrists. One year later he was admitted into the V.A. hospital in Puerto Rico in a coma caused by still another drug-alcohol suicide attempt. He is now in that special Vietnam post-stress treatment program at Lyons V.A. Hospital in New

Jersey—or rather he was until he was arrested again on a weekend pass.

"His instant offense, the sale of cocaine, is a means of accommodating his drug dependency. I'm mindful that it is a most serious crime, especially when one considers the impact on society. I'm also mindful that this court has a difficult choice in this case, balancing the concerns of society against the special circumstances surrounding this defendant. In that light, may I quote one line from his Lyons V.A. Hospital medical report: 'Incarceration of this veteran would exacerbate his symptoms beyond his ability to cope.' Putting it in its simplest terms, sir, the medical people are telling us that he will not survive imprisonment."

Hammond stopped, eyes on Judge Kendall, then delivered the climax of his plea: "Surely the time has finally come for all of us who did not go to Southeast Asia to contemplate and appreciate the sacrifice of those who did. Instead of imprisoning this man, all of us should join together to bring him back—to make him whole—to return what we took from him. To do less would surely surpass the evil of the crime that brings him here."

Judge Kendall eyed the preliminary notes of his intended sentence. He had read the medical reports. His original intent had been to sentence Ferraro to five years. He was a recidivist—he had been given breaks before—and he was still trafficking in drugs. But Hammond had struck a nerve. Kendall had a classmate at law school—a major in the reserves—who also refused to evade his duty and had returned in a body bag. Hammond's plea resurrected how Kendall had always felt about the waste. He tried to put that memory aside now, tried to tell himself that he could not possibly equate his dead friend with lawless drug dealers. But Hammond's words about repayment of the debt applied to all of those who were victims of Vietnam. He stared at Hammond a moment, then proceeded to render his sentence . . .

"Counsel talks of fairness. What, in fairness, does this

defendant deserve? Society, in fairness, needs protection from the injurious effects of drug trafficking. The defendant has been given consideration by other judges, and he has not desisted. It appears, then, that he should be punished. But fairness calls for an inspection of the other side of the coin. I agree with counsel that we have taken too much from this man. Society—and this court is a part of society—owes a debt. We can't forget that debt, not in good conscience. But now, Jesus Ferraro, the slate is clean. By placing you on probation, society is paying its debt. You may not consider this a pass to continue to commit criminal acts. In the future you will bear the consequences of this act or any other crime against society. The Lyons V.A. Hospital says that you have made progress but that you have a long way to go. I wish you Godspeed toward your recovery."

During the entire sentence proceedings, Ferrano had gazed at the judge blankly. But then Judge Kendall saw a tear rolling slowly down Ferraro's cheek, and then another. Words from that medical report that struck him were remembered now . . . "He does not laugh. He does not cry. He seemed incapable of showing emotion. But if he does, his prognosis will improve."

Ferraro's tears, if nothing else, erased Kendall's doubts about his sentence. And now the judge, too, had some need of emotional recovery. He declared a short recess and left the bench.

As Mark Hammond sat in the front row with his client waiting for the court document to bring to the Probation Department, his attention was drawn to the door of the courtroom, attracted by the flurry of activity there. He recognized certain media people, and then, in her regal splendor, came "Evita," the newly elected lieutenant governor of the state of New York.

He remembered her well as a beautiful woman, and in

spite of the strains of her life that were publicized in detail, he quickly noted that her beauty and its impact were undiminished. When she saw him, she smiled. He returned her smile, but he was uneasy. Their lives, after all, had crossed in a manner that could not possibly lead to a friendship. At that earlier trial, in defense of his client, Jorgenson, he was compelled to destroy her husband—the judge who presided at that trial. And although he felt no guilt for what he had done, he always felt sorrow. After all, Judge Alan Sturdivant was a major figure, a distinguished jurist who was heading for the governorship of New York and very likely the presidency of the United States. He had erased his dreams, and Mark had been the agency for it. As he looked into his widow's eyes, he detected no anger but had to assume it was there. He had, of course, no way of knowing that she did not share his reverence for the late Alan Sturdivant. Better than angered, she knew that her husband, behind the facade, had been weak, and that neither Mark Hammond nor anyone else had destroyed him—that his inability to cope with his less tidy emotions had undone him . . .

She found a seat directly behind Hammond, and he turned to greet her.

"Mrs. Sturdivant."

"Mr. Hammond."

"This is the first chance I've had to congratulate you . . ."

"Thank you, and my congratulations to you on marrying such a lovely and charming lady."

He still felt uneasy, and then he realized why she was here . . . The scandal at Mount Olympus, and her daughter Melody Sturdivant being linked with Terry Wilbur. She had made some accusation . . . he couldn't recall the particulars . . . but his lawyer's instinct was telling him that she was not just an interested spectator here.

Terry Wilbur was being sentenced for the same crime as Ferraro—possession of a controlled substance (cocaine), with the intent to sell. Daniel Wilbur, who always made it his business to be aware of every man's ambitions—and thus his weaknesses—chose Charles Poole to represent his son. Charles Poole was the brother of Andrew Poole, who happened to be majority whip of the state assembly.

For obvious reasons, Poole and Poole was among the most powerful law firms in the state. The speaker had taken pains to declare that "Never will we represent a client before a state agency, or one that is seeking state business," but added, "although there is no existing law which forbids us to." Such a law died in committee at least seven times by direct order of the speaker, dutifully carried out by the majority whip. Of course, this self-denial did not stop the firm from being retained in circumstances where its very presence in court could send a message to the judge. Such was the Wilbur case. Nothing was said in that message to Judge Kendall, but much was communicated . . . The junior senator from New York, the Honorable Kenneth Hodkins, was a law partner in Poole and Poole. Although Congress had set a limitation on the outside income of its members, many had wondered about the other compensation that the senator had received from merely having his name on the letterhead.

It was known to Daniel Wilbur, and to Senator Hodkins, that Judge Kendall, a good *and* ambitious man, aspired to elevations to the circuit court of appeals. Kendall, they were certain, would understand his situation. The fee that Daniel Wilbur paid to Poole and Poole to represent his son was considered by him a form of insurance. The deep friendship that Andrew Poole and Daniel Wilbur enjoyed as close political colleagues did, of course, in no way diminish the size of the fee. The speaker eased his conscience by calling Ways and Means chairman Wilbur and explaining: "You know, of course, that I am only concerned with Terry's welfare. I have nothing to do with the fee arrangements."

Wilbur replied that he knew the fee in the case was the last concern of his friend, the honorable majority whip. In fact, Wilbur knew precisely what he was buying, and Andrew

Poole knew exactly what he was selling, as well as the amount to the last dime . . .

The case was called. The prosecution asked that the judge sentence Terrance Wilbur to a term of imprisonment. One could detect a scaling down in the severity of his request as compared to his heated demand that Jesus Ferrano be sent to jail.

Now it was Poole's turn. First, of course, he underlined that this young man "did not waste the resources or time of this honorable court by going to trial but instead entered a plea of guilty at his first opportunity to do so." Then: "Probation would be totally appropriate for this first offender who stumbled once, and will not again—not with the support and guidance of his family, an esteemed and honorable family that will see to it that he not repeat his serious offense, or any other offense, and I, personally, assure the court of this . . ."

Besides having a commanding presence, the tall, gray-haired veteran had appeared before the Supreme Court of the United States. He knew how to plead; he was a real pro. Judge Kendall had no difficulty with his argument, but he was bothered by the obvious maneuver by Wilbur in hiring Poole to intimidate him. At the same time he realized it would be unjust to sentence this young first offender to jail because he, the judge, resented attempts to compromise him. He was just about to go along with his original inclination of probation for Terrance Wilbur—not because of the muscle they attempted to use on him but despite it—when Loren Sturdivant's voice sounded through the courtroom.

"May I be heard before Your Honor passes sentence?"

Kendall knew of her interest, understood it, but was also irritated by the manner in which she chose to intrude on the proceedings. So apparently was Charles Poole, whose brother Andrew was not particularly fond of Loren Sturdivant, and so it followed that he would not be either. He thought of protesting her presence but held his fire.

"It would be rather irregular, Mrs. Sturdivant," Judge Kendall said.

"I'm sure it would," she said, "but I believe I have something to add that has a bearing on this sentence—something that has not been said."

Kendall looked at both lawyers. The assistant U.S. attorney was in no position to object. Poole, not underestimating Loren, kept his silence.

"All right, Mrs. Sturdivant, I'll hear you."

She approached the counsel table and stood next to Poole and Terry Wilbur. She looked at neither, her eyes fixed on Kendall, and with controlled emotion spoke to the judge— and beyond him to the crowded courtroom.

"What happens here today should be of special interest to every young drug dealer in Harlem, Bedford Stuyvesant and the South Bronx. The laws of the state of New York are severe regarding dope dealers. Anyone dealing drugs from the areas I've mentioned would know for certain that he would wind up in jail—and for a very long time. The amount of dope in this case would insure it. Until he was arrested by drug enforcement agents, Mr. Terrance Wilbur had envisioned a bright future for himself. He was well aware of the profit to be made from cocaine trafficking, and had made up his mind to get a goodly piece of it. He would have succeeded in smuggling a sizable amount into the country if he had not been done in by an informer. He would have made his dirty profit, and only a fool could believe that once having succeeded, he would not return to Colombia and repeat his operation.

"His crime, sir, is worse than that of those who buy it here for resale. He *imported* it. In his greed he dispensed his poison wholesale. This was no harmless schoolboy prank. He was doing an international drug run. He had the funds, the supplier, the buyer—and the unmitigated gall to pull it off.

"We now hear that it was all an aberration, a mistake, and it won't be repeated. What kind of casual mistake is planned in such minute detail? He *arranged* for the Colombian connection here. He flew to Colombia and purchased it there. He returned, smuggled it through customs and sold more than two ounces of a drug that debilitates and kills. If this young man goes unpunished the wrong message will be sent out to the poor and the unconnected. Either we maintain equal justice or we don't, and if we don't, our judicial system is not worth a damn. His crime was of such proportions, was so far-reaching in its venality, its greed and its impact on our society that any punishment short of prison would be a travesty . . ."

Poole could contain himself no longer. "I am constrained to reply to the lieutenant governor's unfair attack on my client. Would her plea for blind vengeance be made in the same manner were it her daughter standing here? Her daughter, who, I am informed, is no stranger to drug problems herself . . ."

The sound of sharp inhaling filled the packed courtroom. Loren did not blink. Poole's remark didn't anger her—the smirk on Terry Wilbur's face did. She again turned and faced the judge. "Your Honor, Mr. Poole has made the point for me. He is quite correct. Society is the general victim of Terrance Wilbur's crime, and my daughter Melody is a particular victim. Perhaps she would have been introduced to that sleazy world by someone else in time, perhaps not, but the fact remains that it was Terrance Wilbur who opened that door to her—and God knows how many others. Since Mr. Poole has seen fit to bring my daughter's name into these proceedings, let me enlighten him. Melody is now a residence of Phoenix House in New York City. It has an effective drug program. She's putting her life together. Fortunately she was not seriously burned when Terry Wilbur introduced her to free-basing and caused a fire in a building at the school they both attended. She was hospitalized—but he, in his customary courageous fashion—ran away without the slightest concern for the possibility that she would die in the fire. He was not injured. He has never faced the consequences of what he has done. Forget my daughter . . . the poor and unconnected must know now that immunity for the Terry Wilburs of our society must end, and that he at long last must be called to account."

Mark Hammond had considerable respect for Charles Poole's ability as a trial lawyer, but as he sat there he realized, as Poole probably did, that the old lawyer had made a serious strategic error . . . He had given Loren Sturdivant another shot at his client, and the second was more damning than the first. Hammond knew, of course, of Loren Sturdivant's "iron lady" reputation, that she was called "Evita" and why. But he was still surprised at her displaying her daughter's problems before the world, even in a good cause, as she saw it. The lady was some piece of work . . .

Poole, trying to cut his losses, smiled and spoke in a low, friendly tone: "Your Honor, I don't wish to make this court a debater's forum between myself and the lieutenant governor. Such an exercise would be an indulgence and irrelevant to these proceedings. We will rest on the comments already made. Thank you."

There were days when the occupation of judge left William Lloyd Kendall with a sense of well-being, and then there were days like this one . . . His morning court schedule had involved the sentencing of two people. The first he had intended to imprison, but was persuaded by the sensible eloquence of counsel to change that position. The second he had intended not to imprison, and now he was about to change his mind a second time.

He used the few moments of silence to sort out his thoughts. Am I so "open-minded" that I can be swayed, back-to-back, on positions I had already carefully considered and all but decided on? Or do I show strength in being able to *listen* and be persuaded to go a different way if the arguments make more sense to me than I did to myself?

Well, he was at least sure of one thing . . . Because of what he was about to do, he would be interring any hope he ever had for judicial advancement. He was about to offend the majority whip of the assembly and hurt on a personal basis the family of the chairman of the assembly's Ways and Means Committee and, in effect, spit in the eye of the junior senator from the state of New York. And to put matters in their full perspective, he was certainly getting no mileage out of pleasing the lieutenant governor—a maverick Populist who was out of favor with the traditional party powers. And he was not so naive as to believe that her motives were altogether unmixed. She had made his court a setting for her media event—a pitch to the "people" that she stood for equal justice, when in truth, he believed, her principal goal was a mother's revenge. Still, irrespective of *her* motives, his was to render justice based on truth, and he found himself believing that her words, for whatever reason spoken, were the truth. It would not only have been easy to let Terry Wilbur walk out, it would even seem reasonable, as Poole said. Criticism would have been limited because convincing arguments could and were made for either position. But the search for truth, that was what it was all supposed to be about. Why the lawyers were there, and the litigants, and most importantly himself . . .

"This defendant has never been in conflict with the law before. That is significant. Weighing against this is the severity of his crime, and its effect on society, and how society must deal with it.

"There have been interminable theories presented by criminologists as to what a judge's prime consideration should be in dealing with an individual convicted of a criminal act. But the problem with those theories is that they are generally applied. For example, we hear that judges should consider rehabilitation. But in the real world we have come to know and accept that prisons rehabilitate no one, and it is my firm belief that this would specifically apply to Terrance Wilbur.

"Nor in my view would it be proper, or just, to sentence for revenge. A civilized society is on shaky ground if its courts exist to exact revenge. Counsel is quite correct about that.

"So we are left with the goal of deterrence, which I grant is a compelling motivation in this case. Our aim is to deter the defendant from similar acts in the future, and to deter others inclined to commit the same crime.

"We must first acknowledge that defendant's crime is a serious one . . . no more or less serious because this defendant committed it, as opposed to the man I have just sentenced. But what uniquely applies here is not the performance of the act so much as the manner in which it was performed. On the facts, it was done coldly and deliberately, without any thought to its nature or far-reaching effects. Unlike the previous defendant, Mr. Wilbur did not commit this crime against society because of a physical and emotional dependency resulting from sacrifices for that society . . ."

Kendall removed his glasses, lifted his head from the papers before him and made eye contact with a now frozen-faced Poole.

"Those of us involved in criminal justice must be aware that we are all, so to speak, in a crystal bowl that the public holds in its hands and gazes at constantly. No one that stands before the bar of justice should be judged on anything more, or less, than the merits of his case. Influence and wealth are not proper considerations. This defendant should *not* be punished to a greater degree because his family is prestigious and the power and influence of its friendships may extend to the very top of the social scale. But neither is he to escape punishment if the circumstances of *his* crime warrant it. I believe that the action this court is about to take will deter Terrance Wilbur from repeating his antisocial act. I hope it will deter others similarly inclined to profit from the misery of others. But above all, *on the facts*, the defendant is hereby sentenced to a term of three years imprisonment in a federal penal institution and to a fine of twenty thousand dollars."

The silence after sentence was pronounced was broken by the cries of Terrance Wilbur's mother and the impolitic outburst of Daniel Wilbur: "An outrage, what kind of justice is this, a repeater gets probation, a first offender three years . . . ? You'll regret this, Judge Kendall. And *you* will regret this too, Loren Sturdivant. I promise you . . ."

The U.S. marshals walked quietly toward Daniel Wilbur after his uncharacteristic loss of control, but he and his wife were already exiting the courtroom.

Kenneth Poole, still finding it difficult to accept what had just happened, continued to look in anger and disbelief at the judge.

Loren Sturdivant, who seemed the coolest of all, walked over to the media people in the courtroom and said: "Did you all hear Daniel Wilbur's threat?" And just in case they hadn't, she repeated it for them.


Judge Kendall entered his robing room to await the appearance of the attorneys involved in the case on trial before him. His secretary had received a note that a witness would be slightly delayed. He closed his eyes and tried to take the pressure off by a catnap that he fortunately was able to take from time to time.

He woke up at the buzz of the intercom, glanced at his watch and was gratefully surprised that he had napped for thirty minutes.

His secretary's voice was apologetic. "I'm sorry to disturb you, Judge, but this sounded important. It's Judge Rubenberger."

Kendall shook his head. For sure, this just wasn't his day. The very last person he wanted to speak to at this moment was Everett Rubenberger, judge of the Second Circuit Court of Appeals. He just didn't like Rubenberger, who had preceded him in the Department of Justice and had been appointed to the federal bench by President Carter one year before he was. Rubenberger, in Kendall's view, was not up to his role on the bench. Kendall considered him a "limousine liberal" who responded to the varying winds of politics like a weather vane. Kendall remembered clearly that Rubenberger, to ingratiate himself to the then conservative U.S. senator from New York, expressed opinions that placed him to the right of Attila the Hun. When that senator was defeated and a "liberal" U.S. senator was elected, he did a 180-degree turn and became the darling of the New York City liberals. Senior Senator Kenneth Hodkins made Rubenberger his personal protégé and interceded with Jimmy Carter to advance him to the court of appeals. Carter, badly needing Hodkins in his race against Reagan, obliged.

Since Reagan's ascension, Rubenberger's stalwarts were a bit unsettled by his current decisions on the Second Circuit bench. For example, instead of condemning police, as he once had, with strong accusations of unlawful search and seizure, he now sought to "balance the rights of society." This was a favorite new phrase in Rubenberger's decisions. It was obvious that he was hoping to be noticed by the powers that be in the Reagan administration. After all, it was the president of the United States who appointed judges to the Supreme Court in his own philosophical image. At least the judge was consistent . . . Never in his whole career did Everett Rubenberger allow integrity to interfere with ambition. His ethic was "go with the flow." So far it had worked. But he still needed Senator Kenneth Hodkins, who if lightning should ever strike, could veto him as well.

Hodkins had called him five minutes after the sentencing of Terrance Wilbur, and as a result of that call Rubenberger had to figure out a way to accommodate Hodkins and still not be charged with judicial misconduct. Hodkins, of course, fully understood the serious implications of one judge calling another judge about altering his decision. But Everett Rubenberger was, if little else, resourceful, and

Hodkins had confidence in Everett's ability to "persuade" within the limits of the law, if not of propriety . . .

Kendall reluctantly picked up the phone. "Hello."

"Bill? Everett Rubenberger. Been a *hell* of a long time. How you been?"

"Fine, Everett."

"You going to be at the Judicial Conference this summer?"

"Yes . . ."

"Bring the Mrs.?"

"Yes."

"Me too. Good for marital relations. Right?"

Silence. Get to the point.

"Tell you why I called, Bill . . . I've just had a call from Charlie Poole. He wanted to make a bail application pending appeal of your sentence of young Terrance Wilbur. I told him that I thought it would be better made before you."

Kendall, as was intended, immediately translated Rubenberger's judicial double talk: "They're going to appeal. There's not a chance that we will set aside or reduce the sentence. It was a perfectly proper use of your discretion. The man pleaded guilty so there's nothing to appeal from. I would look damn silly on a case like this if I fixed bail now. Won't you take me off the hook by fixing some bail until we affirm your sentence? He'll only be out for a relatively short time and I can look good to Kenneth Hodkins . . ."

Rubenberger could have had no other motive to call, and now Kendall was glad he did, because he thought of a diversion to lighten the day . . . "Frankly, I'm bothered some by the sentence. Just philosophically, Everett, how would you have handled this?"

Rubenberger paused, excited about the points he could make with Hodkins if the totally unexpected occurred . . . a resentence upon reconsideration. Kendall might do it, but he, Rubenberger, would get the credit for it where it counted. But Rubenberger's survivor instinct told him to move cautiously.

"Now that you ask, and *only* because you ask, I just might have given him probation . . ."

"Why so?"

"Well, he's not likely to do this sort of thing again—"

"Do you suggest I resentence him?"

"That's not for me to suggest, Bill, and you know it."

"Let me put it this way, then. Do you think it would be wiser for me to resentence him?"

Now that was the kind of question Rubenberger understood . . . "Everything considered, Bill, it might be . . ."

"Well, Everett, tell Senator Hodkins and the Pooles, and Charlie Sweeney, and anyone else who has a piece of this contract, that Kendall is an A-one ass, a stupid ass who wants to do what he thinks is the right thing. And I suggest you try that, Ernie. Try it just once. Try to be a man, and a real judge. Sometimes they go together. You'll feel better for it, and it wouldn't be the first time that a whore has reformed."

He slammed the phone down with such force that he chipped the instrument. He then picked up the picture of his wife and two young sons, and spoke to it.

"Folks, your husband and father, respectively, just shut the door on any possibility of being anything more than he is now. And he has never felt better about anything in his entire life."

# Chapter Eleven

JON KLYK was not looking forward to this meeting with Charlie Sweeney—it had been a long time coming and he was no longer able to be put off.

God, but he was *tired* . . . being governor was a very different ballgame from being a mayor. This was all work and no play.

There were, though, compensations. His administration so far had been getting high marks from the pundits. He was willing to take on the political establishment of *both* parties and attempt to govern with a responsibility and dedication which was refreshing and totally unexpected from an old organization war horse. The opposition could claim that the metamorphosis from hack to courageous leader was due to the influence . . . smirk, smirk . . . of the lieutenant governor; and, in fact, there was some truth to those implications. He did listen to Loren and adopted many of her suggestions. On the other hand, their relationship was strictly business, and early in the game he asserted himself as the boss and felt she accepted that. When he came down on one side of a matter the subject was closed and she didn't push him. A perfect colleague, and those who said it was an act were tiresome cynics, as she would point out to him . . .

Nonetheless, there was a price to pay . . . Klyk knew he would have to offend old cronies, and he didn't enjoy it. Neither did they. He was born one of them—and losing old friends, well, it was painful.

Nine months into his administration, he had offended party regulars to the point that Boss Charlie Sweeney received daily complaints from *all* factions of the party—legislators, officeholders, local leaders. They told him that Loren Sturdivant, with nothing to lose—little did they know—spent her days thinking up ways to rock the boat, and Jon Klyk was going along with them. Just look, for example, at her outrageous grandstand play in court to put Dan Wilbur's kid in jail . . .

Most pressing, though, was the new Office of Ombudsman that was snooping into every political sacred cow in the state; and its head, Scott Morgan, was anathema with party regulars.

Scott's sin, of course, was that he was doing his job too well for their comfort. Every letter complaining of governmental neglect or abuse or possible corruption was run down and investigated. Most complaints were unfounded, but the ones that had merit were examined with no holds barred. Inevitably some investigations hit home or close to home with the powerful and politically connected.

The big shots didn't mind Klyk's proclamation in setting up the Office of Ombudsman that no one would be immune from its prying, so long as it was just talk. But action was a shock, not playing the game, which also did not set too well with the attorney general or his own Commissioner of Investigation.

Soon after he took office, Klyk found that the corruption he had inherited from the Beale administration was mind-boggling, extending into every arm of state government. Beale had been, to say the least, evenhanded in his largesse, not limiting the spoils of public office to members of his own party. His operating principle was that as long as benefits were whacked up more or less equally between the two parties, no one could complain he was unfair. What the hell, even Democrats had to eat, he would say.

Jon Klyk and Scott Morgan called it all a rose that distinctly smelled. Klyk also realized he had been relatively passive about a similar system but on a much smaller scale when he was mayor of Buffalo. Well, it didn't play statewide, and he gave Scott Morgan full power to publish all his findings. "No sacred cows, no one's immune." And Morgan was to answer only to him.

Sweeney had tried to tell Klyk he was changing the rules of the game. A well-run government depended on lightened "cooperation." It was a fact of life that the state had to award contracts for goods and services. Whom should these contracts be awarded to? Strangers? Charlie Sweeney, who could have been a stand-up comic had he not been a politician, liked to regale audiences at political banquets with the one about the borough president of the Bronx who was asked why he appointed his brother-in-law to a well-paying job and said: "What should I have done, appoint *your* brother-in-law?"

Charlie Sweeney was not naive, but he felt the appointment of a party regular to a government post should not be offensive to public conscience. On the other hand, he knew there was a lot of dirt under a lot of rugs, and that Scott Morgan was going to uncover it, and the public and the press would eat it up. Charlie was by no means a corrupt man, nor did he tolerate corruption. He believed that those who stole were at best damn fools and deserved the consequences. But he worried that his people who benefited only by being chosen and nothing more would be equally embarrassed by revelations that *implied* sinister acts that were not, in fact, even committed.

Sweeney also doubted Scott Morgan's motives. White

knights on white horses made him nervous. Beware the self-styled pure in heart, and above all the true believer. Besides, it was all a little too easy . . . Morgan needed only to make one well-publicized phone call in order to guarantee his headlines. Good people, he felt, were being embarrassed and hurt. Well, pretty good people . . . and very good friends.

Sweeney had called Klyk and arranged for a meeting. Theirs was a forty-year relationship, formed through genuine mutual respect and admiration. Each considered the other a true friend. Neither looked forward to this meeting.

After dining alone at the mansion they sat in an embarrassed silence. Sweeney broke the ice.

"Jon . . . I've gotten flack over this ombudsman thing."

"I know that, Charlie, and I regret it."

"A lot of people are going to be hurt needlessly." He didn't add that some already had been.

Klyk shook his head. "Not needlessly, Charlie."

Sweeney eyed his old friend. "Jon, I have to ask you this. It's not meant as an insult or a cheap shot . . ."

"Shoot."

"When you were mayor of Buffalo, when you were county leader of Erie County, when you and I planned your four winning campaigns, did you ever need an ombudsman?"

"Charlie, you're too much of a friend to say it so I'll say it for you. There's no one more sanctimonious than a reformed drunk or atheist or whatever."

"I didn't say that."

"Didn't have to. But that's all right. Look, Charlie, I know how I got here. I knew that from day one it took the good workings of party politics to put me here. And along the way everything wasn't always squeaky clean. I used to love the game. Enjoyed every minute of it. I can't afford to now, my responsibility is too big for games. I admit to you there are times when I wonder about my capacity to handle this job.

All I can do is try my best, and I realized early on that that meant taking a very different view of what we both had accepted as business as usual. The bad guys have got to go, Charlie—"

"Does that include nailing Bill Hearn to the cross?"

Sweeney, as intended, had hit him where it hurt. Hearn was an old friend. Although a Republican, he had been kept as budget director, the only holdover from the Beale administration. Klyk kept him because he was an honest, hardworking and dedicated guy, the best qualified to fill the job. But Scott Morgan was a bloodhound. While pouring over a report on overtime excesses, the name of William Hearn kept popping up. Chauffeurs of state-owned automobiles claimed he had used their services in an unusual amount of overtime hours. Then a figure hit Scott's eye and he did a double take: An overtime claim by one of those chauffeurs in the amount of $12,512 on a salary of $24,600—more than fifty percent of base pay. The chauffeur's name was Lonergan, and Morgan called him in.

Lonergan was on the defensive. "I tell you, Mr. Morgan, I earned every damn dime I claimed." Scott reassured him. "Mr. Lonergan, all we're trying to find out is why you were asked to put in the hours claimed." Lonergan was angry. "Hey, Mr. Morgan, I don't have to lie for nobody. Why don't you ask Budget Director William Hearn and his deputy, Mary Knowles?" "And what would I learn?" "You'd *learn* that at least twice a week they left together from the State Office Building and you'd *learn* I drove them to her apartment. Then they'd both go upstairs, say at seven o'clock at night, and he'd come down at ten or eleven. Usually he'd take his briefcase so it would look like he was working. He didn't fool me and he knew it. For the past month or so he's been forgetting to bring the briefcase. I can't say I blame him, she's some tomato."

After informing Jon Klyk and Loren Sturdivant, Morgan referred the matter to the State Investigation Commission.

Naturally the media loved the juiciness of the story, and the fallout was devastating for Hearn. Although almost everyone blamed Scott for leaking the story to the press, the truth was he did not tell them—a source at the S.I.C. did—but in any event, a sex scandal could not be hidden forever.

The Investigation Commission, unhappy that it was unearthed by the Office of Ombudsman, complained to the governor that Morgan was sticking his nose in where it didn't belong. He was confusing jurisdiction . . . But Klyk backed Morgan. "Next time," he said, "you'll maybe catch it first. Maybe a little competition in turning up this stuff will be healthy."

Hearn had no choice but to resign, and Klyk, with no pleasure, accepted his resignation. The governor knew he was losing an unusually competent public servant, but more than that, an old friend was hurt and humiliated. Nevertheless, he'd also been a fool . . . sexual liaisons should be private and every precaution taken to safeguard the privacy. The governor reflected that he was something of an expert on the subject, and was amazed at the naivete of an otherwise intelligent man. Did Hearn really believe that Lonergan, or any other chauffeur that drove for him in the carpool, would not sneer in his beer when telling the tale of the amorous adventures of the budget director and his "hot tomato" of a deputy?

"Charlie," Klyk said, "maybe he should have sprung for the taxi fare?"

Sweeney, knowing of the governor's similar adventures in the past, could not resist taking the shot.

"Oh, come off it, what did you do?"

Klyk was not offended. "I used my own car, Charlie. It's a basic rule of politics. Never use an official vehicle when you're fooling around."

"So for *that* an old friend and competent pro has to be publicly ridiculed and forced out of office?"

Klyk hesitated. "Charlie, this isn't so easy for me. Please let me do it my own way—"

"Go ahead."

"Hearn in a way was unfair. He owed it to all of us not to be so stupid. It compromises us all, and what we're trying to do. Like you say, I'm no saint, but I'm governor now, Charlie. I tell you what that means . . . It means I have to lose a lot of friends, I have to ask a lot of questions I never asked before, and I have to get decent, defensible answers. Good God, Charlie, the man was director of the budget. He had the responsibility to see that public monies were spent wisely and honestly. And he's caught getting laid while public money is paying his chauffeur waiting for him in a public limo downstairs. In the old days this would have been a laugh we could all enjoy at the bar. No more. Put yourself in my shoes, Charlie. What would *you* have done?"

"I'd fire him, but I wouldn't let the media know why. Let him resign for reasons of health. Bill Hearn is at least entitled to that."

"Charlie, that's bullshit. As long as there are file clerks and typists and messengers and any kind of civil servant that can read and can tip off a reporter, the news will get out, and then who's helped? Look, I understand why you feel the way you do, you've got a lot on your side. Yes, as mayor I closed my eyes to a lot of things, and to claim I didn't know or shouldn't have known what was happening would be a damn lie. Sure, I never took a dime, but what I didn't do was almost as bad. I was too concerned with keeping old friends—"

"You make it sound as if all of us who have roots in political organizations are somehow suspect."

"If that's the way it sounds, that's not the way I meant it. It's a cliché but true . . . the bad apples are relatively few, but they're there and they have to be exposed and gotten rid of. I'm sorry, but as long as I'm here, that's the way it's going to be."

Sweeney looked at him, shook his head and left the mansion without another word. Dream on, Governor, he thought as he got in his car. You're going to be eating—or choking on—those words before you're through.

# Chapter Twelve

K LYK'S resolve, and Sweeney's unspoken warning, were tested sooner than either could have anticipated.

A week after the dinner at the mansion, Sweeney saw Scott Morgan as he left Klyk's office. Morgan smiled—Sweeney didn't. Morgan understood that the role he had cut out for himself as the governor's Mr. Clean put him at odds with the very political establishment that was Charlie Sweeney's life; he could never again be in the good graces of *the* old war horse, and it saddened him, because Sweeney was a wonderful character and by far the best of his breed.

Morgan now entered the sumptuous governor's chambers to be greeted by Klyk, and a certain reserve.

"Okay, bearer of bad tidings, what's it this time?"

Morgan's answer was to pull documents from his bag and place them in a neat pile on the table in front of him. "I'm afraid this is really going to bother you, Governor."

"They *all* bother me, Scott. Who, what is it?"

"Paul Medford . . ."

Klyk had hardened himself to Morgan's past revelations, but Paul Medford? Minority leader of the state senate and

therefore its highest-ranking Democratic senator from Long
Island, a Rock of Gibraltar in his support of the governor?
When matters were especially sensitive, or when he needed
maneuvering and arm-twisting for passage of the "governor's bills," it was Medford whom Klyk reached out for.
And almost always Medford delivered. Governor Klyk had
no stronger ally in either house.

Klyk thought of the irony of the situation. He had reached
out for the governorship to stop Alan Sturdivant, Loren's
late husband, whom he believed was too stringent and doc-
trinaire an idealist to recognize the importance of party. But
now, through the amazing set of circumstances that had
placed him in this office, he had to face the fact that he was
doing what Sturdivant would have done. The ex-mayor of
Buffalo found himself in the major leagues, and he yearned
increasingly for the peace of mind that the minors had af-
forded him.

Well, this looked like the acid test . . .

"Sit down, Scott, tell me about it."

Morgan glanced at the documents in front of him. "In
1980, when the legislature enacted the Environmental Conservation Act, it set up the Agency for Environmental Control that you, as mayor of Buffalo, had requested after the
Love Canal thing."

"I remember . . ."

"As you also know, Governor, the A.E.C. was supposed to
be the monitoring agency in the state—the model. At the
time of the law's passage we were told that dangerous toxic
waste disposal would be supervised and controlled. The
A.E.C. was authorized to issue permits to dispose of dangerous toxic wastes. It set up tough guidelines like the federal
standards of the E.P.A. It provided for constant inspection
of any business engaged in disposing or storing or dumping
of toxic waste. It was a good bill, but it turned out to be a
boondoggle. The Agency has issued only four permits statewide since the law was enacted. As far as I could find out,

none of the four recipients were experienced in toxic waste disposal. But the license was priceless, Governor. This is a multimillion-dollar business. The companies using these chemicals, and there are thousands who use them for one purpose or another, were standing in line, money being no object."

"Spare me the prologue, Scott."

"Sorry. Well, I found that one lucky recipient was Dispo, Inc. Its landfill dump site is in Bellport, in the township of Brookhaven, Suffolk County, Long Island. That's smack in the middle of Senator Paul Medford's district . . ."

"Go on."

"One section of the law provided that dump sites can't be located in hydrogeologic deep recharge zones—areas where underground water supply is naturally purified. The town of Brookhaven is such a zone. In spite of the serious risk of poisoning the water, Dispo, Inc., located its dump in Bellport."

"How could they manage that?"

"Governor, you know better than I . . . a troublesome law can be amended. Working with his Democratic colleagues in the senate, who depend on him for good committee assignments, and through his friends in the assembly, he quietly pushed through an amendment that waived the recharge zone ban."

"How could he have sold them on that?"

"His position was that in some areas of the state—Long Island, particularly—the water supply is almost all in recharge zones, and therefore there could be *no* local disposal if the law was strictly applied. The amendment provided for 'all existing precautions' to avoid water contamination. The Agency for Environmental Control then added additional safeguards for disposal in recharge zones—reinforced drum liners and minimum depth of burial. It also banned the dumping of certain chemicals whose toxicity was just too dangerous for containment under any conditions."

"So what's wrong with that?"

"Sounds good, except it was all salad dressing. Oh, at the beginning, right after the license was issued, the rules were followed. But as time passed, the companies who shipped the waste didn't use the reinforced drums and began shipping banned chemicals. After a while everything got dumped. The licensee was not about to lose any part of this lucrative business by demanding strict adherence from customers."

"What about the Agency's inspections?"

"Pro forma. If they'd been for real, they'd have shown that the drums were not lined as the law required, that they were buried too near the surface and that prohibited chemicals were buried at the Bellport dump. The reasons for the casual inspection . . . Dispo, Inc., was and is a corporation owned by one man—Senator Paul Medford."

"I suppose you've got proof?"

Morgan took two documents from his file. "I've got all we need. Dispo, Inc., was incorporated in 1980. The three subscribers were the attorney, Gerald Canfield, and two other people in his office. Then he used the normal procedure when the parties did not want the true owner to become a matter of public record. The one stockholder who was named was Canfield, who in turn assigned it all to Medford. Canfield was given a few shares—probably his fee—but Paul Medford owns Dispo, Inc. No one else shares the profits, no one else sets the policy—no one else, Governor, is responsible."

"Has he committed any crime?"

"It's a close call, but I believe he has. The state Environmental Conservation Act provided only civil penalties for dumping beneath the standards of safety, but the Suffolk County legislature got more specific and banned the dumping of certain specified chemicals under *any* conditions. One of those chemicals was tetrachloroethyline. Violation calls for a jail term and a fine. I found that three chemical firms in New Jersey had shipped tetrachloroethylene to the Dispo dump in Bellport as late as eighty-three. Of course, Medford could always say that he never knew it, and a prosecutor could have a tough time getting a conviction. But in answer to your question, Governor—yes, I believe he did commit a crime."

"You got enough proof?"

"I've got warehouse receipts, Governor. The Jersey firms labeled tetrachloroethylene plainly on their invoices. They had no reason to hide it. Shipping tetrachloroethylene isn't prohibited in New Jersey. It's not prohibited anywhere except Suffolk County because they found that it tends to poison water supplies more than other toxics. Those firms didn't dump the chemicals, Dispo did, which is to say . . . Paul Medford did."

Then Scott spoke what was on both men's minds. "The violation of a Suffolk County ordinance doesn't bother me as much as the insensitivity of Senator Medford and the real effect of his behavior. He was well aware of the problem of water pollution in Suffolk County. I've got newspaper clippings quoting him when he first ran for the senate, demanding that all dumping be banned in Suffolk County."

"I remember," Klyk said quietly.

"And when the county legislature banned the dumping of tetrachloroethylene and other dangerous chemical waste, he's quoted praising them for their 'responsible legislation.' "

Klyk shook his head.

"Governor, and I hope I'm not out of line, I know about your relationship with Senator Medford. I understand the political consequences of your taking action against your close political ally. I also understand that a governor has to get legislation through and he needs legislators who trust him . . . I'm still going to ask you for authorization to go after Paul Medford."

Klyk stared, not at Morgan but through him. Thou shalt not hurt your own. An imperative in politics. But in his inaugural speech he had said, "I promise you that the trust you have placed in me will never be bartered or sold or traded away. The governed have the right to demand from those that govern them nothing less than complete dedication to truth and integrity."

Did he mean it?

He walked to the door, back toward the desk. He looked at Morgan, who was waiting. He sat behind his desk, then, *sotto voce*, said: "Do what you have to do."

Morgan sent his report on Senator Paul Medford to the Suffolk County district attorney, the attorney general, the state commissioner of investigation and the United States attorney for the Eastern District. He didn't, though, want to wait for them to drag their feet, and notified Klyk he was calling a press conference—giving the governor twenty-four hours to give a nay say to the move. None came.

His small office was packed. His office in Albany was larger, but the facilities in the World Trade Center were more accessible to the TV and radio people. It was, of course, a sensational story. Even the most cynical reporters seemed angered by the extent of Medford's greed. Even those who liked Medford—and he *was* likable—silently cursed him.

The story headlined every major New York newspaper, and found its way into evening network TV newscasts throughout the country.

When the first shock waves settled, the man in the street was out for Paul Medford's blood.

# Chapter Thirteen

SENATOR PAUL MEDFORD, a man of considerable personal strength, was wounded by Morgan's attack, but not destroyed. He immediately planned his campaign to reestablish credibility. After all, he'd beaten some big odds in his life . . . Born dirt poor, he couldn't afford a college education and started at sixteen as a part-time clerk in a dry goods store, and when the owner retired he hocked what little he owned for the down-payment on the store. Working eighteen-hour days, he made the business go and bought one after the other until, after twenty years, he had a chain of discount outlets throughout Nassau and Suffolk Counties grossing eleven million a year. All this by a kid who learned his merchandising behind a counter instead of at the Wharton School of Business or, God forbid, the Harvard Business School. Failure wasn't in his resume.

At age forty, he found the challenges of business too tame and got into politics as a candidate for the county legislature. He was a Democrat in a Republican county, the prevailing wisdom said he had no chance, but he saw no difference in the merchandising of himself and dry goods. He won handily. After four terms he ran for the state senate, where the odds against him were even longer. Again, he beat the Republican incumbent. He fought the inner-party battles as well as the public ones, and he emerged minority leader of the senate. He used his power well, knew who his friends were and believed loyalty the only way to run the shop.

Now, though, there were those that shunned him, and he didn't especially resent it. He understood it. P.Y.A.—Protect Your Ass—was prime stuff for all members of the legislature who could not afford to be tainted with too much association with the minority leader. At the same time, they felt appropriately guilty and blamed their crisis of conscience on the governor, who had let loose his "hatchet man."

So Medford accepted that he could not rely on the support of legislator friends, that he would have to depend on his own resources. It was obvious the governor had thrown him to the wolves. There was no way that Morgan could have wielded the hatchet without Klyk's approval. He allowed himself to be personally hurt only by Jon Klyk's treachery— and he believed it to be just that—because their relationship, or so he had believed, had been strong friendship.

Tom McPartland of All World Media brought the matter to its largest viewing audience. Editorials throughout the state screamed for Medford's scalp. One Long Island paper suggested he "drink the water he polluted."

Medford did not panic. He concentrated on trying to convince the people in his district that he had been maligned. He refrained from calling on any Suffolk County officials for help, although most of them were in his debt. He saved them the embarrassment of turning him down.

He had to get off the floor and come back from a nine-count. He did not see it as impossible. It was a selling job—a tough sell, but not impossible. He needed an image man to perform the Herculean task of turning the public's anger into understanding, possibly even sympathy.

Donny Corum landed his first job at National one week after graduating from the Columbia University School of Journalism. He was bright and quick, with the tenacity of a bulldog, the skepticism of a mother-in-law and the burrowing ability of a hedgehog. Danny came to know that politics was not restricted to public officeholders and clubhouse hangers-on. Politics was practiced in boardrooms of large corporations, and in newsrooms of wire services.

National's New York bureau head was Jerry Winston, an amiable drunk who refused to die or go away—which frustrated Donny Corum, who saw himself as a future bureau chief. So Danny turned to public relations, opened a small office on Lexington Avenue in New York City and watched with hopeful anticipation as the block letters spelling Donald Corum and Associates, Public Relations were affixed to the door. He went to work, his motto derived from Patrick Henry—"It is natural for man to indulge in illusions of hope."

Now all he had to do was find a client. He found him in the unlikely person of Cristos Kasouris. Cristos could have been typecast as the ultimate nonentity—bald, short and underwhelming in his persona. He was a lawyer connected with a prestigious law firm, but only because his father was Spyrus Kasouris, who owned Star Togs of Seventh Avenue, which grossed forty million a year and retained the firm that hired Cristos. Naturally, the firm treated Cristos well, although he was distinguished by a remarkable lack of capability. Clearly, Cristos was not going to be fulfilled by the practice of law. Eventually, father decided change was in order. All right, thought Spyrus, he's not a Cardoza, where can his mediocrity be an acceptable plus? The answer: the New York City Council.

Donny met Spyrus Kasouris at a cocktail party thrown at

the Advertising Club, and each answered the other's needs. Donny's notions on "molding public opinion and creating public images" found a ready ear. At first Donny thought he had landed the father or his Star Togs as a client, but when he was told it was the son Cristos he didn't blink an eye or miss a beat.

Cristos, though, was indeed a challenge. Before Donny could begin to build an image he had to change Cristos physically. A fat little bald man whose voice had a decided squeak was not going to win elections, even to the City Council. So Donny put Cristos in an athletic club under the tutelage of Benny Mason, an ex-pug who specialized in changing appearances—in the old days for the worse. He put Cristos through a hair transplant, which didn't take the first time nor the second, but on the third try there were discernible hairs appearing to grow up top. No longer was Cristos a "skinhead." Indeed, he came out of his makeover not like a matinee idol but at least like a presentable candidate. Daily visits to a voice coach eliminated the squeak, but Donny knew there was no treatment for inferior intelligence. Well, he wasn't prepping Cristos for the Atomic Energy Commission. In politics, especially local politics, intelligence was a bonus, not a necessity.

But as a candidate, Cristos needed a cause. What? The plight of the homeless? Donny nixed that immediately. If the homeless were to be housed, it had to be in *somebody's* neighborhood, and even the most "liberal" would say sure but God forbid in mine . . . Pick a safe cause that everyone could identify with and no one could be against. Crime. And it was easy to play to the more than fifty percent of the councilman's district whose family members at one time or another had been the victims of at least a car larceny or a burglary or a robbery. With a near blank check from the father, Donny took ads and television spots attacking the judges, the mayor and the police for "failing the public," and promising all sorts of reforms when Cristos became a member of the

154

City Council. Further, Cristos *believed* in all of this, so he came across as sincere. Donny did not believe it prudent to educate Cristos about the difficulty in carrying out his promises, which could diminish his enthusiasm.

Donny and his creation carried the day; Cristos was a surprise winner in the district against an eight-year incumbent.

Political aspirants now beat a path to Donny Corum's door. Spyrus was his biggest booster, out of gratitude for what Donny had accomplished for his son.

Four years after Cristos's election, Donny was at the top, his clientele was ranging from foreign dictators to U.S. industrialists and when Paul Medford contacted him, Donny thought long and hard about taking him on. Oh, he had turned bad guys around before, that was not the problem. Nor were the funds, which he had no doubt was another blank-check deal. It was just that what Medford was charged with was so offensive that Donny reacted no differently than the average person. But then again, the man was the minority leader of the New York State Senate. The book on Medford was that he was tough, smart, resourceful and a survivor. Donny was also aware that politicians did not forget when they were rejected in their hour of need. Weighing all factors, Donny accepted Medford as a client.

If Medford was to be rehabilitated, it would be impractical to hope to isolate that goal to a small area. In the next sixty days Donny planned his campaign and then began to saturate the airwaves and the print media with brief messages. At first these did not even mention Medford but concentrated on the difficulties of the problem. Then gradually they began taking aim at their goal, showing Medford in a sympathetic light—a man who tried to alleviate the problem and was maligned. After a while the professional announcers gave way to Medford himself. Medford—gray hair, handsome, blue eyes looking directly into the camera—did fine on his very first telecast . . .

"Ladies and gentlemen, I am Paul Medford, minority leader of the New York State Senate. There have been accusations leveled against me which I am obliged to respond to. I am confident that in the spirit of fairness, the people in my senatorial district, and all the people of the state of New York, will listen to my side and judge for themselves. Toxic waste disposal has been a pervasive problem since 1976. When the legislature created the Agency for Environmental Control, certain landfill properties were specified to be used under strict supervision for the disposal of toxic waste. Burial and container requirements were clearly spelled out and severe penalties were provided for any violations. We took this action after considering the other alternatives. We discovered that incineration would create more health problems than it would solve. Dumping at sea or in inland waters would have been downright dangerous. We explored all other possibilities—and every proposed solution was equally hazardous. A company was formed on Long Island to operate and maintain a number of landfill dumping areas. The company operated strictly within the requirements of the state A.E.C. It was efficiently managed, with public safety its highest priority.

"Sometime later, it was discovered that unscrupulous and insensitive people used these landfills to dispose of toxic wastes by merely dumping it without authorization or concern for the consequences. The company tried to secure the area, but it was difficult, if not impossible, to guard against dumping in the dead of night in every part of this large area.

"I am associated with that firm. It was a mistake in judgment for me to be involved with it. It was not prohibited, either by law or by any code of ethics, but in retrospect I would not have done so, because of public misconception of my motives. Yes, it was a profit-making concern. But my

highest priority at the time was lending my business expertise to a vitally important enterprise.

"I ask the people of the state of New York and the people
of my district to withhold judgment on this issue. In the
meantime I am offering a reward of ten thousand dollars for
information leading to the conviction of any trespassers who
disposed of toxic waste on the company's premises. I promise you that those who committed this crime against all of
us will be discovered, and once identified will be prosecuted
to the full extent of the law."

Donny Corum wrote and edited every word of Medford's
speech. As he wrote it, and even after he wrote it, the
thought never entered his mind that he was creating distor-
tions. He was doing a job, which was its own justification.
His clients paid him to present them to the public in the
most favorable light. If the truth was bent like rays of light
through a prism, the resultant rainbow was the desired result. It was very much like the role of a lawyer.

Donny was turning a perpetrator into a victim. And in the
process, he came to believe in his fictions. Which, of course,
at bottom, was why he was so successful. He was rehabilitat-
ing a maligned and valuable public servant. What was
wrong with that . . . ?

# Chapter Fourteen

ON its face, the greening of Paul Medford by that public relations man with the green thumb, Donny
Corum, had little to do with the newly elected lieutenant governor, Her Honor Loren Sturdivant. But in politics, like life, what appears on the surface rarely mirrors the
depths beneath.

At the moment Loren Sturdivant was telling her secretary
to hold all calls—*what* calls? She had had precious few once
the election was over and she found herself relegated to the
same nonentity status that her predecessors as lieutenant
governor had found themselves in. One retainer around the
assembly had referred to her office—and now in her case
with a new poignancy or relevance or both—as being useless
as a tit on a bull.

This was all particularly galling, since without question
she really had won the election for Jon Klyk. Oh, she'd been
willing to lie low and show a diminished profile for a
while—but it had gone on too long and too obviously, with
meetings of the governor's cabinet being called, to which she
wasn't invited, and government operations and decisions
being made without even a routine briefing. She had to

reverse this unacceptable situation, but to do it she also had to face the fact that she had some important fence-mending to do. Busting into the courtroom as she had and delivering the speech that no doubt put the son of the chairman of the Ways and Means Committee, that pernicious little creep Terry Wilbur, into jail, hardly won her points with the assembly or its members. Nor did it help that shortly after Terry's sentencing his mother, Dora Wilbur, had a nervous breakdown, or so they said, and had to be taken off for a "rest cure." And all of this undoubtedly made Klyk's life more complicated, for which she was sorry, but as a mother what less could she have done than defend her child and seek vengeance on the person who had almost killed her? She had had to do what she did, period.

All right, she told herself, but now consider the fallout and, more importantly, what to do about it. Jon Klyk and even Scott Morgan, Mr. Wonderful—at least in bed he lived up to his reputation—acted like a scene out of *The Godfather* whenever she was in sight, literally and figuratively shutting her out of their meetings and deliberations. She heard only secondhand from her executive assistant about Scott going after Paul Medford in the Long Island toxic waste scandal, and how Jon Klyk had thrown Medford to the wolves . . .

Her popularity with the people was by no means hurt by her appearance in court in defense of her daughter, but popular appeal wasn't enough. She needed allies, and powerful ones, in government, or she would soon be yesterday's news, past history . . . like the woman who had run for vice president and lost so badly. What the hell was her name . . . ?

For Loren Sturdivant, in need of new friends and allies, the troubles of Senator Paul Medford seemed to offer just the sort of opening she needed . . .

It would have been an outrageous understatement to say that Donny Corum was surprised by Lieutenant Governor

Loren Sturdivant's call. One just didn't invite them to the same dinner party. Her thing was to attack the power structure. Donny Corum represented the power structure. And although Corum had never represented the Wilbur family, they were close friends, and Corum had not made any attempt to disguise his feelings about that "vicious bitch" who had hurt the Wilburs.

Loren's informants repeated to her the full text of Corum's remarks. She understood Corum. The people she offended were the people that paid him. She chalked him up as another enemy she had to take on along the road to where she was going. But now, circumstances had changed. Now Corum had to be won over. So be it.

When she asked him to her office, he never considered refusing. After all, in his business one never burned bridges to people of power. He arrived at the appointed time.

Her office was as opulent as the governor's—perhaps more so. The paneled walls and the hand-carved desk were solid walnut. One wall was covered with gold-framed classics—Matisse, Renoir, Picasso, Gauguin and a Rembrandt. On the opposite wall hung a single picture, a portrait of the late Judge Alan Sturdivant, as he appeared before his fall from grace—strong, handsome, a commanding figure in his judicial robes, contrasting with the pitiful bloody figure found in a prison shower.

The large white brocade sofa was flanked on each side by two raspberry pullout chairs. Two oversized Oriental rugs covered the floor. A gold leaf coffee table held a large Waterford glass pitcher with freshly cut flowers, and on each side was a framed photograph of her daughters.

Donny Corum was duly impressed with the class of the office—and of the lady who occupied it, even though she presumably was on the opposite side of his political and social level.

She motioned him to the large chair facing her desk, characteristically wasting no time . . . "Mr. Corum, I am very disturbed at the way Senator Medford has been unfairly condemned."

Corum had learned in his professional life as a journalist to expect the unexpected, but he was not prepared for this. The possibilities of support from this formidable lady were mind-boggling. Evita going to her masses—people who genuinely loved her—and asking for justice for Paul Medford . . . He couldn't have possibly hoped for as much, but at that moment he also knew he should control his excitement.

"That's very gratifying, Governor." Nothing more, leave the ball in her court.

"Frankly, Mr. Corum, I am so offended by it that I want you *and* Senator Medford to know that I will be available to help him in any way that I perhaps can."

Corum smiled graciously, asking himself, What's her game? "I'll convey that to the senator, and I'm sure he'll be as pleased as I am. I can tell you, your offer couldn't have come at a better time. The prestige of your office is one thing, but more important, your personal prestige is priceless."

Nice words to hear, Loren thought, after being shut out from the real power of office. Besides, so far as she could tell, Medford was taking quite a beating after years of service. Of course, not being privy to all of Scott Morgan's damning evidence against Medford, she could generate some rationalization for her support.

Corum put Loren's services to work immediately. His plan was geared to persuade people that the attacks on Medford were false. But the problem was that he lacked a motive. Why, after all, would the governor attack an old friend and ally—unless he had a motive? He couldn't leave the public with an answer, so he left them with the question hanging . . . to have the answer come through favorable speculation.

Corum was at first surprised by Loren's cooperation, knowing she had never been exactly enamored of the likes of Medford, or he of her. But why look a gift horse in the mouth? . . . If she had her reasons, who cared? Their purposes coincided, whatever hers were.

Medford's television message was now anchored by Loren's statement: "My friends, Senator Paul Medford is a distinguished public servant who did his best to solve a terribly dangerous problem. He is still trying. And for his efforts he has been the target of unwarranted attacks. I don't know the motives of those attacking him, but as for me, I want to make it clear that I support Senator Paul Medford, a man who has demonstrated in the past that he is worthy of your trust and confidence and will be again when all the facts are disclosed . . ."

Loren did worry at times that her endorsement might be too strong, but so long as she kept the support of the people, she had an escape hatch, that she had been misled. Meanwhile, she was building an ally for an official constituency, now that it seemed Klyk and Scott Morgan had decided to leave her on the outside of their policy decisions . . .

In the weeks that followed, the criticism of Medford lessened. Corum was only partially responsible. Newspapers and magazines throughout the state that depended on the Sturdivant business interests for advertising revenue turned sympathetically toward the minority leader of the senate. Editorials lowered the heat to "reserve judgment until the facts are presented."

Only Loren Sturdivant could pull this off, Klyk thought, not as surprised as Morgan at her apparent change of direction. He'd learned long before that to underestimate the Sturdivant power or smarts or commitment at any time could be a very bad miscalculation indeed.

Scott Morgan, though, was not as accepting. He'd enjoyed, to put it mildly, their one-time sexual encounter, but even as it was happening he kept a hedge in his mind about her . . . and now this . . . Didn't she *know* Medford was a liar? And if she did, then how could she help him?

"That woman is incredible," he said to the governor. "I can't tell you how many times she talked against Medford to me, called him a political profiteer."

"When did she say that?"

"A while ago."

"When you were friendlier?"

"Well—I suppose."

Klyk nodded. He had suspected that Morgan had bedded Loren. They were, so to speak, brothers-in-Loren. He silently apologized to himself for the terrible play on words.

"Scott, I like you. You've got principles, fire in the belly, as the journalists like to say, and you're a hell of an investigator. Just what I need. But watch out you don't turn into a righteous prig. They call Loren 'Evita.' Whatever . . . she's no hustling pol. She's dreampt the dreams, and will do almost anything to make them come true. You're an idealist, good. She's one too, but a pragmatist as well with convictions that her good ends justify her means. She knows how to survive, and she's just shown that she knows the primary rule of survival—that if you don't make a deal you'll be sunk by people who can and do. You never hate or love completely in this game—the blacks and the whites merge into grays. That's politics . . . hell, kid, that's life."

"But she's out to sabotage you—"

"Scott, I knew that from the day we were elected. I expected this. It was only a question of when. She can't be number two. She wants, intends, to be governor of this state. And more . . . and she's ready to make sacrifices for it— including . . . hell, *especially*, yours truly. Getting angry at her doesn't help, but it doesn't hurt half as much as underestimating her. This used to be a man's game. We needed a Loren Sturdivant to show us how it should really be played."

"But why does she defend Medford after drawing such

flack from the legislature by offending Terry Wilbur's father by putting the son away?"

"Because she had some points to make. First, she was proving again to her people that she was willing to fight their fight—be out in front for equal justice, take on the rich and privileged. Second, and more important, she had to show them that because her daughter was the victim—damn near killed because of Terry Wilbur's cowardice—she had to show the world that she wasn't to be trifled with. If that's what she had in mind, she sure made her point."

"I don't know . . . the *lady* has the principles of a cobra."

"Scott," Klyk said, "remember that Loren *believes* in what she's doing, can justify damn near anything and do almost anything to get the power to do what she wants. Trouble is, she's beginning to scare even me . . . turning into a woman on horseback . . ."

Medford knew the winds had changed when he noticed that those legislators who had avoided him just weeks before were now greeting him warmly. He didn't resent them for their revamped attitude. All part of the business of politics. They were just acknowledging the basic rule—survival transcends friendship and loyalties. He'd figured his allies would rally round when it was safe to do so. Apparently, that time was at hand. Even better, he and the lieutenant governor could take satisfaction in that the power structure was beginning to make Klyk the villain of the piece. His popularity with other legislators, already reduced after he gave Morgan free rein, hit near-bottom. He was even referred to as "Judas" Klyk, and he had dimming prospects for any cooperation by legislative leaders.

Jon Klyk was markedly saddened by all this. He had, after all, been "one of the boys." He enjoyed liking people and being liked in return. But he also acknowledged to himself that he knew it was coming when he first gave young Mor-

gan the green light to uncover the state's rot and decay and
show the people that politics didn't necessarily have to smell
like sun-baked fish. The old-time professional politicians
didn't want to change the time-tested order of things. It was
a sort of apostasy. Yet this was the road he chose, and he now
had to live with it. So be it.

Corum kept the pot boiling. "A good man was being
harassed by the powers that be." No question who *that* was.
And then . . . *Why?* Why would the governor persecute such
a good man as Paul Medford? "Unless, of course, the new
governor knows more about the facts of the tragedy at Snyder's Flats and the people who are *really* responsible than he
is telling us . . ."


Morgan did not mind the shots taken at him, but he resented
the tide of condemnation of Klyk, ex-leader of Erie County
and mayor of Buffalo, supposedly an old-time pol, who was
showing more guts and principle than anybody . . . maybe
himself included . . . had ever given him credit for. And the
people's choice, the spellbinding Loren, was, it seemed,
earning her designation as "Evita," North American edition.

His anger at the turn of events was deepened by a call
from Mathew Bradley, the man who had given him that
grisly tour of Snyder's Flats. Bradley came to his point immediately.

"Medford's getting away with it, isn't he, Mr. Morgan?"

Morgan's voice tried to conceal his feelings. "No, Mr.
Bradley, he won't, the public will know the facts—"

"You're a good man, Mr. Morgan. But aren't we kidding
ourselves here?"

"No—"

"Yes, we are, Mr. Morgan. What counts in the world is
influence and power and cover-up, with justice for sale. So

those of us who can't afford the ticket have to get it any way we can."

Scott started to protest but Bradley went on, in a near-monotone now . . . "Do you remember me telling you about my daughter, the one who got cancer of the cervix?"

"Yes, you said she's in remission—"

"Not anymore, Mr. Morgan. We buried her last week."

Scott could not speak. What was there to say?

"Well, what the hell . . . we at least tried, didn't we? It just wasn't a fair fight, but then, I never expected it would be. But you're a good stand-up guy, Mr. Morgan, and I won't forget how hard you tried. Now I guess I'll just do what I have to do."

"What do you mean—?"

"But the line was dead.

Senator Paul Medford was exuberant. He felt his recovery was complete after he received the call from Emmet Quogue, the majority leader of the New York State Senate. The senate was going back to a special session the following Monday, and Quogue, in talking legislative business, told him how pleased he was that the results of Donny Corum's poll were so encouraging.

"Paul," Quogue said, "Your personal thing is over. Now let's get back to good old party politics."

Ordinarily, the Democratic minority leader (Medford) would tangle with the Republican majority leader (Quogue) in friendly combat. It was the job of the minority leader to carry the Democratic governor's bills and the job of the Republican majority leader to criticize the governor and minimize the political capital that the governor could gain from the passage of such bills. Somewhere a compromise was reached and each side salvaged something. But now Quogue was not about to get too much resistance from the

Democratic minority, and especially from Medford. He had had a good working relationship with the governor, but now he said openly that Klyk's attack on Medford was a "Pearl Harbor job," and Jon Klyk was left with very few friends on *either* side of the aisle. In this climate it seemed foolish for Klyk to call this special session of the legislature, since it was obvious that the governor's bills were going to be deep-sixed by the committee.

Medford, of course, welcomed this opportunity for revenge. Quogue was now intent on completely sabotaging the governor's legislative program, and under these circumstances there was no way he would fail. Medford was going to let it happen, proving the old political adage "Everything that goes around comes around."

The session was scheduled for the following Monday, which allowed him to spend the weekend at his beach house in Bellport. The place was an architectural marvel—the very last home on South Howell's Point Road, with a panoramic view of the Great South Bay. He had scheduled an early foursome at the Bellport Country Club. Normally he played at the more exclusive Shinnecock in Southhampton, even though it was at least thirty minutes away. But those were different times. He had to reinstate himself with his people. Shinnecock was not going to see much of Senator Paul Medford in the foreseeable future. Those folks didn't vote in his district.

He loved this time of the day. The morning sun rising over Fire Island filtered its rays through the low clouds, painting golden flecks on the rippled water. The seagulls kept up their chatter, and the air coming in from the east in gentle gusts was salty and fresh and made the lungs feel good. He was about to lift his golf bag that he had temporarily placed on the front porch and carry it to the station wagon when he saw a lone figure on the beach. His lawn extended fifty yards to the waterline, then dissolved into a patch of high marsh grass, leaving only ten feet of sand, which was where the man was standing and waving at him. The sun was shining directly in his face, and he shaded his eyes as he heard the man calling his name. He moved toward the water, then he heard what the man was saying: "I think you got a bad deal, Senator. I want you to know that we're all behind you."

The words brought a wide smile to Medford's face. He'd go there and shake the fellow's hand. He was now about ten feet from the man, moving through a narrow path that had been cut through the tall marsh grass to gain access to the beach. Both men had their hands outstretched. Abruptly the man stopped and reached under the three-quarter coat he was wearing. Medford saw the gun emerge from the coat for a split second before the man pumped the double-barreled shotgun. After the two shells struck him, Paul Medford had no face. The first shell left a gaping hole where his forehead had been, the second all but severed his head from his neck.

The man did not run. He dragged Medford's body into the grass and then walked briskly down the narrow beach. He crossed into a patch of high reeds that covered a small promontory jutting into the water and waded to a small boat that he had moored to a pole behind the reeds that partially obstructed the view from the house. He started the engine, which responded immediately, and the boat sped away from the shore, proceeding south and then west. The man braced the tether between his legs and quickly disassembled the shotgun into two parts. He moved toward deeper water and threw one part over the side, and five hundred yards further threw over the remaining part. He was well out of sight and long gone from the scene before Medford's family discovered the body.


The Suffolk County Police and Sheriff's cars lined up in front of the house on South Howell's Point Road within five minutes of the original notification. The media vehicles found no room in the small cul-de-sac and parked a good distance from the house. There were at least twenty press and police vehicles at the scene, and more coming. The rotating lights of the police vehicles and the constant chatter of radio transmissions gave the scene the sense of drama that the television reporters dearly loved.

The death of Senator Medford was, of course, immediately classified as a homicide. Inspector Brian Leahy, chief of the Homicide Division of the Suffolk County Police, was in charge. Leahy, a respected, experienced cop, was closing out his thirty years, looking forward to retirement and that classy boat he had bought in Boca Raton. He had investigated enough homicides, viewed enough corpses, testified at enough murder trials. This would be his last case, but he was a good and conscientious cop, and he was not about to handle it any differently. Officer Fritz Gorman was chosen to chauffeur him on his detail, and the young cop considered himself lucky.

As they were looking at the body, Gorman shuddered. He had been assigned to homicide for a year and seen his share of corpses, but he had never seen anything like this.

"God, Inspector, I mean . . . the man has only half a face."

Leahy didn't answer. Something caught his eye. It was small and metallic, and it briefly reflected the sunlight that just then temporarily escaped from the cloud cover. It was nestled in the tall reeds. Leahy bent down, digging under the leaves until his fingers closed over it. He put it in his pocket and searched further but found nothing more.

He rejoined Gorman and they watched silently as the medics placed the body in a sack. Leahy did not react, but Gorman bit his lips as they observed the gory process of straightening the corpse's head before placing it in the bag.

"I've seen worse than this," Leahy said, "and before you're through, you will too." The old cop pulled the object, a shell casing, out of his pocket. "This thing talks to us . . . double-O buckshot can sure as hell blow your face away.

I figure he had to be about six, maybe seven, feet away. No more. The fillings didn't have time to spread out. All of it hit him together."

"But he was hit twice. Where was the other casing?"

Leahy looked again at the shell casing in his right hand.

"Probably the shell was never ejected. At least not at the scene."

"I don't understand—"

"I looked hard for that other shell casing but I only found one. I think the killer was using a double-barreled, pump-action shotgun—probably twelve gauge. But whatever it was, it wasn't automatic. An automatic would have ejected the casing as soon as it was fired. He fired once, pumped once and fired again. He didn't pump the second time. If he had, the second casing would have been here—not far from the first one. No, the casing was still in the gun when he left."

Gorman walked the short distance to the cul-de-sac. He looked down the South Howell's Point Road and returned to Leahy. "Nobody saw a car or heard a car this morning," Leahy said. "There are about thirty homes on both sides of the South Howell's leading to South Country Road. The units that arrived here before us asked everybody, and no one remembers seeing or hearing a car driving north between seven-fifteen and eight o'clock. The coroner said Medford died about that time."

"How the hell did he get away?"

Leahy pointed to the bay. "Lots of water out there, Fritz. And lots of boats."

"But, Inspector, there's only two feet draw over here. I go clamming about a hundred yards up. No motor could clear the bottom."

They walked to the water's edge.

"Not now, maybe," Leahy said, "but check the tide this morning at seven-thirty. I'll bet it was high."

He pointed to a wooden pole standing straight up about ten yards from the shore. He crossed the reed-covered sand spit. "He waded out, unleashed the boat, pushed it up a few more yards and tilted the engine till he had enough draw."

"What about the gun?" Gorman asked.

"It's plain he took it with him and dropped it off in the bay. If it were me, I would have disassembled it quickly and disposed of it in separate parts. That way both parts would have to be found to prove they came from the same gun. A fisherman, dragging deep, could possibly pick up one part, but it would be a long long shot to pick up both of them. The two parts are lying on the bottom in deep water in the middle of the bay—a considerable distance from each other."

"But wasn't he in a hurry to get away? Wouldn't he have to take some time to disassemble it?"

"You ever see a Winchester, double-barreled, twelve-gauge pump?"

"I believe so . . . can't remember just when . . ."

"If you'd looked at it close you would have seen how easy it is to turn a pin in the magazine tube, pull the tube forward, then a half turn—and the barrel comes loose from the receiver. It could all be done in less than ten seconds . . . It might be helpful for you to remember when you saw one, and even better, who owned it, Fritz."

Fritz Gorman shook his head. "I'll try."


His trying paid off at about 4:00 A.M. He smiled and turned over and finally slept. At eight he called Leahy. "I was introduced to the guy a couple months ago, had a drink with him. Nice guy, I like to talk to people on my beat. Anyway, he had trouble, family sickness on account of the Snyder's Flats thing. I saw him in his truck a few weeks ago *and* I saw the gun in the truck. I remember it was a big son—pump-action, twelve gauge—and I think it was a Winchester . . . But aren't there a lot of guns like that?"

"Yes," Leahy said, excited by the news. "But most are

automatic or semi–automatic. If this is purely a pump-action I want to know it. What's his name?"

"Bradley, I think. I'm pretty sure, I'm good at names, as you know—"

"Can you find him?"

"Sure, I can ask and—"

"Okay, good. Ask him if he'll bring his gun in, routine checking . . . Give him any story you want. If he refuses, I'll go to the D.A. for a search warrant. If he doesn't have it, and can't explain where it is . . ."

"Yeah, but this is really a nice guy, I don't think—"

"Fritz, that's what the neighbors always say about the killer or rapist or whatever. Don't you ever watch television? Go see your Mr. Bradley . . ."

# Chapter Fifteen

THE United Methodist Church in Bellport had enough historic significance to be listed in the National Register of Historical Places by the Department of the Interior. Founded in 1850, it was a graceful structure, white and clean and stark in its lines and changed little from the day it was built.

It was not, unfortunately, large enough to accommodate the crowd that showed up for Senator Medford's funeral. Some, besides the family, actually mourned his loss. He was, after all, a deacon of the church and its most illustrious member. But others did not attend out of respect for the departed. The minority leadership of the senate now had to pass on . . . and those who coveted that power position—all members of the senate attending—were seated in the second row of pews with appropriately mournful faces. Others were there for other reasons . . . Loren Sturdivant, who arrived with Donny Corum, had been chosen by the bereaved family to deliver the eulogy. Actually, the family had left everything in Corum's hands, and he had told them that she deserved the honor, being the only major political figure to stand up for Paul Medford when he was under attack.

They weren't inclined to debate the point, although the widow had some doubts, which she kept to herself . . . Both were widows, but Mrs. Medford had some questions about Loren's motives, as had her husband . . .

Governor Jon Klyk arrived with Scott Morgan and staff. The ushers had orders to seat them away from the family, where Corum and Loren had already been placed, but Klyk took it in stride. Actually, every detail possible, including the seating arrangements and the program, was orchestrated by Corum with one purpose in mind—to launch his next preeminent client, Loren Sturdivant, on the road to the governorship of the state of New York.

The minister introduced Loren as an "old and supportive friend of the family." She walked to the lectern and stood there dignified and stately. Her tailored suit could not in any way disguise her femininity, and while they watched, her eyes glistened and she threw her head back and took on the aura of Evita. She controlled the pitch of her voice, talked softly about Medford's accomplishments, the respect of his colleagues, the bereavement of his family, as well as the personal loss felt by all who were present . . . Now had come the time to shift gears . . .

"Yes, we grieve today for a leader, a statesman, a father, a husband whose life was snuffed out most cruelly because he offended the powers that be by trying to stand with the ordinary citizen. He was a threat to those who profited from public misery. He did not just talk it but *did* something about it. He was disturbing those who live by influence, money, and he had begun to reach the people. The power barons could not let that continue. They spread false tales about him. It was predictably only a matter of time before a sincere dupe would take their false stories literally and . . .

"Those responsible will be known and remembered for their tragic recklessness. Paul Medford will be remembered for what he tried to do—and the price he paid for it."

Donny Corum did not write this speech, and knew he

never could have. It was at once damning and subtle, making its terrible accusation elliptically but with devastating clarity. She had, in a church, all but made Medford a martyr and the governor a villain. The campaign was launched. And while the governor sat just a few yards away, Donny Corum could only shake his head in wonderment and admiration. What a piece of work was this lady . . .

But the likes of Donny Corum could never quite decipher the enigma of Loren Sturdivant, the layers within layers. Yes, the lady shared his Machiavellian mentality and talent, but she had an informing purpose, a background of family position and service. It was beyond Donny to comprehend, but not beyond his ability to recognize a unique combination of self-server and true believer. Yes, indeed, he had a live one here, he thought as he observed Klyk now. Whatever was boiling inside him did not show. A cool one, Corum thought, which did not come as a surprise. He had, after all, done some work for the governor during the last campaign. But that was then, and now was now . . .

The minister recited the Lord's Prayer. Governor Klyk, still impassive, left the church and waited for the family to appear to pay his last respects, then entered the black state limo followed by Scott Morgan. The reporters tried for a comment on the lieutenant governor's words, but Klyk only smiled and waved them off. Loren, whose car arrived next, also refused to talk to them. When they persisted, Donny Corum, eyes bleeding sincerity, told them: "Heavens' sake, fellas, isn't anything sacred?"


Inspector Leahy saw that his driver Officer Gorman was signaling to him that he had just received a radio communication. Leahy shook his head slightly, indicating that Gorman should say nothing until he entered the vehicle.

The car pulled away from the curb before he spoke up. "You wanted to be told when Mathew Bradley was picked up, Inspector. Well, Rafael and Callus just brought him to the Patchogue Precinct."

"And?"

"He refused to make a statement."

"Did they give him his Miranda rights?"

"Yes, sir."

"Did they say they entered his home with a search warrant?"

"Yes, sir, they said they got one from Judge Davis."

"Did they find the gun?"

"No."

"I didn't think they would."

"But they did find something else—twenty rounds of double-O buckshot—with the same imprint on the casings that you found at the scene."

Leahy frowned. "Better than nothing, but it's not enough to hold him. There's got to be hundreds in this county that use those shells."

"But how can he explain them without a gun to fire them?"

"He doesn't have to explain anything, Fritz. He doesn't have to say a damn thing. But let's give it a shot. Get me there fast."

Gorman activated the siren and they arrived at the precinct headquarters in a few minutes. Bradley was being held in a small interrogation room.

"Mr. Bradley," Leahy said, "I'm Inspector Leahy. I want to make it clear you're just here for questioning.

Bradley shook his head. "I'm not a lawyer, Inspector. But I think I know when I'm being questioned and when I'm under arrest. I didn't come here voluntarily. If I had been given the choice I wouldn't be here."

"Well, the fact is, we believe we can describe the gun that was used in the senator killing. All we want to do is question you and others who might own guns that fit that description.

You are *not* under arrest and you will be free to go after we get this straight."

Bradley stood and faced Leahy. He was a tall man, powerfully built. The police officers in the room eyed him. They had seen suspects before who had reacted badly to questioning. Leahy waved them off.

"Inspector," Bradley said, "I guess I have to use that stale line out of an old Humphrey Bogart movie. 'Book me or release me.'"

Leahy took one more shot.

"All we want to know, Mr. Bradley, is whether you own such a gun and if so, can we see it?"

"Am I under arrest, Inspector?"

Leahy knew then he was trumped. "No, sir."

"Then I'll leave."

Bradley moved toward the door. The two officers stood and looked to Leahy, and again he waved them off.

"Sorry for the inconvenience, Mr. Bradley," Leahy said. "I'll get a police car to take you home."

"No need, it's a fine fall day. I only live five miles from here. I'd prefer to walk." Bradley opened the door and left.

Leahy watched him after he left the precinct building, saw him turn north and walk briskly. Then suddenly he stopped and turned, as if he knew Leahy had been watching him; he turned again and walked at a normal pace.

"The man's playing with us," Leahy said, "but I admit there's something about him I sort of like . . ."

"You figure he's not guilty?" Gorman said.

"No, I think he's guilty as hell."

Gorman waited for an explanation—got none.

District Attorney Ross Montgomery paced nervously on the thick rug of his office. He had read the confidential report that Leahy had prepared, and now was waving it at him.

"It had to be him," the D.A. said. "He had every reason to kill Medford. He had the opportunity. And he had the gun. But all I've got is twenty-five rounds of double-o buckshot. I need some corroboration. If he told someone about how much he hated Medford and how he was going to get him . . . well, that plus the shells is at least enough to go to the grand jury."

"Mr. Montgomery, that's going to be a problem. We've learned a lot about this Mathew Bradley since we began the investigation. This man is so popular he should run for office. He alerted people to the poisoned water problem way before the authorities did. Those that listened boiled their water, and he badgered many of them until they moved. Who knows how much suffering he prevented, how many lives he saved? Remember, he lost his own child. We questioned his former neighbors. When they talk about him it's like he's a savior. Nobody's going to give him up . . ."

Montgomery seemed to have stopped listening, as though not wanting to waste his attention on bad news. "What was the name of that officer who says he saw the gun in Bradley's truck?" he asked suddenly.

"Gorman, Fritz Gorman."

"I want to talk to him again."

"He's my driver, he's outside waiting for me. I'll get him." Leahy walked to the door and called Gorman. The young officer hurried in and sat in the chair indicated by the D.A.

Leahy sensed Montgomery wanted privacy. "Are you finished with me, Mr. Montgomery?"

"No, but if you don't mind I'd like to talk to Officer Gorman for a while."

"Take your time," Leahy said, and closed the door behind him.

"How well do you know Mathew Bradley, Officer Gorman?" Montgomery began.

"Like I told you before, Mr. Montgomery, not too well. I might have talked to him three times in all."

"What did you talk about when you saw the gun in his truck?"

"Nothing much . . . the weather maybe. Hunting. I really don't remember."

"Did you talk about the gun?"

"No, don't think so."

"Did he ever talk to you about the problems at Snyder's Flats?"

"No, sir."

"But you know that his child became ill and eventually died—or so he claims—from the water pollution at Snyder's Flats."

"Yes, I found that out."

"From him?"

"No, sir, from the emergency room physician at Brookhaven Hospital. We get to know all of those doctors after a while. He named the families who were affected."

"Are you sure Bradley never discussed it with you—and that Senator Paul Medford was involved?"

"Can't recall he did, sir."

"Officer, think hard. It would be normal for him to talk about the tragedy, how his family was affected, his neighbors—and how Senator Paul Medford would pay for bringing all that about . . . Saying something like that to you would be enough for an indictment, so you can understand how important it is that you remember. I understand Bradley is a sympathetic character, but he's also a killer. *That* is what counts. You'll be performing a public service, Officer Gorman, a service I and others will remember if an indictment results from your testimony. I see this as a tremendous opportunity for you . . . don't let it go by."

Gorman hesitated. He seemed to be searching for the words to reply. Finally . . . "Mr. Montgomery, corny as this may sound, I like being a cop. And nothing would make me happier than to rise in the ranks. And I agree with you that

Bradley probably is guilty. But, sir, I won't do what you're asking me to do. I don't want it that bad."

He walked to the door and opened it and called Leahy, who seemed surprised at the briefness of Gorman's interview.

"The D.A.'s finished with me, Inspector."

Leahy watched Gorman walk down the hall, his face tight with an anger he had never seen before. When he reentered the room Montgomery was looking straight ahead and shaking his head. "You've got a real squarehead there, Inspector, but never mind, I suddenly realized who's going to help us. He won't want to but he'll have no choice."

"Who's that, Mr. Montgomery?"

"The boy scout who started all of this, Scott Morgan. If it weren't for him Paul Medford would be alive today. Morgan had to have spoken to Bradley, Bradley would be the one who would naturally supply him with the information he came to me with. Nobody knew more about the mess at Snyder's Flats than Bradley."

"Excuse me, Mr. Montgomery," Leahy said, "but if Morgan did speak to Bradley, he may not want to reveal that conversation."

"No? A public official frustrating an official investigation into a homicide? Maybe some would, but not Mr. Ombudsman Morgan. He'll talk, and when he does we'll have what we need. It may not be the strongest case in the world, but it's enough for an indictment. And before Bradley goes to trial we'll get more—"

"If it exists . . ."

"Believe me, it will, Inspector Leahy. Have a little faith . . ."

Leahy didn't like what he was hearing but kept quiet about it.

"How do you intend to get Morgan in here?" he asked instead.

"He'll come, he won't give us any trouble. But if there's any resistance I'll subpoena his ass before the grand jury."

\* \* \*

It seemed, up to a point, at least, that Montgomery had read Scott Morgan correctly. His response to the D.A.'s phone call was immediate and he showed up at Montgomery's office at the agreed time.

However, Montgomery knew that Morgan would not be the most cooperative witness. He didn't expect him to be comfortable in revealing conversations that launched the investigation into the cause of the Snyder's Flat tragedies. But he felt that Morgan would tell the truth.

The small talk was cordial enough until the D.A. came to the point. "Mr. Morgan, in our investigation of the murder of Senator Paul Medford we have reason to believe that a Mathew Bradley is a suspect."

Montgomery eyed Morgan's face carefully, saw no reaction.

"We have," he continued, "certain circumstantial evidence which implicates this person. But at the present time I haven't enough to present to the grand jury. Mr. Morgan, I want you to tell us everything Mathew Bradley ever said to you in connection with Snyder's Flats or about the death of his daughter, and especially any reference to Paul Medford."

Morgan didn't answer, just stared at the D.A.

"Didn't I make myself clear?" Montgomery said.

"Oh, clear as hell, Mr. Montgomery. But I won't answer that question. First of all, it presupposes that I know this Mathew Bradley, much less spoke to him. But even if I did, I won't reveal names or conversations with any sources that helped us uncover the situation. Those people trusted me— they won't suffer because of it—"

"What the hell are you talking about? This is a homicide we're investigating. It's way past the Snyder's Flats thing. There's no privileged communication rule here. You're obstructing justice!"

"Sorry you feel that way."

"Sorry? You haven't begun to be sorry."

The D.A. opened his desk and removed a white form he scribbled Morgan's name on. "I assume you know what a grand jury subpoena looks like, Mr. Morgan. Well, this one has your name on it. You will appear Tuesday where and when indicated. And if you still refuse to answer questions, I will request that you be cited and jailed for civil contempt."

"I know what the penalty is, Mr. Montgomery," Morgan said. "Are you prepared to grant me immunity? That's the only way I'll testify."

Montgomery eyes him warily. Had he stumbled on something here? Why would Morgan ask for immunity if he wasn't involved? Or maybe someone else too? The governor? What a coup to nail the governor's boy to the cross. Mr. Goody Two Shoes involved in a murder conspiracy . . . Whatever, he was afraid of something. Given immunity, Morgan was apparently ready to let Bradley fry and God knew who else to save his own hide. Montgomery decided he would grant Morgan immunity, but for a reason beyond Morgan or Bradley . . .

Montgomery's political life had been a series of frustrations. He ran for state congress twice and lost, he ran for county executive and lost—he ran for district attorney and lost, and succeeded almost by default when the incumbent Democratic district attorney died suddenly and he won in a special election in which the vote was very small. In another two years he had to run again, and up to now his time in office had been distinguished by . . . what? The chances were good that he could lose. And that thought devastated him. He'd been bitten by the political bug, he coveted power. In his case, because he was aware of his own inadequacies, it was more an obsession. What he lacked in intelligence and skill he made up in drive, but he didn't have the goods to use it. Until now. This was his shot. By exposing the conspiracy, as he saw it, every headline would have his name in it. *He* would be the one to expose and destroy the Klyk administration. And when *that* came to pass he would be the shining light of the Republican party in New York State, and who knew how far beyond? . . .

He was going to get his indictment. He was even composing the first of his press releases that would send the message to the public how quickly his office acted, how efficient he was, how he solved the murder in record time. And while he would not directly charge Governor Klyk with being implicated, his words would be such that no one could fail to draw that conclusion. Hell, he might even get Loren Sturdivant on his ticket, get her to change parties. A considerable dish, that woman. Once Morgan spilled his guts he would not have to prove anything on his press release about Klyk, wouldn't have to mention Klyk at all, except to say, "The District Attorney of Suffolk County is investigating the possibility of Governor Klyk's involvement."

Let the people figure out whether Klyk was involved . . .

"All right, Mr. Morgan," he said, "you've got your immunity." And to himself, But rest assured the world will know that you asked for it, and that I gave it to you.

The officer ushered Scott Morgan into the grand jury room, which was large with oak-panelled walls and spacious windows allowing sunlight to flood the interior. The eighteen grand jurors sat in three rows of comfortable swivel chairs spaced about five feet apart. Montgomery was standing in front of them. He was not about to allow any of his assistants to make this presentation. After Scott Morgan was sworn, he sat in a chair facing the jurors.

Montgomery started in a low, calm voice.

"Mr. Foreman, ladies and gentlemen, Mr. Scott Morgan has been called as a witness in these proceedings. He has been requested to sign a waiver of immunity but he has refused to do so. Through the power vested in me by the applicable statute, as the prosecutor of Suffolk County, I have conferred on Mr. Morgan total immunity as required by the statute. In effect that means that he may not be prosecuted for anything he says here, and if it applies to some act he committed in the past he may not be prosecuted for that either. He therefore must now respond to the questions that I ask or you ask, and he must respond to them truthfully."

He turned and faced Scott Morgan, seated so as to be looking at the grand jurors.

"Do you understand what I have just said, Mr. Morgan?"

"Yes."

"Is there anything you wish explained to you?"

"No."

"What is your present position, Mr. Morgan?"

"Director of the Office of Ombudsman of the state of New York."

"And in that capacity did you have occasion to investigate the claims of illness and death due to toxic waste dumping in the area of Snyder's Flats?"

"Yes."

"And in your investigation did you have occasion to talk to an individual by the name of Mathew Bradley?"

Morgan looked straight ahead.

Montgomery edged closer to him.

"Did you hear my question, Mr. Morgan?"

"Yes."

"Then what is your answer?"

Scott breathed deeply. "I never spoke to Mathew Bradley about the toxic dumping at Snyder's Flats."

Ross Montgomery froze, fought to control his voice, but could not disguise the redness in his face. "Mr. Morgan, do you realize that you are under oath and can be prosecuted for perjury if you lie about a material fact?"

"Yes."

"Do you acknowledge that the disclosure of your conversations with Bradley in connection with toxic waste dumping at Snyder's Flats are vital to the investigation of the homicide of Senator Paul Medford?"

"I understand that. But you are presupposing that such conversations took place."

Montgomery's voice began to rise. "Are you telling this grand jury that no such conversation took place with Mathew Bradley?"

"That's what I am saying. At the time alleged I did not know who Mathew Bradley was."

Montgomery saw it all collapse . . . his future, his life . . . all going down the toilet. Now he would be perceived to be a fool. He had leaked the news of the soon to be voted indictment, had telephoned certain media people that "we're going to get an indictment in this case, and more than that, the story will be dynamite . . ." Now there would be no indictment—no dynamite—not even a damned fire-cracker. He couldn't hope for a perjury indictment against Morgan because Bradley wasn't talking, and he doubted whether there was even one witness to their conversations. His frustration was complete, and it overwhelmed him . . .

"Well, Morgan, you better get a lawyer you lying son of a . . ." Not only the words he used but his obvious and abrupt loss of control startled, then shocked the grand jurors and everyone else in the room.

"You're concealing evidence, you're hiding the truth, you'll go to jail and rot there. *I* guarantee it. I won't allow you to do this to me, I won't allow it . . ."

Morgan looked at him with more than a little compassion. The man had fallen apart, and he, Morgan, had made it happen. Still, it obviously hadn't happened as fast as it seemed here in this room. The man had been moving to the edge for a long time. Some of it, looking back, was showing when Scott first had talked to him. Now this ultimate frus-tration had pushed Montgomery over the brink.

Montgomery was beginning to ramble now, still threaten-ing Morgan. Finally he stopped and sat behind a small table facing the jurors and staring into space. His chief assistant put his hand on his shoulder as he spoke to the grand jurors.

"Ladies and gentlemen, this session will be recessed indefinitely. We will let you know in a few days whether there will be a further presentation."

The grand jurors walked out slowly. Scott Morgan stood, took a step toward Montgomery, thought better of it, and left the room.

Morgan reported back to the governor the following day. Klyk had never seen him so upset.

"Scott," Klyk said, "I heard about how you handled Montgomery, showed him to be the fool he is."

"There's more to it than that, Governor."

"I get the feeling I should be careful about the questions I ask you. Maybe you don't want to talk about it at all. If that's the case that'll be okay with me."

"No, I want to talk about it. I think if I don't I'll explode. I can't keep this inside . . ."

Klyk sat back. "Go ahead."

"Governor, I always respected the law. To me it's what saves this country. It had a morality all its own . . ."

"Any doubts about that?"

"Governor, I have doubts about a lot of things now. I'm a lawyer, took an oath to uphold the law. I committed perjury before a grand jury yesterday. Why? Because I'm beginning to doubt that the sterile forum of the court is the only place justice can be served, that a criminal act can be justified in my mind but not in any way the law recognizes . . ."

Klyk waited.

"Is the law too rigid? Does justice really get served by the members? Okay, not original stuff, but new for me . . . It's why I protected someone who killed someone. At the time I felt I had no alternative. For me, there's still no alternative. Because Mathew Bradley was put where he was by Paul

Medford. He was standing in for the others who died at Snyder's Flats. *They* were all punished, and they were all innocent. The law wasn't there for them. Bradley was . . . But I'm no admirer of taking the law into your own hands. I compromised myself and the system, and I compromised you."

Klyk looked at him. "What are you suggesting, Scott?"

"I'm saying, I think, that what I have just told you I'll repeat to the grand jury. I felt I had to protect Bradley, but I had to tell you the truth, and I understand that in your position you're obligated to inform the court of the truth. At least you'll be cleared of all the implications that Montgomery is trying to put out about you being part of a conspiracy. I understand that Bradley, unfair as it may seem to me, has got to face the consequences of what he did, and so must I. I promise you, Governor, I'll confirm everything I told you in this conversation."

Klyk reached for a desk pen and signed some correspondence. He looked up at Morgan.

"What conversation?" The governor continued to scratch his signature on the papers in front of him. He raised his eyes again.

"Scott, are you still here? Haven't you anything else to do except waste my time rambling on about the weather? Get serious. I have a load of work, you're wasting my time. Now get the hell out of here."

# Chapter Sixteen

REGARDLESS of his act in front of Scott Morgan, Jon Klyk shared Morgan's dilemma. His own participation in the cover-up did not escape him. Legally he was obliged to reveal what Scott had told him. But, like Morgan, he also felt that justice pointed overwhelmingly to keeping quiet. He wondered if other leaders, other governors, even presidents or heads of state, buried secrets like this that never got into their memoirs or anybody else's. Sexual dalliances, yes . . . they usually came out one way or the other at some time or another . . . but something like this, a purposeful suppression of evidence, what about that? Did anybody have a right to put his view of what was right and just above the law?

He had to shake his head in some amusement . . . Jon Klyk, ex-mayor, had never considered himself a candidate for sainthood, or to belong among the movers and shakers of society who defied the law for a higher good. He had no such pompous or self-important rationalization now. It took an old sinner to see the light. And now that it had dawned, he wasn't through. He felt *good*, damn it. Not reborn or anything that exalted. Just *good*, and freed up to take the next step. Which meant taking on the legislature, hitting them where they lived—not just money but power and influence—and the devil take the hindmost. If he was committing political suicide, well, what a way to go . . .

Scott Morgan found the Bradley matter more difficult than Klyk. After all, he was a lawyer, Klyk wasn't, and this alone made his responsibility greater, his violation more flagrant . . .

He didn't report to work the next three days, then called the governor, trying to explain his absence, but Klyk knew.

"Take a rest, Scott. You're long overdue. The state of New York and its governor will survive without you for another week."

But he couldn't rest or sleep. Nothing seemed to pull him out of it, until the evening the phone rang and he heard her voice.

He hadn't seen Paula Lawson since Syracuse. He was always on the move and so was she. The only communication they'd had was his letter of congratulation when he couldn't reach her by phone. Smart and beautiful, she had been doing a promo for her paper on a local television station in Syracuse when she was spotted by a network producer. A week later, All World Media announced that she had joined the morning news team in New York.

"Hey, big shot," she said, and his heart jumped.

"Hey, yourself . . . I'm real happy for you—"

"Well, you sure as hell manage to keep it a secret. Here I am, a major TV personality, for all of twelve hours—never mind I could be fired next week—and you still don't call . . ."

"*Mea culpa*, big shot—"

"Never mind, you can atone by helping me find a place to live. I can't stay in a hotel for the rest of my life."

He knew the problem, remembered how he spent most of his time at the governor's New York City office at the World

Trade Center, finally managing to find a one bedroom walk-up on East Twenty-first Street.

"Why don't you move in with me?" My God, just like that it popped out of his mouth. It was his own deep funk that made such an open and unconsidered invitation possible.

She scarcely missed a beat in agreeing . . . "I thought you'd never ask."

That night they didn't bother to sort it out with talk. They got right down to basics—and their lovemaking was not tender, but it was the way they both wanted it and needed it. She was as aggressive as he, and when they finally got out of bed and into the shower at 3:00 A.M. it was with shared feeling of being at once revived and relieved.

Back in bed, she whispered into his ear. "There's something we must discuss."

"Oh, oh, here it comes, well, I'm not the father."

"Bite your tongue," she said. "Listen—there's something we have to work out."

"I've already had my workout—"

"Scott, be serious. I'm a reporter—and, well, you could be my target, or at least your boss could. I know how much you respect him, and between us, I do too, but if he's vulnerable, or good copy, I'm going to go after him."

He propped himself on one elbow, enjoying her body.

"What am I supposed to say to that? I understand and do your damnedest?" But, of course, what her words had done was to bring back the Bradley mess.

"I just hope you'll say that if what we've got is going to survive, then we'll both have to live with what you have to do, and with what I have to do . . ."

"Paula, I go along. *Except* I insist that no questions get answered in the boudoir."

"None will be asked."

"Then let's put it to the test."

And having worked out the ground rules, they resumed playing the game.

Lieutenant Governor Loren Sturdivant, stewing too long in her juices with no outlet as yet in her role as Madam Left Out of the Klyk administration, decided to try an end-run. Paul Medford as an ally was now six feet under, and strangely, the man arrested for the act had never been indicted by the grand jury, in spite of the rumors—and these days she had to go increasingly by rumors—that some sort of hanky-panky had gone on, courtesy of the governor's office and, some said but couldn't back it up, with the involvement of the Ombudsman Scott Morgan.

Well, right or wrong, gain or lose, she needed some action, and it seemed Scott Morgan was the most likely prospect at the moment to provide what she needed . . .

"Scott, how are you?" She had managed to get through to him one lunchtime when his otherwise vigilant secretary was away from her desk.

"I'm fine, thanks."

Not very encouraging, but then she didn't expect him to be. Perhaps he needed a bit of nudging. "Scott, it's been a long time since we had a chat outside of an office." (Or inside one, she added to herself.) "Why don't you drop by my place at the Carlyle this weekend and we'll have tea?" (And whatever else might be usefully indicated. Not only did Scott Morgan have Governor Klyk's ear, he also aroused some remembrances of a most pleasant time past. A double reason to get him to her lair.)

Scott's own memory of their time together was also not dead—though it was hardly burning. He had other diversions, and serious ones, in that area. Didn't Loren Sturdivant know about it? He suspected she did. Even though she was not invited to the inner councils of Jon Klyk's government, she was not without her contacts elsewhere—in the press, the gossip network . . . He wondered if she had somehow gotten the inside story of the Bradley matter, but tended to discount it. She was fishing, he decided. Well, this pond was fresh out of suckers . . .

"Governor, I'd really like that, you're right, we haven't had a good talk in a while, but I've got some official duty that just makes it impossible. Can I have a raincheck?"

"Of course, anytime, Scott. We may have our differences, but we're both after the same thing in this government . . . to make it more responsive to the people. I'm sure you agree?"

"Oh, I agree, Mrs. Sturdivant."

"Good, then maybe you'll be able to find the time to give me some sort of report—from one of your staff, of course, that would be fine—about the Bradley case? It really seemed to disappear awfully fast. I just wondered, there seemed to be some strong grounds for indicting the man for the murder of Paul Medford . . . a valued and important public servant in this state . . . and then nothing . . . You did testify, I understand, and—"

"Loren"—time to take off the gloves—"you know I can't reveal anything that happened in the grand jury room. I think we all just have to rest on the decision of that jury . . . Look, I don't mean to be rude, but I have to get back to the salt mines. And like I said, I hope you'll give me a raincheck . . ."

The line was dead, but so, Loren decided, was Mr. Scott Morgan. Sooner or later . . . he and his boss. Sooner or later . . .

The press room at the governor's office in the World Trade Center was packed.

"Ladies and gentlemen, before I take your questions, a word to brief you on what this is about. Two months ago I asked the legislature to enact a law that would require state agencies to disclose the names of elected officials who are attorneys *and* who represent private clients appearing before them. That bill never got out of committee. My purpose was to reveal sweetheart relationships that, if not corrupt, certainly appear to be. The fact is that firms that are represented by legislators and have a large financial interest in the decisions of government agencies have, to put it mildly, an unfair advantage. I know that this is nothing new. But because corruption has thrived doesn't mean that we can't stop it from being a governmental life style. And it must stop, because every person in this state is affected by influence peddling—more times than not the taxpayer gets the wrong end of the stick.

"Now, since the legislature did not see fit to remedy this problem, the executive will have to. I have this day issued an executive order that mandates the following: One, that all state agencies keep a record of all licensees, contract award recipients or any others seeking a grant of public money. That record will include the names, addresses or law firms of all attorneys, agents and their representatives. Two, that these records be made available for public inspection at all times. The state operations director has been ordered to put this procedure into place, effective immediately. Now your questions."

"Governor," the New York *Times* man said, "could you give us a specific example of what you are referring to?"

"Okay. People who run for office need a lot of money. Right? Big money interest groups are the principal source of campaign dollars. Nothing wrong per se, but it smells when fat-cat lobbyists representing these special interests hire lawyers who happen to be legislators to appear before state agencies that the legislature regulates. It's obvious they're not being hired because they're competition for the late Felix Frankfurter."

Klyk knew that sooner or later they would zero in on the specific example on their minds. It came from Paula Lawson.

"Governor," she said, "in line with your statement, isn't it true that the late Senator Paul Medford applied for a permit to dispose of toxic waste before the state Agency for Environmental Control, and that it was granted, giving him the exclusive right to dispose of toxic wastes all over Long Island, and that many claims were being made about the poisoning of the water, and illness and in some cases death? Isn't something like this the specific by-product of the corrupt influence you were referring to?"

Klyk was well aware that this was a damned if you do, damned if you don't box that he had gotten himself into. But his credibility demanded he come to grips with it.

First, the obligatory regrets over Senator Medford's death, sympathy to his family . . . but unfortunately the granting of that license to the senator is very much what I'm talking about. He had no special experience or expertise in an operation that, if not handled properly, could cause a serious public-health hazard. We all know the tragic series of illnesses and deaths caused by the water pollution. I know that there are some who say the medical proof is not sufficient, but every known expert we've been able to consult convinces me that proof of the connection is really beyond speculation. So in answer to your question, yes, that's an example of what I'm referring to. There's no question that at the time the name of Paul Medford, majority leader of the senate, was all the incentive the issuing official needed. Nothing was said, nothing needed to be said. His name and position were the qualifications. I certainly didn't offer to single out the late senator, but you asked and I'm answering."

"Governor," Paula said on follow-up, "if the legislature doesn't forbid its lawyer members from representing clients before state agencies, how can you stop that practice?"

"My office will periodically publish these records. You people are going to get the lists at regular intervals. It's my opinion that once publicized, those appearances will trickle down to next to nothing. The threat of public exposure makes saints of us all."

He recognized Ray Bowles, Albany correspondent for the *Daily News*, who stood glint-eyed, staring at Klyk and raising his hand for recognition. Bowles hated Klyk and vice versa, and their feelings had been instinctive, almost inborn, ever since the campaign a year before. No words had to pass between the two, they despised each other automatically. Klyk did not want to give Bowles the satisfaction of being snubbed. He pointed at his nemesis, knowing that the questions would now become hostile.

"Governor," Bowles said, "isn't it a fact that in your sixteen years as mayor of Buffalo the very corruption that you describe flourished?"

Well, it was inevitable that his past would come up. If not by Bowles then by someone else. He was prepared for the question.

"When I was mayor I was investigated to the eyeballs. Audited by the I.R.S., probed by the U.S. attorney, the state attorney general's office, the Joint Task Force. They didn't have to subpoena my bank records, or my financial transactions, or my investments. I wrapped all the documents in an envelope and delivered copies to all investigative agencies and sent copies to the local press. Those records were poured over for months, checked, rechecked and they found nothing. *Because* there was nothing to find. I came out clean as even you would, Mr. Bowles."

Klyk had made his point but the question hadn't been answered and Klyk knew it. He saved Bowles the effort of a follow-up.

"I know my answer was not altogether responsive. That was prologue. I'll respond now. But I want to ask you, Mr. Bowles. Are you satisfied with my personal integrity?"

"We ask the questions, Governor."

"Yes, so you do—but you can't tell me how to answer them. You see, it's good to be governor."

Some laughs, not many. Okay, get to it. "As for my permissiveness with people, I won't deny it. Although I didn't know about their shenanigans, I should have."

"So," Bowles persisted, "you're telling us that as mayor you acted irresponsibly."

Before Klyk could answer he felt the burning sensation in his lungs that he had been experiencing the last month. He reached for the water glass on the lectern, but the water could not stop the coughing spasm that continued for several seconds. His press aide moved toward him but Klyk waved it off. Finally the coughing subsided, but it seemed to take the strength out of Klyk's voice.

"Yes," he said . . . "with more diligence I could have avoided what eventually occurred."

Everyone in the room knew what Bowles and the governor were talking about. In the last year of his last term as mayor, the Erie County Grand Jury indicted five of Klyk's commissioners on bribery and extortion charges. Mob money was mentioned, and political cartoonists throughout the state depicted Buffalo as a City for Sale. Beale, then the governor, with the alleged purpose of removing Klyk from office but the real object of getting rid of him as a possible and formidable rival, directed his commissioner of investigation to put Klyk under a microscope. "It's not enough that his commissioners were caught with their hands in the cookie jar," Beale had told his commissioner. "I want evidence that Klyk was involved or at least knew about it and let it happen. That should be easy."

But it wasn't easy, because it wasn't true. Try as he might, that commissioner of investigation could find no such evidence, and to his credit refused to manufacture it. What he did discover was that when it all happened Klyk, bored after almost sixteen years as mayor, had stopped being involved with running the city. He was more involved in the wheeling and dealing of state and national politics within the Democratic party. Without question he was being groomed by his close friend, State Chairman "Boss" Charlie Sweeney, as the next party candidate for governor. But the emergence of Judge Alan Sturdivant, Loren's husband, temporarily sidetracked him until the judge fell from grace. Then, like Phoenix, Klyk rose again. Except while all this was going on, his city became the private corruption preserve of his commissioners.

Other reporters were signaling to be recognized, but Bowles took and got one more shot. "Governor—such frankness by a public official is refreshing. You now have publicly stated that as mayor of Buffalo you were at best irresponsible about corruption in the ranks. Now you've become the white knight of government. Like Joan of Arc, have you heard the voices of truth and righteousness and talked with God?"

Bowles made even the most hardened political reporter present cringe. But Klyk didn't blink.

"No, Mr. Bowles, I sure have not talked to God and I'm not in Joan's league. I'm more in the sinner category. But even sinners can make comebacks. I hope to direct my administration in the path of responsibility if not righteousness."

Klyk won the round. He evaded nothing. He used no double speak . . . no bobbing and weaving.

Then the *Times* man was recognized again.

"Governor, if you discovered that the source of campaign dollars to officeholders comes from special interests, will you also disclose what you find—specifically names of donors and names of recipients?"

"The election law already provides for that, but I understand your question. If you're asking whether I will reveal any circuitous procedures to make these contributions, the answer is yes—you will hear about it."

By such answers Klyk knew that he had offended the legislature even more. The battle lines were drawn. But he was not through . . . "Even if the methods aren't evasive, even if the contributions are of public record, the practice should stop. I am asking the legislature to outlaw *all* contributions by special interest groups to *any* legislator."

"Will you name right now one of the special interests?"

"Yes—the insurance industry for one. It has a vested interest in legislative action. In the last few years medical malpractice insurance is out of reach because premiums have gone through the roof. The result is that more and more physicians have found it economically unsound to continue to practice. And small municipalities and towns and villages face insolvency every day because they can't pay the premiums for liability insurance. The insurance industry demands billions in increased premiums and hundreds of millions in increased profits and the devil take the consumer. Session after session they've gotten most of what they wanted."

"Governor, can you give us another specific industry?"

"Yes, transportation. People in this state whose business gives them a financial interest in highway construction and mass transit contribute heavily to individual legislators— actually more to Democratic and Republican umbrella outfits set up to channel money to them. And there are real estate boards, banks—you name them—they all contribute heavily to these umbrella groups. It's as bad as litigants appearing before a judge who have contributed to the judge's election-campaign committee."

The New York *Post* man threw the inevitable curve. "Governor, have you ever been the beneficiary of such largesse, and if so will you publicize the names of past and future contributors?"

Klyk coughed again—and needed some time to catch his breath. "I have accepted contributions from special interests," he said quietly. "I will never do so in the future. But I defy anyone to produce evidence showing that any contribution by anyone has had any influence on my decisions as governor."

"But you say the *practice* is wrong. So you were wrong to accept them."

"Yes—that's what I am saying . . . And I think, ladies and gentlemen, that I've said all I have to say. Thank you."

As he started to walk away from the lectern the cough was rising in his lungs. He did not want to allow another spasm to get hold of him in earshot of the press. But Bowles wanted his last shot.

"Mickey Goldman has always been your political supporter, and the Civil Service Coalition he heads is on record for having substantially contributed to your campaign for governor. You have been in the forefront in urging the legislature to pass the Uniform Pension Bill, which Mickey Goldman badly wants. Isn't it possible that his political and financial support in the past had some influence on your decision to support a bill that has met with resistance on its merits in the legislature?"

He had hoped that the pension bill would not come up. Yes, he had more or less assured his old friend Mickey Goldman of his full and complete support. He anticipated no problems in a bill that gave parity to all the civil service employees. As it stood, state employees received one-half pay after twenty years but municipal employees didn't. That was unfair, and the proposed legislation would cure it by making half pay after twenty years uniform for all civil servants.

There was no opposition at the beginning of the session and it appeared as if it would sail through. But that was before he started making waves by unleashing Scott Morgan and before the assassination of Paul Medford. The majority leader had been popular, and many in both houses blamed Klyk for Medford's death. He didn't need Bowles' question, but he had to respond . . .

"I know of no one who really doubts the merits or the fairness of the pension bill," he said. And with that, trying to stifle another coughing attack, he quickly walked out of the room, followed by Scott Morgan.


He was parked waiting for her on the Vesey Street side of the huge World Trade Center complex. He sounded the horn as she left the building. Paula saw him and ran to the car.

They drove north on Church Street. It was late afternoon, a rare crisp sparkling fall day that they couldn't fully appreciate because what passed for fall foliage was only to be found across the river in New Jersey or in Central or Prospect Parks.

"It's beautiful at the Finger Lakes now," she said. "You just don't see the reds and the golds and the browns of those trees here. I miss it."

"The price of success," Scott said.

"Scott, this is off the record."

"Okay."

"Is the governor all right?"

"What do you mean?"

She shook her head. "I don't really know what I mean. I just have a feeling he's taking on the world as if he didn't give a damn about the consequences. Sort of fatalistic. I don't think he's well . . ."

Scott nodded. "Still off the record?"

"Yes."

"The truth is I'm worried as hell about him. I've noticed a loss of weight, his eyes seem dull—and that cough is getting worse. He doesn't smoke anymore, but his spells of shortness of breath seem to come more often anyway."

"You really care about this man, you old softie . . . A machine politician from Buffalo has really gotten to you."

"Well, this old machine pol has the courage and guts to change. He's a leader—the kind we need. He has the stomach to take on the crooks and assholes. But like you I get the feeling that his health is lousy and getting worse. I talk to him about medical attention and he brushes me off. Something's wrong, though . . ."

# Chapter Seventeen

IT began about a month before. He found himself tired even after limited exertion. At the beginning he didn't think of it much, but then there were other symptoms. At night, even at normal room temperature, his sheets were soaked with sweat, and when he went to the bathroom he felt so dizzy he could hardly stand.

Then the cough developed. Before, he had been one of those fortunates who scarcely ever experienced a sick day, and the smoker's cough he had developed ten years before had caused him to give up cigarettes. The cough disappeared and he had been fine, until now. This cough resulted from a painful burning in his lungs. Each day it became progressively worse, the spasms came more often, and often he had found himself short of breath. He also noticed a slight swelling in the glands of his neck.

Jon Klyk was of the persuasion that if you stay away from doctors they can't make you sick, and that whatever ails you will go away if you leave it alone. But this, whatever it was, did not go away. The cough persisted, and so did the night sweats and a kind of dysentery that weakened him. First came the loss of weight, ten pounds in less than thirty days, and it showed on his face. Reluctantly he decided to submit to a physical examination.

"Get me Dr. Harlow in New York," he told his secretary.

Jon Klyk and Frank Harlow were closer than brothers—reared in the same poor section of Buffalo, going through the Buffalo public school system together, sharing their adolescence, their mutual failures and triumphs. Each was the other's best man, and although Klyk's marriage failed, Frank Harlow's didn't, and his wife Pat and their six children considered Klyk a family member.

Harlow followed his dream and after years of sacrifice reached the same pinnacle in medicine that Klyk had managed in politics. His world reputation as a cardiologist put him in constant demand. He moved to New York, where the giants of industry and show business celebrities, as well as many indigent poor, crowded the reception room of his office.

He was checking out the C.E.O. of a Fortune 500 firm when the call came. "Excuse me," he said to the patient, who did not appreciate having his examination interrupted, "this is an emergency."

He walked briskly to his study. "Jon," he said after his secretary connected them, "it's been months. When are you coming down?"

"Well," Klyk said, "I've got this special session and I'm buried in work . . ."

Harlow was instantly alarmed at the sound of Klyk's voice—flat and empty.

"Something wrong, Jon?"

"I don't know, I'm not sure. I hate to ask this—it's not as if we don't have damn good doctors in Albany, Frank . . . but I guess I'd feel more comfortable with you."

"Done," Harlow said. "I'll cancel my morning appointments tomorrow. I don't really have to be back here until late tomorrow afternoon. I can fly up and get back in plenty of time.

"That won't be necessary, I'll have a car pick you up at nine, if that's all right. They'll take you to La Guardia and a helicopter will fly you up. I don't think you'll be here for more than two hours at the most and then we'll fly you back . . ."

Harlow's quiet fears about his friend deepened as soon as he saw him. His loss of weight was apparent, but what especially bothered him was that the smiling robust face of Jon Klyk was gone. And when Klyk told him about his night sweats and burning lungs and hacking cough, and his loss of strength, the pattern formed a terrible suspicion in his mind. He examined the swollen glands and tried to smile but found it difficult.

"Okay, Frank, let's have it."

"Jon . . . I have to ask you some questions. They're going to sound crazy and impertinent, but I have to ask them anyway."

"You're the doctor—shoot."

Harlow turned away. He was a professional in every way, but with his friend—his brother—this was painfully difficult.

"Jon, have you ever had a homosexual experience?"

Klyk's first impulse was to laugh. "No, Frank. *Never.*"

"Have you had a blood transfusion in the past five years?"

"Never had one in my life."

"Have you been injected or inoculated in the past five years?"

"No."

"Have you been with many women during the last five years?"

"Bingo," Klyk said, smiling weakly. "Well, not since I've been governor. I've been celibate since my inauguration a year ago. But before that? Yes, old friend, I guess I would say I was promiscuous. I was still mayor of Buffalo, remember. There isn't much more to do in Buffalo."

Klyk smiled, Harlow didn't.

"How many would you say you were with in that last year as mayor?"

"I never fed that particular information into my computer. Maybe twenty . . ."

"Did you use condoms?"

"No, Frank. I believe in taking my whiskey and sex straight."

Harlow poured himself a glass of water from a carafe on the desk.

"Okay, Frank, drop the shoe. I'm a big boy. You think I've got the big C, right?"

"No, I don't think so."

"Then it can't be that bad. Why the puss?"

"I want you to go through some tests today."

"At the hospital?"

"Yes, the tests can't be given here."

Klyk shook his head. "I can't afford the time, Frank—"

"Those tests are going to be given today."

Klyk watched as Harlow called Albany General Hospital, arranging for the tests, then called his office canceling appointments for the next twenty-four hours.


Late that afternoon the results were communicated to Harlow. Klyk, exhausted, slept through until midnight. When he woke up, the nurse sounded altogether too cheerful.

"We're instructed to call Dr. Harlow when you wake up," she told him.

"Can't it wait till morning?"

"He's not asleep, Governor, he's downstairs."

If there was any doubt about the seriousness of his condition, it was gone now. But what the hell was it?

When Harlow entered the room there was no attempt at false cheer. Klyk saw his face and waited.

"Jon, we've got trouble."

"Let's have it."

"Preliminary tests indicate evidence of Acquired Immune Deficiency Syndrome."

"*AIDS?*"

"Yes."

"You're wrong, dead wrong. You made a mistake, you goddamn doctors think you're always right, it's impossible, you're equating *me* with faggots and junkies? That's *their* disease, not mine. How dare you, you who've known me since I was born, for Christ's sake . . ."

The exertion was telling on Klyk. His face reddened and he suffered another coughing spasm, every cough leaving its painful imprint on his lungs. Harlow waited for the coughing to end. He well understood Klyk's initial rage and rejection of the truth. Klyk finally was able to breathe normally, drank water and tried to smile at his friend.

"Sorry, buddy, but I don't understand . . ."

"Who does, Jon?"

"Well, you know plenty more than I do. I'm going to ask you some straight questions, and I'll need straight answers."

Harlow waited.

"I don't really know what this disease is. I want to know what's going on inside my body . . . If I'm going to die, I'd like to know when."

Harlow tried to respond with more calm than he felt. "The human body contains a natural immunity against disease. We catch colds, suffer infections, virus attacks, but we survive because that natural immunity wards off these intruders. But when the immunity system collapses, the line of defense is gone and we're open to that same invasion and powerless to repel it."

"Do you know what causes it?"

"Well, we know it's a virus. We give it different names. Human T-Cell Lymphocyte, known as HTL-3. Also Lymphadenopathy Associated Virus, or LAX. We refer to it simply as AIDS-related Virus—or ARV. Frankly, even with all the research that's been done until now we still aren't sure that the virus alone causes it. Researchers believe that other related factors may be necessary to trigger it."

"You know a lot about it Frank, but it's not your field—"

"But it *is* my field, Jon. It's everyone's field. Heart disease can also result from immunity breakdown. Every organ of the body can be affected."

"It's just that I never heard that heterosexual men can get it."

"Jon, we've come to the realization that when you sleep with a woman you sleep with all the men she ever had."

Klyk nodded.

"Any of those women you had sex with could have been with a bisexual male. That could have done it."

"But wouldn't she suffer from it?"

"Not necessarily. She might only have been a carrier—and transmitted it to you. Although some immunologists doubt that it can be transmitted that way."

"That's what bothers me, there's so much you guys don't know. Frank, I'm not trying to duck the reality, I just want to understand . . ."

"Yes—please don't hold back."

"For instance . . . the last woman I had sex with, well, that was almost two years ago. Why would it take this long to show up?"

"There have been cases where incubation lasted for five years before any physical manifestations."

Klyk struggled with that, then . . . "Frank . . . we've been close a long time. The truth of it is that I'm scared to death. I want to cry. I want to hit something, somebody. At least I want to fight this. I'm not giving in to anything. But I've got to know the odds. Let's get down to it."

Harlow tried to control the pitch of his voice. "Right now around eighty-five percent . . . within two years of diagnosis . . ."

"How's it going to show itself?"

"I'm afraid it already has. We suspect you've developed a

parasitic infection of the lungs called pneumosystis carini pneumonia, PCP. It's a special kind of pneumonia that shows up in AIDS cases."

"Have I shown it yet?"

"No."

"Then how do you know I'm infected?"

"Because we've developed a test to detect antibodies—substances that the blood produces to fight disease organisms. When we isolate antibodies and match them to the AIDS virus we can make a fairly certain diagnosis."

"Can there be a mistake?"

"Yes—we could be mistaken. But I don't think so . . . Your results are clear, the antibodies were positive."

The panic was over, he was now ready to stop feeling sorry for himself and fight his own personal war to survive. "Let's talk battle tactics, Frank. Death isn't going to get me easy. I know the odds. Where do we go from here?"

Harlow was pleased. "There's an immunologist in the city that you're going to see. I'll ask him to come here. He has more knowledge in the field than anyone I know."

"Set it up."

"But first," Harlow said, "I think I better tell you what you face now."

"Yes . . ."

"Jon, it's going to be a bad time. You may suffer pain—sometimes, excruciating pain—mental and physical. You'll have to fight the inevitable periods of depression. You'll be tempted to lose hope. And you'll have to make some hard decisions."

"Such as."

"Such as whether to disclose your illness to the public. Such as whether you'll be able to devote your energies to anything more than fighting this thing. It's a question of priority, and frankly I don't give a damn about your governor's duties . . ."

"Well, old friend—don't count me out yet. I've got no quit

in me. I never had, you know that. If I lose it will only be
after I gave it my best shot. Hey, I'm a great believer in
miracles. It took a miracle to put me here. Don't bury me
yet."

Harlow almost lost control, and apologized. "Sorry, Jon,
the doctor is not exactly professional . . ."

"I'll deduct it from your fee."

Harlow nodded. "Look, Jon, I don't want to give the impression there's no hope. The virus has been isolated. Exper-
imental drugs have shown positive results. There are cases
in remission—"

"Frank—like I said, don't worry about me giving up."

"That's very important."

"And as for your show of emotion," Klyk said, "I thank
you for that. I consider it the ultimate display of friendship."

"Jon," Harlow said, "regular observation and treatment
must begin at once. I hate to throw all of this at the same
time, but only you can decide if you can stay on in your
job—"

Klyk said calmly, "I am not going to resign. There are
things I want to accomplish. And look at the bright side
. . . I don't have to worry about winning reelection. Okay,
okay, false bravado. But bet on this . . . I'll make it till the
end of my term."

Harlow forced a smile.

"Jon," he said as he stopped at the door.

"Yes, Frank."

"Call me. Call Pat. Any hour of the day or night. Talk to
us. Because this is not the kind of thing that you can face
alone."


His upbeat show went out the door with Dr. Frank Harlow.
Alone in the empty hospital room he only began to realize
how tough it was going to be. He knew it would be impossible to erase from his mind that he was living on borrowed

time. Too soon. He had planned, hoped to have someone in his life . . . Frank Harlow had hit it on the head—he was facing it alone.

Well, he'd chosen that route, and now realized acutely what he'd let slip away . . . His thoughts went back—how many years?—to high school. He as the class president, Mary Stevens as the prettiest girl. Smart, too. It was a long-standing love affair, and within two years after graduation she became Mary Stevens Klyk. Happy years, if not affluent ones . . . even Mary's inability to conceive didn't bother him all that much, although it devastated her.

Theirs was a story with a happy beginning and unhappy ending. Success for him in the political world came almost immediately. He seemed born for politics, with a natural ability to attract people to him. When he was nominated for mayor the first time, their marriage was over. Among other accomplishments, he had mastered the lively arts of wine, women and song. Yes, he loved Mary, always would, but he loved the others too, and finally when he came home after a two-day unexplained absence he didn't find her . . . only a note that she had left him, and he knew why. Did he contract this thing then? No, later, as mayor . . .

They kept in touch even after the divorce, until Mary sent him a letter from Hawaii advising him she had remarried and had found happiness again and hoped he would be as lucky. It was then that the full realization of what he had lost, of what he had let get away, hit him. He badly wanted to call her, but at least to his credit he did not—because he knew any contact would cause her pain, and he'd caused her enough of that . . .

But now, this was a loneliness worse than any since the day she had written him. He was here in this hospital room—with, like Frank had said, "not the kind of thing that you can face alone."

How long had it been since he'd prayed? Was he a hypocrite to do it now? Never mind, what, after all, did he have to lose? . . . "Oh, God, this was my doing, nobody else's. And I'm not going to ask for a miracle, because if the truth is told I don't deserve one. But at least I think I finally know what I'm here for. I only pray for time—to finish what I've started here. At least move it along. I need strength, physical and lots more to make it. I'm also scared to death, and I need someone to tell me that it's not too late . . ."

Henry Seldon, the speaker of the assembly of the state of New York, threw up his hands when his secretary told him who was waiting in the reception room. Deluged as he was with work connected with the special session of the legislature scheduled to begin the next day, Assemblyman Egbert Tawpty of Sequoia County was easily the last person he wanted to see. Through the rigid rules of seniority in the assembly, Egbert was chairman of the Labor Affairs Committee. Speaker Seldon once observed that Egbert provided a conundrum and a presence adding up to more than anyone should be asked to bear. To wit: For what unfathomable reason did the people of Sequoia County continue to reelect him? And his powerful voice was connected to a nonfunctioning brain. With an irony missed by Egbert, his colleagues referred to him as "The Brain."

"Couldn't you tell him I'm out?" Seldon said to his secretary on the intercom. "Or dead?"

"Wouldn't do any good, sir. He's settled in for the duration, with magazines and newspapers."

"All right, send him in."

Seldon had found that his most difficult duty as speaker was having to deal with the committee chairmen of his party. The power to push a bill for passage depended on them. So he had an open door and an open ear. But there were *exceptions*. He found some difficulty in dealing with the likes of Egbert Tawpty, who had the I.Q. of a gnat. Still, he had to see Egbert. He was committed to get passage of the governor's Civil Service Pension Act, and for that Egbert's cooperation as chairman of Labor Affairs was essential . . .

Seldon took a deep breath, forced a smile and moved toward Egbert with hand outstretched. "Egbert, *always* good to see you . . ." Actually it was never good to see the assemblyman, whose corpulence was grotesque. When he moved, all of him moved, including his fleshy jowels hanging like pork chops on each side of his face. His eyes were hardly visible through the thick flesh of his forehead. His belly protruded through his coat, through his vest, through his shirt, which rarely had all its buttons attached, due to the strain of his girth.

"Hello Chief," he said, extending his hand and shaking Seldon's in a pumping motion.

"Egbert, what can I do for you?"

"Chief, we got trouble."

It was too much to expect this horse's ass to follow through from his startling opener.

"What's the trouble?"

Egbert sat back in his chair, folded his arm over the mound of his belly and sighed.

"It's the pension bill. I don't have the votes to get it out."

Seldon had hoped this wouldn't happen but was afraid it would. He had just about assured Mickey Goldman, an old and valued friend, that the pension bill would pass. But that was early in the session—before the assassination of Paul Medford and the hostility over it directed at Klyk and his program. Seldon had expected some punishment of the governor, but figured it would be limited to delay on the pension bill during the regular session. He did not expect the resistance to continue on into the special session. Neither did Egbert. His committee members reflected the sentiments of their colleagues—there were other ways to skin a cat. They could get their revenge without being held responsible. They met in executive session, where all proceedings were sealed, closed to public scrutiny, including the way each member voted. The biggest break of the gentlemen's agreement in the legislature was to mention to anyone how any member voted in executive session. Their lips were sealed, and the bill was dead.

Of course Seldon could have it called again, and maybe change the results by individual arm-twisting. But above all he was a realist. There was no way he could twist Republican arms on the *senate* side, and if the Democrats in the assembly expressed their anti-Klyk sentiment, it was obvious to him that the Republican senators, who had been colleagues of the popular Medford and respected him as their leader, would be sure to vote down the pension bill that the governor wanted so badly.

Had Medford been alive, Seldon figured he could have worked things out. It wouldn't have been the first time he and Medford had helped each other . . . Seldon sighed heavily. It was a blow to his self-esteem that it would appear he had let a friend like Goldman down. Not that Goldman could do anything about it, at least to him. It was said in the Brooklyn district that he represented that since the sixties Henry Seldon could have been elected if he campaigned from the Fountainbleu Hotel in Miami Beach. Obviously his potential opponents thought so because one could not remember the last time he had faced a party primary, and when he ran he received the endorsement of all the major parties.

Still, in retrospect Seldon realized he had slipped up. He should have anticipated the degree of opposition, the anger and the hunger for vengeance. Even with his ten years experience as leader he had misjudged the mood of the legislature.

But more serious than his own embarrassment was the mischief that Goldman could now cause, even if not to him personally. Goldman had, of course, gotten advance notice that the bill was in trouble, and he threatened "serious consequences" if the pension act died.

"I'm sorry about this, Egbert," Seldon said, "but I want you to know I appreciate your efforts." (He knew he would need him again another day.)

"Not at all, Chief. We both know that nothing in Albany can be guaranteed by Lords of London!"

Assemblyman Malaprop had struck again. Seldon left his desk, patted Egbert on the back, helped this bulk out of his chair and, firmly holding his arm, steered him toward the door.

"Well, Chief," Egbert said before leaving, "we'll just have to go on to the next one irregardless."

Seldon continued to smile. "Irregardless, Egbert," he said as he finally got him through the door. "You got that right."

"Mickey? Loren Sturdivant here."

"Yes, hello, Madam—"

"Come on, Mickey, we can skip the formalities. It was Loren during the campaign, and it still is."

"Okay, fine . . . Loren. What can I do for you?"

"No, it's what can I do for you, Mickey? I'm not exactly overworked here, but I can still read and think and I haven't changed my loyalties and support since the election. The pension bill, they tell me, has gone down the tubes. I'm not celebrating that, Mickey, although some people think my yardstick of values is what's good or bad for the governor. The fact that resentment against him over Paul Medford may be . . . is at the bottom of this doesn't matter now. I can stand to be on the side of the governor . . . We ran on the same ticket, after all. It's just that he suddenly can't seem to remember who I am or how he got where he is. So, Mickey . . ."

"Loren, I've got a union meeting to get ready for. You're right, you've been with us from the first and we appreciate it. But right now Jon Klyk is governor, you're not, and—"

"And that's what really counts, Mickey. Who sits at the

top in Albany. Well, I just wanted you to know I take no pleasure in the pension bill's defeat, and that if I ever get the chance, I assure you it will never happen again . . ."

"I hear you, Loren." And indeed he did. It seemed clear that the lieutenant governor had officially launched her own campaign for governor.

# Chapter Eighteen

THE meeting room of the union headquarters on Fourteenth Street in New York City was filled wall to wall. Ostensibly, Mickey Goldman called his troops together to vote on a course of action, but he knew the mood of his people, and resistance to the strike authority would be minimal to none. When Goldman entered the room his face reflected his frustration and anger.

He marched directly to the podium. "I've called this emergency meeting because we've been double-crossed and we can't let them get away with it. You folks know me, I've been the leader of this union for almost thirty years. I like to think I've learned *something* along the way. For example, I know that if a union lets itself be screwed, takes no action, it becomes a patsy inviting *them* to do it to us again and again. I think you know who and what I'm referring to. But just in case, I've the unpleasant duty to announce that the uniform pension bill we were suckered into believing would have no trouble being passed is a dead duck.

"Those people up in Albany told me in no uncertain terms that this bill was going to sail through. Either they lied from the beginning or they had a sudden change of heart, who knows why . . . But we have long memories, and sooner or later they'll come to us and we will remember. But we must also remember our friends. I can tell you now that the governor and lieutenant governor have been for us. All the rest can go straight to hell.

"A legislature and its leaders have demonstrated the art of irresponsibility. Because of their petty politics they made us the victims. Did they really think that we would sit still for this?"

"*No . . .*"

"We're at bat now, and we're preparing a message for them. But before we take action we need your authorization. The bylaws call for it, but even if they didn't, it's my policy never to take retaliatory action without the rank and file giving me the green light. Normally, we'd take a little more time making this decision, but the circumstances here are different. We must hit back immediately so there can be no doubt about how we react to a double-cross. So I am now asking for your authorization to take such action by any of the divisions of our union at any time, at any place, without further notice. I'm asking for wider authority than I've ever asked for, but time is of the essence. Do we have it?"

The assemblage rose to its feet and roared its approval.

"Any opposed?" Goldman asked with mock severity.

The answer was scattered laughter.

"Then the ayes have it. Thank you, brothers and sisters, for this show of confidence. After the executive board meeting we will notify each of the shop stewards of the division that will be involved in the job action. They will notify the members of their group. I ask you to be available for phone calls tonight. God bless you all, and God bless this union."

The executive board met at 2:00 P.M. Mickey Goldman already had his plan in mind, but had communicated it to no one. His style was not to waste any time—especially now, when only hours remained.

"Folks," he said, "I guess we all agree that we have to be

totally effective this time. We've got to hit them where it hurts the most."

He stood in front of the long table around which the board members sat. He always preferred to stand. The eyes of the seven men and two women were focused on him.

"The way I figure it, we would have limited impact by calling out the traffic enforcement people. Likewise, it wouldn't mean too much if the court personnel went out or the municipal clerks or the school guards. But we can be heard and felt by striking the bridges—something that has never been done before."

Tony Ovino, the recording secretary, whistled. "Mickey, do you mean we walk off the bridges?"

"Yes, Tony, that's what I said. We have to do something dramatic. Our people have a right to expect that they'll be secure when they're old or sick. Look—I don't want to set the public against us. But we have a duty to our people out there—they're our first responsibility."

Ovino shook his head. "Mickey, do you realize what this will do to the city? We're going to close it down. No one is going to sympathize with us. They'll unite against us—the press, the government, the courts and most important the guy in the street."

"I can't dispute that, Tony."

"But Mickey, where are we going with this? There's no way that the legislature will change its mind if we alienate the voting public."

"Granted."

"Then wouldn't you say this is a no-win situation?"

"No one wins a strike, Tony. Hell, we all know that. It's just a question of who loses more. But there's more to this than winning or losing. Sometimes all you can hope for is respect, because if they don't respect us we're worthless to our members and to ourselves. Our objectives—our reason for being—has nothing to do with making the public love us. It's not pleasant to be unpopular with the good citizens of this city, but it's not our role to be liked by them. There will be other legislatures, and there will be other priorities, and there will be other pressures that we will use to change a future political climate. But for now we can't stand by and let this happen without standing up and saying no with teeth in it."

Ovino nodded. "I just want us all to realize that we may be going in over our heads . . . What about the Taylor Law?"

He was referring to the controversial law that imposed sanctions against public-service unions and individual employees in an "unauthorized" strike. Some unions had been hurt financially by heavy fines the courts imposed without sparing the horses, and in some instances public service union leaders had spent some time in jail when they violated court-ordered injunctions.

"The Taylor Law won't apply here," Goldman told him. "We're going to walk off the bridges, make our point through the morning and evening rush hours, then return back before the corporation counsel of the City of New York can obtain a court injunction and serve it on us."

After a unanimous vote, Goldman grabbed Ovino's shoulder. "Tony, what you said makes sense. Don't think that I don't understand where you're coming from. But there are times when we've got to do things that we don't like, that are risky. This is one of them . . . where the powers that be leave us no other course."

Goldman now addressed his members. "Okay, here it is. Tomorrow morning at seven we walk off the bridges. Ben Nolan will tell us how it's going to be done."

Nolan was head of the Bridge Tenders Division of Mickey Goldman's Civil Service Coalition of Municipal Workers. Although he had no formal education as a civil engineer, his thirty-year experience on the bridge gave him an expertise on the bridges' operations that few civil engineers could equal. When Goldman promoted him to vice president in charge of the bridge tenders, he made the move with mixed emotions—he truly loved his work. Once having decided to strike the bridges, Mickey put Nolan in full control of the operation. Nolan was a large man with a rugged face that reflected his years of exposure to the elements. Nevertheless, he spoke softly now but with authority.

"Like Mickey said, tomorrow at seven we are going to walk off most of the bridges. The ones we choose we hope will have the greatest impact on moving traffic. Macombs Dam, Willis Avenue, 145th Street connecting Bronx and Manhattan. Also the Mill Basin, Gowanus Canal, Flushing Avenue and Greenpoint Avenue in Brooklyn. There are two kinds of bridges—one kind doesn't lift. It rotates on an axis that lets ships pass through while the span itself stops when it reaches a ninety-degree angle to their bridge structure. Then it's perpendicular to the traffic flow and parallel to the river. We're going to walk off the Macombs Bridge, which operates that way. Also, there are the split-span vertical lifts. Each half of the bridge is raised high enough to allow the ships to pass through. And there are some bridges that are single-span vertical lifts, where the whole structure is raised to an upward position. We're going to walk off both of these too.

"I think it's important for us to know all the facts about what we can and can't do. It's a serious violation of the federal law to obstruct navigation. Do that and we all could face a long time in the federal pen. It's one thing to have the public sore at us, it's another thing to go to jail. That's why, under no circumstances, can we ever walk off a bridge leaving it in a closed position. Ships must never be obstructed from passing through. So we're taking all the necessary steps. There's only one nonlifting bridge that we're going to walk off—the Macomb's Dam Bridge on 155th Street between the Bronx and Manhattan. But when the bridge comes to rest in the middle of the river we'll have a little problem. The man in the control shack won't be able to get off."

"Pretty late in the year to swim to shore," Ovino said.

"Right. We're going to use Goldman's navy to get them off."

The tension in the room was broken by Nolan's reference to the twenty-three-foot boat powered by a sixty-horse-power motor that the union had gotten for the bridge tenders to use during spring and summer days off. While it hadn't been cared for as well as it might, it had been the source of relaxing forays up and down the Hudson as far north as the Tappan Zee Bridge.

"There are ladders going down from the shack to the island under the span. Our boat will pick the men up there and take them to shore," Nolan said.

Natalie Cravens, vice president in charge of the Clerical Workers Division, raised her hand.

"Ben, how are the bridges moved?"

It would be Natalie Cravens to get down to basics, Nolan thought. "It's all controlled from the shacks. On a two-span lift we have control shacks on each side. On a one-span lift there's a shack on one side that lifts the whole span. And on the nonlift perpendicular swing-bridge the shack is in the middle. All movement is controlled electrically. A switch is thrown, a circuit is opened, electrical impulses are generated and the motor moves the span."

"And," Natalie asked, "after the bridge is moved and comes to rest in the parallel or uplift position and we walk off—can the motor and the machinery and all the electrical equipment be left unattended, and if so, for how long?"

"A damn good question. There should be no problem with leaving the bridge after they've been moved, but there could be a problem if they were moved back into position by people who didn't know what they were doing. That's why this strike has got to be short. We're the only ones that can put the bridge back in place. We won't screw it up, but other people can, and if they do we'll be blamed.

"How long should the strike be, Mickey?" someone asked.

"Just long enough to make our point and not one minute longer. We've got to hit them in the rush hour—tie them up for a few hours—make them late for work. Then we'll put the bridges back in place. The idea is to prove by this job action that we can't be pushed around. The public will be inconvenienced, yes, but they should not be harmed. Those few hours are all we need to make a lasting impression." (He hoped.)

All the bridge tenders on the 8:00 A.M. shift reported for work an hour early. They took their positions at Mill Basin, Gowanus Canal, Flushing Avenue, Willis Avenue, 145th Street and the Macombs Dam Bridge at 155th Street. The weather cooperated. The day was cold, and a freezing rain left the streets slick and slippery. The wet cold was bone-chilling. Traffic under such circumstances would be affected, but with the stoppage at the bridges the tie-up was complete. As soon as the bridges moved, the traffic lines started to form, and when the spans were not returned in place the lines extended blocks and then miles. At every vital point of transportation from one borough to another the egress was cut off, and in a relatively short time the city was effectively paralyzed. It was inevitable that the frustrations of the public would erupt in violence directed at union members, and the first incident occurred where the Willis Avenue Bridge connected the Bronx and Manhattan . . .

Eduardo Martinez had just reached his sixty-fifth birthday. He had planned to retire on December 31, assuming that the pension bill would pass, as all the union members were told. He had bought a small house in his hometown of Arecibo in Puerto Rico. His wife Reina and he had looked forward to his pension and social security payments after thirty years of service. When he first left Puerto Rico it didn't take all that much to live decently there. But the inflation that hit the mainland affected the inhabitants of the island in spades, stretching budgets all out of shape. So for him this strike was a fight, for Eduardo saw this as *his* strike, so he was the first one on the Willis Avenue Bridge the morning of the job action, and he made up his mind that in appreciation for what his union was doing for him he would be the last one to walk off . . .


A salesman for a large liquor distributor, John Monsey cursed his luck at being the first car stopped on the Manhattan side of the Willis Avenue Bridge. The flashing lights of the guardrail blocking his movements upset him . . . If he had left his apartment on Manhattan's East Side five minutes earlier he would have been across the bridge and on his way. He had made his appointment for 8:30 A.M. at the Rye Hilton in Westchester County, where a buyer for a large hotel chain was waiting. But he had been cautioned that he had to be prompt and that the meeting would be limited to fifteen minutes because the buyer's day was precisely scheduled.

He glanced at his watch. Seven-fifteen A.M. Still no problem. The bridge opening and closing would take five, seven minutes tops—and then no more than forty minutes up the Deegan to the Thruway to Rye. But delays always made him nervous, and this morning was especially unfortunate. He was also puzzled by the combination of no ship in sight ready to pass through, a line of bridge workers in uniform walking off from the approaches to the span, and the workers, once having left the bridge, milling around a pile of placards. He watched with increased apprehension as the men picked up the placards and put them around their shoulders. One of the men turned toward him and he looked in shock at the words in big block letters:


## BRIDGE TENDERS ON STRIKE

To him that read, "Monsey loses fat commission." The message was clear, that bridge was not coming down. Not now, not in the next five minutes, sure as hell not in time to let him cross and make his appointment. He was stalled there, backed up by a mile of vehicles. Monsey looked at the Harlem River and a bridge that did not connect to either shore. He could no longer contain his building anger. He opened the door of his car and ran toward the bridge. The first person he saw was Eduardo Martinez who, according to plan, was the last to leave. Martinez in his enthusiasm held his arms over his head in defiance, which was John Monsey's last straw. Without warning, Monsey aimed a left-handed roundhouse in the direction of Eduardo's mouth. He landed a bull's-eye. Monsey was tall and powerfully built, Eduardo was no more than five foot five and weighed 140 pounds soaking wet. The force of Monsey's blow lifted Eduardo off his feet, and he landed on his face.

It took four strikers to overpower Monsey and pin him to the ground, and then they proceeded to take their own anger out on him. By now, other motorists, equally frustrated and angry, rushed to Monsey's defense. He was rescued from the other strikers after more fists flashed through the air. Two police officers stranded in a radio motor patrol vehicle ran to the melee and stopped it. Eduardo miraculously escaped serious injury, but let Monsey know what he thought of him for smashing his new upper dental plate . . . recently acquired under the union dental plan. Fortunately his verbal assault was in his native Spanish. And even more fortunately the police kept a tight half nelson on Monsey, whose answer back was in pure, unadulterated Anglo-Saxon . . .

Similar reports of violence at the other bridges were being called into headquarters, with the union men outnumbered by irate citizens taking the heat. But things were worse at Macombs Dam Bridge, which linked the Bronx and Manhat-

tan at 155th Street. As planned, the men descended the ladder
to the island and waited for Goldman's navy to rescue them.
They cheered as they saw the boat bearing down on them
from the west bank of the Harlem River. But they cheered
too soon. The boat's motor conked out about fifty feet from
where the men were waiting. The boat, caught in the brisk
current, moved quickly past them.

"Hey," yelled one of the stranded strikers, "you're supposed to rescue us." The man at the engine, trying to acti-
vate the old engine, pulled the starting cord again and again
without success as the boat, at the mercy of the current,
drifted toward the violent swirls of the East River. Said he:
"I know that, you stupid son of a bitch—can't you see that
we're on our way to Paris, France, in this thing? Who's
going to rescue *us*?"

Fortunately for the two sailors of Goldman's Navy the
current edged the boat to shore before it entered the waters
of the East River, but the men under the Macombs Dam
Bridge were still stranded. When news of the naval fiasco
was relayed to Mickey Goldman, he commissioned another
boat from a marina up river, but it was too late. By that time
the union men had to bear the ignominy of being rescued by
a N.Y.C. Police Department patrol boat.


After the first shock of the strike, an outraged city reacted.
The mayor excoriated the union, its actions and especially
Mickey Goldman. For once all of the media agreed with the
mayor. Goldman was burned in effigy and a city councilman
from Staten Island with a limited mentality suggested that
no citizen should be prosecuted for assaulting any union
member.

According to Nolan's plan, the strikers would return in a
few hours. Alas, the best laid plans were demolished by no
less than the U.S. Army Corps of Engineers under the command of Colonel Andrew Boner.

Actually Colonel Boner was a National Guard reserve officer who had been the personal attorney and close crony of the then Governor Beale. Boner loved his lucrative law practice, but he loved uniforms, staff cars, braid and the power of military command even more. When Beale asked him what honorary title he would like in payment for all his good and sound advice—contributions—he told the governor that he wanted nothing except perhaps a commission in the state National Guard. Beale never expected that request, because although the governor was in fact commander-in-chief of the state National Guard, and although such commissions were in fact given as political plums, it had always been a condition that the recipient have some military background. Out of deference to his friend, the governor did not ask what that experience was, which was a good thing. Boner had reached the exalted level of Private First Class in a headquarters unit in World War II, where his service was limited to two years of fighting the battle of paper on Governor's Island. A special provision allowed the governor to grant a commission if the recipient had a special skill or knowledge beneficial to the military. The judge advocate would have been the natural place for a Boner to hang his hat, but that division was top-heavy with politicians and fat-cat contributors who liked the looks of bars, leaves and eagles on their shoulders and were thrilled to be addressed as Captain, Major, or Colonel. So the table of organization for the judge advocate had been stretched to the limit, and there were just no openings, except for one spot calling for the rank of captain, which of course would be an insult to a man of Boner's importance. But as an afterthought Boner advised his friend the governor that he had fallen just one year short of a bachelor's degree in civil engineering. The late calling of the law deterred Boner from completing his original educational goal, and he switched to the prelaw courses in his last year of undergraduate study. Both the governor and Boner solemnly agreed that three years of college engineering were sufficient to qualify him for a commission in the Corps of Engineers on the basis of "special knowledge and skill." Andrew Boner was commissioned a lieutenant colonel in the Corps. Six months later the commanding officer resigned, and Boner was promoted to full colonel and became the C.O. After all, the governor thought, how much harm could he do?

As events unraveled, plenty. Boner woke up to the radio alert about the strike as did millions of others. He felt the city singularly fortunate to have him in the slot, so to speak. He reached for his phone and barked orders to his adjutant, who was awakened by his call and therefore had not yet heard about the strike.

"Who was that?" asked the adjutant's wife—upset when she saw that the clock showed 7:15 A.M.

"It's our commanding officer—Colonel Bonehead. I think he's really flipped this time."

"What does he want?"

"He wants us to retake the bridges."

"Retake the *what?*"

"Retake the bridges."

"Did we lose them?"

"Turn on the news. It seems the men who operate the bridges—the bridge tenders—walked off all the city bridges this morning. They left the boroughs disconnected. I have to report to the Macombs Dam Bridge at 155th Street on the double."

"Take over, Adjutant," the colonel said when he arrived. The adjutant looked at the colonel as if he had addressed him in Latin.

"I beg your pardon, Colonel?"

"I said take over."

"Take over what?"

Boner was clearly upset. "What do you think we're here for?" We've got to put this bridge back in its proper position—and I mean *now.*"

The adjutant scratched his head. "Colonel," he said, "to tell you the truth I don't have the slightest idea about how to get this bridge back into proper position."

"Well—who does?"

The adjutant shrugged. "I guess I'll have to ask if any of the men ever had big bridge experience. You see, Colonel, we're trained to stretch pontoon bridges over rivers and streams, but this kind of heavy stuff, I just don't know."

"Well, get somebody quick. Meantime—deploy the platoon. Have them take positions along the bridge."

The adjutant gazed up and down the span, which had been extended to its full ninety-degree angle, and wondered why the platoon should be deployed. The strikers, continually threatened by the crowd, had decided to leave the scene before the army arrived, and in the absence of a submarine sighting he saw no purpose in having the men—rifles at the ready—protecting the bridge from an assault. But he followed the order, and after talking with the men returned to Boner with a short, pudgy soldier. "Sir, this is Sergeant Petrowski. He says he worked as a bridge tender in Chicago."

Boner looked at Petrowski and wondered how he ever passed the physical—the man stood five feet two, if that much, and was round as a barrel. What's more, he thought he saw a strange glaze in Petrowski's eyes. Boner called his adjutant aside.

"Is this the best you can come up with?"

"He's the *only* one I could come up with, Colonel. Nobody else has the faintest idea how this structure works."

"But this is supposed to be an engineering unit . . ."

"Well, Colonel—we're not the regular army, we're a reserve unit."

Boner let that pass and took another tack. "That man looks like he's on something."

"It's hard to tell, Colonel. I've never seen Petrowski when he wasn't smiling. I guess he's just a normally happy guy."

"Or maybe he's got a screw loose somewhere."

"Well, that's possible too, Colonel. But let's face it—drunk or crazy—he's all we got. We can contact other units but there's no guarantee that we'd do better than him, and we could do worse. He at least knows what moves the damn thing."

Colonel Boner signaled his adjutant to proceed.

And so it was that the fate of the commuters stranded on the Manhattan and Bronx shores of the Macombs Dam Bridge was placed in the pudgy hands of Sergeant Francis Petrowski—civilian occupation, butcher, part-time occupation, sergeant in a National Guard unit with the newly appreciated specialty of moving bridges.

For a while it appeared that Petrowski knew what he was doing. He entered the shack, sat down at the controls and moved knobs and threw switches and turned dials, and the adjutant and the colonel watched breathlessly, unaware that Petrowski knew nothing more about what he had set in motion than they did. Although the bridge did indeed move in what appeared to be the right direction, it did not stop at its original position but continued to swing around until the Bronx end of the span came into contact with the Manhattan moorings. The problem there was that the pieces didn't fit, as attested to by the grinding noise of clashing steel. It was obvious even to the colonel and the adjutant that this was not the way it was supposed to happen. They rushed to the Manhattan side and to their horror saw large gaps that had appeared between the movable section of the span and the stationary section. Boner ran back to the shack with his adjutant in tow.

"You moved it forward, you jackass. You were supposed to move it back. Now reverse it one hundred eighty degrees—REVERSE IT, REVERSE IT, you horse's ass!"

Petrowski was not perturbed by the abusive harangue. Still smiling, he turned the switch in front of him. No response. He turned it again. Still no response. He left the shack, looked at the twisted metal at the Manhattan side and returned to the shack. "I guess I broke it, Colonel."

"Broke it? You broke the bridge? You said you knew how to work it. Do you realize the damage you caused—and what this will do to my military career? What's your rank? Sergeant? Well you're now a shit-ass private . . ."

"Don't bother me none," the former Sergeant Petrowski said. Still smiling, he walked to the Manhattan side of the bridge, jumped the gap and headed toward the horizon . . .

Now the federal law had been violated—navigation was completely blocked. Of course, it would be difficult for the U.S. attorney to prosecute the Army Corps of Engineers, because it alone caused the blockage. The vehicular traffic added to the total snafu.

Colonel Boner at this point evacuated the bridge—mainly because he felt too ridiculous there. The people in traffic whose hopes were raised by the appearance of the military now barked their anger at the retreating platoon, which like Petrowski jumped the gaps to make their getaway. The final ignominy was suffered by Colonel Boner when an overripe tomato, thrown by a motorist, smashed into his bulbous nose.

That experience at the Macombs Dam Bridge was enough to convince Colonel Boner that the New York State National Guard Corps of Engineers was not, repeat not, to attempt to replace any further bridges, and he relayed orders to the other units, instructing them not to attempt it.

Ben Nolan cursed himself for not anticipating that the Engineers Corps would interfere. "Now we got problems," he said to Goldman after they were told of the debacle on the Macombs Dam Bridge.

"What do you suggest?"

"I suggest that we go back to Macombs Dam right now and pray that we can undo the damage those idiots caused."

Nolan took three of his experienced electricians and hurried off to the bridge. The long lines of immovable vehicles had now begun to move—in reverse—retreating into their respective landlocked boroughs. Through skilled manipulation and replacement of fuses that had been burned out because of the incompetence of Petrowski, the span was righted. The men remained on the bridge and vehicular traffic resumed. Mickey Goldman pulled in his horns, and the strike—disaster—was over.

But the reverberations had just begun. That evening every newspaper took potshots at the union and all editorials called for Goldman's scalp. The media also demanded action by the district attorney. Next day the district attorney of New York County, Arthur Hollingsworth, called a special meeting of his two chief assistants.

Notwithstanding public pressure, Arthur Hollingsworth was not one to bow to such pressure if he felt he could not legally justify his actions. He was an introspective man, not a great public speaker by any means and not one to excite the emotions, but he was resolute in doing what he believed was his duty. His tone at this meeting was characteristic of his personality, quiet and reserved. "We are here to decide what action, if any, is appropriate as a result of the bridge strike yesterday."

Barbara Hennesey, one of the two chief assistants, seemed impatient to get going. She was considered a tough lady—tall, dark hair, on the thin side. "It seems to me that the penal law has been violated under the Criminal Tampering Section 145.20."

Hennesey knew her onions. Stan Rogers, the other chief assistant, was not ready to move that fast. "Isn't that the section that prohibits tampering with a public utility?"

"Yes, that's the one—"

"Hold it—that requires intent not only to interrupt services rendered to the public but needs the additional act of tampering with the property of a public utility to bring about that impairment or interruption of service."

"Exactly."

"Well, how the hell are we going to prove the second part? We know that it was those fools in the engineer corps that screwed up the bridges."

Barbara Hennesey's Irish blood was rising. "They put it in motion," she said, "they sure as hell had the intent to impair the service to the public. They're responsible for the consequences of their acts—"

Stan Rogers was equally hot. "These people went out on strike, withheld their services. It was a stupid thing to do but it wasn't criminal. And if we make it criminal when it isn't under law we aren't worth a damn—"

"Spoken like an old labor lawyer," she said.

"No—spoken by someone who respects the law even when it's not so expedient to do so."

Hollingsworth listened intently to the arguments. "How can we tie in Goldman?" he asked.

"Conspiracy," Hennesey said. "That shouldn't be too tough. Goldman ordered this strike, met with his people and they agreed on the action and they took that action. We don't need an overt act from Goldman to tie him in—"

"Tie him in to what?" Rogers asked heatedly. "To telling his people to walk? Do you realize what a dangerous precedent you're setting, indicting a union and its leaders for an unpopular strike?"

Hollingsworth held up his hand. "Barbara, I think the bottom line is would we have indicted Goldman for conspiracy under this section of the law if the press didn't want to see him hung."

"I don't know and I don't really care. He broke the law."

"Well," Hollingsworth said, "if I was as sure as you are

that he broke the law I'd give the green light in a minute. He was reckless, and although up to now he has had the reputation of being a responsible and respected union leader he at least is temporarily tarnished by this strike. But I have to go along with Stan on this one. We'd have no problem in proving the agreement to strike. It's a reasonable conclusion that he gave the orders to the bridge tenders to walk off. But we'd be reaching too far to persuade a judge that he anticipated the intervention of the engineer corps and that he knew in advance they would be inept. I know, Barbara, that your motive is to make this office responsive to the public and I appreciate that. We try to do our job, and as I see it, our job is to prosecute criminals and do justice. But we're not in the revenge business. If we have no legal basis to indict we won't indict, and we'll take the flack because that comes with the territory."

So Mickey Goldman and his union escaped. He was luckier than some others . . .

# Chapter Nineteen

IT had to follow that Governor Klyk would be a casualty of the bridge strike. His friendship from way back with Mickey Goldman as well as his strong support for the pension bill were well known. Ironically, his offense against the legislature in the case of the late Paul Medford was the basis for their turning down his pension bill, which in turn provoked the strike. But who was looking for ironies? His enemies in the legislature and the press were hand-in-hand, spreading the story that he had in some way given his blessing to the strike; and while those giving out the story knew better, the general public did not. And it was the general public that, at election time, made policy. Jon Klyk had offended the powers that be, and for that there was no forgiveness.

By now it seemed clear to Loren Sturdivant that the time was ripe—indeed couldn't be avoided and shouldn't be—to take on the governor head-to-head. He had, after all, rejected her as an ally. So had his point man Scott Morgan, and she hadn't exactly had a responsive reaction from Mickey Goldman after her holding out the olive branch and offering her help. The governor had two strikes against him . . . first the

Medford business, and now a literal strike. What chance did he have of reelection with those odds against him? She had worked too hard for their election to see it go down the tubes by default and come the next election have the state turned over again to the backward fat-cats of the opposition party. Waiting for the other shoe to drop, or—to mix metaphors— for the third strike to put out Jon Klyk, she had decided even before the bridge strike that she needed to find her own ammunition, sad as it might make her, against the governor. It was all in the people's service, after all, that she should save the state from the Republicans, and even more, that she be in a position to lead it as governor herself after the next election.

So to that end she set about to create her own intelligence network—or at least intelligence "asset" as they called it in the CIA—in the house of the governor. From one of her sources she got the name of one Mildred Bostwick, who was the governor's personal maid.

Mildred was on the plump side with a pretty face, usually cheerful, not showing her personal problems. But eventually, through one of Loren's informants, she did show them to Loren Sturdivant, who made it her business "accidentally" to see her crossing the street in front of her limousine. Loren recognized her from the description given to her. She called to Mildred and offered to drive her home. Mildred was thrilled, and when Loren asked for her phone number in a most casual manner she gave it quickly, not stopping to think why such a request was made. At any rate she doubted the call would ever be made.

Two weeks later, however, when she answered her phone late one night she heard the voice of the lieutenant governor of the state of New York asking that she see her in her office at 7:30 the following morning before she reported to work—

and requesting that she tell nobody about the call or the meeting.

Although the police stationed at the capitol were on duty, Loren was personally at the entrance when Mildred arrived. She signaled to the officer to let Mildred through without the normal security questioning of all visitors.

Only the sound of their footsteps could be heard in the ornate marble corridor leading to her office. Using her own key, Loren opened the outer door and the two women walked through the outer office and into Loren's chambers.

Loren motioned Mildred to a large chair in front of her desk, and she sat in her own straight-backed chair—always an imposing figure, Loren was even more so sitting erect behind the imposing desk.

"Mildred," she said, "I've been told that your husband is ill and that you're having a difficult time making ends meet."

Mildred continued to smile but said nothing. Loren had been forwarned about her reluctance to discuss her problem.

"I really don't want to pry into your affairs, but my information is that you are a special person and you deserve some help. *Please* don't consider what I'm about to say as charity. I feel for you, but clearly I want something in return."

Loren then handed her a check for five thousand dollars. Mildred took it, holding the check gingerly as if it burned her fingers. "Mrs. Sturdivant," she said, "I don't know what to say. I haven't made it a practice to talk about my personal problems to anyone. Frankly, I just don't know how you found out about my situation."

Loren detected some annoyance. This lady, despite her troubles, was asking questions—not like the other beneficiaries of Loren's largesse. Loren eyed her.

"Mildred, it's important that I be informed . . ."

"But why about someone like me?" Although she already thought she knew.

Loren, it was now clear, was dealing with an intelligent woman who needed straight answers.

"No one is insignificant to me, Mildred," she said, and meant it in more ways than one.

Mildred had, of course, heard of "Evita's" reputation for compassion, her support of the poor and the under-privileged—a persona that her public relations people had promoted as part of the "Evita" legend since she took office, but one at least partly genuine, which made it all the more effective. But Mildred understood that the other shoe was yet to fall. What did the lieutenant governor want in return?

One thing was sure . . . Mrs. Sturdivant had correctly assessed her situation. Her life was going just fine until Jim's diabetes, which had been under control the twenty years of their marriage, suddenly acted up and became a serious health threat. The doctors tried to explain it to her, but she could not understand why the medication that successfully controlled the disease was no longer effective, and why the man she loved intensely had to have his leg amputated. The emotional crush to both of them was devastating, and it did not give her time even to think about the medical bills that exceeded their insurance and pushed them further and further into debt. Now the judgments against them were piling up and the attorneys were threatening to seize their home in satisfaction of those judgments. This gift from Loren Sturdivant was saving her life, and she could not refuse it, although she realized she was entering into an agreement that would demand something from her she might not want to do.

Several weeks and checks later she faced the subject with Loren the next time she saw her.

"Mrs. Sturdivant," she said after rehearsing her approach, "I'm ever so grateful for your kindness. I don't know what I would have done, or what would have happened to my family . . . How can I possibly ever help you?"

Loren was ready with her answer.

"What I want in return, Mildred, is information. You are an intelligent woman. I've tried to be direct with you from the start. I wanted to help you . . . I *enjoy* helping you . . . and in this instance I'm asking for useful information I need to do my job on behalf of the public. Believe that, Mildred. It's the truth. I want to know anything unusual regarding the governor. It's common knowledge he and I aren't exactly getting along . . . but far more important, I'm being kept out of what's going on in his government, and that's bad for you and lots of other people I represent in this state. Do we understand each other?"

Loren understood what she saw in Mildred's eyes. The maid was being asked to spy on her employer, never mind the good reasons for it, and it was painful to her. Loren was sorry about that, but she had been honest with Mildred, and now she wanted her part of the bargain kept.

"I'm sorry about this," Loren told her, her voice intense, "but I am fighting for something I believe in. I cared about your welfare, Mildred. Now I ask that you care about mine."

And that was that. The issue was never raised again.

They worked out a simple code. Mildred called a private number, identified herself as "Lucy" and provided Loren with items that she had seen or heard in the executive mansion. At the beginning the information she passed on was of little value, but she followed instructions to transmit everything, no matter how insignificant it might seem . . . When "Lucy" told her that the governor appeared to be ill, that a doctor had been called and that it all seemed to be hush-hush, she was told to find out the details of the illness. It didn't take long. The day after the governor returned from the tests—when Dr. Harlow informed him of his illness—she heard him raise his voice in anger and say the word "AIDS." At least she thought she did. But it was so incredible that she told Loren she couldn't really swear to it. It was all but impossible for Loren to believe as well . . . She remembered Klyk's reputation with the ladies—and her own one time with him . . .

She had her sources at the hospital, especially among nurses who remembered how she had campaigned for increased nurses' salaries and participation in medical decisions. One of them soon confirmed what she had been told, after Loren's assurance that she would never be identified as the source.

Now was the time to act. Once this got out . . . that Klyk had AIDS—and it would get out—he would be sure to be defeated for reelection, if he lasted that long. In any case, the stigma of the disease would assure the whole party would be compromised, including herself . . . unless he was off the scene and she could replace him before the election or his death, whichever came first. No time for sentiment now . . .

Her first call was to Donny Corum, who reluctantly begged off for a week because of his involvement in a special project. A well-heeled client conveyed to him his strong desire to become a city councilman. He was ready to give Corum a blank check if he could swing it. However, it appeared that he faced a serious obstacle. The seat this particular client sought was occupied by Cristos Kasouris—the same Cristos Kasouris whose election he had Svengalied just two years earlier. What's more, he had an understanding with Spyrus, the father and patriarch, that the Council seat was just the beginning and that at the proper time he would project Cristos into greater achievements. Donny might not necessarily allow such a commitment to bar him from leaving an old friend for a new one, if such was demonstrably beneficial, but one did not trifle with Spyrus in New York City if he wished to survive.

But it seemed that Lady Luck was Corum's partner . . . the assemblyman from the territorial confines of Cristos's dis-

trict conveniently, if not unexpectedly for his doctor (who
had warned him repeatedly about overindulgence), died
from a massive coronary. Before the ink was dry on the
man's death certificate, Donny Corum was calling Spyrus
before he left for the assemblyman's funeral. After some
pleasant badinage, Corum got right to it, telling Spyrus that
Assemblyman Kramer had died and that this presented a
considerable opportunity for his son Cristos.

"How so?" Spyrus asked.

"Well, the City Council was a nice place to start, but after
a while it's a dead end. Other than a few key spots, like
majority leader or chairman of the Finance Committee, no
one gets heard."

"Go on."

"The assembly. Kramer's seat in Albany. Cristos can
move better up there, he can do things, make headlines."

"Cristos make headlines?" Spyrus hoped that he had
masked his doubt.

"Absolutely—the media covers even better there."

"But where can he go from the state legislature?"

"Bob Wagner became mayor. Andrew Stein became president of the City Council. Jay Goldin became comptroller."

"But Ed Koch was a councilman, and he became mayor."

"Only after he became a congressman. And besides,
Spyrus, you and I know that Cristos can't be another Ed
Koch." (Who could?)

"You're the expert, Corum. What can we do?"

"Cristos runs for the assembly in the special election.
He'll get the blessing of the county leader—especially when
his vacating the council seat opens up another spot for them
to fill." (Of course Donny would not even suggest that *he*
was going to fill that spot. No sense in confusing Spyrus
with all the facts.)

It did not occur to either Corum or Spyrus that Cristos
should have been questioned about what *he* wanted. Had
either done so, he would have learned that Cristos was quite

happy where he was and was bitterly opposed to a move to Albany. But as usual, Cristos's feelings were immaterial.

The governor set the date for the special election to fill the vacant assembly seat. As Corum predicted, Cristos Kasouris received the party designation without difficulty, and Corum made another bundle when his new client became the new councilman. He had, of course, no way of knowing that he would live to regret this particular maneuver . . .

Donny met with Loren in her office immediately after the election, and as usual she wasted little time or breath on amenities.

"Mr. Corum, it's time to expedite matters that will lead to me succeeding Jon Klyk as governor."

"We can't expedite it much more than we have. He hasn't even finished his first year—"

"He's not going to run for a second term, I'm quite sure of that. He's ill, very ill. He might not survive the full three years left. But then again, he might. And if he does, the news of his illness and his inability to campaign will surely become common knowledge. The woods will be full of candidates wanting to run, and I might not be able to control the convention. We can't permit that to happen. It would be bad for my candidacy, worse for the state."

"I've heard nothing about any illness, Mrs. Sturdivant. I only heard that he had an overnight stay at Albany General for a checkup. Nothing more."

"Take my word for it. There is more. Much more. The governor, sad to say, has AIDS."

"*AIDS?*"

"That's what I said."

"That's incredible . . . Is your source reliable?"

"Reliable and corroborated."

"Well, well . . . what course do you suggest?"

Evita stood and trained those beautiful, blue-green eyes on him. "Donny, it seems obvious. For everyone's sake, we must see to it that he doesn't finish his term."

Corum thought he'd heard it all, but this lady was truly
a piece of work. Short of planning an assassination—at this
point he wouldn't be surprised to hear that even that was on
the agenda—there was only one possibility left . . . "You
mean *impeachment*, Mrs. Sturdivant?"

"Yes."

"*That's* a tall order. A lot of risks. Fail and you fall on your
face and you don't get up—"

"I am aware of that," she said pacing across the room.
"This project is worth the risk. When he is impeached I will
become the governor and I will have the power of the incum-
bency, which I will use for the sake of the people I have
always fought to represent. Give me a year, and I will control the convention. I'll give you the ammunition you need,
all you have to do is fire the guns."

Donny Corum looked at her with a respect that only one
of a kind could feel for another . . . except he really was never
in her league, never could be . . . It occurred to him that she
could make Rasputin, or her popular namesake, Evita Peron,
look like Mary Poppins. He admired that she had the capacity of the lioness to go for the jugular and tear out one's
throat if necessary, without reservation or hesitation. In this
world it meant that she was always to be respected, and
always to be feared.

Corum had the intuitive wisdom to know who could
never ever be crossed. There were relatively few in that
category. Spyrus Kasouris was one—and assuredly Loren
Sturdivant was another. Cross her and, he was sure, she
would crush him like a grape. Seventy million—her es-
timated worth—in itself could buy a lot of revenge. If he
wanted to get out, now surely was the time. He might rise
or fall with her, but if he went with her now she would
also own him. This pact, once made, could not be broken.
And how bad could it be? She had a great track record.
This woman had it all—the beauty, the brains, the intellect
and most important, the killer instinct. So she said she was

using it all for the people. Great. So now he could kill for a cause . . .

What appealed especially was her unlimited resources, her willingness to part with large chunks of it and her disdain for specific accounting. He had already experienced her free hand in that regard. He could not pass on this. Besides, they deserved each other.

Or such was his presumption.

As she watched him react to her startling proposals, she had to grant him his due for displaying a minimum of shock. He was a terrible man, no question, but tailor-made for her purposes. A man without scruples was always the most malleable. She remembered how she had tried to manipulate her late husband, the judge, and thinking on it, his failure to go along may well have helped destroy him. A man of great principles, Judge Alan Sturdivant just couldn't handle the shame of his own fall from grace. As for this Corum, he would help her be elected by replacing poor Jon before he could create a disastrous scandal and defeat that would leave the election open to any number of hacks, including the likes of Donny Corum, who didn't fool her for a minute . . . His ambition might have been less obvious to others, but to her—after all, they did share certain antennae—it was clear as the sweat breaking out on his forehead now that he wanted to be a top dog in the party—maybe the mayor of New York, or eventually governor . . . She would be careful to nurture such illusions without for a minute letting them ever come to fruition.

"I'm at your disposal, Mrs. Sturdivant."

"Good," she said, seating herself again behind the desk. "The first thing I want you to do is to arrange a meeting with Jesse Case—just the three of us."

Corum paused. "Pardon me for saying so, Mrs. Sturdivant, but if I remember correctly, the last contact you had with Jesse Case was not exactly a happy one."

She dismissed that with a wave of her hand. "Immaterial—he only dislikes me, he hates Jon Klyk. When you tell him the purpose of our meeting, and that I intend to call upon him for advice and guidance when I become governor, I suspect he'll meet with us."

Her prediction, of course, was exactly right. Jesse Case not only was willing—he was anxious. They met over a private dinner in her suite in the Carlyle Hotel. Loren had redecorated the suite after her husband died. Donny Corum thought he had seen it all, but this was surely something else. She had the knack of having her surroundings reflect both her strength and her beauty . . . the gold moire fabric that covered the walls from ceiling to floor, the thick cream carpeting, the imported crystal chandelier acting as prisms for the light that reflected on the Limoges dishes and the Waterford glass and the crystal vase centerpiece that held roses of all colors.

Corum consumed the beluga caviar, escargot and cold poached salmon, but wished he could have enjoyed the meal in a more relaxed atmosphere.

Loren, who if so disposed could charm the fangs out of a rattlesnake, was playing perfect hostess. Not a word of business passed her lips until the meal was over. Then, Corum thought, "Evita" surfaced and, as was her style, there were no preliminaries.

"Mr. Case," she began, "I trust that any disagreements we may have had in the past are now forgotten."

Case merely eyed her. "Such disagreements happen, Mrs. Sturdivant. Intelligent people do not allow such things to interfere with their mutual interests."

"Of course. So let us get to our mutual interest. I believe Mr. Corum has indicated to you why we are meeting."

"He did."

"I'm interested in your thoughts on the project, Mr. Case."

"I think that before we discuss ways and means we should get something straight, Mrs. Sturdivant. This project, as you call it, requires total commitment. There can be no retreat down the line—no changing of positions."

"I agree. I am committed to Jon Klyk's impeachment," she said flatly. "After all, I will be the major immediate beneficiary, and you will soon realize that retreat is not in my vocabulary."

"No offense intended, Mrs. Sturdivant."

"None taken."

She then reviewed the situation, the arsenal to be used, finishing with the news of the governor's shocking illness. At which point she was surprised by Case's reaction—or lack of it.

"You don't seem surprised by the news of the governor's ailment, Mr. Case."

"I was when *my* informant told me about it last week."

"*Touché.*" And to herself, a warning not to underestimate Case.

"Well, then, that's all of it, Mr. Case. I believe we can now proceed."

"No, Mrs. Sturdivant, not quite yet."

"Oh?"

"What you have reviewed for me adds a motive for his enemies in the legislature to impeach him. What we still don't have is a *basis.*"

She waited.

"We're not, after all, talking about a local alderman here, we're talking about impeachment of the governor of the state of New York. Over seventy-five percent of the members of the senate and the assembly are lawyers. Lawyers use phrases like 'probable cause,' and 'reasonable grounds,' especially for such a drastic action as impeachment. They might hate Klyk's guts—and at this point, because he wants to hit them in the pocketbook with his ethics bill, most of them probably do. But they will not take such an action unless they feel they are on solid legal ground. We need more, Mrs. Sturdivant."

"I respect your view, Mr. Case, but I know nothing at all about the governor that would taint him with personal corruption."

"I said we do not now have legal grounds. I did not say we can't provide them."

Dirty tricks, thought Donny Corum.

"I'm glad to hear it, Mr. Case."

Corum once again considered how vulnerable he would be the minute he should be perceived as expendable by either or both of these people. Well, forwarned was forearmed . . .

"I believe now would be as good a time as any to set forth a full understanding of where our interests lie," Case said.

"I was thinking the same thing," Loren said. "It's clear what I want. And you? . . ."

"I have numerous business interests in this state, as you know. From time to time the smooth operation of these interests is interrupted or interfered with by bureaucratic snags from certain state agencies. The individuals who place these annoying obstacles in my way are usually pencil-pushing hacks who feel obliged to do something to justify their existence. What I want, Mrs. Sturdivant, is the right to call the governor when that occurs, and be carefully listened to, with a friendly ear. I had no problem with Governor Beale in that regard. But my relationship with this governor has, as you are aware, badly deteriorated."

"Mr. Case, as governor my door will be open to you, and I shall do my best to find solutions to any difficulties that you may encounter. Unless, of course, such assistance would compromise me. At that point, all bets, as it were, would be off."

"We are in agreement, Mrs. Sturdivant," Case said. He could hardly press her for more, she thought.

They stood and shook hands, both smiling. Corum smiled too, unable to escape the impression he was viewing a replay of Molotov and Von Ribbentrop setting up the Hitler-Stalin Pact.

Bennet Sloane pushed the papers away. Although well paid as an expediter for the Mansfield Oil Company here in California, his heart was not in his work. He missed the action of backstage politics, his specialty. As he had been doing for some time, he cursed the circumstances that had driven him to California like a whipped dog. He cursed Jesse Case, too. The man was a total ingrate. Hadn't he served him well? Hadn't he carried out all the rotten assignments that Case ordered? Just because he failed once, he was banished forever. Not *fair*, he thought, missing the irony of that condition being offered to him.

Granted, it was no small failure. The election of the governor of the state of New York could have turned on that mistake. And Jesse Case allowed no margin of error. Still . . . well, it was the old question—what have you done for me lately?

Such was Sloane's state of mind when he received a most unexpected phone call. His secretary buzzed him on the intercom.

"Mr. Sloane, you have a call from New York City. A Mr. Case on line two."

He was excited and a little frightened. It was sort of weird, the call coming just as he was cursing Case. He didn't consider how Case was able to locate him—the man had unlimited resources. He breathed deeply, tried to sound calm. "*Hello*, Mr. Case. What a wonderful surprise."

Case reacted as he had before when he heard the high pitch of Sloane's voice—with distate. At the same time Case acknowledged that in his experience there was no one more devious, cunning, and untainted with morality. All basic qualifications for Sloane's job classification—slime bucket.

"Bennet, I have an important assignment for you. I need you back in New York tomorrow."

Case's imperious tone did not surprise Sloane. In all the

time he worked for Case, he was never asked—always ordered. And he never rebelled against it—he accepted it. But now, for the first time in his life, Bennet Sloane had a card to play . . . "I'm afraid I would find that difficult, Mr. Case. I have a position here that gives me the security I never had—"

"How much, Bennet?" Case asked, rushing over this obvious attempt at dignity.

"Seventy-five thousand a year, three-year contract—unlimited expense account," came the answer without missing a beat.

"You've got it. I want you in my New York office tomorrow at noon. Catch the red-eye tonight."

Case hung up.

Sloane then marched into his employer and gave him what amounted to three hours notice of his resignation.


Of course, the chilling thought had occurred to Loren Sturdivant that the governor's disease was a worrisome thing for her. In their happier days, when they had joined forces for their mutual political advantage, she recalled again how they also allowed their respective high-voltage sex drives to merge as well. It only happened once or twice, but Loren remembered the experience as exceedingly pleasant. She thought it unlikely he had infected her—the odds, she knew, were greatly against it—but she had also learned that the AIDS virus incubates for a lengthy period, and it was at least possible that it existed in his body then . . . So rather than worry she arranged for a complete checkup. Her specific inquiry about the presence of the aids virus did not raise any eyebrows because she had received a blood transfusion after she was shot. When tests indicated, as she presumed they would, that she was healthy, that no trace of the AIDS virus or any other infection indicating a breakdown of the immune system was found, she was able to concentrate fully on her settled purpose—the impeachment of the governor of the state of New York.

Governor Klyk had been forwarned by Dr. Harlow. The mental and physical pain was getting fierce. Yet he maintained his fighting spirit, which to him was always a manifestation of personal courage. There were down times when he could not block the reality of what that recurring pain in his lungs signified, but he did his best to concentrate on the positive and threw himself into getting well with the zeal and fortitude that were his style. His courage was all the more remarkable because he knew what the odds were, and the pain never entirely left him—not for a moment—and slowly seemed to increase in intensity.

He fought with knowledge. He read all he could about his affliction. He learned that alcohol was nonsupportive of the immune system, so he became a teetotaler, no mean accomplishment for a man who enjoyed the grape. Shortly after Dr. Harlow's diagnosis, he contacted the immunologist who was considered the leading researcher in the AIDS field.

"Dr. Myron Paul," Harlow had said, "is fighting this thing like it was Hitler reborn. He puts in fourteen hours a day. He's working on a grant and he lives for nothing else but to beat AIDS. He doesn't take on private patients, it interferes with his research. But I got him to make you an exception. And Jon—not that it's important, but I think I should tell you—he's gay himself. He lost his lover to AIDS."

Klyk shook his head. "You know, Frank, it's high—or low—irony, but I never liked *those* people. I didn't hate them, don't think I really ever hated anyone, but I sure didn't like them. I always just felt that because of their sexual practices they were unnatural—sick—perverts. Too damn bad I had to contract 'their' disease to understand how horrible and frightening this must be for all of them, and how

252

senseless and ignorant my bias has been. I guess tolerance comes quickly if you walk in the shoes of those you're prejudiced against. Suddenly I'm no longer concerned with their life style, or their sexual preference, or their private worlds. Suddenly I can only share their pain in a society that despises them without reason . . ."


Dr. Myron Paul was aptly described as a tall drink of water. He stood six foot four, no more than 150 pounds, with a large head topping a reedlike body and a shock of black untrained hair. The horn-rimmed glasses that perched low on the bridge of his ski-jump nose could not hide the brilliance of his blue eyes, which seemed to be moving in cadence with his whole body.

He had flown up to Albany on the governor's helicopter, having assigned just an hour's interruption to his long day. He moved constantly and spoke rapid-fire. He had hardened his shell, trying to be immune to emotion. Now he examined Klyk and read the charts that Harlow had provided him. He had already studied the results of the tests, but he read them again.

"Where's the pain?" he asked.

"Right here," Klyk said, pointing to his chest.

"When you breathe heavily or cough?"

"Especially then."

Paul examined his eyes and took his blood pressure. When the preliminary examinations were finished, Klyk said, "I've got some questions."

"Shoot."

"I know that my particular condition is called PCP, right?"

"*Pneumocystis carini pneumonia.*"

"Clearly a link to the immune deficiency virus."

"Clearly. Governor, you've done some research. That's good. It's always good to know all you can about the enemy."

"Can we attack this with an antibiotic?"

"No. PCP has taken hold because the AIDS virus has broken down your defense against it. Antibiotics work against diseases because of bacteria, not by viruses. They hold bacteria in check only until your own immune-defenses regain strength and take over."

"So what's the next step?"

"Since you've done some research on your own, I assume you've read about azidothymidine."

"Yes—AZT—I sure as hell have. That was going to be my next question."

"Well, we're beginning to learn more about AZT. And what we've learned is good news and bad news."

"Give me both."

"You're at the early stage of the PCP infection. You will start on AZT immediately because, frankly, without it, you could be dead in a month."

"Can AZT save my life?"

"I wish I could tell you that. The fact is that all we've been able to prove is that it provides a holding pattern. I'd be less than frank if I told you it will beat the PCP out of your body. It won't."

"Fair enough . . . I'll settle for an extension of my lease."

"Well," Dr. Paul said, "we may need several extensions. We're about a year away from a vaccine, governor. Maybe two. So be prepared for more pain and hang tough. I'm going to see you regularly, and test you and maybe even experiment with you."

"You've got a deal," Klyk said, feeling cold all over.

"I'm afraid that was the good news. The bad is that you will be taking this therapy every four hours and it may be needed for the rest of your life."

"The rest of my life . . ."

"There are side effects. Chances are you'll develop anemia as a direct result of AZT's use. You'll require regular transfusions, at least once a month."

"Look, Doctor Paul, I'm prepared to pay any price to live a day. I'll do what I have to do. Anything else about the vaccine?"

"Well, one problem is that we have to come up with a whole new approach. Conventional vaccines are given before a patient is infected. Once the virus is in the cells, antibodies can't eliminate it. But that's only for now. We're working on a procedure to develop antibodies that will attack the sick cells and isolate them. I tell you in time we *will* develop such a vaccine—it's not a scientific impossibility—and when we do we'll have a ballgame. What we need to do now, Governor, is keep you alive until we can use it."

"I'll just refuse to die," Klyk said, not bothering to force a brave smile.

"That's it, that's it," Paul said in his machine-gun style. "Refuse to die. Curse the pain. Scream if you want. I'll always be there for you—your helicopter only takes an hour. But promise me you will bear down and take everything it can dish out. Try to remember we will do better than we are doing now. I think you can do it, I think you have the guts to hang on. Just don't die on me, goddamn it!"

Klyk looked with some amazement at the young doctor who seemed to have worked himself into a kind of frenzy. Who the hell was the patient here?

At the door Paul stopped and turned. "I will arrange for you to come down to Sloan-Kettering next week for more detailed tests. See you then."

He literally jumped through the door opening, ran to the main entrance and continued running to the waiting 'copter. Once airborne he looked down at the mansion and permitted himself to surrender—just briefly—to the sorrow and melancholy of these encounters. But as always, he pulled himself out. He could not afford to be diverted by anything as mundane as heartache.

# Chapter Twenty

THE HONORABLE HENRY SELDON, Speaker of the Assembly of the State of New York, enjoyed the trappings of power as much as any other man. But at this point his responsibilities were wearying, and he wished he were two thousand miles away on a white beach in the Caribbean.

He looked at the clock, which read 7:00 P.M.—and still a mound of papers to attack. No way that he could tackle it now. His thoughts were zoned in on the crisis that dogged him and was not about to go away. He had put off facing up to it long enough.

Naturally he was aware of all official and unofficial happenings on the assembly floor, its offices and its corridors. He knew—or thought he did—every move that Loren Sturdivant made when she began her campaign three months earlier to deep-six the governor. Even those legislators who sided with this "Evita" and were in her camp informed Seldon. He was, after all, a popular *and* powerful leader, and so they felt an obligation to make their positions clear. As their numbers increased, Seldon was concerned by the momentum. It became clear to him that the assembly believed that Jon Klyk was expendable.

She had certainly done her job well. A clear majority of his people on the Democratic side of the aisle were anti-Klyk. Some were turning on Klyk for reasons of principle, more were guaranteeing themselves seats on the boat before it left the pier, as well as jumping off a sinking vessel—as they perceived it. Loren Sturdivant was the future, and Jon Klyk, "rumored" to be dying in the mansion, was yesterday. There was little incentive for any practical politician to remain steadfast in his or her loyalty to the titular head of the party.

Yet there were those, a minority but more than Seldon originally imagined, who were opposed to impeachment. Some, even though they were not in agreement with the governor on some of his policies, were put off by "Evita." They doubted her integrity, whereas they had never doubted the governor's. She could overwhelm people with her charm, but to them she could not disguise her ruthlessness from practitioners in a profession where ruthlessness was often lifted to its highest level.

There were also those in that minority group who believed that Jon Klyk deserved something better than being impeached, especially when he apparently had a death sentence hanging over him. They failed, of course, to grasp the exquisite rationalization of this concern that Loren had quite sincerely managed for herself. They remembered Klyk from other days, other times, and they remembered his unqualified service to the party. There were legislators sitting in that assembly who owed their presence to Jon Klyk.

Yet a political leader had to learn how to count, and the numbers for impeachment were there. And Seldon was also acutely aware of how a change of administration would suddenly open up hundreds of prestigious vacancies for commissioners, administrators, directors and the like that the legislators, hopping on Evita's bandwagon, saw as cushy spots for themselves or family members. Seldon was a realist. One had to be a realist to hold the position of Speaker. He was personally opposed to the impeachment, and while he could exact some loyalty and control over his people, there were times when even the power of his position was not enough. The failure of his influence on the governor's pension bill was an example. Of course, members at that particular time had been partially motivated by the death of Senator Paul Medford, their well-liked colleague. But if it wasn't one thing it was another where the governor was concerned. In the past year the animosity had come from many quarters . . .

He looked again at the clock—as if by the power of his gaze he could stop the hands from moving closer to the appointed time of his conference with Assemblyman Jackson Clafford. When Clafford asked for the meeting he didn't have to tell Seldon the subject they would discuss. He was, after all, the leader of the group who was out for Klyk's scalp. And he wasn't just another legislator. Jack Clafford was majority leader, personally appointed by Seldon. It was his job to carry out the Speaker's wishes on the floor and, incidentally, to inform him about the concerns of the troops. Of course Clafford would not personally defy the Speaker's spoken intent on any issue, but on the other hand, all concerned knew that Seldon would not arbitrarily rebuff the will of a clear majority. Seldon had made his loyalty to the governor known, but wearing the other hat as Speaker gave him little choice.

What bothered Seldon was the influence that Jesse Case had on the movement to unseat Klyk. Case was calling in his markers—for contributions to various assembly campaigns that Case or his corporation had helped finance. Seldon disliked Case—and personally was not dependent on him or any other so-called power broker. He understood that the prime objective of any elected official was to get reelected. He well knew that because of the prohibitive expenses that campaigning for public office required, many of his people on the Democratic side of the aisle would have lost to the Republicans had it not been for Case's help. He could not ignore, and he had, of course, been made aware of the rapprochement between Loren Sturdivant and Jesse Case. An alliance of that dimension could not be hidden—especially when neither party tried too hard to keep it from public knowledge. On the contrary, it was an advantage to Loren to let the political world know that she was making her move and had aligned herself with the state's leading power broker. The steamroller had assuredly been set in motion . . .

Seldon respected Clafford's integrity. Clafford was not in Case's hip pocket, and his desire to impeach the governor was sincerely motivated. He held the Democratic delegation together, a sort of party whip, and he delivered. Seldon just could not oppose him. Long before Clafford had taken such a firm position, he grumbled to Seldon about Klyk's insensitivity to the daily bread-and-butter problems of his colleagues . . . "The man is heading in a dangerous direction, Henry," he had told Seldon. "First he wants us to pass legislation prohibiting us from receiving contributions from individuals or corporations having business dealings with the state. God, that could apply to anyone and everyone. Who doesn't do business with the state in some way or another? We regulate every business and industry, every vocation and every association. Damn it, he knows better than anyone else what a primary costs, and after that, what a general election costs. Who's he kidding?"

"I think he's only referring to abuses, Jack," Seldon had said.

"Abuses . . . they're in the minds of the beholder, Henry. And frankly, if you want to talk about abuses, what about his cheap shot—publicly demanding that lawyer legislators be banned from representing clients before state agencies. The man and his boychik Morgan read corruption in everything we do. If he had his way we couldn't receive contributions to finance our campaigns, and we couldn't earn the funds. It gets even more bizarre when you consider the road the governor himself traveled to get where he is. He's a *product* of this system, but in his conversion to righteousness, he has conveniently forgotten everything—including, don't hurt your friends in the pocketbook."

Seldon had no good arguments in favor of the governor. Even worse was Klyk's demand that "no show" jobs be eliminated. It sounded wonderful for public consumption, Klyk's demand that everyone employed by the legislature in any capacity must appear in Albany and records in the legislative office must be kept of their presence.

But many saw this as posturing by a man who knew the facts of life when it came to the grease that made the wheels of politics roll along. The word was "patronage," and Seldon, as every other Speaker before him, accepted a system that in his heart he disapproved of. Ninety percent of the candidates for the assembly were handpicked by the party leaders of the county he or she represented. It was the obligation of the elected assemblyman to fulfill his debt by putting members of the party faithful on the assembly payroll. It made no difference whether these people had zero intelligence or ability, and certainly the assemblyman did not have the right of veto. He was told, not asked, by the county leader, and he dutifully placed those who were sent to him in one of the "public tit" jobs with salary ranges from twenty-five hundred to sixty thousand dollars per annum. They were assigned fancy titles like "legislative assistant," "research coordinator," "assistant committee clerk," etc. When the legislator's quota for his personal staff was reached, he would dump the rest on committees, which had thousands of hidden jobs, most of them admittedly unnecessary. Committee chairmen, however, sympathetic to the county leader's problems in taking care of the party faithful, seldom failed to find some place for them.

Klyk had been a part of this politically revered practice,

Clafford pointed out. Now he attacked it without warning—embarrassing the legislature, putting it in a ridiculously defensive position before the public. In many instances these public payroll beneficiaries were relatives of the assemblymen, and after Klyk's call for reform of the "no show" practice, many a legislator had to order many a "no show" to stop, for God's sake, calling him uncle in public.

Personally, Henry Seldon agreed with abolishing the no-shows. He was one of the few who refused to pad his payroll with parasites, and since his was the biggest payroll of all, he had incurred the anger of some political leaders who resented his refusal to play the game. Every member of the Speaker's staff, whether in Albany or New York, put in a full day of legislative business. They did not work in his law office nor did they "work" at home. He weathered the resentment of the political honchos, and there were *some* who believed as he did and insisted that employees put in a day's work for a day's pay. But the Speaker's refusal to participate in the practice did not mean he was about to condemn those who did. He had to work within the system. His own standard of morality could not be imposed on the members who elected him to top spot in the assembly. These were his facts of life—these were the rules of the game.

Yet Seldon still tried to make at least a limited pitch for Jon Klyk.

". . . But Jack," he said, "is that enough to move members to impeachment?"

"Not that alone, Henry. He's been on a collision course with us ever since he stirred up the public in a way that led a dangerous bastard to kill Paul Medford. There's no question in my mind that since that time he was out to get us. Well, like they say, what goes around comes around. Now *we've* got something to get *him* with."

Seldon shifted in his chair, waiting for Clafford to drop the other shoe.

"Henry," Clafford said, "we have strong evidence that

Mickey Goldman conspired with the governor on the bridge strike. We understand that after we turned down the pension bill, the governor gave Goldman the green light. Someone is going to leak that to the press. Once the public hears it, they will be after his scalp more than we are. And impeachment will be the natural the inevitable consequence. I think you have to admit that if he did conspire with Goldman, or even if he knew about the strike and did nothing to prevent it, then he absolutely deserves to be kicked out."

"*If* he is guilty of that, I agree he would have to face the consequences."

"Exactly."

But Seldon still had his last card to play. "Isn't there something else we should consider?"

"Such as?"

"Jack, I haven't seen him in a month, but all we've heard indicates that Jon may be dying. Why can't we wait a while? He isn't going to run again, what's the rush? God's going to take him shortly . . ."

"I'm not insensitive, Henry," Clafford said, "but I understand that shortly can be up to three years. That's too long. And who's to say he won't try to run again and lose it all for the party?"

Seldon could not argue the point. But the radical movement of impeachment still bothered him, and he gave it his last shot. "Jack, I understand all the rules of the game. *But the man is dying,* and I'm finding it difficult to reach that level of insensitivity I'm often accused of."

Clafford understood the tough position that Seldon was in, and he was aware of the once deep friendship between Klyk and the Speaker that went way back. It had to affect him . . .

"There *is* another way, Henry," Clafford said quietly. "He could resign. It would be a natural thing for him to do. He's a governor who can't govern. Even if we felt differently about him we would eventually have to find that he's unfit to pursue his duties. If he resigns now we can praise him to the skies and he could leave with his dignity intact."

"A dignity he damn well deserves," Seldon said abruptly.

"Okay, I'll buy that."

At least they had the making of a solution. But something else bothered Seldon. "Have you given thought, Jack, to what the consequences could be? You are going to dispose of one problem and create a worse one."

"You mean 'Evita'?"

"I do."

Clafford nodded. "I'm not exactly comfortable with her. I know you're not and a lot of our colleagues aren't. But she's there, Henry, and we can't do anything about it."

"But you know damn well that without her and Case the impeachment move would never have gotten off the ground. Here's a former running mate and second in command going after him."

Clafford shared some of these sentiments, but not enough to alter course. He had no reason to condemn Loren Sturdivant, increasingly known as "Evita." She hadn't tried to put the legislature out of business. As a matter of fact, she had passed the word via one of Jesse Case's functionaries that she would probably honor in the breach the so-called reforms that Klyk had proposed. That, of course, helped sell her on both sides of the aisle.

"She's made the right kind of noises, at least told us what we want to hear, Henry. If she's conning us, and I agree that that's a good possibility, we'll just have to deal with it when and if. She can be a mean bitch, but for the time being she's *our* mean bitch. Besides, face it, she's inevitable. I don't think she can be stopped. Any problem with her is in the future. Our problem with Jon Klyk is now. If he gets the public demanding these reforms . . . well, his illness aside, he's a real threat he is out to destroy us, so we have no choice but to go after him. I'm sorry, but that's the way it is, Henry. We've got to focus public attention on the man who conspired to shut a whole city down."

The Speaker nodded, resigned to the argument, and moved to the next square. "About his resignation. We're friends, but I'm not close enough to make that suggestion. There's only one person who can . . . Charlie Sweeney. They're close as brothers, fought the political wars together."

"It will be tough for him," Clafford said, "but I agree—and he *is* state chairman. The party has become polarized because of the statements and acts of the governor. The longer Klyk remains the worse it's going to get. If I know Charlie Sweeney, as much it will hurt, he'll give his obligation to the party a higher priority . . ."

The next day Seldon called Sweeney, who happened to be staying over in Albany, and they met in the Speaker's office. Clafford had appraised the situation correctly . . . Sweeney had been besieged by complaints from county leaders all over the state. The reforms Klyk asked for hit at the life blood of his political organization—patronage. Taking care of the faithful was the Golden Rule—and it was being violated. Worse, was the way Klyk was going about it—holding the legislature up to public ridicule, making them all out to be crooks.

Ironically, Sweeney had quietly asked the county leaders to stop the practice of no-shows. It wasn't too much to ask those on the public payroll to do more than just appear in Ablany once in two weeks to sign for their paychecks. But he also believed the way to get rid of the problem was through quiet persuasion . . . Klyk's way, public and scornful, was sure to get backs up. But Jon Klyk's breach of political protocol—including the damage he was doing—concerned Sweeney less than the illness of his old friend. He went along with Seldon's request to ask Klyk for his resignation mostly because he wanted Jon to use all his dwindling energy in the fight to survive.

Sweeney had visited Klyk often after he'd first heard of his illness, but the rush of recent business had kept him away for over a month. When he entered the bedroom, he managed to keep a smile on but inwardly he was torn apart by Jon's appearance. The deterioration was terrible . . . He was not the same man Charlie had seen on his previous visits. His eyes were sunk deep in their sockets, his face seemed to have shrunk, patches of baldness showed through what once was a heavy shock of hair and his color was grayish.

Sweeney sat on a chair next to the bed. Klyk opened his eyes, his slight smile acknowledging Sweeney's presence. He held out his hand and Sweeney took it.

"Charlie," Klyk said, "this isn't the way we planned it."

"Nothing we can't handle, Jon."

Sweeney had made up his mind that there was no way he was going to deliver the message about resignation. Impossible. And then Klyk, though gravely ill, demonstrated that his powers of perception were still not affected.

"Charlie, old friend, I appreciate your caring, and it doesn't take a genius to understand that you came to ask me to bow out."

Sweeney shook his head. "You think you're a psychic? Come on, Jon—"

"Can it, Charlie . . . If I were in your shoes, and you were in mine and giving me the same headaches . . . well, friendship is one thing, the party another. I know what I've been doing and saying the past year has been nothing but trouble for you . . ."

"Then why?"

Klyk laughed softly. "Charlie—the only thing that bothered me about what I've done is that you would be embarrassed, and I was sorry about that . . . but I can't quit now. Especially not now."

Just talking about it seemed to energize him, and Sweeney thought he saw a light in his friend's eyes that wasn't there before. It wasn't over yet . . .

"Charlie, I'm sorry, but I'm not going to quit."

"Then the hell with it," Sweeney said softly.

"Absolutely—the hell with it."

They shook on it, and sat there silently because there was nothing left to say.


Henry Seldon was grateful that Charlie Sweeney got back to him as soon as he did.

"Henry . . . I spoke to the governor. He is *not* quitting. Knowing the man, I should never have even thought that he would. I know you'll do what you have to do, but please don't expect any help from me. I will not talk to one legislator. I will not twist one arm. I will have no part in it."

"I'm sorry, Charlie," Seldon said.

"I am too, Henry. I'm sorry that I'm chairman of this party and I can't go public against these efforts to knock off the likes of Jon Klyk. I'm just sorry I don't have the guts to match his."

Sweeney hung up abruptly then, leaving Henry Seldon all alone at the telephone.

# Chapter Twenty-one

THE lovemaking had recessed, and Paula Lawson, on impulse, ran to the window and lifted the venetian blinds so that the pearly light of the cold February moon filled their bedroom, then quickly went back to bed with him. They clung to each other, looking north at the alignment of the full-moon-and-winter-stars backdrop to the lighted spire of the Empire State Building.

What was that song, "Having It All"? It seemed to be happening to her, and she told herself she'd better watch it or the gods that kept score about things like this would start evening it up . . . She had progressed at All World Media at a pace she'd never hoped for—appearing regularly on the six and eleven o'clock news, assigned the first of several special interviews. There was even talk that she was heading toward an anchor spot. Still, she'd earned it . . . She was intelligent, attractive, professional. All this and the love of a good man too. Scott Morgan.

Not that it was such an easy relationship to keep going. He was a part of government—she was a reporter obliged to be objective, critical when the situation called for it. There were things they couldn't ask each other—things they wouldn't even discuss for fear something would be said that shouldn't have been. But after she moved in with him they were mostly able to adjust to the needed delicate balance. He respected her obligation, she his.

Actually, Paula cheated just a bit every now and then. If she felt a small piece of information could be very helpful to Scott, and not compromise her, a remark would slip through. She knew of his loyalty and dedication to the governor, and when she did break her own code the information usually involved something that had to do with Jon Klyk. Tonight was one of those times.

"I interviewed Mickey Goldman today . . . It's going to run on the Sunday morning news."

"How was it?"

"Good. We discussed his relationship with your boss."

"Oh, oh—I better not watch it."

"No, it wasn't bad. Goldman praised him, called him the best governor since Herbert Lehman. And he emphatically denied that the governor had anything to do in any way with the bridge strike. As a matter of fact, he says that the governor was angry and let him know it."

"I know that's a fact," Scott said. "I was there when the governor called him right after he first heard the bridges went up. But do you think the public will believe they weren't in cahoots?"

"Probably not, since Case and Loren have been feeding innuendoes to all of us. And some of them get printed and broadcast, with the 'usual reliable sources' cited."

He knew better than to pursue it. But there was one other thing she felt free to say.

"Scott . . . Charlie Goldman is an old charmer. We did the interview in his office on Fourteenth Street, and when we finished he asked me to lunch so that we could talk off the record. He took me to a quaint tavern across the street from the union headquarters."

"And you're going to tell me everything he told you? Right?" (Knowing, of course, that she wasn't.)

"Wrong—but this I will say. The place was filled with union people and it took five minutes for him to say hello to them. The owner took us to a booth on a balcony and gave the waiters orders to tell everyone we weren't to be disturbed."

"So? . . ."

"Most of what he said was general stuff about the labor movement, about his frustration over the pension bill. He gave me chapter and verse how he and other municipal union leaders helped save the city from bankruptcy in the early seventies. His big complaint is that the public has a short memory."

"The public is entitled. Hell, our survival is still a problem."

"All right, all right, lighten up, lover. Anyway, as we were leaving, guess who I saw at a table in a corner of the bar talking to some man?"

"Come on, Paula, cut it out."

"Okay, it was our old friend Bennet Sloane."

*That* news was both surprising and upsetting to Scott. He'd heard that Jesse Case had banished Sloane into permanent exile after he failed to sabotage the Klyk and Sturdivant campaign . . . "Which means one of two things," Scott said. "Either he's in business for himself or he's back on Case's payroll doing his thing, which is imitating the lowest species of rodent."

"Could there be any connection between him and Goldman?"

"I doubt it. Goldman probably doesn't know him, and Charlie wouldn't spit on him much less talk to him. No—I figure he's back working for Case."

Sloane wouldn't dare come back unless Case approved. But what was he doing there—in that saloon across the street from Goldman's union? "Paula, do you think you would recognize the man Sloane was talking to if you saw him again?"

"Maybe—I'm not sure."

Scott kissed her. "Well, when I know Mole is back I know dirty tricks are coming down. He and Case are cooking up something, and I suspect the worst."

He kissed her again and sealed it in a way they both appreciated.


Henry Seldon had played his cards. The intensity of the impeachment movement would allow no further delay. Loren had, if anything, increased the pressure. She sent messages to those who had made commitments to her that she expected immediate compliance. Jesse Case contacted the people he controlled.

Assemblyman Lester Floyd, who, it was said, squatted at the raising of a Case eyebrow, was chosen by Loren and Case to make the formal impeachment motion. Floyd was a part-time preacher, a part-time farmer, a full-time con man. His holy-roller oratory scored well with the voters in the northern agricultural county that he represented. He spoke, said he, for the Little Man, but he voted the way the Big Man, Jesse Case, so ordered. For this total obedience he was given the spotlight for this moment in state history. Abiding by the wishes of Case and Loren, who had planned the orchestration of the process from the beginning, the others who sought that particular honor stepped aside.

After recognizing Floyd, Henry Seldon turned the gavel over to Clafford and kept on walking until he had exited the chamber. It was his only way of demonstrating his personal feelings about the proceedings. A few others joined him, but the rest were obliged to listen to an harangue by Floyd calling for, among other things, the vengeance of the Lord in the disposal of the governor. Because of the nature of the motion, he had been granted the unlimited time he requested, and the longer he spoke, the lower he descended . . .

"And what ye sow, so shall ye reap, and the governor of this state, through his chosen life of immorality, suffers with the disease that plagues our land. It is the disease of the wicked and the damned, which the devil himself has seen fit to proclaim as just retribution . . ."

Afterward Seldon was obliged to name the select committee for the impeachment hearings. Seldon, despite his personal feelings, insisted the makeup of the committee represent the sentiment of the assembly. His own poll showed an amazing seventy percent for impeachment. He decided on a committee of seven. The three Republicans could be expected to vote for impeachment, because of their allegiance to the dead and now almost revered Paul Medford, but the three he named—Bert Sheridan, Adie Clark, and Martin Gerard—were fair-minded men by reputation and just might fool the conventional wisdom. Or so he hoped. He named Majority Leader Jackson Clafford as chairman of the committee. Seldon knew where Clafford's sentiments lay, but he believed he'd at least conduct a fair hearing. As the second Democrat, he chose Daniel Wilbur, who as chairman of the Ways and Means Committee had been a diligent legislator and a man whom Seldon had grown to rely on. He too had expressed his anti-Klyk sentiments because the no-show attacks were especially applicable to his committee. Seldon had little doubt about the way he would vote.

Which left only two that he could in good conscience appoint whose sympathies were for the governor. Both were from New York. The first was Sarah Tannenbaum, the assemblywoman (she didn't care for the designation assemblyperson) from the Riverdale section of the Bronx. She had beaten the previous incumbent in an upset—partly because he was a sanctimonious bore who presumed he would serve forever. It had certainly seemed that way when the voters returned him to Albany in five straight elections. But Sarah

Tannenbaum had the wit to make her opponent appear as
wooden as a dummy on a ventriloquist's lap, which he was.
She made the voters laugh, and then she made them think,
and when the incumbent refused to debate her she debated
the empty chair at her rallies. But what they heard was not
just comedy. They heard about the issues, about the government and politics itself. She identified with the long-suffer-
ing taxpayers and they with her. There were no sacred cows
as far as she was concerned. Her favorite description of
political elections was the "evil of two lessers"—a phrase she
did not originate but was glad to use. She also avoided taking
herself too seriously, overall a most refreshing change of
pace. Her victory was no mean accomplishment. The incumbent had been the darling of the self-proclaimed intel-
lectuals of Riverdale and had the advantage of being chairman of a prestigious committee. He was also an overbearing
type who believed he himself divinely entitled to the job. In
any case, for once the system showed that the mighty could
fall when someone better came along . . .

When Tannenbaum reflected on her past, she freely admitted that she had been something of a swinger in the
sixties, had been married three times and after her last divorce said she was "clearly fated for single occupancy."
Now in her early fifties, all her children having left the nest,
she was having the time of her life. She was not above a
harmless flirtation now and then, and she could still swing
her hips a bit as she walked, even though she was the first
to admit that "Father Time has broadened my beam."

Despite the fact that she was in the minority on the Klyk
and the no-show issues, she was by far the most popular of
the women legislators, and though she tended to have a good
word for almost everyone, she found it difficult if not impossible to find one for its lieutenant governor. She had been a
schoolteacher in her prepolitical days. Her subject was history, and she felt in Loren Sturdivant she was seeing a dangerous version of those historic figures who rationalized

their yearning for power by the good works they would perform for "the people." And her open and frank nature would not permit her to keep these opinions to herself, which guaranteed a well-financed primary against her the next time she ran. But, as a colleague from Tonandaga County once told her in admiration, no one in the legislature had a bigger pair of balls than she. She thanked him for the compliment. She was also a defender of the governor.

Naturally, Tannenbaum was grateful for the honor of being named to this high-visibility committee, but her honesty compelled her to tell the Speaker: "Henry, of course you know how I appreciate your thinking of me, and I'll try my damnedest to keep an open mind. But you also know my sentiments. It's no secret that Loren Sturdivant and Jesse Case are coaching this ballgame from the sidelines, and that impeachment is a *must* for Evita. I'm prepared to listen to everything that will be said at the committee hearings, but I frankly can't promise how objective I will be."

"Sarah," Seldon said, "the very fact you're telling me this assures me you will be as fair and objective as anyone has the right to expect."

And that was that.

Javiar Rios, representing the lower East Side of Manhattan, was the final Democratic appointee. There was no mystery about *his* feelings. Rios idolized Klyk, and the governor respected the bright Hispanic lawyer enough to call on him from time to time to talk about the problems of his district. He was capable, engaging and hard-working, and Seldon was in truth especially rewarding him by placing him on the select committee. Such exposure could go a long way in making him a candidate to succeed the incumbent congressman in his district. When Rios called Seldon to thank him, he made no pretense of being objective. He simply could not be objective. Well, his pro-Klyk vote was offset by a predictable antivote among the Republicans.

So there it was. The three Republicans, Clafford and Wilbur probable votes for impeachment. Only Tannenbaum and Rios likely votes against. The task of creating this committee was painful enough, but knowing its composition, which he in good conscience had to make to represent the will of the assembly, was even more troubling. This impeachment was, at this point at least, a certainty. Once voted out of the committee it would sail through the assembly, and the necessary votes to try and convict Klyk in the senate were there as well. The Speaker felt as if he was swept away on a current he could not control. The humiliating removal of an outstanding public official, governor of the Empire State, seemed just a matter of time . . .

# Chapter Twenty-two

I N order to dispel the widely held notion that it was without a heart, the New York City media formed an organization called the Inner Circle. This organization staged an annual dinner, called the Roast, where the tickets went for some $300 per head and more than two thousand attended. The proceeds went to charities throughout the city.

Usually held in March, it attracted the politicians for many reasons, not the least of which was the secret hope that they would rate the publicity of being pilloried in the show. Business interests bought tables because they wanted contact with top-level leaders, such as the governor and the mayor and their immediate subordinates. All major municipal unions also took tables—many a hard-nosed negotiation was known to be softened if not resolved in the relaxed, informal atmosphere of the evening. The event, in short, was a must night for all who had an axe to grind, which included everyone with political aspirations or who did business with the city or could profit from contact with a particular officeholder. The Inner Circle could charge a thousand dollars a ticket and the ballroom would still be jammed. As one old-timer wryly observed, "When money is no object, what's a thousand or two?"

But underneath it all was the desire of those present to watch the Lions eat the Christians. The performers and writers of the Inner Circle were media people. Fair enough when one considered that in the final analysis it was only the press that could bring the mighty down. The voyeurs enjoyed the sight of the mighty falling.

There were no sacred cows, which was amply demonstrated by the attacks in the skits on all minorities—the Catholics, the Jews, the women, the gays, the blacks, the Hispanics and all other groups whose flexing of political muscle would normally cause political types to quiver in fear. Some rare, hardy souls like Charlie Sweeney could handle being cut up, chewed and spit out for all the world to see. He had long accepted that being and remaining in politics required the capacity for digesting poison.

When Paula Lawson was asked to be on the writers' committee, she was especially pleased because she was assigned to "do something on Evita." She not only wrote the parody but her talents as a singer, dancer and comedienne made her a natural to perform it as well. This would be the first time that Loren Sturdivant was to be put on the firing line. She was "Evita"—the darling of "the people"—and everyone looked forward to the way she would respond to the roast. Of course, she had faced criticism in the press from time to time, but mostly those critics had treated her mildly compared to their coverage of other political figures. Evita's influence with most publishers was considerable to awesome. She was very popular with the average citizen, and she, like her pejorative namesake, spoke more in protected Albany corridors than publicly, making sure that the many charitable foundations bearing her name were well publicized. As one reporter remarked, "You don't knock Ms. Santa Claus."

After her 6:00 P.M. newscast on the Wednesday before the

Inner Circle Dinner Show, Paula was summoned to the office of Merril Baines, local news director of All World Media and Paula's immediate boss. Baines, truly a newsman, had been around longer than he cared to admit. He was not happy with the administrative duties that came with his present job. He had accepted the post only on the specific promise by the people upstairs that he would shortly return to hard news and that his term as news director was temporary: It didn't work out that way. He proved to be too good and too admired by all the news personnel—a rare quality in the business.

When Baines saw Paula enter his office he felt the "agita" rise in his stomach. "Sit down, Paula," he said, puffing on the cigar that seemed to be a permanent fixture of his face. His deep-set blue eyes, usually lit by a mischievous twinkle, appeared to be saddened by the reason for her presence. "By the way," he said, "if I haven't had a chance to tell you lately, you've been doing a hell of a job."

Paula smiled and nodded, but she knew that neither of them had the time for compliments. She sat and waited for the real reason he had summoned her.

"Oh hell, Paula," he said finally, "I'm a messenger boy on this one. This comes from upstairs. They just told me to tell you that the lady has heard about the parody. They don't want to stop you, don't even suggest that you change a damn thing. But they want you to know that if you do it the way you wrote it you'll be making a serious enemy. They'll back you up, but someday she could buy this network—or could manage to have a controlling interest via a third party. If that happens you'll be dead. And so will the folks upstairs."

Paula was not surprised by this. She was aware of the risks in taking on Loren Sturdivant. But she also had to live with herself, and the last time she looked, the press was still relatively free. But still . . . Maybe she was being foolish, maybe she hadn't thought it out . . . "Merril, if you were in my shoes, what would you do?"

Baines twisted his chair around so that he faced the vintage Underwood typewriter that he had never replaced.

"I can always think better when I write it." He typed on a blank sheet and handed it to her. The words jumped off the paper.

"I'd tell Evita to go fuck herself."

Paula folded the paper and put it in her purse. She kissed Baines on the cheek, and nearly floated out of his office.


Henry Seldon tried to keep his cursing low key. His wife, dressing in the bedroom of their hotel suite, continued to remind him that the use of such language was inappropriate for the Speaker of the assembly. But, damn it, the tie just didn't lie right—it slanted to one side. No matter how many formal dinners he was obliged to attend, he never felt comfortable in the monkey suit that custom required. Thanks— or no thanks—to the paunch he had developed in the last few years, his shirt never fit right either.

At least he had the luxury of taking his time. Taking the room at the Hilton was a good idea. The Inner Circle Dinner Show was usually a late night. He felt comfortable with the thought that he would be ending the event by riding an elevator instead of driving to Brooklyn.

He was making some progress with the tie when the phone rang.

"Get it, dear," his wife said. He cursed again—but quietly—as the tie returned to its half-mast position.

"Hello."

"Henry, it's Dan Wilbur."

"Dan—a pleasant surprise."

Wilbur chuckled. "Nice of you to say so, but bothering you like this just before a big social evening can't be pleasant."

"Don't give it a thought, Dan. Comes with the territory."

"Well, it is sort of an emergency. I think it's news that you should hear now so that you can act on it if you think necessary."

Problems, Seldon thought, always problems . . . He waited for the other shoe to fall.

"Henry, I'm really honored that you thought of me for the Select Committee on Impeachment. But I've given it a lot of thought and, well, I have a problem with it."

"Oh?"

"I think I'm obliged to tell you that I can't forget that Loren Sturdivant carried out a vendetta against me and my family. Because of her, I believe my son is in jail and my wife needs constant care. I can't erase that from my mind, and I can't overlook that she will be the greatest beneficiary from the governor's impeachment. You know my views on Klyk. Although I was prepared to try to be objective about him, I'm afraid I can't be objective about *her*. If I sat on that committee it would tear me apart . . ."

"I understand, Dan," Seldon said.

"I knew you would, Henry. I regret this, I know I've created a problem for you—"

"No problem, Dan. I would have preferred to have you, for a lot of reasons, but under the circumstances . . . well, don't give it a thought. And please give my regards and best wishes to Mrs. Wilbur."

He hung up and stared out the window. Damn it, he had hoped to have one night—just one—free from pressure. The hearings were scheduled to begin the following Tuesday. He tried to put it out of his mind but could not forget that he had an important choice to make within the next forty-eight hours—a replacement for Dan Wilbur on the Assembly Select Committee on the Impeachment of the Governor.

They began to congregate in the massive lobby of the New York Hilton at 6:00 P.M. The same people usually attended similar functions, eating the rubber chicken and trying to keep awake during interminably boring speeches. But to-night—ah—tonight was different, and the anticipation of what they would soon witness elevated spirits. The mood was jolly.

Those who attended the penthouse party had limited op-portunity to mingle—the suite was spacious but it could not accommodate the wave of humanity that entered it between 6:00 and 7:00 P.M. Nevertheless, the conversation continued until a few minutes after seven, when the management flashed the lights, signaling that the festivities in the ball-room were about to begin.

Only one elevator descended from the penthouse suite to the ballroom. Most of the people walked one flight down through a narrow corridor to two elevators, which was only a slight improvement on the traffic problem. Finally the guests were freed from the restraints of the relatively small elevators and the ballroom quickly filled.

Henry Seldon, the third most important elected official in the state government, still preoccupied by the problem that Dan Wilbur had dropped in his lap, was happy to see Spyrus Kasouris approaching him. Spyrus, in addition to being a major contributor to the party, had become a friend. He had supported him when he sought the Speaker's post, and Sel-don never doubted that in the close vote that put him over, Kasouris' influence was felt.

"Spyrus," he said, "how the hell are you?"

"Henry, can you give me a minute?"

They found a corner away from the mainstream, making it clear that they did not want to be disturbed.

"Henry," Kasouris began, "I am embarrassed to ask a favor of you."

Seldon smiled and patted his friend on the back. It was rare—very rare—for Kasouris to ask for something in re-turn. Which was a reason Seldon especially valued his friendship.

"If I can do it, Spyrus, you know I will."

Kasouris said slowly, "Henry, I heard earlier today that Dan Wilbur might be pulling out of membership on the Select Committee."

Seldon was not surprised that the contents of a supposedly confidential call made less than an hour before were known to Kasouris. Kasouris and Wilbur were tight—had been for years. Obviously, as a gesture of friendship, Wilbur had advised Spyrus in advance to give him an advantage in pushing his son Cristos for the spot. The ploy was obvious but Seldon did not resent it. It was how things were done.

"Well, Henry, I don't have to tell you that Cristos is a good young man but he doesn't have what you would call charisma. He's not exciting. We had hoped when he moved from the New York City Council to the assembly that he could make a few headlines on his own, but he just can't generate that excitement. I got plans for him for high elective office in the city, but he won't get anywhere unless people hear about him."

Privately, Seldon rated Cristos higher than his father did. True, he was basically a quiet young man, he worked hard, never missed a vote and put in his hours.

"I think he's got potential," Seldon said.

"Good . . . Henry, I know it's a lot to ask and if you turn me down on this one I'll understand, but I'm asking you to name Cristos to replace Dan Wilbur on the committee."

Seldon was expecting it. And wasn't all that put out. Kasouris had proved himself, over and over, a true friend. He knew how much this meant to him. "I'll appoint Cristos to the committee, Spyrus," Seldon said. "He will work very hard, I believe he will be an asset." What he did not add was that he had little doubt that Cristos's vote would be controlled by Corum, who in turn was Loren's representative. It was one anti-Klyk vote replacing another, so what really was the difference . . .

But with it all he still did not share Kasouris's low opinion of his son. He had taken a few moments to talk to him privately during the legislative session. He did not believe Cristos to be a fool—far from it. Once drawn out of his shell the young man was capable of talking intelligently and knowledgeably. It's just that he said nothing if there was nothing to say—an unusual and agreeable characteristic rarely found in a legislator.

In any case, the Speaker was relieved. The vacancy was filled, and now he could enjoy the evening.

She walked in with her entourage. There was, of course, no announcement or warning—but it was almost as if ruffles and furbelows had sounded. The lady was, no question, a show-stopper. People stopped and stared. She walked tall, with her customary grace. Her blue eyes flashed in the light, her face was framed by her raven hair falling free over her shoulders. Her gown was white satin trimmed with crystal beading—strapless, low-cut, form-fitting. Perhaps tight-fitting for a lieutenant governor, but she was herself above and beyond a mere official designation.

On her way to her table she passed Mickey Goldman. They were adversaries now, of course, but Mickey was important enough for her at least to begin to make an effort to win back . . . she stopped and turned and Goldman was obliged to rise from his table and shake her hand.

"Mickey," she said, "we really should chat. I'll bet we could still find things to talk about . . ."

Sure we could, Goldman thought, like how you're putting out stuff that the governor and I were in bed on the bridge strike. All right, for the evening, it was a game and he would go along.

"It would be my pleasure," he said, a smile creasing his face.

She smiled back at him—but not with her eyes—clasped his hand and walked on to her table.

At which point the lights dimmed, the noise abated, the orchestra played its opening medley and the show began.

The skits, as usual, aimed for the jugular. By intermission, most notable targets were drawn and quartered. The waiters moved quickly to finish serving the main course before the lights dimmed again.

The second act began with a skit about the governor. Reference to his illness was omitted, but nothing was spared. They especially leaned on the war between him and his "Evita," which was the lead-in to Paula's number.

Paula parted the curtain to look for Loren Sturdivant, located her at the third table from the stage, directly in the center.

Okay, you can dish it out, let's see if you can take it.

"Here comes the lieutenant governor now . . ."

That was her cue. The chorus parted at center stage and she slithered to the front.

The sight of her generated gasps—followed by loud applause. She wore a pink body-stocking with only the legal minimum underneath. She bumped and ground to the music, then stopped as the orchestra played the intro to her parody—"Bewitched, Bothered and Bewildered," from Rodgers and Hart's *Pal Joey*.

She sang it slowly, with an English-accented voice—accompanied by pelvic punctuation.

> It's me again
> With glee again
> Just watch me become the Queen Bee again
> A plain ordinary vulture, am I.
>
> I scheme a lot
> And dream a lot
> To make myself Lady Supreme a lot
> A sweet unassuming vampire, am I.

# THE POWER

\* \* \*

*All I want*
*Is the Power*
*Just to make*
*Me the Boss*
*And I scheme*
*By the hour*
*To give the Gov-Er-Nor*
*The Toss.*

*They say I'm mean*
*O.K. I'm mean*
*But that's just my way to make the scene*
*A sweet, lovable Evita, am I.*

The orchestra increased the tempo, and Paula did likewise with her bumps and grinds, and brought down the house. It took the room several minutes to calm down before she moved in wide-eyed innocence to the mike for her final stanzas.

*When I think back*
*I didn't lack*
*The joys of those afternoons in the sack,*
*No chaste, virginal Evita, was I . . .*

She stopped again, and the orchestra stopped—and a white spot focused on her as she slowly sang the clincher:

*Cross my heart*
*I did not start*
*This thing that they're calling*
*A coup d'état,*
*Not sweet, lovable Evit-ta*
*Not I . . .*

She held the last note, milking the audience for applause and laughter, hips still swinging in lascivious circles—then she exited.

They rose and applauded loud and long, and the cries of "Encore" rose from the floor and persisted. She returned for a reprise but Loren Sturdivant was not about to sit and hear it again. She and her group rose as one and proceeded to the exit, stopping only at Mickey's table to say *sotto voce:* "I believe you're a friend of hers. Give her this message. I enjoyed the performance. Too bad about the performer. Such a pretty little thing too . . ."

After she passed by, Goldman turned to Joe Mori, his first vice-president.

"Well, at least we're sure of one thing."

"What's that?" Mori asked.

"Evita can't digest pretty poison."

# Chapter Twenty-three

THE New York State Constitution sets forth: The procedure for the impeachment of a governor of New York is initiated in the assembly, where a simple majority is required. The second stage involves a trial before the Court for the Trial of Impeachment, "comprised of the senators, or the major part of them, and the Judges of the Court of Appeals, or the major part of them."

There was such certainty about the assembly vote on Governor Jon Klyk that all potential members of the Court were alerted that their presence would probably be required within two weeks.

Eric O'Brian, counsel to the majority leader, was given the responsibility for moving the entire scenario. A former prosecutor, he was an intensely ambitious young man who, like so many others, saw this situation as the opportunity of a lifetime. He was of medium height, built like a tree trunk, with flaming red hair. There had been only one similar proceeding—over seventy-five years before—when Governor William Sulzer was the victim.

O'Brian was a plodding, exact and tireless worker. He chose the largest hearing room for the purpose of accommodating the media turnout, expected to exceed anything in legislative history. Although technically the committee would have to vote media coverage, he rightfully assumed that they would have no objection to his arrangements for coverage by the press.

Chairman Clafford pounded his gavel three times to call the proceedings to order. O'Brian was seated to Clafford's right, reviewing a stack of papers and documents he would refer to during the hearings. According to the prearranged format, he would call the witnesses to the witness chair at a table approximately ten yards in front of the podium where the committee members were seated. Clafford would then administer the oath, and O'Brian would ask the preliminary questions. Next he would turn the witness over to the committee, where Chairman Clafford would, if he wished, ask questions and then recognize any member who wished to do the same.

O'Brian's job, of course, was to make the best case for impeachment. Realistically, based on the survey of the committee members and of the assembly, the result was predictable. Nevertheless it was up to O'Brian to make it look good—the result had to appear to be justified by the testimony. If the ending were known, O'Brian had to write the script to justify it.

Originally he had wanted to go with more than the governor's alleged complicity in the bridge strike. It was a simple strategy of turnaround. Level the same charges against Klyk that he leveled against the legislature. It wouldn't be too difficult to find incompetent and even dishonest employees in the mass of the executive bureaucracy. But the more O'Brian searched the less he found.

In fact, he found that the governor acted quickly when he discovered corruption. O'Brian had intended to make headlines over the sex scandal involving former Budget Director Bill Hearn and his deputy, Mary Knowles, and all that overtime racked up by that chauffeur Lonergan while he waited for them to finish their sexual research. He anticipated how the press would pounce on that one. But O'Brian's investigation showed that the governor fired Hearn immediately after hearing of it. He was not there to make the governor look good, and that is just what could have happened had he pursued the Bill Hearn scandal, which he wisely abandoned.

O'Brian would not dilute his strength. He decided that proof of conspiracy with a union leader to foment an illegal and devastating strike would be sufficient to persuade the committee and the assembly and the Court for the Trial of Impeachment to find that the governor should be removed from office. He developed the scenario of his presentation skillfully. The first witnesses were called to set the scene, to educate the committee about the full effect of the strike and to show its recklessness and its impact.

Witness number one was a statistician who represented the Department of Hospitals of the City of New York. He testified to the medically debilitative effects of the strike on the city's population. With charts and graphs he showed how the five-hour closure (only two hours charged to the union and three to the Army Corps of Engineers) caused transportation delays in emergency cases, as well as loss of medical facilities to nonresidents of Manhattan.

He was followed by an ambulance driver who dramatically evoked one particular incident in which his patient had a cardiac arrest *because* of the delay.

Financial loss and costs to the city were testified to by a third witness.

Having set the scene, O'Brian was now prepared to move forward with a specific description of how the bridges were affected. He had, though, some reservations about his next witness. His interview of Colonel Andrew Boner touched an instinctive message center in his gut which told him that Boner was not as expert on the subject as he appeared to be. But he had no alternative . . . he really had to call the Commanding Officer of the Corps of Engineers of the New York

State National Guard who was, after all, present at the time and could describe the chaos. The colonel had called O'Brian and all but demanded to be heard—Boner was not about to lose that television exposure. He arrived in a staff car looking very military in his uniform, with shiny silver eagles on his shoulders. He was accompanied by his adjutant, who unlike Boner was uncomfortable in his captain's uniform, which normally was taken out of the mothballs only when absolutely necessary. But Boner, gray-haired and ramrod straight, walked as if he were auditioning for a John Wayne movie. All that was missing were medals, because other than the Good Conduct, there was nothing else he was entitled to. His two-year sojourn at Governor's Island during World War II could not exactly be considered either overseas or combat duty.

Well, there was no more time for second thoughts as O'-Brian opened the questioning.

"Colonel Boner, will you please state your current assignment with the New York State National Guard."

Boner replied in a voice firm and authoritative, trying very much to sound as important as he looked.

"I am the Commanding Officer for the Corps of Engineers."

"And was that your assignment on November seventh of last year?"

"Yes, sir, it was."

"And did there come a time when you, in the furtherance of your duties, were called to respond to an emergency situation in New York City?"

"Yes, sir."

"Would you describe the emergency and what you discovered when you arrived at the scene of the emergency?"

"I received a communication from headquarters about 0745 that the bridge had been struck. I ordered personnel to each of the bridges in the city that were involved. I personally arrived at the Macombs Dam Bridge at 155th Street connecting the Bronx and Manhattan at about 0830. When we arrived we saw the central portion of the bridge parallel to the shore—at a ninety-degree angle to the main structure. Naturally we couldn't gain access from the Bronx or the Manhattan approach. The only way we could get across was from the sea."

Assemblywoman Sarah Tannenbaum, anxious to tweak the bulbous nose of the weekend colonel, moved in: "Pardon me for interrupting, Colonel. You don't mean from the sea, do you? The last time I looked, the Bronx River was nowhere near the sea."

Boner hastily consulted with his adjutant.

"I stand corrected, Assemblywoman—er—Assemblywomanperson." Boner was flustered and Sarah loved it.

"Mrs. Tannenbaum will be good enough, Colonel," she said.

"Yes, Mrs. Tannenbaum—we gained entry from a boat on the river."

"Well," she said, "please excuse me, Colonel, I didn't wish to be picky, I just wanted the record to be clear."

Boner smiled.

"No offense taken, Mrs. Tannenbaum."

Sarah smiled back. We are dealing here with an idiot, she thought. This may turn out to be some fun.

O'Brian, no fool, was echoing her thoughts, and cursing the system that could grant such responsibility to such a fool . . . And he was stuck with him. Knowing that Sarah's tongue was as sharp as her mind and that she did not suffer fools lightly, he worried about how much damage she could do to the effectiveness of Boner's testimony.

"Please continue, Colonel," O'Brian said.

"Well, we landed on an island under the bridge and we mounted the steps leading to the structure. We then secured the bridge."

Sarah moved again into the opening.

"Secured, Colonel? Secured against what? Were the motorists going to attack?"

Boner finally got the message that Assemblywoman Tannenbaum was less than entranced by him, which rattled him even more. As his face reddened he placed his hand over the microphone and again consulted his adjutant . . . "What did we secure against?" he whispered.

The adjutant shielded his whispered answer with his hand. "If you remember, Colonel—that was the same question I asked you at the time."

"Well, how should I answer?"

"Beats the hell out of me."

Boner was silent for the next ten seconds, until an improvisation hit him.

"Sabotage," he said finally.

Sarah smiled, pleased with the looks of astonishment on the faces of the committee members. She then whispered to Javiar Rios, "Did you ever see such a horse's ass?" And turned back to the witness.

"Please forgive my rudeness, Colonel. I won't interrupt you again."

"Well, we proceeded to the control shack and tried to restore the span to its normal position. But although we were able to move the bridge, we found that we could only move it clockwise—not counterclockwise. Obviously the fuses had been tampered with—either removed or defaced in some way—making it impossible for the span to revolve correctly."

Boner's revision of history made good press and would have been impressive had it not been for a question from an unexpected source—Assemblyman Adie Clark.

"Colonel, just for clarification, you said the machinery was sabotaged and therefore you could not reposition the bridge in its original state."

"Yes, sir."

"But you did move it clockwise."

"Yes, sir."

"Well, then the fuses *were* present."

Boner was beginning to sweat. "I can only assume that the fuses for clockwise movement were present and the counter-clockwise fuses were removed."

"At any rate," Clark said, "there did come a time when you and your men left the bridge. Correct?"

"Yes, sir. Approximately one hour later. There was nothing more that we could do."

"Well, we know that the bridge was eventually righted. Who fixed it if you didn't?"

"The very people who sabotaged it in the first place, sir. The union technicians were called in and they replaced the fuses, or did whatever was necessary to undo the mischief they had caused."

"Thank you, Colonel."

At that point Clafford called for a short recess and Sarah Tannenbaum cornered Adie Clark in the corridor. They were generally fond of each other, this odd couple—the conservative Republican lawyer from upstate New York and the feisty Jewish lady from the Bronx. Adie liked her, as did most of her colleagues, partly because she always said what she thought, which could be dangerous but was also most refreshing.

"Adie," she said, "I get the feeling you have some doubts about Colonel Boner."

"Oh, Sarah, you wouldn't be working your wiles on your old friend Adie to help your old friend Jon Klyk?"

"*Moi?* Would I do that? But seriously, you must admit, the colonel was trying desperately to make himself look good. If you believe him, I have property on Long Island I'll sell you at a very reasonable price. Of course most of it is under water."

"Yes, I agree." Clark had to laugh. "If we were invaded by Pennsylvania I'd feel more secure if you were the C.O. of the

Corps of Engineers. But, Sarah, the fact remains that the idiot colonel didn't set this terrible thing in motion—Mickey Goldman did. Boner's incompetence was just one of the consequences. It was a miracle that no one died.

"Granted," Sara said, "it was a reckless thing to do, out of character for Goldman, by the way. We both know how provoked he was over the pension bill defeat. But we're not here to impeach Goldman . . ." Adie did not say the obvious . . . that the charge was Klyk's colluding with Goldman in this irresponsible act.

When they were back in session Clafford went down the line, giving each member the opportunity to question Boner. But Sheridan, who had been a close friend of Paul Medford's and was out to get Klyk at any cost, skillfully questioned Boner, even managing to rehabilitate him somewhat. Clafford then asked a few perfunctory questions. Gerard, Rios and Kasouris had none, and day one was completed as they recessed.

Having set the scene, O'Brian now let the public have its say. Day two was devoted to representatives of various taxpayer and civic groups who vented their outrage over the strike. It was window dressing, but it made good press and gave Assemblyman Gerard (who, like Sheridan, was convinced that Goldman and Klyk had conspired to bring about the strike) the opportunity to lead the witnesses and join in their indignation. The witnesses were impressive; typical was the statement of the executive director of the Citizens Union: "A chief executive who would tolerate such an interruption to public service, causing possible danger to an entire municipality—even if he felt the cause was justified—does not deserve to remain in office."

When Mickey Goldman received the expected phone call from Eric O'Brian requesting his appearance before the committee, he called Mark Hammond. When they met at the union headquarters, Hammond's legal advice was direct and clear: "You have to invoke the Fifth."

"Why?"

"Because they will find something in your testimony that could be used to incriminate you. You could be nailed by the most innocuous response."

"But if I had committed a crime the D.A. would have gotten me indicted in a minute. My information is that he decided it didn't even require a grand jury inquiry."

Mark Hammond shook his head. "That's because he hasn't got anything, Mickey, and while he won't manufacture it like other D.A.s I can think of, he could very well find something from your testimony. Why take the chance? Besides, there are other D.A.s looking at this—some who would love the headlines. I can never forget what Sol Wachtler, the Chief Judge of the Court of Appeals, said about the grand jury—'A district attorney can indict a ham sandwich.'"

Goldman stopped to think about it. "Well, you make sense, Mark. If I invoke the Fifth, what exactly does that mean?"

"It means that you will not be compelled to testify unless they give you immunity. Then anything you say, or anything you might have done that your testimony reveals, cannot be the basis of prosecution."

"If I ask for immunity will they give it to me?"

"Probably not. Technically, the whole thing is still under investigation. Testifying under immunity would protect you forever from any future prosecution. I'm betting the D.A.s, or the attorney general, or maybe even federal prosecutors have asked Clafford not to eliminate their chance to get at you."

"So by taking the Fifth I can in effect refuse to testify."

"Exactly."

"But my refusal to testify—that wouldn't make Eric O'-Brian too unhappy, would it?"

Hammond was puzzled. "Come again?"

"It would serve his purpose to discredit the governor by creating the inference that in taking the Fifth I was hiding something—and that maybe I was protecting the governor as well as myself."

"Well, that's right. It couldn't help Jon Klyk, that's for sure. But I don't think he would expect to have you put yourself on the line that way."

"Maybe not, but I've got to live with this, Mark. We're playing for high stakes here. They're seeking to bounce the Governor on any pretense and I'm not going to be a part of it. Let's go with the truth—Jon Klyk had nothing to do with this. As a matter of fact, he gave me hell when he first heard about it. I think this committee's vote is a foregone conclusion and so is the full assembly's, but if there's a shot at turning it around it will be lost if I don't testify that he had no part in the strike. It might not make any difference, but at least I'll be able to look at myself in the morning. And if the tables were reversed, Jon Klyk would do the same for me . . ."

The afternoon session of the third day began with Mickey Goldman being sworn in. He sat quietly as the photographers took their pictures. Finally, Clafford asked them to leave and O'Brian began.

"Mr. Goldman, what is your occupation?"

"I am president of the Civil Service Coalition of Municipal Workers."

"And were you president of that union on December eighth of last year, when the members of your union walked off the bridges pursuant to a prearranged strike?"

"I don't want to be overly technical, or nit-pick, but it's important to describe it accurately. It was not a strike."

"If it wasn't a strike, what was it?"

"It was a job action."

"What's the difference?"

"We didn't intend a strike in its usual sense. There were no plans for a prolonged period of withholding services. We *only* wanted to make a point, and then go back to work."

Assemblyman Sheridan, hostile to Goldman and Klyk, grunted his interruption. "What *point* were you making, Mr. Goldman?"

"We were trying to establish that a government supposedly dedicated to equal justice won't allow discrimination by its elected representatives."

"You can speak plainer than that," said Sheridan. "What discrimination are you talking about?"

"Sir, I'm talking about a law that grants pensions of fifty percent of highest salary after twenty years of service. That law applies only to civil service workers who are employed by the state. We tried to have the same terms apply to city workers. As you know, the legislature refused to enact such an obviously fair law. If that isn't discrimination, then I don't know what is. And it is puzzling, because we were assured by legislative leaders that a parity bill would be passed. It didn't even get out of committee. Would you like me to spell out why?"

"That's not why we're here," Sheridan snapped, figuring he'd already given Goldman too much of a platform and noting a slight shake of O'Brian's head. "Enacting legislation is our business, Mr. Goldman, not the business of labor unions. We're here to determine what . . . agreements you had with Governor Klyk after the legislation didn't pass."

Mickey Goldman's face reddened, in spite of his earlier lecture to himself to stay cool. "Well, Mr. Sheridan, we might as well put that one to rest right now. Governor Klyk never, at any time, had advance knowledge of the job action we took at the bridges. When we walked off, the governor contacted me by phone and called me names that can't be repeated."

"But he was in favor of the pension bill, was he not?" Sheridan asked.

"You know he was. He sent a public message to the legislature asking for its passage."

"And prior to his issuing that message, didn't you discuss it with him—many times—urging his support?"

"I didn't have to urge his support. He openly supported pension parity from the outset—"

"And when the legislature did not approve it, did you contact him?"

"No."

"Did he contact you?"

"No—it wasn't necessary for me to contact him. I knew it wasn't his doing that the bill didn't pass."

"Would you say that the governor and you are close friends, Mr. Goldman?"

"I'm proud to say he is one of my closest friends."

"Well, close friends communicate with each other and exchange confidences, don't they?"

"I suppose so . . ."

"But after this terrible disappointment, your testimony now is that you didn't even ask the governor what went wrong?"

"That's right."

Sheridan smiled for the first time during the exchange, eyed the paper in front of him, removed his glasses, and leaned forward in his seat. "Well, sir, isn't it a fact that you met with the governor on or about the twentieth of October of last year—approximately two or three days after the strike?"

Goldman, never a poker face, winced—only for a brief moment, but the camera caught it. Damn it, what a fool thing to visit the executive mansion at that particular time. But he had wanted at least to explain to his old friend why he felt he had to take an action that would embarrass him. As angry as the governor was, Goldman knew he wouldn't refuse to see him. Klyk should have, but he, Goldman, should have had the sense to know that the wrong impression would be created and spread by those who learned of the meeting—which meant all of Albany a few minutes after he entered the mansion. But Jon Klyk was strong on friendship—maybe too strong—and he was not about to freeze out a friend who wanted to make amends.

Now that unwise visit was hurting both of them. Well, he had no choice but to tough it out . . . "Yes, Mr. Sheridan, I did meet with the governor."

"And what was the purpose of that meeting?"

Goldman was stuck and he knew it. How could he answer that question? Actually, besides his intent to apologize, he had also been concerned about the persistent rumors about Klyk's mysterious illness. He wanted to wish his friend well, see for himself how he was. But any reference to that reason for the visit, with the national press hanging on every word, would not, to say the least, serve the governor's interests. When he answered he spoke slowly, trying to persuade, knowing that the odds were against that . . .

"Mr. Sheridan, Governor Klyk and I have been close friends for more than thirty years. As good friends we meet occasionally for informal chats of a personal nature. That is the *only* reason I met with him in October."

Like most politicians, Sheridan was something of an actor. This was *his* moment. He again moved forward in his seat—aware that all the cameras were on him—and after the requisite pregnant pause, he boomed the next question in his best oratorical fashion.

"Mr. Goldman, are you telling this committee that two or three days after this devastating strike, you met with Governor Jon Klyk and only talked about *personal* affairs?"

"Yes, sir, that's exactly what I'm telling you, and—"

"And that the subject of the strike and the incalculable damage it did to the city of New York was not discussed?"

"No, sir. It wasn't. I also want to disagree with your characterization—"

"Not even as to how it would effect the governor's career?" Sheridan said, riding over Goldman's attempt to correct him.

"No, sir."

Sheridan sat back. He had won the round—no doubt about it. He turned to Clafford. "I have no more questions for this witness, Mr. Chairman."

Which ended day three.

The press people followed Goldman into the corridor and surrounded him. Mickey smiled but added nothing to his testimony. They drifted to O'Brian, who was also close-lipped, saying only that the witness scheduled to be called the following day would give "some very interesting testimony."

Paula Lawson stayed with Goldman. She was about to ask him a few off-the-record questions when she saw the anger in his face as he watched Eric O'Brian talking to a short, stout man before they both entered the elevator. She looked at the man, who appeared extremely nervous after he noted Goldman looking at him.

"Did you see a ghost, Mr. Goldman?" Paula asked.

"Off the record?"

"Okay."

"The son of a bitch that O'Brian has with him is Marty Polenka. He's an ex-member of our executive board. He had a position of real trust with the union. We bounced him last month. We'd suspected he had sticky fingers for years, but up to then we could never prove it. Now he's here with O'Brian. Something smells, I'd say . . ."

Paula went directly to the Albany outlet of All World Media to do her remote segment on the six o'clock news. She gave her effective analysis of the day's proceedings, then said she was just too bushed to join her colleagues for dinner and opted for room service, a hot bath and a night's sleep.

But when her head hit the pillow sleep wouldn't come. She felt she had missed something of importance . . . That man, the one that Mickey Goldman had identified as Marty Polenka, an ex-union bigwig . . . She had seen him before, but where, damn it? And when?

Scott Morgan, who had to stay in New York, called her in the morning, and she told him how much this elusive memory was bothering her.

"Well, maybe it will come to you," he said.

The next morning the media was notified in the hearing room that they would have to wait until 2:00 P.M. A crucial budget vote required the presence of all the committee members on the assembly floor. There were long and loud grumblings about unnecessary loss of sleep. Then they proceeded to kill the five hours the same way many had spent the hours the night before, and after a while no one was angry anymore. Their only problem seemed to be that the ice had run out.

The members and staff of the committee began to come in at two, but it wasn't until a half-hour later that everyone was in his place. O'Brian's hints of sensational testimony had spread through the capitol, and the hearing room was packed. It took some time for Jack Clafford to get it quiet enough to proceed.

Marty Polenka now walked in with his attorney and stood at the witness table as he was sworn in. He was obviously nervous. After he was seated, beads of sweat lined his forehead and his very bald head.

O'Brian, aware of Polenka's insecurity, wasn't comfortable with this witness—didn't like him too much—but he was the closing act and the star of his production. He led him slowly.

"What is your full name, sir?"

"Martin J. Polenka," he said while mopping his brow and reaching for the glass of water.

"And what is your occupation?"

"I'm unemployed . . . at present."

"What was your last employment?"

"I was third vice-president of the Civil Service Coalition."

"And were you also a member of the executive board?"

"Yes, sir."

"And did you serve in that capacity on November sixth of last year?"

"Yes, sir."

"And were you present on or about that day when the executive board discussed a strike, or so-called job action, that was to take place on the seventh of November?"

"Yes . . ."

"Will you tell this committee, to the best of your recollection, the events leading up to that meeting and what was said at that meeting, and by whom?"

Before responding he made a last check with his attorney, who was sitting next to him.

Paula, sitting to the left and behind Polenka, in the press section, had to muzzle herself when at that moment she finally realized who he was. It was his profile that jogged her brain, and she also remembered when and where she had seen him. Her sense was right on the money . . . It *was* important that she remember, damn important. She realized she couldn't leave and call Scott, the phone call would have to wait until Polenka's testimony.

Polenka cupped his ear as he listened to the instructions of his attorney, then faced the microphone. He was obviously referring to, if not reading from, a prepared statement.

"The legislature had been called for a special session in the first week of November to vote on the pension bill. Mickey Goldman had told us that it was a done deal—that the governor was giving it full support and that the legislative leaders were for it. When we heard that it didn't come out of committee, Mickey Goldman called an emergency meeting the next day. All the shop stewards were there and Mickey riled everyone up by telling us again and again how we'd been double-crossed. He then called for authorization to call a strike . . . I mean, job action . . . and we unanimously voted it."

He took a drink of water, looked around, then went on. "That afternoon we held a meeting of the executive board. We discussed details of how the strike was to go down. We all got our assignments. After the meeting Mickey called me into his office. We talked awhile and then he picked up his private phone, it didn't go through the switchboard, and dialed a number . . ."

"Go on, Mr. Polenka."

"Well, I remember he said, 'Marty we're going to do this, but I think I owe the governor the courtesy of letting him know in advance.' Then I heard him ask for Governor Klyk, and when he told the operator at the mansion who he was she put the call through right away and the governor got on the phone and they started to talk . . ."

"How did you know it was the governor talking?" O'-Brian asked him.

"Because while he waited for the governor to pick up the phone he said to me, 'I want you to hear this,' and he pushed the button on the amplifier so that I would hear both sides of the conversation." Polenka looked momentarily pleased with himself for that bright answer. It pleased O'Brian too. At least Polenka remembered his prehearing instructions . . .

"And, Mr. Polenka, will you relate that conversation to us, as best you can recollect it?"

"Well, I can't remember the exact words, but after they said hello Mickey said, 'What the hell happened, Jon?' and the governor said, 'They're getting at me through you,' and Mickey said, 'We can't sit still for this,' and the governor said, 'Absolutely not.' "

The little creep, Goldman thought. Like hell, he can't remember. He's memorized O'Brian's script . . .

"Then Mickey said," Polenka charged on, " 'If we act

quickly maybe they'll understand we mean business.' The governor said, 'What do you have in mind?' And Mickey said, 'We're going to strike the bridges,' and then I heard the governor whistle and he laughed and said, 'That ought to do it—but don't keep them out too long. I don't want the city to suffer any prolonged effects.' "

"When Mr. Goldman told the governor that he was going to strike the bridges, did the governor appear angry or upset?"

"Definitely not. Like I said, he whistled and laughed."

"Please proceed," O'Brian said, fighting back an inappropriate smile. Polenka was a rat, but at least a rat with an excellent memory.

"Well, then the governor said, 'Make sure that the bridges aren't damaged,' and Mickey told him not to worry, but to make his point he had to show the public that only his union people could restore the bridges to their normal positions. And when the governor asked him what he meant by that, Mickey said he was going to see to it that no one . . . not the police, not the National Guard, no one else could do it. The governor said, 'Okay, give it a shot, maybe it will have an effect on the legislature. They probably won't reconsider, but I understand that you have to do what you have to do.' And then he wished Mickey good luck and told him to keep in touch and they hung up."

"Did you have any conversation with Mr. Goldman after the phone conversation?"

"Yes, sir. When he hung up, Mickey said that the governor was going to protect us on this one. I asked him would he have done this without first getting the governor's okay and he said if the governor had really objected he owed it to him not to do it. Mickey said that the governor had a stake in this too, that he had a point to make too. I didn't understand that at first, but then Mickey explained that the legislature was irresponsible in not passing the pension bill and that the chaos the strike caused could be blamed on the legislature."

O'Brian nodded, ended his questioning.

Polenka again went to his handkerchief. By this time his face was shining, the perspiration highly visible. His nervousness was not lost on the members of the committee, but in spite of it O'Brian felt that Polenka had done well, had served his purpose.

Those members of the committee who wanted to believe him, would—Polenka had given them more than enough to hang their hats, or prejudgments, on.

The last hurdle was getting through the questioning of the committee members. Sheridan and Gerard asked their questions in a friendly, supportive fashion—in effect reinforcing the impact of Polenka's damning testimony. But after the few perfunctory questions by Jack Clafford, it was Sarah Tannenbaum's turn.

"Mr. Polenka, you say you were a member of the executive board of the Civil Service Coalition, is that correct?"

"Yes, ma'am."

"Do you still serve in that capacity?"

"No, I . . . left the union last month."

"Why was that, Mr. Polenka?"

"Well," he said, "on account of some differences I had with Mickey Goldman."

"What differences?"

Polenka placed his hand over the mike and again consulted with his lawyer.

"Professional differences, Mrs. Tannenbaum," he said.

"Such as?"

"Well, such as my opposition to the strike, the harm that it could do and that it did do to our union. I always said the strike was wrong, and we continued to fight about it after the strike. After a while there was no way I could stay."

"A professional difference . . . very high-minded of you, Mr. Polenka. Did you express this opposition at the emergency membership meeting?"

"No, I didn't. I should have, but I didn't—"

"Did you express this opposition at the executive board meeting the same day?"

"No—"

"As a matter of fact, Mr. Polenka, you never expressed your outrage over this strike in front of any witnesses, did you?"

"No . . . but there was a reason for that. Maybe it was a false sense of loyalty, but I wouldn't oppose Mickey publicly. Now that I look back on it, I should have."

The man was no dummy, Sarah thought. "Well, after the executive board meeting, did you privately express your opposition?"

"Yes, I did."

"And nevertheless, as Mr. Goldman's long-trusted confidant, you were permitted—no, invited—to remain in the room when he called the governor and allowed by him to hear this alleged conspiracy unfold. Is that your testimony?"

"Yes, ma'am."

"How inconvenient that there are no other witnesses to corroborate your story. Or perhaps . . . how convenient? Mr. Chairman, I want to thank Assemblyman Rios for yielding earlier. I know that he has several questions for this witness, and after he finishes I may have a few more of my own."

"And I may have a few, Mr. Chairman," Adie Clark put in.

Clafford looked in the direction of Cristos Sakouris, who had not participated in any way in the hearings other than sitting in his chair. Sakouris, true to form, did not react to Clafford's inquiring glance.

Clafford then called for a recess. He knew, of course, that Polenka was O'Brian's last witness, and his plan was to finish the hearings no matter how late so that the vote could be taken the next day.

*　*　*

Paula Lawson stayed in her seat while other media people moved about. Her experience was that these "short recesses" took forty-five minutes at least—long enough, among other things, to become fortified at the local gin mill. Normally she would have been pleased to join them, but she had a matter of conscience to resolve and needed her privacy to try to resolve it.

She thought of the words used by an esteemed professor at the Columbia School of Journalism . . . "Your job is to report the news, not to make it." He was talking about journalistic ethics—and the reporter's obligation to keep all sources confidential, and never to disclose to anyone for any purpose what was learned from those sources. Certainly Goldman's off-the-record disclosure about Polenka was a confidence, and even if Goldman might now want her to disclose it, that was beside the point. She knew, as she approached Sarah Tannenbaum and Javiar Rios when they were about to enter the outside corridor together, that she was about to violate this basic journalistic canon. And by the same token, she felt that if there were no exceptions to that rule there should be . . . and, damn the consequences, she was about to create one.

# Chapter Twenty-four

POLENKA took his seat as the hearing resumed. Clafford now recognized Javiar Rios, a former assistant district attorney in Manhattan and well-trained in the art of cross-examination. That knowledge was not lost on O'Brian, who told Polenka during the recess to answer the questions asked of him by Rios but not to volunteer any information.

"Mr. Polenka," Rios began, "would you say that you were Mickey Goldman's closest confidant on the executive board?"

"I don't know how to answer that, Mr. Rios."

"Well, let me put it more plainly. You testified you were the third vice-president of the union, correct?"

"Yes, sir."

"Which means there were two people higher ranked than you."

"Technically, yes . . ."

"It's more than technical, isn't it? If Mickey Goldman should die or retire there were two ahead of you who would succeed to the presidency."

"Yes . . ."

"Yet he didn't call either of those two into the room to hear this highly confidential phone call, did he?"

"No, sir . . ."

"Nor any of the other officers or directors? How do you account for your being the only one he called into the room?"

Polenka shook his head. "I guess I happened to be the only one present at that particular moment."

Sarah Tannenbaum felt she had to speak up. "Or was it that he trusted your loyalty more than any of the others, which you are so interestingly displaying now?"

Clafford had thought of admonishing Sarah for the obviously improper question, but she took him off the hook.

"I wish to apologize again, Mr. Chairman, for interrupting Assemblyman Rios's questioning." But Tannenbaum realized, as did O'Brian, that her point was made about the character, or lack of it, of Polenka.

Rios nodded in acknowledgment and continued.

"Mr. Polenka, are you acquainted with a man named Bennet Sloane?"

Was that an involuntary twitch in Polenka's neck?

"What was that name again, Mr. Rios?"

"Bennet Sloane. He is widely known as a representative of Mr. Jesse Case, usually acting on Mr. Case's behalf. You've heard of Mr. Case, haven't you?"

"Yes."

"Then have you heard of Mr. Sloane?"

Polenka answered after again consulting with his lawyer. "Assemblyman Rios, I meet a lot of people. I can't always remember their names. It's possible that I met this man at one time or another."

Rios was having difficulty controlling a Latin temper that was coming to the boil.

"I'll try to be more specific," he said. "On or about January fifteenth of this year, did you have a conversation with Bennet Sloane at a bar and grill named Swifty's across the street from union headquarters on Fourteenth Street in New York City?"

Polenka stared at the ceiling, trying to convey the impression that he was concentrating on remembering. He was a bad actor and a worse liar.

"I can't recall having such a conversation—"

"Well," Rios said, "perhaps I can refresh your memory by referring to the subject of the conversation."

Rios threw down his pen, his anger no longer reined in. "Did you discuss with Mr. Sloane or any other representative of Mr. Case, at any time, the subject of the testimony you have given this committee today?"

"No, sir—"

"And have you been compensated by Mr. Case or Mr. Sloane or anyone else for giving this testimony?"

"Absolutely not. My only motivation is that the truth be told—"

"Or is it that you had revenge for being discharged as a union official on account of repeated questionable financial activities?"

"That's what Goldman told you? That's a *lie.*"

"Then we are to rely on your statement that philosophical differences caused you to leave the union? Never mind, I have no further questions, Mr. Chairman."

The derision in Rios's voice made his point of disbelief in Polenka's testimony.

Clafford then turned to Adie Clark. "Mr. Clark, I believe you said you had some questions of this witness."

"Just briefly, Mr. Chairman."

Adie Clark smiled at Polenka, but then, Adie smiled at everyone. Many a political gravestone had been placed over those who took Adie's smile too literally. Always the gentleman, he could carve you up and almost make you like it. And while at the moment he was not prepared for radical surgery on Polenka, he wasn't too happy with him either. This was an exploratory procedure.

"Mr. Polenka," he began, "when you heard that telephone conversation between Mr. Goldman and the governor, what was your reaction?"

Polenka, mistaking Clark for a friendly interrogator, got back some of his confidence. "Well, I was amazed. I really couldn't believe what I was hearing. Here was the governor conspiring with a union leader to do something that could threaten the health and safety of the people."

Clark noticed that at this point he seemed to be reaching from the paper in front of him on the witness table.

"Do you have a prepared statement that you would like to make, Mr. Polenka? If so, you are still free to do so."

Polenka reacted as Clark thought he would. He pushed the paper away.

"No, sir . . . I have no such statement."

"All right, then. Mr. Polenka, did you express your amazement and disbelief to Mr. Goldman?"

"Yes—I did."

"Did you express it to anyone else at that time?"

"No, sir—I did not wish to wash our dirty linen, as it were, in public."

As it were, indeed, Clarke thought. What a pompous little liar . . . "Very commendable, Mr. Polenka. But there came a point, did there not, when you told *someone* about it. You had to tell our counsel, Mr. O'Brian, for example, or else you wouldn't be here."

"That's correct. After I heard about the impeachment resolution, I called Mr. O'Brian and told him the whole story."

"And that was toward the end of March?"

"Yes, sir."

"But you didn't see fit to tell a public official, or a prosecutor, or a reporter—or anyone else until then. Why did it take five months to reveal this compromising act?"

"Well, I had a very tough time coming to grips with what I had to do, Assemblyman Clark. I finally decided that telling the truth was more important than anything else, even my friendship with Mr. Goldman."

Clark's only response was to peer at Polenka over the half-glasses perched on the tip of his nose. "Thank you, Mr. Polenka. I have no further questions, Mr. Chairman."

"The hour is late," Clafford announced, "and it has been a full day. Keeping in mind the importance of this committee's action, I suggest it would be wise to get a good night's sleep and vote in the morning. Any objections, or do any of the members desire to question the witness further before we close?"

There were none, and except for the vote to be taken the following day, the hearings of the Select Committee for the Impeachment of the Governor were concluded.


Donny Corum, having planted himself in the last row of the crowded hearing room, rushed out immediately after the questioning of Polenka. Once out the door, a black stretch limousine with nondescript license plates approached him, he entered and the vehicle moved quickly away.

"How did it go?" Loren Sturdivant asked.

"Frankly," Corum said, "it could have been better." He gave her a full report on Polenka's testimony and his grueling cross-examination, especially the reference to Bennet Sloane.

"Will it seriously affect the vote?"

"I doubt it. Polenka was an eyewitness to a conspiracy. Any doubt about his credibility will only make the back pages, if at all. Public outrage, that's the ticket, and the committee members will feel justified, and more important, supported by the public. We may lose Adie Clark, although I doubt it. He likes to play with witnesses, but more than once he told me how outraged he was over the way that Jon Klyk and his sonny boy Morgan contributed to Paul Medford's death. *And* he said that your eulogy at the church in

Bellport was right on the mark. At any rate, even if we lose Clark, as well as the divine Sarah and Rios, Sheridan and Gerard and Clafford and Kasouris are definitely our votes. It will either be five to two or four to three."

"I don't want to see any last-minute surprises," she said, "such as Bennet Sloane showing up. They could always reopen the hearing for that."

"No problem," Corum said. "Jesse Case took care of it. He sent Bennet on a long vacation—long and far away."

"You sound confident, Mr. Corum. I hope for both our sakes you're right. The media has quite correctly called the impeachment of Jon Klyk crucial to my political future, and if I may say so, the future of this state. If we don't get it out of committee, my credibility and influence will be permanently damaged. And, most assuredly, so will you."

The press occupied the first ten rows. Every network and independent television outlet was represented. Cameras were in place directly in front of the podium where the decision of the committee would soon be announced. Donny Corum sat with Spyrus Kasouris in the first row of the audience section, directly in front of Cristos's position on the podium. Spyrus was almost visibly puffed with pride, eagerly awaiting his son's vote—which, it occurred to Corum, when it came would be the only indication that the fellow was breathing.

The tension of the moment made it easy for Clafford to restore order.

"This committee will now vote on Resolution 221, introduced by Mr. Floyd, to impeach the governor of the state of New York, Jon Klyk. Pursuant to the rule, we will take a voice vote, unless a member wishes to make a statement prior to registering his or her vote. All those in favor signify by saying aye."

Sheridan, Gerard, and Clafford said aye.

"All opposed, signify by saying nay."

Tannenbaum and Rios said nay. Adie Clark *and* Cristos Kasouris—surprise, surprise—said they wanted to make a statement before voting and had abstained on this first call.

Spyrus Kasouris, completely bewildered by his son's action, whispered to Corum: "What the hell is he doing?"

Corum had to restrain himself, because Cristos was, after all, the son of an important client. But his anger and frustration were too great to hide completely.

"Spyrus, I haven't the slightest idea, and frankly I don't think he has either."

Clafford first recognized Adie Clark.

"Mr. Chairman, I make this statement because I do not want my vote to be misunderstood. Let me make it clear that I suspect that Governor Klyk did at least have advance knowledge of the bridge strike, and that he took no steps to prevent it. Keeping in mind the potential serious consequences for the safety of our citizens, that, in my opinion, if credibly established, is in itself sufficient grounds for this action. But having said that, I am constrained to add that as an old country lawyer who has represented a lot of people charged with committing crimes, the case against the governor has not been made. I am well aware that the governor's culpability does not have to be established beyond a reasonable doubt. All that is needed for the purpose of this committee's decision is credible evidence. But my observation of the one witness who links the governor to the alleged conspiracy leaves me with serious doubts as to his credibility. Perhaps I'm overly influenced by an old lawyer's instinct, but this story just doesn't ring true. I repeat, I have my strong suspicions about the governor, but American justice does not allow suspicions or hunches to determine liability or guilt, and I am not about to vote to impeach a governor based on a gut reaction. Even my own educated gut. Failing the requisite *credible* evidence, then, my vote must be nay."

This time Chairman Clafford had trouble controlling the

noise. The press was buzzing among themselves. One of Paula's colleagues from NBC said it all: "This was supposed to be a lock. Now it turns out to be a ballgame and thereby a story. Who would have thought that it would come down to Mr. Silence himself, Cristos Kasouris?"

Clafford got their attention when he said in a loud voice: "Mr. Kasouris."

The room was instantly dead quiet. The only sound was of the cameramen moving to the side of the podium and placing their equipment directly in front of Cristos Kasouris. Cristos, of course, was not aware of all that had happened behind the scenes for him to be placed in this unique position. But now, stout, balding, shy young Cristos was, indeed, very much aware that he was to determine in some major degree not only the issue of impeachment but the political futures of the lieutenant governor and perhaps hundreds of others.

Out of the corner of his eye he saw his father trying to get his attention. He avoided making eye contact and faced the center of the podium, looking uneasily at Jackson Clafford.

His voice was calm but so low-pitched he could barely be heard.

"Mr. Chairman, I have always respected this body, and was proud to become a member. But at this moment, I am not proud. For the last few days we have been promoting a sham. Our objective, presumably to consider malfeasance by the governor, is not the reason we are here. We are here because the governor has accused *us* of malfeasance, and while our charges against him seem to have little merit, his charges against us have substantial merit. We are conducting these proceedings to undo the damage that his charges have done to the public perception of the legislature. We have used this device—this impeachment proceeding—to obscure the truth.

"The governor has charged that we place individuals on

the assembly payroll and that the taxpayers pay their salaries for services related to private purposes or political purposes or for no purposes at all, certainly no good ones. He has charged that we indulge in obvious conflict of interest when the lawyers among us represent private concerns doing business with state agencies—knowing that those very agencies must come to us for appropriations so that they may continue to function. He has charged that we accept substantial campaign contributions from the private sector and vote favorably for legislation benefiting those contributors. We all know that there is merit to these charges. We know, but we continue to stonewall and pretend. We take the position that these practices have a history of being acceptable and we object to changing the rules in the middle of the game. Not fair, we say.

"Mr. Chairman, we are living a lie. We pad payrolls, we grant preferences, we violate election laws, we call bribes legal fees, we break our trust under the guise of 'business as usual.' And woe to the man or woman, governor or clerk, who blows the whistle on us. When the governor tells the truth about us we simply turn the accuser into the accused and commence proceedings to rid him of his office.

"What we have done is put ourselves above the law. We owe people the truth—we owe them honesty—we owe them accountability. And we owe them the right to expect that we refrain from conducting future sham proceedings such as this one, in which, as Assemblyman Clark aptly puts it, we have resorted to incredible testimony to divert public attention from our own sins. I vote nay."

There was no way that Jackson Clafford could maintain order. People, at first stunned silent, broke into applause. Many moved toward Cristos, but the first to get to him were Sarah Tannenbaum and Javiar Rios, both of whom embraced him.

Clafford, seeing the uselessness of even attempting to restore order, announced, "The nays have it," and walked off the podium.

The reporters, cameramen and photographers had now encircled Cristos. Sarah Tannenbaum and Javiar Rios walked out of the building together.

"What irony," Rios said. "The best statement of truth and candor about the legislature comes from a member most of us thought was a mute."

"He had things to say, and none of us bothered to listen. We were too busy listening to ourselves."

"He's our own too often silent but decent majority," Rios said. "What Cristos did today lets the rest of us hold up our heads . . ."


Paula called Scott in New York as soon as she left the hearing room. His joy was to be short-lived. He called the mansion and was told that the governor had slipped into a semi-coma that morning. The local physician was present, but Scott insisted on calling Dr. Frank Harlow. They met at La Guardia and boarded the state police helicopter. They were at the governor's bedside in an hour.

Jon Klyk was unconscious when they arrived. Scott sat with him while Dr. Harlow consulted with the attending physician in another room. When Dr. Harlow joined him he shook his head negatively.

They sat silently, watching. Finally the governor moved and opened his eyes. He managed a smile.

"How did we do?" His voice was a hoarse whisper.

"We kicked their butt," Scott answered.

"I go out a winner?"

"And still a champ," Scott said, clearing his throat.

Dr. Harlow reached for his friend's hand and held it.

"Is this a pass, Doc?"

"No, governor, you're not my type."

Klyk smiled weakly and with his other hand reached for

Scott Morgan's, and they gently held on to him as his consciousness was leaving him for the last time.

"Goodbye, friends," he said.

And it was over.

# Chapter Twenty-five

THE lab technician scratched his head and reread the report he was holding.

"I can't understand this," he said to his associate.

"This woman's blood sample tested positive HTL-3 virus in October. The second test taken in January shows negative. The AIDS virus doesn't disappear in three months."

"Let's look at the log," the associate said, and opened a record book. "What name did you have on the test tube?"

"Roxanne—taken October tenth—result positive—Dr. Klein."

The associate examined the log again, scanning the fictitious names given to each of the patients by the referring physicians whose understandable demands that their patients remain anonymous were strictly enforced. "I have a Rosanne here," the technician said—October tenth—Dr. Wooster—negative."

"Did you say Dr. Wooster?"

"Yes."

"Oh God. We screwed up—"

"What do you mean?"

"I mean we mislabeled Roxanne for Rosanne. Look at this—Roxanne—October tenth—Dr. Wooster—negative. The similarity in name did it. We mixed up reports. Dr. Klein's patient is *Rosanne*. She does not have AIDS. Dr. Wooster's patient is Roxanne. She does. We've got to call Wooster immediately."


When the lab people informed him, Dr. Wooster did not use the intercom, his nurse came running in at the sound of his yell. "Mary," he said, "do you know what those idiots at the lab did?" He didn't give her a chance to respond. "They mixed blood sample results. Do you remember them sending us a 'negative' on Loren Sturdivant in October?"

"Oh, my God," said the nurse, "are you saying that Mrs. Sturdivant's blood showed AIDS antibodies in October?"

"That's exactly what I'm telling you. We've got to get her in here right away. She may need medication. She certainly has to be watched. We're way behind—at least five months."

"Shall I call her now?" the nurse asked.

Dr. Wooster nodded, but as she moved toward the outer office to make the emergency call to Albany, he stopped her.

"No, Mary," he said, "let's not call her today. It's her inaugural today. She's the new governor. We'll call her to-morrow."